I ALWAYS
cry at
weddings

For love and courage,
Sara

I ALWAYS
cry at *weddings*

SARA GOFF

WhiteFire Publishing

This is a work of fiction. All characters and events portrayed in this novel are either fictitious or used fictitiously.

I ALWAYS CRY AT WEDDINGS

WhiteFire Publishing
13607 Bedford Rd NE
Cumberland, MD 21502

ISBN: 978-1-939023-56-8 (digital)
        978-1-939023-55-1 (print)

In memory of John V. Goff

Goodbye to all those sentences that sought
to puncture the illusory world - like the warning
on the polyester Halloween outfit for my son:
Batman costume will not enable you to fly.

~ "Warnings" by David Allen Sullivan
from *Strong-Armed Angels*

Chapter One

Ava stood on the steps of City Hall under a bright sun. The white lilies she had picked up at the florist glowed, full of promise. It was a gorgeous day for a wedding. She checked the time on her phone. Strange. Wouldn't Courtney and Brad be on time to get married? She tried Courtney's cell. No answer.

Josh must've gotten caught up at work, which meant he'd arrive in a bad mood. She wiped her forehead with the back of her hand.

Courtney had said they couldn't be bothered with the general nuisance of a formal ceremony. Couldn't care less what their parents' friends thought or how many tabloids they made it into. They loved each other too much to wait another day.

Ava held tighter to the lilies. *It's a matter of personal style. They're from the unbridled passion party; we're from the cautious side of the aisle.*

Josh flew out of a cab with a bottle of champagne. "What a nightmare!" He met her on the steps. "Where are they?"

She accepted a perfunctory kiss on her cheek. "Can you believe they're not here yet?"

"And I rescheduled a client meeting." He pulled at his tie. "This is unbelievable."

"I'm sure they'll arrive soon. Let's see, I've got flowers and a pocket full of birdseed, and you've got the bubbly...is there anything we're missing?"

"Are we supposed to have a gift?" His cheeks flushed red; just the thought of a social faux pas embarrassed him. "We only got the invite yesterday."

"Oh, I have a little present for them, something I wrote."

"Just what they need." He checked his watch. "I'm giving them five more minutes, and then I'm going inside. Why'd they insist we wait out here? I'm dying in this heat."

"Please don't die on me." She touched his shirt, feeling his firm chest beneath designer fabric.

Do I Have to Give Up Me to Be Loved By You? The title of her latest self-help book had a haunting effect. Reading relationship books at this point was like cramming for an exam. After five years of dating—since sophomore year at NYU—how could she not be prepared? In a way, it seemed she'd been preparing since childhood. Every penny in every fountain went toward one wish: a husband who would love her more than anything else in the world.

Josh was quiet.

"Your mother is going berserk trying to get us featured in *The Times*."

"Why?" He looked out over a river of yellow taxis. "Where *are* they?"

"Because of our wedding, dummy. The Vows column in the Sunday Style section. She had some editor come by work this morning to hear the story of how we met. I think Phoebe bribed her." Ava smiled at his mother's knack for sneakiness.

"How'd we meet again?" He shielded his steel-blue eyes from the sun, keeping watch for the bride and groom.

"You're kidding me."

"I know my mother had something to do with it—but where'd she find you? On a street corner?"

"Very funny, Josh. At Bergdorf, on the Beauty Level. An embarrassing story to publicize in *The Times*, if you ask me." Ava sat down on the hard concrete steps. "It's muggy out, like August in June."

Josh slouched down beside her. "This is such a waste of time."

"I remember the day I met your mom like it was yesterday." Ava rested her chin in her hands. "She was dressed in Chanel, no surprise, a pink and coral sleeveless dress with yellow pumps that somehow complemented the dress perfectly. She was buying state-of-the-art age-defying face cream, while I was spending my student loan money on a bottle of Allure to get the free gift bag."

"What are you rambling on about?" Josh's expression read physical pain.

"The first time I met your mother. I'm trying to pass the time. If you'd rather sit here in silence, then fine."

"Talk away." He stared out at the congested sidewalk.

She hesitated, suddenly uncomfortable with the sound of her own voice. "So, anyway...Phoebe pointed to the perfume in my hand and said something like, 'Oh, that's a perfectly sweet scent,' and then in the same breath, 'Say, are you single?' Now here we are."

"Here we are." Josh checked his watch. Again.

"Oh, I almost forgot." Ava sat upright. "We have a potential wedding disaster. Table Twelve. According to your mother, it's 'dangerously mismatched.' Do you think she's obsessing?"

"It gives her something to do." He let out a long breath, as if deflating. "I thought this was only supposed to take an hour."

"We can't leave. I promised Courtney we'd be here." Ava looked at Josh, noticing—not for the first time—how much he looked like his mother, from their light-blue eyes and flawless skin, a shade of pale olive, to their regal noses and high-angled jawline. The only prominent difference between them, beside Phoebe's ever-bouncy spirit, was the color of their hair, his tar black and hers constantly changing. "Did you know that for the wedding your mother is thinking of dyeing her hair amber with violet highlights? To complement the flowers on the chuppah."

"You gotta love her."

"You really do."

The chuppah. It symbolized the future home they would share, but it was hard to imagine standing under one, being Catholic. Thank God for Father Luke. Most priests wouldn't do an interfaith ceremony. Of course, it would've helped if she belonged to a church.

The steps of City Hall grew harder. "Do you think they're having second thoughts?" she asked.

"That or they forgot they made the appointment. It's not like this required a lot of planning. Think of what we've been through the past twelve months."

She tried *not* to think about that and looked out at the Brooklyn Bridge—its gothic towers shooting up from the glistening water. "Hey, remember that time we decided to walk across the bridge in the middle of the night?"

Josh smiled, and everything felt right again. "That was a great night," he said.

She touched his hairline at the base of his neck. "Seemed like the city belonged to us. A perfect night with the sky full of stars and no one else around—"

Little bells clinking and the clip-clop cadence of shod hooves on pavement interrupted the memory. Parting traffic, the bridal couple arrived in a horse and buggy.

"Oh!" Ava jumped up with the lilies in one hand and swiping long brown strands of hair out of her eyes with the other. "Okay, remember, they're getting married. Be happy for them."

Josh stood and squinted as if they were hard to spot. "I'd give anything to be at The Whiskey Bar..."

She ignored the comment.

"Hello! Hello!" Courtney caroled pure joy, waving as she and Brad stepped down from the carriage. Her playful kiss on Brad's cheek turned into a moment of passion, right there in front of City Hall. Ava watched with envy...strangling the lilies.

"Thank you so much for coming," Courtney said when the kiss was finally done.

"We wouldn't want to be anywhere else!" Ava gave her a hug. "We're so happy for you." She stepped back so Josh would know it was his turn to congratulate the bride. He kissed Courtney's cheeks in his typical fashion, simultaneously avoiding physical contact.

Ava handed her the lilies, such as they were. "It's so hot out that—"

"They're gorgeous!" Courtney took the flowers and threw herself on Ava with another hug. "I'll press them...to keep forever."

Ava gave a hopeful smile and exchanged a glance with Josh. The last couple they expected to go simple and cheap was Courtney and Brad. They had the money to throw a knockout wedding, like theirs would be. Plus they had a vow of chastity to wrap up. Wouldn't that be all the more reason to go big? In a church, or under a chuppah? What about God's blessing? Instead, they opted for a public building with fluorescent lighting and stale air. A room where couples and their witnesses waited in long, grim lines to get their licenses signed, stamped or whatever. How unromantic. How could they?

Ava looked down at her skirt and blouse, her long legs in red opaque tights, and then to Courtney, who had on a pair of low-cut jeans and a pink T-shirt, both on the clingy side. Brad wasn't dressed any better in grass-stained khakis and an old yellow polo shirt. Here they lost her completely. A bride wore a white dress of some kind. White wasn't just tradition. It symbolized the innocence of a new beginning and the purity of commitment. Without white, it wasn't a wedding.

"I guess we overdressed." Ava blushed as it became obvious that she was staring.

"You guys have seen these outfits before." Courtney winked. "The Bridgehampton Polo Club, a year ago today..."

"When Josh and I introduced you, of course!" They had gone divot stomping at halftime, Courtney and Brad competing and hitting it off at once. "That's so cute you're wearing the same clothes. Wow, our first date was so long ago..." She turned to Josh. "Remember? I wore a vintage bubblegum-colored dress with pleats down the front. Ugh! I was going through a 'Carrie Bradshaw' phase, on a budget." She pictured the elegant French restaurant, *Daniel*, and her meal of goat cheese stuffed escargot and peppered filet mignon...warm and buttery madeleines...a taste of champagne.

"I remember you got a little tipsy." Josh smirked.

She laughed, as if it were a silly mistake. After dinner, she had naively gone back to his apartment. In a dream-like moment, which she could barely recall, she had given up her virginity. Gone. She felt the sting of regret now, thinking that their first time could've meant something if they had waited until marriage, until they knew and loved each other, like Courtney and Brad.

"You look beautiful," Ava said, softly, almost to herself. Courtney didn't need the white dress, the veil. She still had that special glow.

"Thanks, but bridal magazines are going to want *you* on their covers!" Courtney touched Ava's hair. "You'll look stunning in Vera Wang, without a doubt."

"Thanks." As if that were her ultimate goal. The happy-bride smile Ava had been rehearsing came naturally now—but would she glow with love on her wedding day?

"Lose the tie, Buddy." Brad slapped Josh's back. "What do you think this is? A funeral?" He took out a DVCAM.

"Give me that." Ava snatched it from him, suddenly overtaken by a restive energy. "It's your day, not ours."

Through the lens, Courtney and Brad hugged and kissed, *really* kissed. How long had it been since Josh kissed her like that?

"Ahem." Josh cleared his throat. "My guess is that you two are ready to get this ceremony over with."

"Josh!" Ava slapped his arm, rather violently. "You're supposed to *encourage* wedding couples to kiss, not break them up."

"No, he's right." Brad took Courtney's hand. "You guys need to witness more than us making out. Come on."

Josh gave the bottle of Dom to the carriage driver to hold until after the ceremony, and they all went inside the cool gray building.

On the second floor of City Hall, they found a room marked by a piece of paper that read, *Marriage Licenses*. The manila-painted room with crooked rows of chairs had the ambiance of an under-funded public school classroom. An old chalkboard stood forsaken at the rear. It was like being a student again, but in the wrong class.

She and Josh took seats in the back, while Courtney and Brad waited in line to sign in. Josh was brooding, probably hating the wait. Or it was the room, clearly beneath him.

He shot up from his chair. "I'm gonna find the john," he mumbled and took off.

She was left alone among the various couples, some whispering sweet dreams, others staring nervously off into space.

By the time Courtney and Brad were at the front of the line, Josh returned with parts of yesterday's *New York Times*.

"Hey,"—she leaned over, keeping her voice low—"isn't it cool that they've waited for marriage?"

He looked at her with a blank expression.

"For sex," she whispered. "Just think of the night ahead of them!"

Josh set aside the paper, leaned over, and gave her a gentle kiss on the crease of her mouth. "Before marriage or afterward, Ava, it's all the same."

The honeymoon phase of marriage generally starts with the engagement and lasts up to a year after the wedding. She'd read it in one of her books. *Relish this remarkable stage of matrimony, the longing for togetherness and the irrepressible desire to make love, because it will, you can be sure, fade.* Their honeymoon phase had ended long before Josh finally uttered, "I love you," as if, for them, saying it and showing it were exclusive to each other.

Courtney and Brad appeared. "It's time!"

Chapter Two

Josh glanced at Ava as if to say *save me!* They filed into the chapel, which must have been a walk-in closet or storage room in a former life. Courtney and Brad beamed as if they had entered the Sistine Chapel.

"Here we go," Courtney whispered, and then giggled.

The Justice of the Peace, a tall Hispanic woman with tangerine hair, stepped into the diminutive space and shut the door. Immediately, Josh went white. Claustrophobia. Ava took his clammy hand in hers, but he quickly recovered and pulled away. The letdown every time he distanced himself seemed palpable now. She looked down, fingering her engagement ring.

"Don't be shy." The Justice of the Peace smiled as she motioned for them all to step forward.

They shuffled up to the pale wood pulpit, which didn't match the dark wall paneling. Behind the pulpit was a small stained-glass window. Ava glanced at Josh as he nervously shifted his weight. "I'll do the filming," she said, taking up the camcorder. She focused the lens and once again had herself an up-close look at love.

Courtney and Brad faced each other, smiling confidently with interlaced hands.

"Brad, I love you," Courtney began.

"Even when I let you down?" Brad asked, gripping her hands.

"I'll love you," she replied. "I'll encourage you. I'll help you to be your best."

"Will you always try to understand me, my dreams and desires?" he asked.

"I'll listen. I'll give you what I can. I won't stand in your way.

I'll never desert you."

Brad smiled and nodded. Now it was his turn. "Courtney, I love you..."

When the *Do You Takes* were said and done, they sealed their union with a kiss. Ava switched off the video and blinked away tears. Sincerity, she thought, caught in their moment. It was that simple. The afternoon light sprinkled the newlyweds with deep colors from the stained-glass window.

She looked over at Josh.

"What," he said and then noticed her tears. "Oh, Ava."

"I'm fine."

"Why do you always cry at weddings?" he whispered, or rather, hissed.

"The anticipation...I don't know." Couldn't he see that she needed more from him? That she was succumbing to doubt? Maybe he had cold feet, too, but wouldn't admit it. He chose his emotions as carefully as he picked out his tie each night for the following day, always planning ahead. Now, emotions chosen, his fate was set.

After the marriage license was signed, the four of them left the chapel. Josh took a call on his cell, and she waited by the marble stairwell, while Courtney and Brad collected their papers. *Our wedding won't be big*, she mused, *but high-end, bordering on snobbish.* There'd be her and Josh, her maid of honor, his best man, and seventy-five guests, with accommodations at The Surrey. Phoebe called it a "weekend event" and assured her that it would be the most wonderful and exhausting forty-eight hours of her life. *But would it feel sincere?* Ava gripped the railing, fighting vertigo.

"Let's go, you two!" Courtney and Brad raced down the stairs to the door. Josh, one step behind them, slipped his phone into his pocket.

"Hey, wait!" Ava rushed after them, people getting in her way. "Wait, Josh!" She caught up to him at the bottom of the steps. "I have an idea. We should write our own vows."

"Forget that. It's time to uncork!" He flew through the open front doors and vanished into the sunlight.

She walked down the steps of City Hall, ready to fight for something in their relationship: a wedding that felt sincere.

The horse and buggy waited across the street beside a few trees and a patch of green.

"Oh, Ava!" Courtney said, grabbing her arm. "Say something poetic, please? I want it on tape, so say it loud and clear, okay?"

Say it loud and clear. Ava looked at the lilies in Courtney's hands...flopped over as if in prayer. Mom used to tell her to speak out loud and clear when she was a little girl. Today it seemed she still needed Mom's coaching.

"Well, actually, I wrote you guys a haiku." She hesitated. "Do you want to hear it?"

"Yes!" Courtney exclaimed.

Brad laughed, putting his arm around Courtney's waist. "That's what we love about you two. You always come prepared."

Ava took a deep breath and spoke out: "Love, Courtney and Brad / Blesses you as you declare / Dependence today."

They stared at her as if expecting something more.

"Don't rack your brains over it," Josh said. "Ava obviously doesn't have enough to do at work."

"Thanks, Josh." She glared at him, thinking of their vows. What would she write?

"I think 'dependence' says it all." Courtney hugged Brad's arm, and they were at it again—lovers, kissing.

The driver took up the DVCAM and started filming. Ava imagined the night ahead of them and threw the birdseed in one fistful without thinking. Josh seemed to be making up for the civil ceremony, spraying champagne as if Courtney and Brad were William and Kate leaving Westminster Abbey. Giddy, in love, the newlyweds climbed back into their carriage. The driver took his seat, gave a shake to the reins, and the horse was off at a swift clip.

Ava stood beside Josh, waving farewell with the feeling of being left behind. The carriage rounded the corner and disappeared.

"Wow."

Josh tossed the champagne bottle into a trash bin and started quickly down the sidewalk, as if he couldn't get away from the wedding experience fast enough.

"I can't believe they're married." Ava walked alongside him, her long legs in full-stride. "Just like that. Done."

Spying a mailbox, she pulled a "get well" card out of her handbag and dropped it inside. She'd been sending one home every week for a year. Some were real cute, like the one that pictured a sick puppy with a thermostat in its mouth. The stick figure cards were just plain funny. This week, she'd picked out one with a cat that read, *Heard you're feline crummy!*

"Now what?" Josh asked.

For a second, she'd forgotten about the wedding and Courtney and Brad. "They're going to the airport and jumping on the first flight that grabs them. Hawaii, Paris, Amsterdam... so exciting. Don't you think?"

"Sounds like coach seating, bad layovers, and booked hotels." His eyes scanned the streets. "There are never any available taxis downtown. Anyway, that's not what I meant. What are *you* doing now? My mother just called. She has an extra ticket to some show on Broadway. My dad must've bailed. Do you want to be her date?"

Going to the theater with Phoebe was always something special. They loved romances. "Remember Roxie Hart in *Chicago*?" she'd say, passing the Ambassador Theatre on 49th Street. The Broadway Theatre. The Marquis. The Palace. They'd gaze up at the gilt-edged billboards and relive the storylines: the drama, the passion, and sometimes the tragic endings.

Josh looked at her, waiting for an answer. Would she be his mother's date tonight? It was the kind of mother-daughter evening she couldn't have with her own mom. For now, chemo came first.

"I have to get back to Bergdorf and finish a style analysis. Sales are down, la, la, la. I feel bad disappointing her, but Bucksly will kill himself, or me, if it's not done. Luxury handbags must go on!"

"My mother will live if she misses a show." It would've made Phoebe's year if *he* went, being her only child. But not Josh, not the theater.

"I'm sorry. If it weren't for work..." Oh, the guilt. But Phoebe would sense her reservations about Josh like a dog senses fear, and then what? Phoebe was *not* the one to confide in; her happiness in life, her very *raison d'*être, depended on their wedding.

Josh consulted his watch. "Well, I think I deserve an hour at The Whiskey Bar." He leaned in for a kiss, and her lips touched his before he pulled away.

"One second," she said, touching his arm. "If I had asked you to wait until marriage...as in sex, what would you have said?" She thought of her old high school vow, strongly encouraged by Sister Ann and Sister Mary Joseph, God bless them. But they didn't follow her to NYU.

"Like the two ding-a-lings we just witnessed recite poetry, or whatever that was? No."

"I'm not kidding. What if I believed it was the only way to tie the knot? Or what if it was a spiritual thing for me, and I had made a promise to God?"

Josh feigned a pensive look. "Hmm...abstinence. If you had thrown a vow of chastity at me on our first date, I would've left you with the bill."

"What does *that* say?"

"I like sex? Regardless, it's too late now. Why are you even asking me?"

"I don't know. We've been so caught up in the wedding...we barely talk anymore."

Josh sighed. "Come here." He put his arm around her shoulders. "You're right. I've been kind of tuned out lately. I'm sorry."

She liked the feel of his muscles, his flawless skin. His attention, though sparsely rationed. He held her face, his lips to hers, and the gap between them seemed to disappear. "I'd be an idiot to lose you, Ava." His voice reached her like a gentle massage. "You're beautiful, sincere, giving...without you, I wouldn't know myself."

"Me, too," she whispered. Blame it on nerves. She could

already hear the bell choir ringing, feel the patter of birdseed on her beaded silk organza gown. Of course, the reality of marriage was nothing like the fantasy of a wedding. Twenty-five years old, she knew that. And at least she was prepared for the post-honeymoon letdown.

Chapter Three

Ava descended the concrete steps into the seasonal smell of brewing garbage, worn by the subway like a signature scent. Her blouse stuck to the sweat beading down the center of her back. Waiting for the train, she dug her cell phone out of her Prada tote. Password: josh.

With Phoebe micromanaging the wedding, there had hardly been any need for a maid of honor, until now. The line rang. "Come on, Maggie, pick up."

"Hello, lovely!" Maggie's voice brought immediate comfort, while little Melanie babbled like a hidden brook in the background.

"You two sound happy," Ava said.

"Melanie just woke up from her nap. Listen, Ava, if you keep postponing my dress fitting, I'll be holding your train in my bra and underwear. Now, unless stretch marks are the latest fad at weddings, your guests do *not* need to see mine."

"Sorry. I just haven't been able to focus on it, but that's not why I'm calling. Maggie, I want Josh's love spelled out. Is there something wrong with that?"

"Yes! Tattoos are way too permanent! Crochet it on a pillow or something. A pillow you can keep forever or sell at a garage sale. Seriously."

"No, I'm talking about personal vows. Is it wrong that I want Josh's feelings written out? Is it wrong that I want words I can return to...when I'm having doubts?"

"Oh." *Silence.* "Whoops!" A loud clatter came through the phone. "Sorry about that. My darling Melanie grabbed the phone out of Mommy's hand, didn't she? I no longer decide how long I talk on the phone. Okay, so...doubts?"

"It's hard for me to talk about this. I remember when you got married you were all dreamy and blissful. The way a bride should be."

"That means nothing. Listen, talk to Josh and see what he says. He'll probably write something foolish and adoring that will make you cry."

"I guess so. I guess that would help." Ava sighed, feeling lost in a wedding maze. A swell of hot air enveloped her as the train approached the platform. "Got to go. I'll call you later."

People pushed off the subway while others piled on. Ava took a seat. A man slid in to her right with a boxy old suitcase, which he planted between his feet. She made a point not to look and kept her hand with her Bvlgari platinum 3.3-carat solitaire engagement ring deep inside her pocket.

The lights on the train flickered. The man to her right shifted in his seat. She automatically disliked him for sitting too close. *Do you mind?* She didn't ask, afraid that if she harried him, something heated would start for sure. Now his leg bobbed, touching hers.

She looked up at dark-brown hair hanging to his shoulders— which were broad, she noticed, before looking away. Eye contact wasn't necessary. A white undershirt, broken-in jeans, scuffed sneakers—he could've been anyone, except for that old suitcase which oddly enough looked familiar.

The train stopped, the doors opened, and more people got on than off. A middle-aged businessman stood directly in front of her. He was reading *The Financial Times*, entirely sure of himself, not even bothering with the subway strap. Impressive. The train jolted into motion. He lost his balance, lurched forward with his attaché case, and smacked her square on the forehead.

"Ouch!"

"Relax. People fall." He hardly looked at her as he straightened his suit.

She expected an apology, and instead he blamed her? Suddenly all of New York City felt heartless and mean.

"Too proud to apologize, bro?"

Oh, great, the guy to her right had to get involved. His voice was steady, unaffected. Did she hear an accent?

The businessman glanced at him and moved away.

"Only a coward can't bring himself to say he's sorry!" The guy beside her chuckled. "It's amazing how out of touch some people become."

She looked up at her travel companion in disbelief. Square jaw, intense dark eyes...he couldn't be. But he was. She knew him, or rather had seen him many times before. She was sitting hip to hip with the homeless guy who lived below the stoop of her apartment building.

"You okay?" he asked.

"Sure. Thanks." She looked away fast, hoping to avoid conversation. *Please don't recognize me.* But how could he not, when she walked past him every other day, going home to repack her overnight bag for Josh's apartment? He'd been around since the beginning of April with a piece of cardboard and a dog panting by his side. A guy's-guy sort of dog. Friendly-looking. So who was taking care of it now? Funny, but for someone living on the streets, he didn't smell bad, and she never saw him begging. Maybe he had a job, washing trays at McDonald's or something.

Brakes screeched as the train rounded the bend, pulling into Union Square Station, 14th Street. He picked up his suitcase, smiled at her with dimples between wisps of dark hair, and left. Good, she was glad he was gone. More ear-piercing squeals and the train sped for Grand Central Station, and then her stop, 59th.

She got up and stood near the door. Above the windows of the train car were advertisements for Black Label Scotch and Curiously Strong Altoids. Another read, *Get Back to Mischief*, an ad for Viagra.

Josh would never take Viagra, nor would he get up to "mischief." Their problem wasn't physical, though; they could have sex morning and night, and she'd still crave his attention... his affection. If only love could be enhanced with a pill.

A sticker randomly stuck at the bottom of the ad read, *Eve's*

Garden ~ Where Women Go for Love. It seemed like an answer to prayer. *Eve's Garden.* But what was it? A lingerie shop? A dating service? *Where women go for love.* She'd Google it at work.

The train stopped, and she made her way out, weaving through a throng of people gathered around a group playing Peruvian flutes. Above ground, a new flow of life in a new part of town: Madison Avenue, the New York address for haute couture, where taste was world-class and good manners were protocol—most of the time. She touched the sore spot on her forehead left by the man's Hermès attaché case. *Only a coward can't say he's sorry*—the homeless guy had one thing right.

Turning the corner to Bergdorf's corporate offices, she nearly collided with her boss. "Hi, Bucksly!"

"Hi, yourself." He smoothed down his frosted coiffure. Sporting slim black slacks and his favorite salmon-colored shirt, he appeared to be posing for something...or waiting for her, more likely. "So, the prodigal employee returns," he sneered.

"Come on, I'm the good son!"

"What son?"

"The parable." She noticed the cigarette. "Oh, are you smoking?"

"Does it look lit to you?" He held the unlit cigarette to her face, chomping furiously on a piece of gum.

"I'm glad you're staying the course. It's such a harmful addiction."

"Who does the lecturing around here?" He scowled at her without the slightest indication of joking. That was his sense of humor.

They entered the revolving door and walked through the cool lobby, giving the usual nod to security. The day's floral arrangement still occupied its corner of the check-in desk. "Very Caribbean," Ava said, thinking of her honeymoon. "Birds of paradise aren't really my style, though."

"Oh, it totally took me to Saint Barth's this morning." Bucksly closed his eyes and inhaled. "I could just smell the Hawaiian Tropic—as in, tanning poolside. But I'm over it now." He turned to her as they approached the elevators. "I thought you deserted us, Ava."

"Why would I do that?" She smiled to assure him. A new career sounded like a great idea as she was about to work another late night. They stepped into the available elevator, and the door slid shut with a *clang*.

"You look a wreck." He surveyed her, leaning against the mirrored wall.

She glanced at her reflection and saw limp hair and dark circles. He was right. Her best effort was up against restless nights and an overwhelming feeling of apathy come morning.

"So, where were you this afternoon?" Bucksly dipped his chin and raised his eyebrows, accusing her of slacking-off before she could answer.

"I told you I had a wedding to go to. At City Hall."

"City Hall? Yikes. No hors d'oeuvres, no Macarena. What did you do?"

"Well, I witnessed an exchange of vows. It was nice, actually. I witnessed true love."

"You don't say. I haven't had a true love sighting in...I don't know how long."

He had RSVP'd to her wedding invitation, solo. Fifty-something and no romantic love in his life, other than Bogart, his cat. The photo on his desk of a disinterested tabby made it even more sad. What did he have to live for, other than his absolute dedication to fashion?

On the 14th floor, the air had the sweet-ambery scent of Rhonda, even though she had already left reception for the day.

"I can't go to weddings anymore without getting acceptably plastered," Bucksly said as they walked down the narrow white corridor.

She thought of Josh, whose sole focus at weddings was the open bar. Would it be any different at their wedding?

"I'm looking forward to yours, though." Bucksly stopped in front of her office. "It will mean the end of appointments: florists, caterers, bands..."

"I'm looking forward to that, too, actually."

"By the way, did I tell you we need adjustable shoulder-straps on our Givenchy bags? No. What we *really* need is to get that Prada denim with ostrich feathers in stores. The mark-up on that bag is kill-er! It's going to make our year."

"Right." She inched toward her office door. *Eve's Garden ~ Where Women Go for Love.*

"Just two more weeks before it hits stores. Right?" he said, carrying on about some bag.

"Right." Just two more steps to her computer.

He looked pensive—another thought was coming. "When exactly will our first delivery arrive?"

"Oh, what style?"

"Come on, Ava, get with the day. That little denim creation with ostrich feathers! It's going to be *the* handbag this summer. Every woman who's anyone will own one. You used to tell me these things before I asked."

"I've got more than ostrich feathers on my mind at the moment. Only twenty-eight days to my wedding."

"And after the wedding there'll be births and anniversaries and funerals..."

She saw her mom, bald and pallid, fighting it out.

He seemed to realize his slip. "The point is, Ava, there will always be something competing for your time. When you're here, be *here*. For M-E."

"I am. I have been since the day I started." She stepped inside her office. "I've spoiled you."

"Ha! Do you think you work for free?" His voice carried down the hall as he walked to his office. "That's a good one, Ava!"

She closed her door and breathed. *Eve's Garden.*

The webpage gave a midtown address and a mission statement: *We empower women of all ages to celebrate their sexuality as a positive, nourishing, and creative force in their lives.* She read it again, not fully comprehending the purpose. Well, they had to have something for a terrified bride-to-be.

Chapter Four

Ava walked with determination toward Eve's Garden, feeling the energy of the city at rush hour. Sidewalks overflowed with tourists venturing out from their hotels and with New Yorkers hurrying to put distance between themselves and their desks. Low, hazy clouds veiled the skyscrapers, making their lights look blurry. She breathed in the scent of car exhaust and roasted peanuts and couldn't imagine herself being anywhere else.

The glamour and commerce of midtown made a striking contrast to her apartment in Chelsea. Her building seemed lost in Manhattan's rush for transformation, fiercely clinging to its pre-war status. Then there was that guy below her stoop, an accomplice to the deterioration. What were the chances of sitting next to him on the subway? He could've been following her. Shivers chased the thought away.

She turned her attention back to the city, to Sixth Ave, Avenue of the Americas. A supper club—a throwback to the Big Band era—flanked a new hotel. Posters on the door shouted GIRLZ SENZATIONAL! STUNNING & SAVOIR-FAIRE! A crowd waited outside. The lights would dim, and the curtain would open...

She pictured herself as a young girl in a jazzy costume, taking a bow and savoring the applause. Twelve years of recitals and competitions...amazing how Mom never missed a performance, always in the front row, always smiling. *You could become a Rockette*, she used to say. Just one of those "what if" things, a career in dance. The closest she'd been to a Broadway stage was the orchestra section, Phoebe's treat.

Another city block, and she passed a hardware store, a Vietnamese take-out restaurant, and a nightclub called The

Encore. No windows, just a tinted glass door and a notice that read TALENT WANTED. Out front, a middle-aged woman smoked a cigarette, talking into her cell phone. "Listen," she said, exhaling a trail of smoke, "it's not about pretending you're someone special. It's a lot more than pretending." Her voice grated, and gold bangles hanging from her wrists clanged as she took another drag.

Ava moved on until finally she reached 119 West 57th Street. It seemed odd that Eve's Garden was in an office building. She took a deep breath and went in. An elevator ride to the 12th floor, a short walk down a drab corridor, and she came to the door: *Where Women Go for Love.* A fertility center? A day spa?

Eve's Garden smelled like the rose-shaped soaps that Phoebe displayed in her guest lavatory. It was a small store, pink like the inside of a hatbox, but not so innocent. Right in front was a display of edible panties and furry handcuffs, romantic stuff that would turn Josh off faster than she could coo, *Come to me, my sweet love*, eyelashes batting. Time to leave. But a quick glance around and more "practical" items stood out: massage oils, bath salts, scented candles, books, and...Dr. Lindquist? Her gynecologist, standing by the bookshelves, waved.

Ava smiled and quickly turned to the scented candles. She wasn't about to have a casual chat with her doctor here. What would she say she was looking for?

"I know you," Dr. Lindquist said, approaching. "Don't tell me. Ava, right? And you're about to get married. Or, no, you already have. Which is it?" She had youthful skin, for someone broaching her sixties. Her slight frame and wide eyes gave her an elfin appearance. It was strange to see her without her lab coat. In jeans and a Yankees T-shirt, she looked like someone's spunky grandma.

"I'm about to be married, and please don't ask me what I'm doing here." Ava looked down at the cherry-red candle in her hand called *Je T'aime Toujours.* "I'm wondering myself."

"How's it smell?" Dr. Lindquist asked. A small black book peeked out from under her arm.

"Spicy, like those little red candy hearts. Not for me. Want

31

to try?"

Dr. Lindquist gave it a sniff and made a face, setting it back on the shelf. "I'm guessing you're here honeymoon shopping." A wink and a sly smile.

"No, just looking around." How could she get out of this situation? *Butter Cookie.* "Oh, this one's the best so far." She handed it to Dr. Lindquist.

"Yum. So, how's your fiancé doing? Is he starting to get the jitters? They all do."

"Actually, *I'm* the one getting nervous."

"Really. Is there anything bothering you in particular?" Dr. Lindquist raised her faint eyebrows. "Lay it on me. I've heard everything."

"Well, we've been together so long and...sometimes I wish we had waited for marriage. You know, like save yourself?"

"That's a new one. Chastity in retrospect. Normally if a sexually-active couple makes it as far as you have, they don't even think about the benefits of waiting." Dr. Lindquist frowned, visibly concerned about something.

"I think if we had waited, we might still have romance. And maybe I'd feel more certain about our relationship."

"Maybe. But love and sex have very little to do with each other. Sex dies, while love...Ava, love can look death in the face and grow stronger." Dr. Lindquist handed her a cinnamon-colored candle called *Sin-A-Bun.* "Wow, try this one. It smells like the real thing, hot, straight from the oven."

"It really does." Ava stared at the candle. "Maybe I'm expecting too much."

"Oh, I'm not saying to give up on romance." Dr. Lindquist took the black book out from under her arm. "It's called *What Today's Woman Wants in Bed, Third Edition.* I wish I could say it's for my husband." She paused. "George passed away seven years ago. I'm just keeping up with the times. One decade, women prefer the bottom, and the next, they're crawling up on top. These days, I don't know. There's a chapter in here titled 'Sperm for Hire.' I'll tell you, though, if there's *one* thing that never changes, it's the male psyche. Men like to satisfy their women. It makes them feel good about themselves."

Ava looked absently at the book. Not Josh, not lately. A clean apartment made him feel good about himself, eight hours of sleep, The Whiskey Bar...

"Here, maybe this is something you should read," Dr. Lindquist said, holding out the book.

Ava didn't reach for it. "Thanks, but I'm more the traditional type. What I want most in bed is to feel loved."

"Then what are you doing here sniffing candles?" Dr. Lindquist gave her a hug. Ava felt twice her size, but she had a strong embrace.

"Thanks for your advice."

Dr. Lindquist went to buy the book, while Ava stood alone with the scented candles. Should she buy something? Or forget about love and just get married?

Another glance around the store, and she noticed a wall of books and videos. She browsed the shelves, refusing to give up. *Urban Friction: a Modern Romance* might be appropriate. The cover pictured a young couple clinging to each other against a city skyline. Perhaps she and Josh needed to work harder for love, experiment.

But...was pornography the answer?

Mom, loving toward David in the most natural, honest, and self-respecting way, would be ashamed of her. But they lived in the country and didn't have the distraction of twelve million people, all-consuming careers, and The Whiskey Bar, if you're Josh. Of course, cancer could be a big distraction in a relationship, but it seemed to bring Mom and David closer together.

Ava glanced over her shoulder. No one was watching.

Dad. He'd send an e-mail, a long one, full of warnings and worry. She touched the cover, expecting the fire of passion and sin to burn her fingers. It felt like a video cover.

How could it be bad if it helped? A little guidance, that's all. Maybe they just needed to laugh, loosen up? The strangest, most unexpected moments could spark love.

She bought it, along with the *Sin-a-Bun* candle.

Two subway stops and she was on the Upper West Side—a safe place to raise a family, as Josh often pointed out. It did have some of the best museums and private schools, just a few blocks from his apartment building. Not to mention, Central Park at their fingertips. Without question, the Upper West Side was reputable.

Standing on Columbus Avenue, she arched her neck for a vertical view of his condominium, a tower of tinted glass. Traffic and the bustle of city life couldn't penetrate it. His building, soon to be her building, was a city in itself with a gym, lap pool, full-service spa, Starbucks, drycleaners, and a shoeshine. It even had an Italian bistro with her favorite take-out. Such a bubble-like lifestyle made it easy to float along, unquestioning.

"The bride-to-be!" Benny, the night doorman, greeted her when she entered the lobby. A soaring ceiling and black marble floor gave her the feeling of falling through a dark abyss, not the warmest of welcomes. "So, you nervous yet?" he asked.

"Do I look nervous?" She walked to the elevators, clutching the plastic bag from Eve's Garden. A twisted version of their wedding announcement came to mind: *This bride believes sex tapes and scented candles are the secret to lasting love.* Phoebe wouldn't be so eager to get that one in *The Times.*

The floor seemed to separate beneath her feet. She didn't really believe this was the way to love, did she?

"I'm sure you've got everything under control," Benny said, laughing. As always, her eyes were drawn to the bald spot on top of his head. He was just being his usual chatty self, innocuously prying, but it made her particularly uncomfortable now. Yes, she was nervous—for tonight! She'd been rejected by Josh before. It hurt, and it could happen again.

"Thanks, Benny." She stepped inside the elevator and willed the doors to close.

"Have a good night!" he shouted, disappearing from view.

On the 41st floor, she let herself into Josh's apartment. He was half-asleep on the couch, TV on, lights off. "Hey! I have a surprise for you."

He groaned. "What surprise?"

"Just wait. You'll see." She kissed his head and went to change out of her work clothes, tossing the bag on his bed. His bathroom smelled of lemons and ammonia. Marta had come. Ava imagined her dirty laundry at home washed and folded, knowing a good cleaning lady should *not* be a consideration in getting married. She splashed water over her face, washing away the city streets in fine particles on her skin.

Back in his bedroom, she lit the candle she'd bought and placed it on his nightstand. Next, lingerie...except she didn't have any. Weren't boyfriends supposed to keep a separate budget for lacy teddies and matching garters? Or maybe she was supposed to buy that stuff for him? Comfortable PJs were more her speed—a sky-blue shorts-and-halter set would have to do. Bare toes sank into soft carpet...his place was a luxury.

Her stomach rumbled. She hadn't eaten a thing all day, other than a small fruit salad and twenty raw almonds. Phoebe's Perfect Bride Diet didn't count as food in her mind. It was a taste of poverty, really.

She walked down the hall to the kitchen and raided his refrigerator for a leftover sandwich or anything edible. The usual tonic water and condiments he kept on hand were a disappointment. "You want to order chicken marsala from downstairs?" she called out to him.

Heavy breathing and a quivering sigh wasn't the response she expected.

"Hey!" She ran into the living room and found that her video was no longer a surprise. "You were supposed to wait, Josh!" The couple on the cover was now kissing on his plasma HDTV. They held each other, naked, on a canopy bed. Their pleasure embarrassed her. She and Josh weren't vocal...or greedy about making love. They never even kept the lights on.

"What *is* this?" He made a face as if watching toxic waste

35

removal.

Oh, baby. I love you, the man said between kisses. *Love... you.* His muscular back glistened with sweat, which looked more cliché than sensual.

*More...*the woman moaned, digging long red nails into flesh. *Love me MORE!*

"Oh, dear." Ava watched, hoping for a redeeming scene...a tender moment.

"Seriously, can you tell me what this is all about?" Josh asked, looking straight at her.

"The plot isn't exactly clear to me at this point." She started to smile, but he didn't follow her lead. "Okay, I went to this store in midtown and—"

"You went to a porn shop? You could catch something in those places! What if someone saw you?"

"Who would see me?" Dr. Lindquist came to mind, winking with her sly smile. The couple in the video swapped positions, making Ava's throat constrict. "I was hoping it'd be about returning to love," she whispered, "when you've lost the very core of companionship and showing affection has become a last priority...but it's more explicit than that." She sat down next to him on the couch and carefully put her hand on his leg. "We could just kind of watch and see what happens?"

"Sure. Let's see if I throw up. Are you joking? Take it to your place and throw it out. I don't want this trash in my apartment." He brushed her hand away and stood up from the couch. "I'm curious, Ava. Who do you think we are? I mean, talk about tacky. Really, throw it out."

He left the room.

She counted one...two...trying for composure. *Enough trying to please him!* She jumped up from the couch. "We're a couple who doesn't make love anymore, that's who we are!" Jabbing the eject button, she grabbed the DVD and followed the buzz of his Waterpik into the bathroom. "Men are supposed to *want* to please women!"

He raised his perfectly arched eyebrows. "Don't give me that

Cosmo magazine propaganda crap. You're wasting your time."

"That's *exactly* what I'm afraid of!" She held *Urban Friction* in the air as though it were proof of their disconnect. "I can't keep going like this. I'm lonely with you. Am I supposed to just accept that? Because I won't. I can't, Josh."

"What are you talking about? All because I don't want any part of your pathetic video?" He started his electric toothbrush.

"Okay, I'm sorry. It was an impulse purchase, a dumb idea. I regret it." She set the video down on the bathroom counter. "I actually thought it might get us in the wedding spirit. You know, lovey and excited about sharing life together."

He spit paste into the sink. "Watch the video yourself and see what happens. I bet nothing."

"Are you saying I should get into the wedding spirit without you? Alone? Come on, Josh, can't you see how much I care about us? How much I want to love you?"

"We're focused on the wedding right now, that's all."

"We *are* the wedding!"

"You know what I mean, Ava. It's late. Your parents are coming tomorrow. Sunday we have Kitty's wedding. Can we go to bed? Seriously."

"Fine. Just don't forget I tried." She went into his bedroom, blew out the candle on his nightstand, and lay down on top of the covers.

Josh wrapped himself in the comforter, his nightly cocoon, and fell asleep.

She stared at the ceiling. How had she come so far with him only to end up feeling so unsure?

The regularity of his breathing filled the silence. Had his mother gone into marriage knowing that she would feel lonely, too? Ava forced her eyes to close, but her mind kept going. It had taken her own mom nine years of marriage to figure out what was missing.

Unable to sleep, Ava slid out of bed, tiptoed into the bathroom, and picked up the video from where she had left it on the counter.

God, bear with me. I'm trying to understand what love is. At least now I'm trying.

She dropped *Urban Friction* into the trash, ashamed that she had gone into a sex shop looking for the answer.

Chapter Five

The plan was to meet at the bus stop by Macy's Herald Square. Through a crowd of Saturday shoppers, Ava saw a charter bus parked at the curb. A pale woman wearing a long jean skirt and a billowy purple blouse stood next to it, holding two plastic shopping bags. Wrapped around her head was a light blue scarf, the same color as the clear June sky. Mom.

Even with the scarf, it was obvious that she was bald. And her skin wanted color, which she more than made up for with the purple blouse. She was so thin now; her clothes might as well have been on their hanger.

David stepped off the bus and stood behind Mom, his beard neatly trimmed. Wow, he actually made an effort. Years could pass before he'd find a reason to take out his scissors, and even then he'd just trim the strays. Today, for her, he almost looked professional, except for the jeans.

She could just imagine Josh and his parents taking it all in: David's red and blue plaid shirt and crisp blue jeans, Mom's rainbow of colors. Hicks. Beatniks. Hillbillies.

Mom waved gaily. Ava went to her, while the Copelands and the cancer and everything else slipped away. How wonderful it felt to be her daughter.

"Honey!" Mom set down the shopping bags and opened her arms. "It's so good to see you! And to be back in the city!"

Ava hugged her thin body, breathing in a scent of soap and medication. Two months had made a difference she didn't want to see. Why had she put off going home?

"Well, here we are," David said, "for the day anyway. How are you, Ava?" He put his arm around her shoulder. "So what's the agenda? All I know is that we have to be back here for the bus by 6:30. I'd like to aim for 6:00, to be on the safe side."

"Don't worry, I'll make sure you don't miss the bus." Ava smiled. David considered running errands traveling. She understood the sacrifice he was making coming down to the city for this lunch. "I love the new beard, by the way."

He grunted.

They pushed through sidewalk traffic to a less crowded street where there was a better chance of finding a taxi. "What's in the shopping bags, Mom?"

"Oh, you'll see in a minute. A little surprise from home."

"Well, I've got a surprise for you, too! Matinee tickets for us all to see *Wicked*. Orchestra seats!"

Mom gasped. "Oh, my word! Orchestra seats? But we didn't bring that much money."

"It's my treat! For making the trip here, and to the Copelands for the wedding. It's something I wanted to do." And could do, she thought happily. As of July, no more rent payments!

Ava stepped to the curb and threw up her hand. "Taxi!" The driver pulled over.

"Leigh, you're in the middle," David said. Afraid of an accident, no doubt. Mom loved taking the subway, experiencing the *real* New York, but no one had questioned the decision to take a cab. Mom needed to conserve energy, not tackle stairs, and being above ground just felt...safer. They buckled up.

"I hear it's an amazing play." Mom's dark, sunken eyes shone with excitement. She looked happy.

"Sounds like a big to-do," David said. "Am I dressed for the theater?"

"No. You're dressed for carpentry. All you're missing is your tool belt." Ava winced at the bite in her tone but kept it up. "Couldn't you have helped him out a little, Mom? I told you the Copelands dress up. Suit jackets. Ties."

"Goodness, Ava, I don't think David has ever worn a tie."

"I swear I just washed this shirt." David gave it a whiff and smiled.

Ava glowered at him. "I know you own one decent jacket,

40

at least."

He made a face, as if trying to think really hard. "Yes, I recall there was a brownish jacket at some point. I believe I last wore it at your college graduation. Must be up in the attic, waiting for your wedding day."

"You'll be wearing a tux to my wedding!"

Their cabbie lay on the horn at a truck blocking the intersection.

"A tuxedo!" David protested. He obviously hadn't read the invitation. "You know my philosophy about visiting this city, Ava. Dress poor and people will leave you alone. If I show up in a tuxedo, every bum in town will expect a handout. I'm a total sucker. We'll go broke, for sure."

Mom touched his arm and laughed. "We're already broke, honey."

Ava thought of the homeless guy living below her stoop. He didn't dress like a bum, didn't *look* like a bum, but when he was on his cardboard, people sure left him alone. Kind of sad, actually. He had no one to talk to, as far as she knew, other than his dog.

"Not all homeless people beg, David," she said. "A lot of them keep to themselves. Anyway, if you don't wear a tux to my wedding, Phoebe won't let you in."

"I can't wait to meet this all-powerful woman." He put down the window. "Anyone need air?" Their cab crawled up Central Park West.

Mom fingered her gold cross necklace, which had become a habit over the past year. Ava thought about asking her to take it off, just for lunch. Josh and his dad already considered her family a bunch of religious freaks for going to church every Sunday. And Phoebe would compliment it every five minutes, her way of fixating on things. There they would be at a white-clothed table and Mom's cross glinting under recessed lighting. Phoebe: Such an exquisite necklace...now, what does it mean, exactly?

Ava took a deep breath. "Mom, would you mind tucking your cross inside your blouse? I'm not sure the Copelands will understand why you wear it."

"I wore it the first time I met Phoebe. That lunch went well. I don't think religion even came up."

"We weren't planning a wedding then."

David sat forward. "Gosh, Ava, don't the Copelands know you well enough to understand our differences?"

"I can't take it off," Mom said. "I mean, that's just what I *shouldn't* do. Let it open dialogue! So we have a conversation about faith. Great! I'm not saying I'm right and everyone else is wrong. I'm saying this is what works for me."

"But it doesn't work for them." Ava looked again at the cross. "All right, fine."

"I almost forgot!" Mom opened one of her shopping bags and then stopped. "Is there time for a quick make-over?"

"Makeup? You never wear makeup. You don't need to be someone you're not."

"It's not makeup. These times call for...well, hair!" She pulled a carefully wrapped wig out of each bag. "I brought two options: a blond, which I think is too flashy, but David loves, and this plain brown one with curl in the back. The style seems a little dated, but I wanted a conservative option. You can't imagine how hard it is to pick out hair."

David chuckled. "My opinion, every woman dreams of being a blond at some point in her life."

"I'd go red." Ava looked out the window to see how far they were from the restaurant. "Okay, let's see the blond one. We've only got a few blocks, though, so hurry and fulfill David's fantasy."

Mom pulled the scarf off her head, revealing a bald stranger. This person could've been Sinéad O'Connor. A punk rocker. A monk. Or a very sick woman. But not her mother.

"Well?" Mom smoothed the long, straight hair, which was blond as in overripe corn. With her narrow face and wide, dark eyes, she looked like an abandoned doll. Blond wouldn't work.

"Quick, let's see the other one." They were a block away and trying on wigs.

Mom become the bald woman again, and then a frazzled

waitress in a diner. Alice from the '70s sitcom.

"I don't like it at all," David said, taking it off her head and reaching for the blond.

Ava wanted to say forget the wigs and go with the scarf, but the restaurant was in sight with Josh and his parents waiting out front.

"You look great as a blond, Mom." Ava smoothed it down. "Okay, there they are. Remember, don't bring up money, politics, or religion."

"Oh, Ava, honey, you're making way too much of this lunch. It's not an interview. Josh isn't going to feel differently about you because of us. If his parents don't like us, big deal!"

Mom had a way of seeing straight to the heart of a situation, but she was no comfort this time. Obviously, at the heart there was a resounding lack of confidence. Ava closed her eyes for a moment, shutting everything out.

Their cab pulled to the curb, and she put on her happy-bride smile.

"Hello!" Phoebe waved from the sidewalk. The Copelands looked like a window display for Ralph Lauren with Josh and his father in navy sport coats, pastel shirts, and tan slacks, and Phoebe modeling a knee-length blue and white striped sundress, the accent, tying the display together.

Ava paid the driver, while Mom and David struggled with their seat belts, surpassing the acceptable amount of time it takes to exit a New York City cab. Finally, David backed out in an effort to help Mom. The Copelands looked on in silence, as if watching an accident.

The café was on a quiet, tree-lined street, neighbor to opulent brownstones. Phoebe had said they'd grab lunch someplace casual. Maybe casual to them.

Ava tried to read Josh's expression. A good mood? Annoyed that they were a few minutes late? His lips suddenly landed on hers, a total surprise. "Hey, Ava." He just as smoothly moved on to greet Mom and David, a kiss on the cheek, a firm handshake, respectively. "Good to see you in the city, David. Is this a first?"

"It always feels like a first, although I see it's still loud and crowded."

"No worse than the country, quiet and desolate." Josh laughed. "I think the longest I've lasted upstate is three days."

"Two." Ava recalled his brief visits to her childhood home upstate. He sat on the old couch in the living room, drinking diet Coke after diet Coke.

"I've been waiting for this family lunch since the day I met Ava!" Phoebe said, hugging Mom like an old friend. "It's so good to see you again, Leigh. You look amazing. And I love your new hair. I could *never* pull off blond, but you wear it like a natural!"

"Thank you. It was a last-minute decision." Mom's eyes met Ava's, repressing a smile.

Mr. Copeland stepped forward, extending his hand. "Barry." He was a piranha, with a permanent frown and a protruding under bite. He had eyes like reflecting glass, silvery and cold.

Mom braved his handshake. "I'm Leigh," she said, "and this is my husband, David."

"You'll get to meet my father and his family at the wedding," Ava said.

"Looking forward to it." Mr. Copeland spoke as though it required effort. Phoebe nodded in earnest agreement.

"It looks to me like I might be underdressed," David said as they approached the restaurant. Ava tore at her thumbnail, fearing they would be turned away at the door, and she'd be to blame.

"Well, yes, you are," Mr. Copeland replied. "But not to worry, they keep extra jackets on hand. As for the jeans, we know the owner. He'll let it go."

"Sorry," Ava said, "I should've given them better instructions." She double-checked her pressed white pants and yellow blouse.

"David has this silly philosophy about dressing for the city," Mom explained. "Dress like a bum, and people will treat you like one."

"Actually, the idea is you won't get mugged," David said.

Again, Ava thought of the guy below her stoop. He could keep a million dollars in his archaic suitcase and no one would bother to look.

"I've lived in this city my whole life and have never been robbed," Mr. Copeland said. "And I don't dress like a bum."

Phoebe held open the door for them. "Well, we'll all be safe in here."

The restaurant, beige with warm lighting and wall-to-wall carpeting, reminded her of a private doctor's waiting room. The maître d' helped David into a dark green jacket.

"I think this should inspire us to buy you a new sports coat," Mom said. "You look like a golfer winning the Masters Tournament!"

Having passed inspection, they were seated. "Josh, I'll sit next to you, darling," Phoebe said, doing what she did best. "Ava, you can take the seat to his right. Leigh, you're next to Ava, of course, and then David. Barry, you're fine where you are, next to me. Perfect. Round tables are my favorite."

Mom sat down, smiling. "Usually when I come to the city, it's hotdogs from a street vendor and a walk through Central Park. That's our little ritual, right honey?"

Ava smiled, suddenly feeling very shy. "It's the only time I let myself eat a hotdog."

"Well, this is quite a place," David said, decibels above fine-dining volume. "And Ava tells us she picked up theater tickets, too."

Phoebe put her hand on the table as if laying down a card. "I wanted to pay for them, but Ava flat out refused to let me."

"Well, thank you, darling," Mom said. "It means a lot."

Menus arrived, and David opened his. "Would you look at this, we're in a French restaurant!"

The couple at the next table looked amused.

"Is that a problem?" Josh asked, crouched behind his menu.

"I don't think I've ever eaten *authentic* French food."

"We'd love to see Paris," Mom said, "but there's always some project keeping us at home."

Ava pictured them at the old farmhouse: repairing the roof... tending the garden...chemo.

"David has been getting steady orders for his custom-built furniture," Mom continued, "and I'm busy teaching music, when I can."

"Don't forget our folk band," David said. "We're booked year after year at all the local festivals."

"Leigh is a fiddler, and David plays the piano and bass," Phoebe said to the Piranha. "Isn't that something?"

"Can't say I know much about music," he replied. "I'm more a baseball fan. When I come home from work, I like quiet, actually. Phoebe and I will catch the news before bed, I suppose."

"Hold one minute." David peered at the menu. "Is this right? Forty-two dollars a plate...for lunch?"

Ava returned to her thumbnail.

"Never mind money." Phoebe fluttered her hand in the air as if shooing away hundred dollar bills. "Leigh, you haven't been able to visit all year. I wanted today to be special."

"But these prices—"

Mr. Copeland cleared his throat, drowning out every conversation in the restaurant. "It's true my wife knows nothing about what things cost in the real world, but please, just enjoy our hospitality."

"That's right," Phoebe added, although with some uncertainty.

A waiter appeared, and Phoebe opened the wine list, back into the spirit of the moment. "Well, I'm going to order a bottle of 1998 Cuvée Louise Brut. We have our beautiful children here, and we're going to celebrate. They're getting married!"

The waiter congratulated them, while Mom clapped.

Ava looked at Josh. Now seemed like the appropriate time for a shared smile or kiss, some show of enthusiasm.

"Does the whole restaurant need to know?" he asked. "Seriously. It's not like we're the first couple in the world to get engaged."

"I agree," Mr. Copeland added. His father being present didn't help; it never did, as if Josh were afraid of his criticism for being in love.

"Some people shout it from a mountain top," Ava muttered.

Josh closed his menu and turned to the waiter. "Your top

shelf whiskey and the tartare de bœuf."

"Do you all mind if I toast with water?" David asked. "I'm not a drinker. And Leigh, I'm not sure you want to drink, either."

"Yes, I do! Oh, one glass won't kill me. I'd love some champagne and the charcuterie. I'm up for anything today!"

"Ava, will you have some?" Phoebe asked.

"I'll have a glass to toast." She smiled at Mom but felt unsure about her sudden carpe diem.

"And your order?" The waiter looked at her expectantly.

"The soup du jour. Thanks."

"So. The wedding." Phoebe beamed with excitement. "We'll just zip through the marriage contract and the seven blessings, so there'll be enough time for...oh dear, what's his name... Father...you know, your guy."

Ava laughed. Not again. "Father Luke."

"Right. That's right. I don't know why I can't remember his name. Now, are there any family traditions that you want to include in the ceremony, Leigh?"

"I always love the unity candle." Mom glanced at Ava, looking for an okay.

"Sure, fine with me."

When their drinks arrived, Josh downed his whiskey.

"Nice of you to wait for the toast, Josh," she snapped. It was hard not to sound bitter.

"Waiter!" He raised his empty glass. "Make it another." It arrived in seconds.

Phoebe held up her flute of bubbling champagne. "Ava and Josh, to a long life of love and happiness, children and grandchildren!"

Everyone cheered, not too loud.

"That gets right to the point," David said. "Do you both want children?"

"Isn't that how it goes?" Josh asked. "You get married, buy a place with a couple extra bedrooms, and fill them."

"My word, that makes it sound like you're on a conveyor belt!" Mom exclaimed.

"Call it what you want." Josh picked up his drink, about to

down another.

Mom clinked her glass with her fork. "Now I'd like to make a toast. To the loveliest, most giving and caring daughter a mother could ask for. You'll make a wonderful wife, honey."

"Thanks, Mom," Ava said, blushing. "I *aspire* to be all that."

"Well, I feel like the luckiest mother on the planet." She sipped her champagne.

"Go easy there, Leigh." David shot her a knowing look.

"Oh, pooh," Phoebe said. "We're celebrating life!"

Conversation turned to seating arrangements for the wedding reception. Phoebe had them memorized, which gave her the authority to make daily changes. "That'll be fine," Ava said, letting Phoebe have her fun. Mr. Copeland checked his watch.

"So, Barry, what's your line of work?" David asked.

Ava felt a headache coming on. "Let's talk about anything but. It's Saturday."

"Hear, hear!" Phoebe exclaimed. "I'd rather learn more about that folk band, playing at festivals and country dances. Wouldn't you, Barry?"

Several waiters arrived with their orders. Mom finished her champagne and smiled hazily.

"I've been in banking for forty years," Mr. Copeland said as he cut his duck rillette into bite-size pieces. "I started the current fund in 2000, a true milestone, if I say so myself."

"You're very rude to ignore me," Phoebe said, her cheeks as pink as her lipstick. "Most people don't even know what hedge funds are."

Mr. Copeland chewed and swallowed his food. "The focus of the fund is currency, which is a four trillion dollar marketplace right now. Anyone who knows what the words 'low risk' and 'diversify' mean can understand currency investments."

Phoebe opened her mouth to protest further.

"It's all right, Mom," Josh said.

"Moving money around is your passion, too, Josh. Isn't that so?" David asked. "After all, you followed in your old man's footsteps."

"Not exactly." Mr. Copeland grunted. "Six months ago he joined another fund."

"Oops, I think I'll bow out of this conversation." David took a mouthful of pasta with clams. "Excellent food!"

Mom was hardly eating.

"My fund invests in property," Josh explained. "We're not in competition."

"It's not a matter of being in competition," Mr. Copeland said, exceeding a comfortable volume. "It's about taking the heat. I might actually respect your decision to quit the firm if you continued in currency."

"They say in fashion that without competition no one would care," Ava said—not the first time she'd tried playing the peacemaker.

Mom stood, both hands on the table. "Phoebe, could you tell me where the women's room is?" Her voice was strangely somber.

Ava held her breath as the weary woman, who couldn't be Mom, looked around the restaurant, unsure of her balance, unsure of herself. "Want me to go with you, Mom?"

"I can go alone," she replied with a resolute look in her eyes. "You stay here."

"Are you sure?"

They watched her leave the table and cautiously cross the dining room. She clutched the back of an empty chair for support, and Ava stood. But then she continued.

"Your mother is a strong woman," Phoebe said. "I could never be so strong."

"If you'll excuse me a minute." Ava left for the rest room.

A bald woman stood in front of a gold-framed mirror, wig in hand. "What a waste of money." She stuffed the blond rendition into her handbag and wrapped the blue scarf around her head. "I'm dying. There's no hiding it."

"You are not!" Ava stood behind her, looking in the mirror. "How could you say that? Fighting cancer is *not* dying. You're strong, Mom. Phoebe just said how strong you are. You *have* to be!"

Mom inhaled a deep breath and let it out. "Sometimes it feels like I'm out-running the cancer, like I'm way ahead of it, beyond reach. And then all of a sudden I stumble, and it catches up to me. It shouts horrible words, like, *you won't be there when Ava gives birth! Your grandchildren won't know you!*"

"Stop it! Just stop it!" Tears came at once, as if Ava had been saving them for this day. "You're drunk! Why'd you go and drink when you knew you'd fall apart?"

Mom covered her mouth, realizing her mistake. "Oh, Ava, I'm so sorry. Forget what I said. It was self-pity talking. Really. You know I'm fighting this, every step." She gripped Ava's shoulders. "Honey, are you all right?"

Ava couldn't look up. "I'm okay."

Mom hugged her, and Ava felt the stranger in her arms. If only this frail woman missing so much muscle mass was someone other than Mom.

As soon as Mom let go, Ava stepped back. The truth: she could feel cancer's significant lead in their lives and wanted no part of it; love was asking too much.

Ava glanced in the mirror, seeing guilt, and then remembered the Copelands. Red eyes and nose forced her to say, "They'll know I've been crying." She blinked several times and reapplied lipstick.

Mom gently pulled back Ava's long hair. "I used to love to comb your hair when you were a little girl."

Ava smiled and took her hand. "We should go back. Leaving David alone with them makes me nervous, like leaving my diary open on the table." They left the rest room. "No more champagne, Mom. Right?"

"No more. I don't need it to celebrate."

The Gershwin Theatre was warm and filled with the excited chatter of a sold-out show. Ava sat in her front-row seat, relieved to forget about life for the next couple of hours.

"Here we go, again," Josh said as the lights dimmed.

"What do you mean? We've never seen *Wicked*."

"I have, with clients. Didn't I mention it? You'll like the storyline."

"When? I bought these tickets months ago. How could you forget to tell me about seeing a Broadway show?"

The curtain opened. "Shhh." His face glowed from the stage lights.

Josh never took clients to the theater. At least as far as she knew he didn't. What else had he forgotten to mention? Paranoia obstructed her view, so that all she could see was Josh excluding her...alienating her...disappointing her...living a separate life. Sitting beside him in forced silence turned her theater experience into a punishment.

She looked to her right. Mom, tucked under David's arm, rested her head on his shoulder. She looked so trusting, happy just to be held...and safe.

The sun was much lower in the sky when they returned to Macy's to catch the bus. "Thanks for making the trip," Ava said. They waited on the sidewalk for boarding to start. "Next weekend I'll come home for sure."

"We'll see how things go this week," Mom replied. In other words, chemo. She might not be up for a visit.

"I can help out around the house or even cook for you," Ava pressed, knowing it was useless. Mom didn't want her hanging around, in tears. That didn't help anyone. "Well, call me when you get home, okay?" She looked away. She wasn't giving enough. It felt impossible on so many levels.

"We had so much fun, Ava." Mom held tight to her hand. "Thank you."

"And we didn't get mugged!" David leaned in for one of his

brief, yet firm, hugs.

"I still want to see you in a tux at my wedding," Ava said, and it occurred to her that she was speaking for Phoebe. If it were her choice, she'd want David to be comfortable.

He and Mom smiled vaguely.

Bus tickets were being collected, and David had theirs ready. "Well, I guess this is it," he said.

Mom pressed her soft lips to Ava's cheek. "I like Phoebe," she said in a whisper. "I'm glad you have her." She turned away, and they boarded the bus.

Chapter Six

The battle of the weddings was on. Ava entered The Plaza Hotel with Josh, arm in arm, feeling as tense as steel wire on a suspension bridge. Maybe Kitty's caterer wouldn't show, or something would catch fire...

Such horrible thoughts! Ava shook off the competition, feeling ashamed. How did she get caught up in this? The reception of Mr. Copeland's business partner's daughter had nothing to do with her wedding reception. Nothing. She took a deep breath.

The grand ballroom glittered in pink and gold under a spectacular chandelier. "This is really nice," she said, determined not to make petty comparisons.

"I see my parents." Josh pulled her toward the bar where Phoebe stood waving to them as if she were stranded on a deserted island.

"The contenders!" The Piranha actually smiled when he saw them. "Twenty-six more days, and we'll know if you can top *this* event," he said. "Kitty's gone all out."

As if on cue, the eight-piece band started "Up Where We Belong," and the newlyweds rose on a heart-shaped platform above the center of the dance floor. Everyone clapped, while smoke machines blew a grayish haze, aiming for billowy clouds. Ava searched her handbag for a tissue, eyes burning from the gaseous smell.

Josh looked at her and his jaw dropped as if watching the Knicks lose to the Mavericks by 50 points. "Don't tell me—the *anticipation*?"

"No, it's just so—"

"Lovely." Phoebe, dabbing tears, nudged her arm. "I think every wedding is its own accomplishment, don't you? Honey, if you need another tissue, I have plenty." Her chartreuse gown hung to the floor. Today she had golden highlights in her hair.

"I'm okay. Thanks." Ava smoothed her favorite bridesmaid gown...fitted lavender satin to mid-calf and puffy sleeves. "Remember this dress from Maggie's wedding?" she asked Josh. "It was the first wedding we went to together, like a million weddings ago." She pictured herself catching the bouquet. Of course, Maggie threw it right at her.

"Our wedding will top this," Josh said, obviously not listening.

"You've always been an optimist." Mr. Copeland tipped his empty glass to the bartender.

"Let us *have* the wedding before you criticize it, Dad."

"Well, if you're hoping for pink hearts," Ava said, brushing at the pink heart confetti scattered over the bar, "you'll be disappointed."

"What I'm *hoping*," the Piranha retorted, "is that it'll be worth the hole it's burning in my wallet. I just saw the catering bill. My God!"

"Pooh, pooh the bill," Phoebe said. "It's your son's wedding! Isn't family why you work so hard? Seriously, I wonder. Oh, there's Gabby! You'll have to anticipate our wedding without me. I haven't hugged her yet." Phoebe scurried off after the mother of the bride as fast as her heels and gown would allow.

"Marriage," Mr. Copeland muttered. "You two have no idea what you're headed for."

Ava had sensed the Piranha's disapproval of her from the beginning. The first time she was invited to their townhouse on the Upper West Side, she'd overheard him say to Phoebe, "Where'd Josh find *her*?" as if she had been picked up in a back alley.

He threw back his Scotch and excused himself.

"Well, if you're gonna go pink," Josh said, looking around the room, "you might as well go PINK."

"Sure, if you're Frenchy in *Grease*. You don't really like it, do you?"

"No," he replied, much to her relief. "It's tacky. Come on, let's eat."

They looked for their seating cards on a pink-draped table at the back of the ballroom. "I don't see our names."

"My parents are at Table Two," he said, "so I assume we're at Three or Four."

"Oh, here we are." She reached over and picked up *Mr. Joshua Copeland* and *Ms. Ava Larson. Table 54.*

"What the—?" He took the card from her. "You've got to be kidding me."

"Never mind. Let's check out the international buffet."

As they made their way across the room, Josh didn't even say hello to the guys he used to work with at his dad's hedge fund. She knew him well enough not to acknowledge the affront; it would only send him deeper into his rotten mood.

"Can you believe all this food?" she asked. "It's enough to feed underprivileged weddings around the world!"

He grunted and went for dim sum from the Asian station, and then heavy on the mushroom ravioletti with chèvre. She loaded up on salad. Kitty had obviously stuck to her diet. She looked perfectly starved in her princess gown, sitting amongst her bridesmaids squeezed into pink satin and tulle.

Ava thought of Maggie, her dress-less maid of honor. Outfitting her was the last purchase before the wedding. The amaranth floor-length gown and dyed-to-match silk pumps only needed its final fitting. What was she waiting for?

"Look at that." Josh stood before their table as if on a cliff, reluctant to take a step closer to the edge. He held his plate with one hand and his drink with the other. "Number fifty-four."

Okay, so it was next to the service entrance, at the furthest corner from the bride and groom. "Maybe they're putting the younger generation in the back." Kind of like a kids' section, she thought, but kept that to herself.

"I went to summer camp with half of Table Four," Josh whispered. "Even Greenberg is at Table Five."

"Who?"

"Our family's lawyer."

"Don't let it ruin your fun." She sat down and began introductions with the others at the table before Josh's snobbery became apparent. "Josh's family has been friends with Kitty's since the Stone Age. Well, practically. Kitty was like a sister to you growing up. Wasn't she, Josh?"

"You could say that. My parents are at Table Two, but I don't work for 'the company' anymore." His tone discouraged any further questions.

"Hey, at least no one will notice if we sneak out," she whispered, knowing it would be hours before they could leave. Five hundred guests. A pink rose bush on each table. Mini heart-shaped crystal dishes with pink candy hearts for gifts. The speeches were bound to drag on.

She leaned over to Josh. "What's the groom's name again?"

"Who knows?" He downed his drink.

"Great. Another wedding with you halfway to the moon."

"What do you want me to do, Ava? Sit here and tick off all the ways our wedding is going to be better? Or not. I'm so sick of weddings." Josh looked around, holding his empty glass. "They're short-staffed."

Like a lighthouse in a storm, the little chapel at City Hall flashed in her mind. "You know what, Josh? I really think we should write our own vows, like Courtney and Brad. Bring some meaning to it all."

"Please, don't remind me of those two. That civil service was the longest ten minutes of my life."

"I'm serious. If our wedding felt more personal, maybe we'd be more excited about it. Think about what our own words would add."

"Hmm, let's see. Embarrassment. Boredom. A hokey, melodramatic flair."

She fought a surge of anger. "Hey, I'm trying, at least. Our wedding should be one of the happiest days of our life."

"Ask any married man if his wedding day was the happiest day of his life. Or was it the most stressful?" Josh ate his ravioletti, taking small angry bites, just like his father.

"Fine, then we can look forward to getting our wedding over with. Might as well dread our honeymoon, too!"

"Keep your voice down. I just don't see the reason for personal vows."

She couldn't look at him.

He sighed. "Then tell me, what would writing our own vows add?"

"Us! How much we love each other. Why we want to spend the rest of our lives together. It takes *guts* to put that down on paper. I have a lot of respect for Courtney and Brad."

A steamed dumpling hung precariously between his chopsticks. "Honestly, I had no idea what they were saying."

"That doesn't matter because those were *their* vows. We'll write our own. And I don't mean anything long or poetic. Just to the point."

Silence.

"A few words from the heart, Josh. Please?" Did her begging sound as pathetic to him as it did to her? Not even the homeless guy below her stoop resorted to desperation.

"I don't know, Ava. Vows shouldn't be a creative writing assignment. They're a formality. God and State. I think we should stick with tradition."

She forked a radish. "Will you at least consider it?"

Josh dipped a dumpling in mustard sauce, three quick dips, ate it, and wiped his mouth with his napkin.

"Well?" she asked, hanging on his every movement.

"Well, what? Kitty and whatever-his-name-is didn't get all crazy with their vows."

"Right, and we don't even know who she married."

"But you see my point. Bottom-line, they were married. It is what it is." Josh looked around. "I'd really love a drink right now."

"I feel like I'm losing my mind. I really do."

Josh stopped a waiter who had strayed to the back of the room. "A double whiskey, please." He turned to her. "Forget the vows, Ava. Do you *really* think it makes any difference?"

"How many ways do I have to say it? Yes!" She raised her

hand, sending her water airborne and Josh flying from his seat, only too late. The front of his pants took the spill.

"That didn't just happen!" Heads turned. He sat back down. "Real nice. Draw attention to Table Fifty-four."

"I'm so sorry!" She tried to dab the wet spot with her napkin.

"Forget it." He shoved her off. "I can't believe you. Was that on purpose?"

"On *purpose*? Of course not. I'd never throw a drink at you, Josh."

"You know what? Write whatever you want. Just give me the script when I get there. I'll see you later." He stood, flung his jacket over his shoulder, and walked out the double doors.

Phoebe came up behind her. How long had she been there? "Oh, just pretend he's home sick with the flu or something. Be my date tonight! We'll feast on salad together...and maybe splurge on cake!"

Ava smiled, relieved, in a way, for the replacement. "I don't want to make Mr. Copeland jealous."

"Please, do! Nothing would make me happier!" She took her hand. "Come on. He's at the bar, anyway. You can take his seat."

She went with Phoebe to Table Two.

Ava unlocked Josh's apartment door and went inside. The living room was dark, but a light shone from under his bedroom door. Feeling unusually calm, she opened it without knocking.

Josh stood in his briefs in front of the mirror, deliberating over the next day's tie. "I hate it when the simplest decisions become the most difficult," he said.

"I'm sorry about the spill. It was an accident."

"I know."

"And, Josh, I'm sorry that your dad can be a jerk, and that we were seated at the crummiest table, but...you walked out on me."

He put one tie back on the hanging rack in his closet and hung another over the suit he had ready for the morning. "I'm sorry. It was inconsiderate. Once I started walking away, I couldn't stop. I needed space."

"Well, your mother is a great date. We ate and laughed and danced all night."

Josh turned to her, as if alarmed. "It was a good wedding?"

"We had fun, so I guess it was...I even danced with the groom. His name is Sam." Still in her lavender bridesmaid dress, she sat down on his bed. "I have something to tell you, Josh. It's something I've never mentioned before."

He came over and sat down next to her, brows furrowed, as if expecting bad news or a confession. "What is it?"

"You'll probably think...well, I just want you to know that I pray for you. To God. I pray for us."

Silence.

"O-kay. I'm not sure what I should say to that, other than I'm not big on prayer, which you know."

"I'm not expecting you to start praying for me, or anything. It's more about how much I care—that you're happy."

"Well, I am. Thanks." He put his hand on her leg, got up, and went back to his closet. "You know what I'm afraid of?" he asked, facing a row of hanging dress shirts.

"What?" The rest of her life seemed to hinge on what he would say.

"I'm afraid that you're hoping to 'save' me. Get me to church or synagogue, whatever."

She didn't know what to say. In a way, she did wish he believed in God, something more. Maybe he'd be a happier person.

Josh turned out the light and crawled into bed. "And really, Ava, leave the vows alone, okay?"

She took her time undressing and then carefully hung the lavender gown. Vows. Jewish, Buddhist, three-day long or three-minute short, it didn't matter. It wouldn't change a thing. Without love, vows were empty words.

She lay down beside him, finding no comfort in his soft

sheets, the down pillow.

"Basically, Ava," Josh murmured from inside his cocoon, "we owe it to my family to have a traditional wedding. It's what they want, and after all, they're paying for it."

She didn't say anything. She couldn't. Not yet. But the truth she'd been pushing away finally planted itself firmly in her mind. She had to call off the wedding.

Chapter Seven

4:15 a.m. Ava stood in front of floor-to-ceiling windows and looked down at the lighted streets below. There had to be a plan B out there.

The easiest way to leave Josh would be to run out the door, take a plane to Timbuktu, and call him on a phone card with limited minutes. How else would she tell him that the life they were to begin was over? Especially when their families approved. And when Mom... Tears blurred the streetlights below, a long way down. Ava closed her eyes and heard a miniscule voice inside her heart: *Let him go.*

She walked quietly into the bedroom and opened the bottom dresser drawer where she kept a few clothes. After folding them neatly into her Burberry bag, she noticed her *Sin-a-Bun* candle on the nightstand. Leave it. Her lavender bridesmaid gown, too. It was time for a break from weddings.

The urge to run grew. Go now while she had the courage! But it wouldn't be over until she told him they were through.

Returning to her place beside him, she waited for morning.

6:10 a.m. To the blast of an alarm, Josh exploded from his cocoon and bolted for the shower. For the first time, she let his typical start to the workday annoy her. His bursts of energy belonged to his job and the gym. She got his leftovers, and often after The Whiskey Bar.

"No more." She climbed out of bed and went into the

bathroom, light-headed from lack of sleep. "Josh?"

He poked his head out the shower door, condensation fogging the glass and leaving a layer of moisture on her skin. "What are you doing up this early?" he asked.

She aimed for the right tone: determined and resolute. "I—I'm calling off our engagement." Her voice cracked, landing on heartbroken and afraid.

He stared at her through the steam escaping from the shower. She held her breath, while unspoken thoughts swelled in the space between them.

His eyes narrowed. "What did you say?"

"I know the wedding is planned and everything, but I have serious doubts about us. You don't seem to want all the love I have to give. And I wonder if you can love me the way I need to be loved. It's like...we're out of sync." She hoped her words made sense.

"What are you talking about? Our vows? Write whatever you want, if it's that big a deal. Forget my dad and what he thinks."

"Vows won't fix us. It's more than our wedding." How could she explain a gut feeling? She longed for a love they didn't have, but what kind of love was that?

"What's your problem, Ava?"

Her face flushed as vague ideas of meaningful love dissolved in her mind. It was as if an executioner had asked for her final statement and she couldn't find the words. "From the beginning, I've wanted our relationship to work, but now—"

He pulled the shower door shut. "Is this some kind of payback for deserting you yesterday?" he shouted above the sound of pounding water.

"What? No! Yesterday was just one day." The humidity made it harder to think. "I haven't felt close to you for months. I don't know. Have I *ever* felt close to you?"

He laughed and turned off the water. "You're losing it, Ava. You really are." The door opened, and he appeared wrapped in a towel, his hair and face still dripping wet. "Look, we've made a commitment. The Surrey is booked. My parents' guestroom is full with gifts. People will be arriving in—"

"We're not getting married for our guests and their gifts! I'm talking about *us*. We never hold hands. When we kiss, it only lasts a few seconds. I keep wondering how much affection I'll get *after* the wedding. But I'm not going to wait until it's too late to find out!"

"Too late? We've been together for five years, Ava. *Too late* is right now! Seriously, don't drag me into this inane conversation. I should be dressed and on my way to work." He attacked his hair with a towel.

"Ignore me, Josh. Just keep on ignoring me. Maybe when you're standing alone under the chuppah, you'll remember what I said."

"I get it. You woke up in a bad mood, so now I have to be late for work and have a rotten day. Is that how it goes?"

"No, you don't show me that you love me, and I break our engagement. *That's* how it goes!" A painful sob expanded in her throat. Please, no tears. Not now.

"What do you want me to say? Fine? Cancel the wedding? Listen, I love you. You know I love you. And I'm sorry I left you at Kitty's reception. Is that better?"

She walked out of his bathroom.

"Don't involve my mother in this!" he hollered over the buzz of his electric shaver.

Ava paused. *What about Phoebe?*

No, she couldn't marry him for his mother. Holding tight to her overnight bag, she walked out of his apartment, taking the first steps out of his life.

Downstairs in the lobby, the sliding glass doors opened to the city where she was one of millions, a single woman, and scared. A light rain washed out her tears as she looked for a southbound taxi. Heading home on the West Side Highway, she pressed her face to the window and fixated on the black swirls and swells of the Hudson River. Her cab seemed to travel without moving through a gray, unfeeling city.

"Three-twenty-four West Twenty-second," the cabbie announced, stopping in front of the vine-covered brownstone where her one-room apartment waited. She paid the fare and stepped onto the rain-slick street. Through the mist, her building showed once-white windowsills flecked with peeling paint. She'd always thought of her place as shabby chic, even though Josh swore it wasn't safe. Now it looked downright hazardous.

She watched as the cab drove away. On sunny days, the leafy trees lining the sidewalk played shadow games in the flowerbeds below. But not today. Her street, masked in fog, told a different story, maybe the real one, of want and neglect. But this was her life, and there was nowhere else to go.

The guy from the subway, now tucked beneath her stoop, didn't look up. Judging from his downcast eyes, he wasn't happy with the weather either.

He appeared to be her age, give or take a year. He wasn't bad looking for someone in serious need of a haircut. His face had an innocence about it, the way a daydreamer looks content.

The dog at his side was the sheepdog type with longish-legs and black fur, a patch of white here and there curling up every which way. The banged-up brown leather suitcase looked like something her stepdad David would use, at best. And what was his allegiance to that notebook? A starving writer perhaps? He appeared perfectly healthy and had a sturdy build, which she'd noticed more than once beneath his white T-shirts. Maybe he was a modern-day Joe Gould, documenting the life of a homeless man. "Joe." It was a good name for him.

Walking past Joe, he glanced up, eyes dark, but didn't say a word, thank God. She went inside and carried her stuff up five flights of worn stairs. Once a month the super came through with a mop and bleach, doing nothing to lighten the fusty smell.

Number 5C. The lock on her door felt loose. The door groaned. She stood in her entrance hall, looking with new eyes at her studio apartment. Hazy morning light filtered through grimy windows. Beneath them, her futon bed occupied most of the floor space. Then there was her kitchen the size of a walk-in closet...the refrigerator, empty. She held tighter to her bag as loneliness flared to panic. What motivation did she have to make her place a home? Marriage was the plan, and then a *real* home. Instead, here she was alone, broke, and feeling old for twenty-five.

"I can't do this." She turned toward the door, took one step, and stopped.

You can do this.

Her hand released her overnight bag, and it hit the hardwood floor with a *thud*. The sound of independence was anything but victorious, but she could hope.

Ava surveyed her apartment, again. She'd accumulated so little over the past five years: a geranium, some throw pillows, and a stack of crates holding her favorite romance novels. Oh, and her hope chest—made from a cardboard box—guarding bridal magazines, color charts, and trade show brochures piled beside meticulously wrapped white satin gloves and silk pumps. She could legitimately call it a Depression Chest now.

Outside her kitchen window, the fire escape—complete with bird-doo and a dirty clothesline—acted as her "balcony." Her red geranium, which occupied one corner, was alive at least, though barely. She wrestled with the window frame, determined to get a bit of fresh air, and then remembered...

"My lease!" Chills shot down her arms. Three months ago she had cancelled it in anticipation of the wedding and moving in with Josh. She'd even spent her rent money on tickets to *Wicked*! Technically, she didn't have an apartment.

It was too early to reach the managing agent, so she left a message: "Hi, this is Ava Larson of 324 West 22nd Street, apartment 5C. I previously gave notice to terminate my lease on July first. My plans have changed, and I'd like to continue renting my apartment. Actually, I don't have anywhere else to go. Please call me back."

That was only one of many pressing phone calls she needed to make. The amount of work it would take to undo the wedding was overwhelming, but she was too hungry to think about it. The upside to resigning from bride-to-be was she no longer qualified for the Perfect Bride Diet, which, by the way, would *not* have made her a perfect bride.

"Deli." A man answered the phone, curt but familiar. His

voice was a comfort; she wasn't the last person on earth—other than the homeless guy.

"It's Ava, apartment—"

"5C on 22nd Street." He spoke above people shouting orders in the background as if his deli were the Stock Exchange.

"You remember me! I haven't called for delivery in nearly a year."

"Will it be your usual?"

"Yes, iced coffee, scrambled eggs on toast, and a side of bacon, extra crispy." Food freedom, at last!

"Ten minutes," deli man replied. *Click.*

Still holding the phone, she sat down at her kitchen table for two. What about work? There was no way she could focus on handbags this morning, not right away, which meant she'd have to call Bucksly.

"Wha?" His nasally voice sounded like a crow's squawk.

"It's me. I'm going to be a few hours late. I—I've had a setback and can't function."

"Is this a prank? You *have* to function. Our morning meeting, Ava. Gucci will be here in an hour!" Bucksly, at his wit's end.

"I'm sorry, but I can't. Anyway, Gucci puts us off all the time. We can reschedule this once, can't we? It's important."

"Unbelievable. Are you pregnant? Is that what's going on?"

"No. A few hours, Bucksly, that's all. I just need some time."

"Sure, get here when you get here, and we'll see if you still have a job!"

"Bucksly..."

"What do you want me to say?"

Silence became her answer.

"Fine," he muttered. "I'll reschedule Gucci. See you in a few. Functioning."

"What a rat." She hung up the phone, hoping he didn't catch that last bit.

Desperate for air, she forced open the kitchen window and climbed out onto the fire escape. A garbage truck compressed its collection, kids called to one another from the street. Frank Sinatra crooned about love on the radio across the way, a love

like no other, come rain or shine. At least she still had Manhattan. A gritty breeze made her geranium shudder.

Chapter Eight

First things first, she had to call home. Mom would likely be sleeping in, but Dad rose at dawn. She called his Montana number. Be calm and keep it short. Let *him* get riled. He could wrestle with her decision on his own.

"You're the first to know, Dad," she said.

"Nonsense. You wouldn't do something as foolish as that."

"I already have. And it's not *foolish*...not from my perspective." Gripping the phone with one hand, she pulled her hair back out of her face with the other. Their relationship wasn't what she would call smooth, but they never argued.

"I can't believe what I'm hearing, Ava. We have plane reservations and everything."

"I'm sorry. I can't go through with it." She knew what he was thinking. *Fickle, scatterbrained, just like her mother.* Would she ever just be *Ava* to him?

"So you're saying I should cancel our flights? There'll be some kind of penalty, I assume."

"I'll pay the penalty." She didn't want to think about what the canceled wedding would cost her in total.

"Have you given this sufficient thought? I mean, really considered the consequences? The bills. Your reputation. You're not getting any younger, Ava."

"Yes, I'm aware of all that. It feels right, Dad."

"Sure, today it does. What about tomorrow, the next day, the rest of your life?"

"I can't see into the future, but there's got to be more to love than...routine. I don't know."

"Oh, for heaven's sake. The very nature of routine is that it works. But I suppose you're going to see it your way. I'll cancel our flights and get back to you on the penalty."

He didn't ask if she was okay. Opening the conversation to feelings would overstep the boundaries of their relationship, as sad as that was.

An e-mail would come next. She had only lived with him for the first eight years of her life, but she knew how he operated. He'd put down the phone, walk promptly into his office, and craft the proper response to what he of course believed was a complete lapse of reason on her part. Ava opened her laptop. Five minutes later, there it was.

> *Ava, I find your news upsetting for reasons which pertain to both of us. First, I question your motivation in canceling the wedding and wonder what could have driven you away from a life that would have secured your future.*
>
> *Pertaining to my own concerns, I fear the financial consequences. You agreed to Josh's proposal, whereupon the Copelands offered to pay the wedding cost as a gift, which I am sure is not refundable at this stage. Are you prepared for such a bill? Would Mr. Copeland have taken out wedding insurance? Would it even apply? As you know, Kelly and I have two teenage daughters to see through college. I'm in no position to help you financially.*
>
> *To fulfill my role in this matter, I will leave you with this advice: Have patience with Josh.*
> *Your Father*

Dad required all her patience. She wasn't looking for a handout. And did he really think she'd get married to avoid a bill? Never! No matter how big. *Wedding insurance?* Whoever heard of such a thing? She called him back, set on being heard.

He wasn't answering. It appeared the conversation was closed in his mind.

Feeling the sting of rejection, she started to hang up, and then heard his voice, talking to someone else. "I'll be right there."

"Dad?"

He sighed, making his disappointment audible. "They're just my thoughts, Ava. That's all."

Her determination faltered. "I'm sorry. This isn't how I wanted it to go."

"I only hope that a romantic fling isn't behind your decision. There'll be regrettable ramifications."

"Of course I'm not having a *fling!*" She paced the length of her futon, three steps...turn, three steps...turn. "It's just that I'm not completely happy with Josh. I know it's hard to accept at this point—"

"Completely happy? Who's ever completely happy? You're living with the sun in your eyes, Ava. Making blind decisions, who knows where you'll end up?"

A part of her understood his thinking. Dad always said he had spent a lot of money to put her through twelve years of Catholic schools. He cared about her security.

"But marrying Josh feels like the *wrong* direction."

"I don't see why. Josh seems very good for you." He paused, perhaps trying to understand, or at least accept, her decision. "All I can say is stay true to the path which God has shown you. Be grateful."

"I am grateful, but which path?" God wasn't hanging any arrows. "I have to trust my heart on this one, Dad."

"Your heart can't think things through. That's what you need to do. Make a list of pros and cons."

"Pros and cons are shape-shifters. I used to think that his father's company was a pro. But Josh pulled out of it, and now his father holds it against him. I used to think that because Josh was dedicated to making money he'd be a dedicated husband and father. Dedication has to go further than a good salary."

"You're being short-sighted. He's young and still proving himself in his career. This decision will determine the rest of your life."

"I understand that." She didn't need his support. "I have to go, Dad. I have to get ready for work."

"It's okay to be scared going into marriage, Ava. It happens to a lot of people."

And a lot of marriages failed. She didn't say it; divorce was too close to home for them.

"Let me know if anything changes. I'll hold off cancelling our tickets."

"Okay. I love you."

"Well, think it through, Ava. That's all I'm asking." He hung up.

Her hand shook holding the dead line. Ever since the divorce she felt like the offspring of a mistake in his eyes. She never stopped wanting to change that, even now.

Breakfast arrived, though she barely tasted it. A hot bath helped, hot enough to turn her skin bright red, as if guilt could be burned off. She was dressed for work and about to leave when her landline rang. She waited. The answering machine clicked on, and Josh's voice filled her empty home:

"Hey, it's me. Turn your cell on. It's so annoying when I can't get through. I called your office and Rhonda said you're coming in late, something about you malfunctioning. At least that explains your mood this morning. My mom said not to forget your veil appointment this afternoon. She'll probably call. Guess that's it. Feel better. And call me when you get this."

"No!" She pulled off her engagement ring and chucked it into her hope chest. It landed softly on the white cloth bag holding her satin gloves and glimmered, as if laughing.

Had anything changed? Phoebe's hair was likely a different color today, but Josh's stress level sounded the same. He actually thought they were still getting married! Obviously, she had to tell his mother. Someone else to let down.

Outside, the air was damp, but noticeably warmer. Stepping off the stoop, she heard the rustle of movement and glanced back. Joe was arranging new cardboard, bigger pieces than his old ones. The smell of strong coffee came from his paper cup.

"Housekeeping," he said with a smile. His dog looked up.

She smiled back, a little, and kept walking. He made her uncomfortable.

In a split-second decision, she hailed a taxi. New financial constraints would likely come with breaking her engagement, but that was a problem for another day. The cab careened to the curb. "Fifty-eighth and Fifth," she said, getting in. The driver sped off, taking the streets like an obstacle course.

Walking through the white reception area on the fourteenth floor, she felt as though she had died and gone to Bergdorf. The office was her refuge now. Here she had to leave her worries at the door—Bucksly's orders.

Rhonda folded her arms on the glass reception desk. "Five calls from that bubblehead woman," she said. "How do you cope?"

"Josh's mother?" Ava felt a tightening in her stomach. So much for her escape. "There's no real emergency is there?"

"Something about your veil." Rhonda rolled her eyes. "You actually make me feel better about being single."

Single. Should she give Rhonda a good piece of gossip to spread throughout the department? For all they knew, she was born dating Josh. But Mom and Phoebe had to hear the news first.

She shut her office door and picked up the phone. This call felt harder than telling Josh, as though she and Phoebe had more in their relationship to lose.

One ring and she heard, "Ava! Thank God. Josh told me you weren't feeling well and—"

"Phoebe, wait, I have something to tell you."

"Wait, wait. Me first! I have an idea. I'll meet you at The Moment boutique to pick up your veil, and afterward we'll go to Serafina for our favorite lunch. Spinach salads! To celebrate!" A pause. Phoebe expected spontaneous enthusiasm. "Your *veil*, sweetheart! This is it!"

Ava's hand gripping the phone started to cramp. "Phoebe,

this is not it." She stopped. The words to explain wouldn't come.

"Well, you've got the dress and today we're picking up your veil. I'd say you're close!"

Silence.

"Ava? Where are you?"

"I'm here, it's just that—"

"I know, I know. Josh told me. You're not feeling well. It's wedding jitters, sweetie. Don't worry, I had them, too."

"I can't do lunch today, Phoebe. I came in late and Bucksly isn't happy." She stared at the stack of reports on her desk, the boxes of sample handbags on the floor.

"But your veil, Ava. This is a once-in-a-lifetime—"

"I can't. I'm really sorry."

Hurrying down Broadway through the Garment District, Ava envisioned her two-tiered cathedral veil, its lace motif and scattered pearls...and dreaded asking for a refund. In and out, she thought. Don't lose focus. Don't get emotional.

Heat rose from the sidewalk as she walked impatiently behind lunchtime crowds. Her task was to dismantle the wedding, one vender at a time, but she didn't know where to begin. It was like trying to decipher the direction of a tornado from its eye... while wearing her veil? It would've looked beautiful.

At least David wouldn't have to put on a tux. Ava wondered how Mom would handle the news. Her and David's wedding was a vivid childhood memory. They had the ceremony under the giant oak in the backyard. She was eleven. Mom wore a white cotton dress and jasmine in her hair. There was music and dancing, and after the picnic, she cuddled up on Mom's lap to hear a secret: "Love is the greatest gift of all," Mom had said, "but you have to give it back."

The memory felt reassuring. Her decision was the right one; Josh didn't give love back, at least not noticeably. Maybe in her white gown and veil she would've become a beautiful bride, glowing and happy, but she couldn't go through life wearing them.

Waiting to cross Broadway, the Don't Walk sign changed, and she stepped off the curb. The Moment bridal boutique's white awning was visible up ahead.

"Yoo-hoo!" Phoebe, pulling one of her surprises, came toward her in raptures. "Perfect! I was hoping to catch you before you got there."

"You don't accept no for an answer, do you!" Ava smiled at first, happy to see her, and then filled with panic. *Now what?*

"We're doing lunch. You tell that hardnosed boss of yours that I said to have a heart. Have two while he's at it! This is a very special outing, and since your mom can't be here with you, well, I'm going to do my best to fill her shoes."

"Phoebe, I appreciate it. I really do, but we need to talk."

"Absolutely." She took Ava's arm firmly in hers. "While we walk. Sweetie, you know, you really do look pale. Are you getting enough sleep? You *need* your sleep."

Ava nodded, imagining the sleepless nights ahead...

Phoebe patted her hand. "It's a good thing I got you those body bronzing appointments at my spa, that's all I have to say."

Body bronzing? She had to douse Phoebe's wedding dreams now. Only, how, here on Broadway, surrounded by people who couldn't care less? How could she hurt her deeply and then walk away?

"It always gets complicated when feelings are involved," Phoebe said, on to worrying about seating Table 12.

Kitty's wedding came to Ava's mind—she and Josh stuck in a corner at Table 54. "Phoebe—"

"Make a match at your wedding and your marriage will last! What do you think of that? I don't know if I made it up myself or read it somewhere, but I like it."

Ava stopped. "Phoebe, a lasting marriage comes from a mutual and balanced give-and-take of love. Man, I sound like I'm quoting text!"

"Oh, but I know all that." Phoebe squeezed her arm. "Josh

told me that you want to recite your own vows. I think it's a wonderful idea."

"You do? But he said—"

"Josh doesn't want the criticism from his father. You know him."

"I suppose." They started walking again, just yards from their destination.

"So you really can't blame him," Phoebe continued. "Rabbi Green wants to say a few words on love, of course. You don't mind, do you? Most of our guests know him, and they don't know Father...what's his name?"

"Luke. Father Luke. Like luck, but Luke." Why was she having this conversation?

"Luck," Phoebe repeated. "I'm such a dummy. I won't forget next time, promise. But, don't worry, Rabbi Green will keep it short. A little mention about patience when one of you leaves hair in the shower drain. That sort of stuff."

"Is *that* all I have to be afraid of? Hair in the shower drain?" She sounded bitter and explosive.

They stood in front of The Moment. Phoebe looked her straight in the eyes. "Darling, the *real* vows come from your heart. You've just got to trust that."

Ava stepped aside for two women entering the boutique and noticed their excitement, their conviction and entitlement. "But I don't...I don't trust his love."

An unfriendly silence planted itself between them. Phoebe blinked, as if the words *don't trust his love* had gotten into her eyes. "What are you saying?"

"I can't go inside for my veil."

"Of course you can. You have an appointment."

"I've called off the wedding, Phoebe. I'm so sorry. I never thought this would happen." She wanted to hold her and cry together. "I hate that I'm hurting you."

"Hurting *me*? What about Josh? This is silliness, Ava. It's just nerves. Pull yourself together."

"It's not nerves, or silliness. Please trust that I know what I'm doing. That it's the right decision. Okay? I'm sorry."

"But we all love you! We want you in our family, Ava. You can't do this. You can't walk away now."

"I'm sorry. I wish I had known sooner. I have to go, Phoebe."

She turned and quickly backtracked through the Garment District. When her cell phone rang, she turned it off.

Chapter Nine

Ava ran to get distance from Phoebe and The Moment. A Krispy Kreme sign in neon flashed by, but the smell of hot dough and powdered sugar lingered. The scent carried everything she'd been deprived of over the past year. She stopped and went back for a doughnut. If her life was going to change, then let it change.

"A chocolate iced with sprinkles, please."

The man behind the counter plucked it off the shelf like ripe fruit. She should be sad right now. The image of Phoebe standing bewildered on the sidewalk was branded on her mind. But she only felt relief.

"Most people, I've noticed, order at least two." The man standing in line behind her spoke. She glanced back at the hard-worn face of someone who might have lived in the wild or maybe did extreme sports for a living. He could have been twenty-five or forty-five; it was hard to tell with the long greasy hair and the holes in his jeans. She smiled to be polite. Doughnut bagged and paid for, she headed for the door.

"My problem is deciding." That guy again. "Any advice?"

"Me?"

He nodded.

She glanced hurriedly at the counter. "Try a custard filled. They're good."

"Okay. And?"

"Well, if I were going to have a second, I guess it'd be a cinnamon twist." The longer she talked to him, the better looking he became, though he dressed like a freeloader.

"Everything she says," he told the clerk, "and make that

two twists."

She turned away.

"Hey, you've got a cinnamon twist coming." He threw a bill down on the counter and wrote something on a Krispy Kreme napkin.

"No, thanks," she replied. It was obvious where this was going. "One is it for me."

"Here." He put the napkin into the bag with the twist and held it out to her. "Today you get two."

"All right. Thanks."

"Don't mention it. Have a good day." He took off.

Of course, his telephone number was on the napkin. Clever, but no way. Too random. She'd take it as a good omen, a sign of moving in the right direction, and that was it.

Back to Bergdorf. As she walked into her office, the phone rang, double rings, an outside call. Setting the Krispy Kreme bag on her desk, she pitched the balled-up napkin into the trash, just missing.

"Hello?"

"I hate to bother you at work, but—"

"Mom! I wanted to call you this morning."

"Honey, I have news."

"What? Is everything okay?" Ava sat down at her desk, seeing Mom, a bald stranger with watery skin, sitting beside her in the cab...staring at her through a gold-framed mirror in the restaurant bathroom...boarding the bus. *I'm glad you have Phoebe.* Her parting words.

"Well, depends on how you look at it," Mom said. "This chemo isn't working, obviously, but they have a new treatment, a miracle-worker, according to Dr. Eastly. It knocks you out, initially, but it's gotten good results. I started my first dose today, so I should have my strength back for the wedding."

The wedding. "Mom, that's really great. I can't wait to see you beat this. You're almost there."

"Thank you, again, for your cards, by the way. They give me so much hope. You can't imagine. I feel like I have this last arrow to shoot, and it's going to be the one."

"I think so, too!"

"Ava, I'm sorry about that episode in the restaurant, staggering off to the bathroom. I'm a little embarrassed by it all. Can you tell me Phoebe's address? I want to thank her for the wonderful lunch, and apologize, as well."

"You don't have to do that. In fact, please don't."

"But I really feel I should explain. I never could handle alcohol. You're the same way."

"Mom, I have something to tell you."

"Uh-oh. You never preface *good* news. What's going on?"

"Well, like you said, it depends on how you look at it. I've called off the wedding. I told Josh this morning and his mother about a half-hour ago."

"You what? Why?"

"I don't think he loves me. Maybe he does, but then we have two different definitions of what love is. Anyway, I shouldn't have to wonder. It's something I should know. Something I should feel. Right?"

"Yes, that's right. You should feel loved. Wow. I'm stunned. You canceled the wedding?"

"I can't believe it, either. I canceled the wedding! I feel like I want to run and hide somewhere, or burst out laughing and celebrate. How do you de-bride? Do I sit at home and eat pizza? I've been on the verge of tears for the past month and now I'm laughing. I'm a total wreck!"

"Go ahead and laugh, if that's what you feel like doing! Or cry! I guess I can be honest now and say I always thought you could do better. You know what? I'm relieved. Go out and find someone more like yourself, Ava. Take your time, meet lots of men, until one clicks. You're free of Joshua Copeland!"

"I'm free!" Ava laughed, tears fell. "Am I crazy? I had what I wanted and then I gave it up! Now I have to cancel everything, mail out apologies..."

"It must've taken a lot of strength. What gave you the push to do it in the end?"

"I had a 'true love sighting,' as Bucksly put it."

"That boss of yours?" Mom sounded like Phoebe.

"I went to a wedding at City Hall. Never mind. I'm just doing what I believe is right and trying not to look back. I'm sorry I'm so much trouble."

"What trouble? As long as they don't sue you! But thank God you figured it out now. Maybe I should've voiced my suspicions in the beginning. But you seemed happy, and then six months turned into a year and so on. Maybe I've been too caught up in my own life."

"It had to be my decision." Ava stood up from her desk. Just talking about Josh made her feel confined.

"Of course," Mom said. "It couldn't have come from anyone else. How did Phoebe take it?"

"I didn't give her the chance to say anything, but I'm sure I haven't heard the last of it. I'm going to miss her. I wish we could stay friends."

"Don't count on that happening. She must feel deeply offended. I'm hoping they don't send you the entire bill. They shouldn't. You let Phoebe plan the kind of wedding *she* wanted for her son."

"I know."

"Listen, you did the right thing, for yourself and for Josh. You both have your whole lives ahead of you. Please, don't waste a day of it worrying about the past. Get out and meet new people. Keep an open mind!"

"I will. I promise. Thanks for understanding, Mom. I don't know what I'd do if I didn't have your support." Ava hung up, and for a second, she felt as though she could fly.

The Krispy Kreme napkin lay crumbled on the floor. She bent down and picked it up. Among the crumbs and grease marks, the guy's number was barely legible. Strange that he didn't leave a name. She tucked the napkin back inside her handbag, a keepsake from a momentous day, if nothing else.

Chapter Ten

A quick *tap* on Ava's office door and Bucksly barged in. He had a pencil in his mouth and a stack of reports in his arms. His hair reached new heights, which gauged his caffeine intake. Fully charged, he was ready to make her pay for having a personal life.

"Thanks for canceling the Gucci meeting this morning," she said. "I appreciate it."

Unable to speak with the pencil between his teeth, he motioned with his head for her to clear a space on her desk. She jumped into action, and he dropped the reports as if into a garbage bin. Pencil removed, and showing bite marks, he laid out the next twenty-four hours of her life.

"We'll deal with Gucci later. I scheduled Givenchy for nine a.m. tomorrow and decided to give you the spotlight. You'll prepare and present the line list, including selling history, competition, and what's trending. This is an opportunity for you to look good, Ava. Are you with me?"

"Givenchy? Tomorrow at nine?"

"That's what I said."

"Right. No problem. Hey, if I take the afternoon off to get my hair done, will that make me look good?" She hoped for a smile.

He glared at her. "I'd get busy on the line list if I were you." He walked out, leaving her door open.

She looked down at the reports on her desk, a five-year history of Givenchy's sales. The numbers on the paper blurred as her mind wandered. Six months ago, she was begging Bucksly for the chance to run a meeting. Now, it just felt like more work. What was the point? She took out the cinnamon twist and ate it, only to feel nauseous moments later. Long-term happiness did *not* come from a doughnut.

She reached for the phone. Givenchy could wait five minutes. Her maid of honor needed to be fired.

Maggie picked up right away. "Ava! It's about time you called."

"How's it going in Mommyville?"

"You mean Looneyville." Little Melanie quacked like a duck in the background. "So, are you ready to dress me, or what?"

"The alternative. I broke our engagement."

Melanie's *quacking* escalated. "Shush! Mommy's talking. Ava, did you just say—"

"At least I'm not out the full price on your gown. Funny how I kept putting off your last fitting, even when I believed I was getting married. My subconscious must have been working ahead of me."

"Wait a minute. The last I heard you were writing your own vows."

"Well, obviously that didn't happen. Maggie, I need your help."

"To do what? Sounds like you've made up your mind. Melanie, no!" A shrill cry came through the phone. "Not the knife, honey. I'm sorry. She moves so fast, like a hummingbird. I can't look away for a second! Here you go, hon. Drums!" Frantic banging on pots ensued. "So, is there going to be a wedding or not?"

"The wedding is off," Ava said above the commotion, "but now what? Do I send out note cards? Beg for forgiveness? Join a monastery? Phoebe is devastated. I feel so heartless."

"Most people get married and deal with the problems after the honeymoon. It might be easier if you just go through with it and then get a divorce, like six-months or a year later."

"Are you crazy? I've been living Josh's life since college. I need to start my own life, figure out what makes *me* happy. I need to meet the man I'm supposed to be with!"

"I think you should write the book: *The Former Bride's Guide to Breaking Her Engagement—And What Comes Next.*

It's a sure best-seller." Melanie screeched. "Not mama's tea! Oh, shoot! Listen, I've got to go. I'll call you later, okay? You're not suicidal or anything, right?"

Ava looked at the work Bucksly had dumped on her desk. "Maybe I should be. But, no, I'm not. Call me when you can." She hung up.

It was futile to try to work when life demanded her attention. She took another baby-step forward and changed her cell phone password from "josh" to "ava." Maybe she should do something for herself, like a reward. Dye her hair red? No, she wasn't ready for such a bold move. Join a church? That way the next time she planned a wedding—hopefully there would be a next time—she'd know the priest, at least. Which church, though? Not today. Dance classes...that would be fun. Yes, that would feel great.

You Should Be Dancing, a studio on Eighth Avenue near Penn Station, had a choreography class every Thursday night, fifty dollars per class. She registered online.

Ava looked out her office window, dizzy from number crunching. A luminous reflection of the setting sun looked like wet paint on the skyscraper across the street. On clear evenings, the fiery mirror image lit up the top floor and then slowly descended, dripping down the building's façade.

The intercom buzzed, and Rhonda's high-pitched voice reminded her where she was. "Ava, you have a delivery."

Right. The pizza she had ordered for dinner in another fit of wedding rebellion. "I'll be right there."

"Please do, and get this thing off my desk."

Maybe it wasn't the pizza. Rhonda would've announced she was helping herself to a slice.

Josh. Ava walked to reception with her jaw clenched and her hands in fists, as if following a call to duty. This was just like him. Josh was a good boyfriend when it came to surprise deliveries, any way he could say *I love you* from a distance. The model gourmet chocolate chuppah was his most original idea. She'd wanted to keep it forever—to have and to hold—but it tasted too good.

Now a three-foot teddy bear with outstretched paws sat on Rhonda's desk. It wore a sign around its neck that read, *Love Me!*

"No card," Rhonda said, thrusting the bear at her. "I think it talks."

A few people had gathered. Bucksly, along with the pizza deliveryman, stepped out from the elevator. "An office party?" Bucksly asked, waving an unlit cigarette. "Nobody told me."

"Squeeze the bear, Ava," Rhonda urged. "I bet it's a singing teddy gram."

Ava squeezed, regretting it immediately, as a recording of Josh's voice began: "I won't let you go, Ava."

Flustered, she searched for an off switch.

"I understand you're scared," the bear continued. "I'm scared, too, which is probably why I've shut down in bed. Just give me a chance. I can do better. I love you." The recording stopped.

Bucksly looked from the bear to her. "Having troubles?"

"Oh, hon..." Rhonda touched her arm.

"I can't believe this." Ava looked into the bear's adoring eyes and felt conflicted.

The pizza guy cleared his throat.

"Here." Bucksly pulled a twenty out of his wallet and handed it to the man. "You owe me, Ava."

Still holding the bear in one hand, she took the pizza in the other. "Thanks. Anyone want this?" She offered the hot pepperoni pizza to her wide-eyed audience.

No one stepped forward, as if breaking up were contagious.

Rhonda chuckled. "Sorry, but you look like you're coming from a carnival, holding the grand prize."

"Except people who go to carnivals are happy." She looked at Bucksly. "I'll get back to those reports now."

"Tomorrow at nine," he called after her, "looking good!" She slinked into her office, out of sight.

10:00 p.m. Ava shut down her computer. "Enough." She spoke to the bear. "If Bucksly doesn't go for this line list, I'll *never* make him proud." She grabbed her handbag and switched off the light. "Good night, Ted. Sorry your mission failed."

Outside, a town car waited, her perk for working late. She sat in the backseat and watched people stroll the city sidewalks... couples laughing and cuddling as they walked. It was like living in exile, banished from meaningful love. And a talking stuffed bear was *not* meaningful love.

Car voucher signed, she got out in front of her building. Joe was taking the leash off his dog. Just arriving home, as well? As she neared the stoop, he looked in her direction. A quick glance and she bolted up the steps.

Inside, she flopped down on her futon with *Women's Wear Daily*, wishing she could fall into a deep sleep and forget that her life had been reduced to work and more work. Instead, she reread the same caption, wide-awake, retaining nothing: *Fashion Turns to Layers in a Slow Economy.* So this was being single. The emptiness felt like a life-sentence. She reached for the phone and called home.

"Hello?" Mom sounded far away.

"Hi, it's me."

"How are you, sweetie? Is everything okay?"

"Fine, I guess. How's the new treatment going?" Ava felt hope rise.

"All I know is that I'm tired, and sleep does nothing. You're calling late. Are you sure you're all right?"

"I'm sorry. I didn't even think of the time. Wow, breaking up with someone is like having jetlag."

"You'll adjust soon enough. Hey, remember that music

elective I wanted to teach at the university this fall? It got approved! I'm calling it *Folklore and the Fiddle*."

"That's great news, Mom! You'll be amazing." She could see her playing live for the class and envied the students for having her energy, her passion. "They'll love you." Ava hesitated. "So, I was thinking of coming home this weekend."

"Honey, you know this weekend won't be a good one."

The treatment. One month off, two months on, every other week. It knocked her out.

"I can stay with you while you're sleeping. Give David a break."

"Ava..." The tone in her voice said, *Why are we going through this again?*

Ava recalled past visits, spent teary-eyed. Mom had to be the strong one.

"If you can't sleep, I can read to you, like David does."

"I just don't see the point of you sitting around here, dwelling on my cancer. You get upset, and then I feel worse. I can't stand to see you suffer, too."

"But this time will be different. I'm stronger now."

Mom was quiet—thinking it over or just tired?

"Mom?"

"I'm proud of you, Ava. It took guts to walk away from Josh."

"I gave him so much of myself, I feel like I've got nothing left. I don't even know who I am anymore."

"Sure you do. Hey, at least you're not getting divorced."

Does that even qualify for a bright side? Ava closed her eyes a moment. "I'm not getting married, either."

"I couldn't believe him at the restaurant, embarrassed to toast the wedding. I noticed he wouldn't kiss you at the table. Did he even touch you once? What's wrong with him?"

"He's a lot like Dad. Maybe that's why I tried so hard to make him happy. There's no winning with Dad, either."

"Your father loves you. Not in so many words, but in his heart he does."

Ava laughed out loud. "What good is it, kept there?"

Mom sighed. "You're asking the wrong person."

"Exactly. I should give up on him, too."

"No, whatever you do, don't give up on your father. You'll regret it. Keep trying, don't stop loving him. Promise me?"

"I suppose."

"Listen, take this transition period one day at a time. Stay in the city this weekend. Get together with friends. Have fun!"

"All right. I'll try. Love you, Mom."

"I love you, Ava."

The worst of one day at a time was now. She looked at the phone in her lap, her only companion. Kind of like a cat, without fur. Normally when feeling sorry for herself, she avoided the phone. But it wasn't self-pity she felt...it was fear. She had to start over, on her own, which meant taking risks. Reaching out. Exploring the unknown. *Oh, heck, just call him.*

The Krispy Kreme napkin made the inside of her handbag smell deep-fried. Her heart beat faster as the line rang once, twice, and then, "Yo."

It was him.

"Hi. Remember me? We met—"

"Nina!"

Nina?

"I thought I'd never hear from you again!" He was unquestionably thrilled, thinking she was Nina. "Listen," he said, his tone suddenly somber, "about the other night—"

"I think you've got me confused with someone else."

Silence.

"Then who's this?"

She hung up, taking the hint that Mr. Krispy Kreme was *not* meant to be. This time the napkin made it into the garbage.

The air in her apartment suddenly felt hot and stuffy. She grabbed the phone and a pillow and climbed out the kitchen window onto the fire escape. Nick from college might be able to help her out with the single scene. They had kept in touch, kind of.

He answered on the second ring. "Ava. Wow."

"Hey, Nick. I see you still have my number in your cell."

"Why not? What's going on?"

"Just calling to say hi. We haven't caught up in a while."

"I bet you're getting married. Women always 'check in' with their ex-boyfriends before they walk down the aisle."

"No, not me. Well, I was getting married, but...it's a long story. What have you been up to?"

"Don't ask. My life's out of control. I'm closing more deals than I have ties in my closet. Seriously! In fact, I'm looking to pick up a bargain in the Hamptons, fourteen bedrooms! I'm telling you, New York is doing me good. Definitely, doing me good."

"That's great, Nick." Horns honking in the background muffled his voice. She pictured him striding down a crowded avenue, on his way to something *big*, no doubt.

"So, Ava, is that guy Jim or James still in the picture?"

"You mean Josh. We broke up." She left herself wide open. Why'd she call Nick in the first place? She turned him down in college; she didn't want to date him now.

"Sorry, A, but I've got something going at the moment, fresh out of NYU."

"Neat, our alma mater," she said, imagining a young girl with barely a clue—much like herself when she fell for Josh.

"Met her at the gym, blah, blah, blah. She follows me around like a puppy. Gotta love her for that!" He laughed to the piercing scream of an ambulance in the background.

Ava choked inhaling. "So, uh, where're the hot spots in Manhattan these days?"

"Like I said, I've settled down. Listen, A, if I know of anyone, I'll definitely hook you up. Are you into blind dates?"

"No!"

His other line clicked. "Uh, there's puppy now. Gotta jet. Hey, I hope you're keeping yourself up."

Keeping myself up? "Uh, yeah, of course."

"Don't want to waste my buddies' dime, that's all. I'll ring you." The line went dead.

He might as well have slapped her across the face. It appeared she was in a whole different category now. Like the day-old muffins at Pick-a-Bagel. No longer hot and fresh.

Marked down. Not worth standing in line for.

The fire escape suddenly felt like a slippery cliff, and she was going over. She climbed back inside through the window, into her barren apartment where monochrome walls closed in on her. Unable to breathe, she ran for the door, down five flights of stairs, and barreled outside, collapsing on the stoop, gasping for air.

"You okay?"

It was *him*. She peered cautiously over the edge.

"Everything all right?" He glanced up.

She moved back quickly and said nothing.

"Hell-o?" he called out, insistent.

"I'm fine." What did he want to hear? Her life was so hard? To which he'd probably respond, *I'll tell you about hard*, slapping the pavement where he slept. She'd rush to explain, N*o, my mom's really sick, and she's so young, younger than I feel, so unbelievably old*, and in no time, there she'd be, swapping sob stories with a homeless man.

She wasn't able to make out his face in the hazy yellow light escaping from the windows above, but she could picture his dark eyes and his wavy brown hair falling to his shoulders.

Silence hung in the air. His dog sighed loudly. At least he didn't smell bad. And why didn't he? Was there a bar of soap in that beat-up suitcase of his, which he carried around like a prop? Next to the soap, a razor? Kafka's *Investigations of a Dog*, maybe. She'd seen him reading it once. Another peculiarity, Kafka being so warped.

He must have a can opener stashed away. How else would he open those cans of Pedigree for mature breeds? Unless they were flip top. How did he afford them? She was becoming obsessed. Weekdays she saw him reading *The Times* as she stumbled to work half-awake. Sometimes she saw him in jogging shorts and a sweaty T-shirt, he and his dog back from a run. He lived a different life, not playing by the rules.

A peek over the edge. He had on black and white checked pants, perhaps all he could find at the Salvation Army. Somehow he managed to get by.

"Well," he suddenly spoke up, "as my dog would say, if there's food in your dish, life is good. It's a variation on Kafka. Nice to know life can be that simple."

She didn't know how to respond. He had compassion in his voice, when she expected bitterness, and would've preferred it so she could legitimately go on ignoring him. Now what? She stood up and moved for the door. "I just needed some space to breathe."

"Who doesn't?" he said as she stepped inside.

The door closed behind her. She stood beside the little tin mailboxes in the dirty-yellow foyer and felt like a fool. Her life wasn't any more significant than his. She dragged herself back upstairs.

Chapter Eleven

One hour until the Givenchy meeting. Waiting for her computer to boot, Ava jotted down a list of vendors she had to call to cancel the wedding. If only there were a service that canceled weddings for you—a party untangler, as opposed to a party planner. She'd pay someone to take on the burden... except she had to pay for the canceled wedding first.

Her cell phone rang. Phoebe. *Calling already?* Ava let it go to voice mail and tried to focus on her immediate task of printing and making copies of the line list report. Handbag styles appeared on the screen: tote, clutch, satchel, hobo, and messenger. She glanced at the blinking message light on her phone. *Oh, all right.*

"It's me, Phoebe! Did you get Josh's not-so-little surprise?" Ava looked at the bear, which seemed to watch her reaction from the chair in the corner. "This mood swing isn't like you, Ava. I hope it's not Josh's bachelor party. All men do that *Vegas* thing. I hate it, too. Anyway, we can have our own fun this weekend... in the Hamptons! Yes! Shopping and Shiatsu massages, salads at Babette's, and wheatgrass cocktails at sunset!" She sounded desperate with her treats and cheery voice, the way someone might pacify a crying child. "And what do you say to the word *Sincerity* inscribed on the wedding favors? Just the touch you wanted. Ring me back!"

Ava pressed Stop. So much eagerness, which used to bring a smile, now depressed her. It hurt losing Phoebe.

Her meeting with Givenchy had to take precedence right now, her once in a lifetime opportunity to "look good," according to Bucksly. She scrolled through the report to check the bottom-line, expecting to see a decent eighty-seven percent mark-up. Wait a second. Ninety-three? It *grew* after she shut down her computer last night? No. Ninety-three percent was last year's mark-up.

As fast as the mistake sank in, her adrenalin spiked, as if she should run for her life. Hadn't she saved her report under a new year? Would she really have replaced it with the old file? Her hand shook dialing the Help Desk.

"Someone will be free to look into it at eleven o'clock," replied Dan, Manager of the IT Department.

"I have a meeting in an hour. Can you find someone to look into it now? This is an emergency."

"We're upgrading our inventory system. We ran it last night, but ran into some glitches. Eleven o'clock is the best we can do at the moment. Sorry."

"Sorry doesn't fix anything!" She pounded her fist on her desk. Highlighted sales reports slid onto the floor.

"We're IT, Ava, not 9-1-1." He took another call.

Nothing would make her look good now.

Givenchy sample handbags were lined up on the conference room table as if on trial. Four Givenchy sales reps, their head designer, two assistants, and Bucksly watched with concerned expressions as Ava stood at the head of the table.

"There's a reason why you don't each have a copy of the line list," she started. "If you remember in our focus meeting in February, we specifically asked for adjustable shoulder straps. While your line looks saleable and fresh"—she motioned to the handbags—"there are only two styles here with adjustable straps. Two!" A nervous Bucksly flagged her down with his brows, sending out flares with his eyes. She shot back a furious glare. *I'm functioning. Be happy.*

"We made it absolutely clear: the number one request from

our preferred customers is adjustable straps, did we not? It was established that *not* having adjustable straps was partly to blame for last year's drop in sales! Now, what's the point of holding focus meetings if you don't focus on what we focused on in the meeting?" For a second, everything blurred and it seemed she spoke in a foreign tongue. "We *need* adjustable straps!" She brought her hand down hard on the conference table and coffee cups trembled on their saucers. The designer's sanguine expression had been reduced to a look of pleading. "It comes down to this," she concluded. "Give us what we asked for, and we'll show you a line list."

"Okay!" Bucksly stood with a nervous smile on his pale face. "Well. Ava made her point. Adjustable straps. Can you at least say please to the nice people, Ava?" A glint of wrath flashed in his eyes.

He might never put her in charge of a meeting again.

Back at her desk, still pumped up from the meeting, Ava got on the Internet: *What to do after breaking your engagement?* She was in control, and it felt good.

Bucksly appeared at her door, too soon. "Ahem, do you have anything to say?"

"Good meeting?" The waver in her voice proved that it wasn't a good meeting and she knew it. Whatever control she had felt vanished.

"Can you explain to me your *act* for Givenchy?" he asked. "I'd like to think you were trying to impress me with your hardline negotiating skills, but I assume there's more to it than that."

"So I impressed you?" Keeping it light felt critical but had no effect. His reply was an icy stare.

"The report didn't save," she explained, "and admitting defeat wouldn't have, you know, 'looked good.' I guess you could say I found a different way to shine, more or less."

"I guess you could say you weren't prepared."

"I'm sorry. At least we'll get adjustable shoulder straps."

Bucksly gave a long, drawn-out sigh, obviously not seeing the upside. "I'd like a meeting, just the two of us and your line list."

"The Help Desk will get back to me at eleven. We had an eighty-seven percent—"

"I don't have time today." His tone was uncompromising. His eyes showed his disappointment. "Tomorrow morning, eight o'clock sharp."

"Right." Her office phone rang, an outside call. How long could she ignore Phoebe and Josh?

"The pressure is on, Ava," Bucksly said, glancing at the bear. "Are you with me or not?"

"Of course, I am."

"I hope so. Conference room, tomorrow at eight. Prepared."

After he left, she listened to Phoebe's voice mail, knowing it would make her feel even more cornered.

"You're obviously not returning my calls," Phoebe's message began, "which I find very hurtful, but I'll get right to my point. No relationship is perfect, Ava. You have something very special with Josh, something you may never find again. Please, call him. And then call me!"

Talking to Phoebe would be like talking to the bear. She wouldn't listen, either, even though Phoebe of all people should understand. She and Mr. Copeland seemed to share nothing in common, and it was doubtful he showed her any more affection at home than he did in public, unless patronizing jabs were code for *I love you*.

Back to the Internet. The first hit read, "What to Do After Ditching Your Wedding." She pictured bagging the whole thing—dress, flowers, live band—and tossing it into a dumpster. Unfortunately, life didn't work in images.

The canceled affair was a waste of hopes and dreams and a beautiful veil, actually. With so many marriages ending in divorce, where did the white dresses and blue memorabilia go? The poems and dried bouquets? The senseless party favors and unused gifts? Beyond waterfalls of broken glass, perhaps there was a Land of Forgotten Weddings, where it rained champagne and wedding dresses told their stories.

The good news was that everyone from eHow to Wiki offered advice. She had thought of mailing out a letter, trying to put into words why she had called it off, and concluding with a sincere apology for being born. But About.com had a different opinion on apologies: *Regardless of how you let folks know that your wedding has been canceled, remember that you do NOT owe anyone an explanation.*

This made complete sense. It was her wedding, not theirs. Why apologize? She didn't feel sorry for anyone but herself and Josh. And Phoebe, of course. They were the only injured parties with shattered dreams. Friends and family would have to make new plans for the Fourth of July. Big deal. Right? She supposed she could apologize for their trouble.

The engagement of Miss Ava Larson and Mr. Joshua Copeland has been broken. All gifts will be returned.

She read it over and added: *Most sincere apologies for any inconvenience.*

A second call to the managing agent of her building resulted in leaving another voice mail: "It's Ava Larson, again, at 324 West 22nd Street, apartment 5C. I need my apartment and have no plans to move out July 1. I'd appreciate it if you could get back to me."

Gusts of wind shuffled the heat and dust as she walked down Broadway to Krispy Kreme, anxious to sink her teeth into a chocolate iced doughnut. It would make her feel like the inside of an oilcan later, but she needed the immediate sense of fulfillment. A moment of calm. One-a-day was becoming her fix.

"With colored sprinkles," she told the man behind the counter.

One bite into her remedy stopped time, and bliss was hers

to savor...until she heard his voice.

"Your backside is very familiar to me. And I mean that in a good way."

Swallowing a mouthful of sugar and fried dough, she turned to see the same man smiling at her, exactly as before. Except his rough-and-tumble image was replaced by a yoga mat slung over his shoulder. His hair was back in a ponytail, and he had on forest-green harem pants and a T-shirt that read, *Namaste, Nincompoop.* A yoga junkie?

"Hi." She wiped her lips of icing.

"Say, were you at The Outcrop last Saturday night?"

"Where? No. We—"

"I swear I've seen you somewhere." He made a point of studying her face.

Okay, it was one thing for a man to hit on a woman in a doughnut shop, and entirely another thing for him to hit on her again the very next day and not remember. She was the *nincompoop* for talking to him. "You must be thinking of someone else." She slipped the rest of her doughnut into a bag and turned away.

"Gotcha! Come on, do you think I buy every woman I see a cinnamon twist? You didn't call! You probably wiped your mouth on my number and pitched it into the trash, like any old Krispy Kreme napkin. I know, I know, it's risky business meeting someone new. Most people are afraid to give a stranger a chance. Or just too lazy."

"Actually, I tried, but didn't exactly get through."

"Let's start over. I'm Julian."

She hesitated, but then remembered Mom's advice to get out and meet new friends. *All right.*

"I'm Ava." They shook hands. His firm grip held on a second longer than was protocol.

"My full name's William Julian Knox. Julian, or Jules, stuck back when I was a kid, and that's how it's been ever since." He had a childlike grin. Friendly. Appealing.

"Jules is catchy. I like it."

"So, Ava, what brings you to the Garment District? Are you

a model? Cheesy question, I know, but the thought did cross my mind."

He was all eyes. She looked down at her conventional navy blue skirt and pumps and felt like a uniform model, if anything. "I'm a handbag buyer for Bergdorf and come here occasionally to check out the showrooms...and pick up a doughnut."

"A buyer in the fashion industry—very savvy." He glanced around the store and leaned toward her. "I just moved here and am keeping my options open."

"You're new to the city?" He was so confident...so outgoing. He looked like he belonged to the city, or it belonged to him.

"How about showing me around one day?" he asked as they walked outside. Buying a doughnut must not have been that important to him.

"Maybe I could do that," she replied. His smile was contagious. They stood on the sidewalk, people brushing by.

"Great. Give me your number." He took out his mobile. "I don't trust you with mine."

She hesitated, again, thinking of her first attempt to call him. Who was *Nina*? Apparently not his girlfriend. She gave him a hard look. *Here goes taking a chance.*

He entered her number into his phone as fast as she could say it. "I'll call you soon." Another flash of his charismatic smile and he disappeared into a crowd.

She went back to work, feeling his lively eyes on her skin, and tried not to smile.

Seventy-five cancelation cards in the mail! Ava walked out of the post office and wanted to celebrate. A big sky brought cooler temperatures that evening. Life was all right.

She arrived at her building and found Joe kicking back on his cardboard. Counting cars? Plotting a shooting spree?

He nodded hello. "What a night, huh? The heat finally let up."

"At last. It's refreshing," she replied but kept moving.

"Everything okay from last night? I thought you were running away from someone."

"From myself, I suppose." She stopped before going up the stoop. "A new day can change everything."

"For better or for worse. I'm glad you're doing better."

"Thanks, and, um...thanks for checking in with me last night, asking if I were okay."

"Just being a good neighbor." He stood up but said nothing more.

She felt him watching as she moved quickly up the concrete steps.

Inside the musty stairwell, a faint smell of roses made her doubt her senses. On the fifth floor, a red petal in front of her apartment proved it wasn't her imagination. She rushed with the lock and swung open the door.

"Josh?" No one else had a key, although anyone could break in. But what robber would come with roses?

As she walked down the hall, the usual silence greeted her. She turned on the main light and discovered a basket of crimson roses lying on her hope chest. She went to it, shaking, unnerved. Nestled in the thorns was a black velvet jewelry box and a scrolled letter tied with white ribbon. She carefully unrolled the silk-woven paper and read:

Ava Larson, will you take me, Josh Copeland, as your partner in life? Knowing the breadth of my love for you, knowing my sincere dedication to you, knowing my dream of raising a family with you, can you accept me for who I am now and throughout the ever-changing seasons of life?

Ava, our love is this simple. Please, let's take up life together and be happy. Forever, Josh

Inside the jewelry box was the wedding ring he'd chosen for her. She held the golden band of diamonds in her palm and reread his vows twice more...feeling love for him and completely confused. Was it too late? He wrote: *Can you accept me for who I am?* Was this Josh?

A cool breeze blew in through the window. Everything was

still, except for her thoughts, which seemed to fill the room with loud, overlapping conversations. Would they make love more often, kiss and hold hands? Would his affection be out of obligation? Or worse, guilt? It was better to be lonely with the hope of finding love, than committed in a lonely relationship. But he was trying. Could she love him for that alone?

He wasn't home when she called his apartment. She tried his cell phone and it went to voice mail. Eight o'clock on a Tuesday night...she knew where he'd be.

Back outside, her thoughts were on Josh and picking up where they had left off—only this time in love. If only she hadn't mailed out those cancellation cards! How embarrassing to have to cancel them.

"Have a good night," Joe said as she stepped off the stoop.

"You, too." She didn't stop. Maybe she had spoken too quickly. What was a good night for him? She remembered his dog's philosophy: if there's food in your dish... Could it really be that simple? She pulled her cardigan tight around her chest and set out to find Josh.

Just a short ways down the street, a black town car pulled over to the curb. A woman sitting in the backseat stuck her head out the tinted window. "Did you get his vows?"

"What? Phoebe?" Ava barely recognized her with slicked-back hair. Her pale, thin lips looked lost without lipstick. But then familiar blue eyes peered out from behind dark sunglasses, and happiness spread through Ava's heart, followed by apprehension. "What are you doing here?"

"Did you get them?" Phoebe made no move to get out of the car.

"Yes, just now. Are you trailing me?"

"If I can't get you on the phone, then yes. Do you want a ride?"

"All right."

Phoebe swung open the car door and slid over in the backseat.

"I've never seen you in all black before," Ava said, getting in.

"Not many people have seen me incognito."

"*What?* Have you followed me before?"

"No, never. Only Barry, one time, and it didn't lead to anything. Thank goodness." Phoebe pressed a button on an overhead panel, and the tinted divider lowered.

"Where to?" her driver asked, a rather burly-looking man to be driving Phoebe around.

"Josh's apartment," she replied.

Ava took out her phone and tried his home number again, letting it ring. "I think we need to go to 79th and Amsterdam. The Whiskey Bar. And, Phoebe, would you mind not hanging around? I don't mean any offense, but this is between me and Josh."

"Fair enough," Phoebe took Ava's hand and held it tight. "Fair enough."

The Whiskey Bar. Warm, stale air. A boxing match sounded its bells on a wide-screen television suspended above the chatter. Ava had been there a few times before with Josh, but now she felt edgy and paranoid. She moved slowly, not knowing what to say or do...or what her life would be like afterward, when all was said and done.

Most of the stools at the bar were taken. She noticed the back of a dark-haired man sitting with a woman, his hand on her knee. The woman wore a short skirt, and Ava watched his fingers tighten around her bare leg before letting go. It couldn't be him. She looked away, positive she recognized his stature and the back of his neck. A low, contained laugh made her look again. It was Josh.

Her heart took a blow that stole her breath. She stood motionless with her mouth open.

"One more?" he asked the woman—a brunette. High cheekbones and slender shoulders.

"Sure. Your choice this time." She laughed, glancing back.

Ava made eye contact, and the woman's red lips came together like velvet stage curtains.

Josh turned to see what she was looking at. "Ava!" He scrambled for a smile while his eyes read fear.

She stepped back. "The flowers are beautiful," she whispered, inaudible.

Josh motioned to the woman. "This is Jess, my assistant. Jess, Ava."

The initial blow passed, followed by rage stronger, more untamed than a herd of incensed bulls. "I'm his fiancée!" Ava shrieked in a voice she didn't know she had. People turned and stared.

"Hold on," Josh said. "*You* broke it off."

The woman, Jess, got up. "I work for Josh. I've heard all about you."

"Super. I haven't heard a thing about you."

"I should go." The woman touched his arm. "See you tomorrow." She rushed off.

"She's one of the guys," Josh said, as if that explained anything.

"When was the last time you put your hand on *my* leg?"

"You're freaking out for nothing. What are you even doing here?"

"What are *you* doing here? Why would you leave me wedding vows, and then go out drinking with 'one of the guys'—some assistant in a miniskirt?"

He ran his fingers through his hair and groaned. "My mother..." He didn't have to finish the thought.

"You had *Phoebe* write our vows?" Ava looked toward the door in disbelief and half expected Phoebe to run in trying to explain. "Please, tell me it's not true."

Josh looked at the floor. "She's good at that kind of stuff."

"I'm so embarrassed—"

"She mentioned the idea yesterday," he said. "I didn't think she'd do it without showing me first. I can't believe this. She's out of control."

Ava closed her eyes for a moment, searching for sensibility.

"I'll go now."

"Ava," he said, following her out the door, "Jess is a buddy. You need to believe me. It's you I want to marry."

"Your mother wrote our vows, Josh. Can't you see how wrong that is? Was the bear her idea, too? The chocolate chuppah?"

"You don't know what you're doing to me," he replied. "What you're doing to my family. I don't understand why we can't just stick to the plan."

"The *plan* isn't working. I only wish one of us had seen it earlier. Tell your parents I'm sorry. There's nothing more I can say." She walked away.

"Ava!" he called after her. "Ava!"

She didn't look back.

Chapter Twelve

Morning sunlight greeted Ava as she stepped out of her building with the basket of roses and wedding vows in her arms. It was garbage day.

Phoebe's last attempt to salvage their "weekend event" joined a pile of plastic bags at the curb. There. She stood back admiring the visual display of her decision to leave Josh as if it were art. Finally free of guilt and second-guessing, a tomb-like sense of closure sealed off that blip in her life.

Looking down, she noticed bits of glass encased in the sidewalk reflecting the sun. Above her, the sky was clear and blue, and a breeze blowing from the east carried a hint of the sea. She took a deep breath. Today was her meeting with Bucksly, and she was prepared with her line list. The help desk had come through, saving her report, after all. Tomorrow, her first dance class. Friday straight after work, she'd go home for the weekend and be there for Mom, for a change.

What should you do after breaking your engagement? Move on!

The smell of coffee and liver enticed her to glance back. Joe was scooping a spoonful of mush into his dog's tin dish, a steaming paper cup nearby. He looked up—his dark eyes catching hers—and smiled.

"Hi." She quickly turned in the direction of the subway. What was it she saw? That he might actually be a normal guy? Impossible. How could a normal person end up on the streets? There had to be issues, addictions, a troubled past. He had to have made serious mistakes, or been a victim of abuse. Something went wrong at some point in his life.

"Hey," he called out, "I've finished my *New York Times*, if you want it."

Was he talking to her? It'd be rude to keep walking. "Excuse me?"

He stood, holding out his newspaper. "You can have it."

Early risers were out jogging, opening shop, or pausing by a tree with their dogs, a leash in one hand and an iPhone in the other. It was daytime; she was safe.

She went back and took the paper from him. It was easier than saying no. "Thanks."

"Sure. It never hurts to save a buck twenty-five. If I gave you my paper every morning, you'd notice the savings." He smiled, and his dog glanced up from its breakfast.

"Well, I don't normally read the paper." Not counting *Women's Wear Daily*. She didn't want his *Times* every day.

"You watch TV news? No, I bet you listen to the radio. NPR." His dog pawed its dish, having finished breakfast. Joe squatted down. "Good girl."

Ava found herself smiling at them. "I don't have a television, for various reasons. I'm more of a novel reader, some self-help."

"No TV for me, either. We're a rare and dying breed. It wouldn't hurt to read the newspaper, though...and know what's going on in the world."

"Right. Well, I'll remember that." *It wouldn't hurt for you to have a job and a real home.* She walked to the sidewalk. "Have a good day."

"Thanks, I will. Enjoy your *Times!*"

Riding the subway, she skimmed the paper and noticed that a recipe had been neatly clipped from the Dining In/Dining Out section. He cut *recipes*? Was he crazy? A pair of scissors appeared on her mental list of things he kept in his suitcase. He could be dangerous. She wouldn't talk to him anymore.

Bucksly was in the communal kitchen, pouring black sludge into his coffee mug. "Hello, Ava."

"Good morning, Bucksly."

"You appear chipper this morning. Is the wedding back on?" He held his mug suspended before his mouth as if her answer would determine whether or not he'd drink his morning coffee.

"Not a chance, and I'm not spending another day of my life thinking about it."

"Huh." Now he was brooding. "All that time you took off from work, running around the city, planning that wedding, and now there's the chance you'll be doing it all again someday? For my sake and for the sake of our bottom-line, stay single. Please."

"What? I hope you don't put fashion above love!"

"I prioritize my immediate concerns. You should know that about me by now, Ava."

She sighed. It was his roadmap to tunnel vision.

"Anyway, it will take you awhile to find someone else," he said, as if he knew.

"Who's to say I'm not going to find someone today?" Julian from Krispy Kreme might call, ready for her to show him the city. Picturing his cocky grin and dirty-blond hair, shivers plunged down her back—an attraction with no grounding. She could get to know him on a tour of Central Park. Or she could take him downtown to Battery Park for a view of freedom, the Statue of Liberty! Manhattan would become her city to show off, and she'd see it brand new through his eyes.

Bucksly sighed. "Well, save yourself from looking like a fool holding a teddy gram and get to know him first." He set his coffee down on the counter, untouched. "Whatever you figured out about Josh in the eleventh hour, I'd love to know. A talking bear...the poor guy is desperate."

"Poor guy?" He didn't look desperate at The Whiskey Bar, mourning their wedding with his cute assistant!

"And another thing, Ava. I know you've been putting in the hours, but your career deserves a lot more serious attention than you've been giving it lately. All right? It defines you, and don't forget it determines your lifestyle. If you'd put your mind to it, you could run this division one day." A glance at his watch. "That's all I'm going to say. See you in the conference room in ten? I assume you have the line list ready?" He walked out of the kitchen. "A little tough love, Ava! It never hurts!"

She went into her office and shut the door. *Tough love.* She'd had enough tough love in her life. Sometimes she wondered if there was any other kind.

Later that morning, with Bucksly's meeting behind her and a ton of work ahead, she cleared off her desk and sat down with her list of vendors: *Father Luke, Venue, Rehearsal Dinner, Band, Flowers, Hotel.* A deep breath. She'd take it one at a time, starting with Saint James Church.

"This is Ava Larson calling about the Copeland wedding, July Fourth. May I speak with Father Luck—I mean Luke?" *Darn it.* Phoebe had obviously snuck into her subconscious.

"This is Father Luke. Hello, Ava! You're on my list of people to call. We need to set a time to talk about the point of marriage. With all the wedding details to think about, couples do forget! Now, the agreement was two meetings prior to the big day. Shall we get out our calendars?"

"Father, I've called off the wedding."

"No. What a shame! Have you tried counseling? You'd be surprised how talking things out can help."

"I'm pretty sure we're beyond counseling." She glanced sheepishly at the bear and made a mental note to get rid of it already. "I apologize for the late notice. It was a hard decision."

"I can imagine. Ava, do you have someone you can talk to? A support network? You may not realize it, but you're experiencing a death, the death of your dream."

"It does feel that way sometimes. But I think I'll be okay."

"Well, just so you're aware, you might have some drastic mood swings. Keep someone on hand, someone you can call, day or night. This isn't something you want to go through alone."

"Right." She thought of the other night out on her stoop. Who happened to be there for her? Joe, the homeless guy.

"Have you gotten angry yet?" Father Luke asked.

"Excuse me?"

"Angry. The most insignificant, completely unrelated setback might trigger an outburst you never saw coming."

"Actually, I was kind of hot-tempered at work yesterday." She glanced at the line list set aside on her desk.

"That's good! A hot temper is natural in your situation. Try not to get down on yourself about it. Acknowledge that you feel angry. Punch a pillow! Throw a glass against the wall! Just promise me one thing...you'll put the glass in a plastic bag first. Do you know what I'm saying? Let it out, but don't hurt yourself."

"Right. Thanks, Father Luke. I'll remember that, and, again, I'm really sorry."

She finally got off the phone with him and looked at her long list of calls. Hopefully, they wouldn't all be so involved. It was exhausting.

Next, the venue and caterer. A brief conversation told her there was no refund on the total cost—$44,800.

The rehearsal dinner. The standard cancelation policy of $75 per head—$1500.

The band. *Not* happy, and another deposit gone—$6700.

"Tell me you're joking." The lead singer wouldn't let it go. "July Fourth is one of our biggest weekends. There's no way we'll find another gig!" He was making her pay with guilt, too.

"It's not the way I expected things to turn out, either. I'm sorry."

"What happened?" he pressed.

"I'd rather not talk about it."

"You catch him running around or something?"

"I did, actually, with a bitch. I called the ASPCA right away. There are worse things than not having a gig on the Fourth, you know!" She slammed down the phone. Did she really just say that? Father Luke was right; she felt explosive. Two calls to go.

The Flowers: pre-ordered orchids—$12,500.

"Oh, you poor thing," the florist gasped.

"It's for the best." Pity invited tears.

"You know," the florist said, lowering her voice, "I almost called off my first wedding. I was so young, I probably should have. The marriage only lasted three years. Then I fell in love with a man from Missouri and had the whole big white ceremony all over again. That marriage survived almost ten years. Not bad. With my third true love, I said what the hay and eloped. We'll have our twentieth anniversary next year, and divorce hasn't come up once."

"I'm glad you found him," Ava said, appreciating the happy ending.

"So, about your bouquet and the orchids for the centerpieces," the florist said, "I'll have to charge you the full price. The other bouquets, boutonnieres, and corsages we can cancel, no problem. How would you like to pay?"

The orchids were Phoebe's idea, along with all the other exquisite, though pricey, details. Ava gave her MasterCard number over the phone, again.

The only cancelation she could make without being charged was the block of hotel rooms plus brunch at The Surrey. She was a week past the one-month cancelation policy, but they were kind. Very kind.

Current Wedding Debt: $65,500, plus $400 for Maggie's bridesmaid gown. Ava was still paying off school loans; it would take her years, many years, to pay off the wedding. Dance lessons were out of the question.

And still no word back from the managing agent of her building. Would she lose her apartment in all of this, too?

Joe might soon have some company under the stoop.

The sunset was a fiery blaze outside her office window. Ava had no plans to go out, and no desire to go home. Julian hadn't called. Probably had better things to do on such a balmy night, perfect for going out with friends or on a date. Even Bucksly had bailed for a men's fashion show. It was just her and the eerie quiet halls and dark offices.

Her cell phone vibrated on her desk, and she took a chance on an unknown number. "Hello?"

"A!" Nick from college burst through her phone. Back to boost his ego already?

"What's going on?" she asked and braced herself for another rundown of his happening life.

"Plenty. But forget me. You doing anything tonight?"

"Not really. You know, it's a Wednesday night—"

"Good. You're going out with a buddy of mine."

"Uh, I don't know if—"

"Can you be at Raoul's on Spring Street at eight?"

She went to the window, as if her answer were outside. "Well, I—"

"Perfect. He's a catch, trust me." *Click.*

She hadn't even gotten her date's name. But a meal in the garden of Raoul's might be worth it.

Rushing home to change brought back the good times with Josh. *No. Don't go there.* It was a beautiful night to be out, even on a blind date.

Ava ran down the stoop, the pink halter dress she'd put on invigorating. Joe and his dog were apparently out on the town, too. Doing something illegal? He never appeared to be drunk or on drugs, but that didn't mean he was honest.

She dropped a card into the mailbox on the corner. This week she picked out one with a baby pig that read, *This little piggy went to the market, and this little piggy cried GET*

WELL SOON *and ran all the way home.* It was corny, but Mom would smile.

A cab ride later, Ava stepped inside Raoul's, into the rich scent of aged wood and spiced meat. Standing at the packed bar, surrounded by people in conversation, she tried for a look that said she was comfortable standing alone, waiting for a stranger. She forced her facial muscles to relax while sweat accumulated under her arms.

A heavy-set man in pinstripes shimmied off his barstool and sauntered her way. Her smile dissolved, and she quickly tried to recreate it. He was attractive, sort of, with a friendly smile and very white teeth. But his cheeks—was it petty of her to notice?—were so much larger than his eyes, which were kind of squinty. She couldn't even decipher their color.

"You must be Ava," he said with a radio announcer's voice, smooth and cheerful. "Am I right? Nick warned me you were a knockout. The name's Hale."

"Hi, um, nice to meet you."

"My pleasure, Ava." His fleshy hand engulfed hers, and his gold pinky ring shimmered. Her hand came back damp. She stared at it, wanting a napkin, before blatantly using her dress.

He looked at her as if in a quandary, unable to decide if he should spring for a bottle of reserve or play it safe with last year's vintage. "Okay then, should we go to our table?"

They were seated in the garden beside a rose-covered trellis. Ava felt a laugh begin in her chest and then spiral up her throat. She bit her lip. Father Luke had warned her about mood swings. Hale peered over his menu. She commanded herself to be calm, but it was beyond her control, like sobbing to Mom—except Mom knew why she was crying. Laughing, crying. *What am I doing here with this guy?* She wiped her eyes.

"Is something funny?" he asked.

"No, nothing." She took a long breath...*easy.* "This is all very nice. I've just got some personal stuff going on, and perhaps the contrast..." She glanced around at the other couples, all of whom looked comfortable with their dates. Happy. In love.

Their sommelier appeared, a small man with a pinched face.

"Wow me," Hale said, cocking his head to one side.

The sommelier turned to her and opened his eyes wide. "Lucky you!"

"It's not necessary, really. I hardly drink." A glass of champagne for a special occasion, sure, but tonight didn't qualify.

"I insist." Hale handed back the wine list, and the sommelier dashed off to fetch something to impress her.

"It's been a crazy summer so far, for weather," she said.

"Totally. A hot one."

A waitress came over and gave Hale his order. "The usual, rare?"

"So it still moos." He laughed, humored by his standing meal. "I'll have the salmon, medium."

The waitress smiled as if she knew it'd be the salmon. Ava imagined her doing a cross-comparison of all the women Hale brought to Raoul's.

"So, I hear you're a fashion designer or something," he said when the waitress left them.

"I work in fashion, buying handbags for Bergdorf."

His eyes glazed over, introducing a lull in conversation. They were headed straight for an awkward moment.

"What do you do?" she asked.

"Accounting. I won't bore you with the details. I've gone on enough dates to know my work only interests me."

"I wouldn't mind hearing about it."

The sommelier returned, and that was the end of accounting. "May I present our finest?" he asked, bowing as he presented a dark bottle.

Hale took a whiff of the cork. "That's what I'm talking about!"

"I'm glad you're 'wowed,'" she said, trying to look appreciative. Pretending to drink it would be the real challenge.

The sommelier filled their glasses, and Hale raised his. "To new beginnings."

"As opposed to *old* beginnings?" She chuckled.

"What'd you say?" he asked, still holding out his glass.

"Never mind." She raised her glass to his and took a sip,

letting the burgundy-colored wine wet her lips. "Have you been single a long time? This is all rather new for me."

"On and off," he replied. "Six years, maybe?"

Six? She suddenly felt bad for him. "Does dating get old? I think I'd get frustrated after six years."

"What's frustrating about being an eligible bachelor?"

"Oh, I see. You like the single life."

"I didn't say that." He drank half of his wine in one gulp. "Are you hungry? Our food will be out in no time. They take care of me here."

Soon enough, he was digging into his bloody sirloin. "*This* is the good life," he said and took another mouthful. The bottle of wine was half empty.

She nibbled at her salmon, wishing she had an appetite. "Delicious. Thank you for bringing me here."

"Of course." He sat back in his chair, napkin balled up on the table. "A lot of women go for my steady career, Mercedes E-Class Coupe, et cetera, but I get the feeling you're different. Can't say why, really. Just a hunch."

"I wouldn't hold your Mercedes against you."

"I like your sense of humor!"

Ava reached for her water.

He glanced at her full wine glass. "It's an excellent year. I was inspired to splurge."

"Thank you. But I warned you I'm not a big drinker."

"Right. So what else...I just got back from Spain." He nonchalantly swirled the noble wine in his glass. "I work hard and play harder. You know?"

"Not exactly," she replied, "but I get the idea."

"Love to travel," he went on. "Normally I shoot down to the Caribbean with my buddies every couple of months. I'll take a girlfriend, if I happen to be dating someone special. How do you feel about spontaneous getaways?"

Josh's opinion came back to her verbatim: *They sound better than they really are, what with coach seating, bad layovers, and booked hotels.*

She smiled. "I like to think I'm spontaneous."

"Precisely!" His small eyes opened wide, revealing a handsome jade color.

She looked at him, and for the first time that evening saw a possibility, like a narrow inroad to love. She had never envisioned herself with someone so loud and so flashy and somewhat conceited...but they were only first impressions. Maybe he was just the spontaneity she needed in her life.

Dessert menus came. "The apple tart looks good," she said. "Want to share a slice?"

"I'd love to."

Waiting for the kitchen to pick, peel, and bake the apples, she struggled to follow his gym routine.

"With my upper body I can do four reps of twelve, no problem. Legs, that's a whole other story. I'm psyched if I can squeeze out eight counts. Of course, squatting 280 is totally awesome. But that's just my opinion."

Their date felt like strenuous exercise. She longed for her claustrophobic apartment and hard futon.

One crumbly apple tart arrived with a scoop of vanilla ice cream acquiescing to its warmth. Here was the perfect union. "It does look good," she said.

"Honestly, the desserts here are pure nirvana," he replied, and again, genuine excitement joined their table.

"Allow me." He leaned over and brought a spoonful to her lips. The crisp and creamy delight collided with repulsion. No open mind could change bad chemistry.

An hour later, or so it seemed, he cut the last tiny bite in half for them to split. She couldn't believe how someone with a mouth as large as his could take such small bites.

Finally, the bill arrived.

"I can get you a cab," he said, looking over the damage. "Or you could come back to my place." His eyes sidled to hers... expecting a *yes*?

"I think a cab would be best. I had a good time, though. Thank you."

"Of course." He reached into his suit jacket for his wallet, came out with nothing, and then checked his back pocket. His face donned a look of shock. "What the..." He searched more pockets. "I can't believe it. I don't have my wallet. I must've left it at the office. I'm so sorry, Ava. I would've picked up the bill, no question."

"I'll split the bill, no question, but are you asking me to pay for the whole tab? I didn't choose this restaurant, and our meal is over two hundred dollars with the tip. I don't have that much extra cash sitting around—or any, actually."

"I feel awful, really, but there's nothing I can do. I don't have my wallet."

"Can't you stop in tomorrow and pay?" Her voice shook with anger. "I'm sure they won't mind, since they know you so well."

Laughter oozed from the back of his throat. "An I.O.U.? Sorry. Not a chance. I take clients here for work almost every week and have a reputation to uphold." He took a deep breath, puffing up his chest. "Call it pride, if you want."

"Are you *proud* to stick me with the bill?"

"I'm fully prepared to make it up to you on another date, of course. It's not a matter of money."

"Is this a test? Or some sick way of getting a second date?"

"Think of tonight as an investment." He raised his wine glass before finishing off the outrageously priced wine he'd ordered to impress her.

"An investment in learning not to go on blind dates is more like it!"

They waited in silence for her MasterCard to be approved. Ava scribbled her name on the bill and stood up from the table. "I hope you find your wallet, Hale, and some dignity while you're at it." She walked out of the restaurant. Having the last word was no consolation.

The night air felt refreshing, but it was late and tomorrow morning Ava had to be at work. After spending more money on cab fare, she stood on 22nd Street, grateful to be home. The ivy clinging to her building glowed in the moonlight. Joe was sound asleep below the stoop, curled up on his cardboard, the dog by his side. His head rested on an inflatable pillow, and a russet-colored blanket covered them both. She felt an odd tenderness, a mixture of pity and admiration. They were managing, a man and his dog, having only each other and a home under the stars. The dog lifted its head and barked, just once and not loud, as if undecided about making a fuss. She ran up the steps and went inside.

On the fifth floor, she opened her apartment door and stopped. Down the hallway, a light shown from the kitchen, a light she always turned off when she went out.

"Hello?" She remained absolutely still, her pulse racing. A shadow moved into the light, and before she could react, Josh appeared.

"Out on a weeknight?" he asked.

"What are you doing here?" Feeling uneasy, she walked toward him.

"Your keys." He tossed them on the kitchen table. His smug expression and steely eyes made her want to physically kick him out the door. He didn't fit in with her place anyway, with his pressed designer suit and gleaming Italian leather shoes.

"I haven't seen you wear that dress in a while," he said. "Where were you? Out on a date?"

She wanted to lie, falling back into "good girlfriend" mode, as loyal and unthreatening as a Golden Retriever. But she didn't.

"Yes, I was." A flutter in her stomach preceded the thrill of progress. Independence.

"Great! Get your revenge, if that's what you need. Whatever." He put out his hand. "I also came for the rings."

"Oh." She had actually forgotten about the rings. "They're right here." She opened her hope box, and her hands shook taking out the two glistening bands.

He saw them and brought his hands to his face, pressing on his temples. "I can't believe this..." His eyes became glassy.

"I'm sorry." She could barely speak.

"So I've been a little distant." His voice turned soft, pleading. "That doesn't mean we just give up, or that things won't change."

"I won't go into marriage hoping you'll change, Josh. I can't." She held out the rings.

He extended his hand, and she dropped them into his palm, seeing their brilliance one last time before his fingers closed. He turned away, inhaling deeply and holding the air in his chest. There was nothing she could say to make this easier.

With the rings in his breast pocket, he ran his fingers through his hair. "My father refuses to pick up the bill, just so you know. You'll use the wedding gown someday, I'm sure."

"Except I'd never! And I wouldn't have bought Vera Wang if your mother hadn't insisted. The dress is eight thousand dollars. I'm paying for a wedding that met *your* family's expectations!"

"If you're looking for sympathy, forget it. You trashed the wedding. You clean it up. Don't blame me, don't blame my mother, and don't come looking to us for help!"

"You know what, you're right. I'll pay for it all. The dress and veil, too!" What was she up to in debt now? Seventy thousand or more?

"I just don't get it, Ava. Why are you ruining your life like this? You're making a big mistake. You know you are." He stood at the door. "Oh, there's one thing I'll pay for. The fireworks. They were supposed to be a surprise. My gift to you." He left, slamming the door behind him. A deafening bang that stole her breath, as though she'd fallen from a swing.

Lying on her futon, staring up at the ceiling, tears spilled from her eyes. "God, help me." But she felt alone...and unheard.

Chapter Thirteen

A *New York Times* had been left on the ledge of her stoop with FOR THE PERSON WHO KNOWS THIS IS HERS written in black marker across the front page.

Why me? She was receiving charity from a homeless man, and not only that, something she didn't even want. Looking over the ledge, Ava could see his cardboard and the dog's bowl, but neither man nor dog were there. If he returned, she could lie and say she never saw it. Or just ignore him, except that was no way to treat someone who was trying to be nice. She sighed and stuck the paper into her workbag.

At the N-R subway station, a fast-moving stream of people ascended the concrete steps. That always meant a train was approaching or already there. She pushed her way into the downward flow, swiped her card and sprinted across the platform, squeezing inside with no time to spare. Among put out glances, under bright lights, she found herself wedged between three heavyset men carrying knapsacks and hardhats. The air was hot and smelled like oily hair. Oxygen was poorly rationed. If she had wanted to read her *Times*, space was an unattainable luxury.

Later at Bergdorf, her office did little to relieve her lingering claustrophobia from the subway. Sample handbags, sales reports, and a talking bear left her a narrow path to her desk. At least she had made it inside before Bucksly could thrust his watch in her face.

She sat down and called home. It was day four of Mom's miracle treatment.

"Hello?" David's voice sounded unusually soft, like a slippered footstep. She could see him sitting in the old upholstered armchair by their bed, a book on his lap, music softly playing. She missed the lived-in comfort of their farmhouse, the simple times...breakfast by the woodstove... shucking corn from the garden...picking flowers for the kitchen table. The merry times when Mom and David's folk band would practice, and they'd barbecue chicken in the pit out back. So many memories...

"I'm sorry," David said, "but she's sleeping. The new treatment has wiped her out."

Ava stood up at her desk. "This is awful. I can't speak to her. She doesn't want me to see her. She might as well be locked up in prison!"

"Ava, I'm here by her side, and I feel the same way," he replied in a whisper. "Wait, one minute...she's waking up."

Blankets rustled before Ava heard wheezing through the phone. "That you, honey?" Mom asked, breathless, as if she had just run in from the garden. This cocktail had no mercy.

"Hi, Mom. How are you?" Ava's throat tightened like a clenched fist as she sunk down in her chair. How did David face this, time after time? Was it their vows, said over twenty years ago, to love each other in sickness?

"I'm doing fine," Mom replied, not entirely there.

"Hey, I'm trying your approach to life, keeping an open mind, looking for the positive. You know, like your music class this fall. Things to look forward to." Ava tried with everything she had not to cry. Could Mom hear it in her voice? "I'm even taking up dance again. Can you believe it after so many years? If I make it into a recital, you'll come and watch me, right? Just like old times."

"My music class?" she asked, fading out.

"You didn't forget about Folklore, did you?"

"I love you, honey."

Ava gripped the phone, as if that would keep Mom close. But the drugs made her smaller, weaker, transparent...taking her further and further away.

"I love you too, Mom."

David came back on the line. "She has to sleep, Ava."

"I know. I just...I understand. Maybe tomorrow." There'd be no going home for the weekend. She hung up and cried.

Throwing herself into work seemed like the only thing to do. Markdowns needed to go into the system to move summer inventory and make way for fall.

She ticked off old styles that hadn't sold through, handbags from April and May presentations that felt years old as July approached. Her intercom buzzed. "Yes?"

"Uh, Ava?" Caution and uncertainty were not Rhonda's style.

"What is it?"

"You have a visitor." Her voice dropped to a whisper. "His mother."

"No."

"Yes, and she's on her way to you now!" Rhonda said through the intercom.

"Tell her I'm in a meeting right now but will call when—"

Phoebe appeared in the doorway, frowning. She had on a red pantsuit and matching red scarf and looked like a walking panic button. "Don't bother making an excuse." She spoke in a low, shaky voice.

"Phoebe," Ava said, releasing the intercom, "I can't talk to you now, not here."

"You don't need to." Phoebe shut the door, gripping her handbag, also red. "I'll talk." Moving the bear, she sat down and closed her eyes, as though looking inward for her script. "I used to have a son and a daughter-in-law," she began coolly. "Now it seems I have nothing. You won't talk to me. Josh won't talk to me. I understand that you are both hurting, but just so you know, I'm hurting too. I've put my heart into this wedding. My life! How can you just abandon it and leave me like this?" All constraints broke, and she wiped tears from her cheeks. Phoebe never cried; her job in life was staying happy and keeping everyone else happy, too.

"I don't know what to say." Ava stepped toward her. She'd do anything to take away her pain—except marry Josh. "I wish we could stay friends. It's not that I don't love you. You're like a mother—"

Phoebe put up her hand, rejecting sympathy, a hug, love. "I'm not finished. I used to brag to my friends that Josh was marrying the kindest, most considerate and devoted woman in the world, but what you're doing now...it's unforgiveable! I don't understand. Was he unfaithful?"

Ava stepped back. "No. I don't know. But I feel cheated on when he won't kiss me in a restaurant or hold my hand in a chapel."

"That's Josh! He doesn't show his feelings in public. He never has."

"It's not just in public, Phoebe. My affection doesn't make him smile. He never asks for it. I reach out to him, wanting to make him happy, and he acts as if I'm taking something from him. I once hesitated before touching his arm; afraid he'd pull away. His arm!" She shuttered, recalling the feeling of rejection that he had planted and fostered inside her. "I know what I want now, or at least what I *don't* want, and that's a relationship that leaves me out in the cold. I think you know how it feels with Mr.—"

Phoebe shot up from her chair. "This isn't about me!"

"Yes, it is!" Ava stood a head taller than petite Phoebe, which accentuated the strength she felt at that moment. "I'm sorry to say this, but maybe if you were happier in your own marriage, you wouldn't have put your whole life into our wedding. You have to realize that I can't get married to save you from more disappointment."

"How can you be so cruel? I only want what's best for you

and Josh!"

"You also want what's best for *you.*"

"Shut your mouth!" She raised her handbag to strike. Ava ducked, but Phoebe stopped herself. "I'm sorry," she said, pulling her handbag to her chest. "God, look at me..."

Neither of them spoke. Phoebe closed her eyes as if shutting down...or rebooting.

"Phoebe," Ava said softly, carefully. "I'll pay for everything. I'm trying to be as fair as possible."

"Fair?" Phoebe opened her eyes still burning with anger and pain. "Do you even know what it means to be fair? You led us on for years! Fair would be getting married, like you agreed!"

"I'm sorry. I wanted it to work with Josh more than anything else, and I gave everything I had. But now I'm putting my happiness first, or at least my dream of happiness."

"Oh, isn't that great!" Phoebe thrashed her arms and handbag as if she'd been thrown into deep water. "Well, then go after your dream, knowing that you're hurting two people who love you very much!" She walked out, slamming the door behind her.

Ava opened it and followed. "Love is understanding!"

Phoebe didn't stop.

The city lit up the night, and people celebrated the start of the weekend. Outdoor seating was the ticket at all the restaurants, while horns honked like a symphony on the streets. Ava refused to work later than 9:00 p.m. just because Bucksly was still there "catching up." *On a Friday night?*

Arriving at her building, she felt like she had come in last in a marathon. Even worse, no one was there to care that she had finally crossed the finish line. Well, almost no one.

Joe sat below the stoop, writing in his notebook with a penlight. He didn't look up as she approached. A voice in her head said to keep going, but she stopped. "I got the paper you left this morning."

He stared at her as though trying to place where he'd seen her before.

"*The New York Times*," she said, wishing she hadn't opened her mouth.

"Oh, okay. Sure. I'm...glad you got it."

"It was for me, wasn't it? I just assumed, since we had talked about *The Times* and knowing what's going on in the world..." Twilight masked her bright red cheeks.

"Right! Of course. That's fine." He paused. "Do you know Shirley? She lives in the building."

Ava shook her head. She didn't know anyone in her building.

"A real thin woman with bright yellow hair. Must be in her nineties. And no balance whatsoever. She walks like we're having an earthquake."

"I've seen her."

"Well, she was complaining that her dog, Nuisance, is too old to go outside anymore, and Wee-Wee Pads would cost her her heart medication."

"That's terrible!"

"I know. I told her this morning that I'd give her my newspaper."

"I'll never take it again!"

"I would've left a note with her name, but I didn't know it at the time. Now I do." He closed his notebook. "I'm Chris, by the way." He stood, extending his hand.

"Ava." She glanced at his fingers—long, lean, no apparent dirt under his nails—before shaking his hand.

His palm felt soft against hers. His grip was strong. *So it's Chris, not Joe.* She quickly released his hand.

"What'd you think of yesterday's news?" he asked.

"Which news?"

"Any of it." He looked at her, expectant.

"Yesterday's news." She couldn't think back that far. There was only today's news. Mom, too weak to talk. Phoebe, hurt and angry. How could she even begin to make room in her life for world events?

"There was this one article," Chris said, "the headline caught my eye. *Memories of a Doomed Utopia*. Did you happen to see it?"

Ava shook her head.

"It was about a man named Janusz Korczak. He ran an orphanage in Poland, until the Nazis forced him and his orphans into a ghetto in Warsaw. That was in 1940. Two years later, they were deported to Treblinka, a death camp. The article said he led the children, each with a toy, in a silent march to the train."

She listened in awe. Even his dog seemed to be listening.

"The thing is, he could've left the orphanage and fled Poland long before it got to that point, but he stayed with the kids to the end."

Drawn in by the story and the sound of his steady voice, she thought of the children, their innocence, and the unimaginable crime. Seventy-some years ago, a continent away, Korczak touched them both now. "That's love."

He nodded. "So what about you?"

"Me? Oh, I'm just coming home from work. A long day, as usual. My boss expects me to be like him and live to buy and sell handbags. Sometimes it all seems so meaningless and I wonder why I don't quit. But then my rent check becomes due..." She paused. Chris stared at her, listening as if she were sharing a story as tragic and beautiful as the children's silent march to Treblinka. "It's silly of me to complain."

"Sounds like that's his passion in life, or all he has at the moment. What do you live for, if it's not your work?"

"Does paying off bills qualify?" She laughed and then felt as though she had shared too much. "I promise I won't take your paper next time," she said, going up the stoop. "Nuisance's paper, rather."

"No worries," Chris said from his spot. "It's the weekend. Have fun."

"Thanks. I'll try."

Inside her apartment, feeling lost, she remembered Mom's

advice, and Father Luke's, as well. Call a friend.

Maggie answered in her cheery mommy voice. "Hey-ho!"

"Hi, what are you doing tomorrow?" Ava asked.

"Changing diapers, watching *Blue's Clues*, why?"

"This is late notice, I know, but how about coming into the city? We'll have a girls' night out!"

"You're joking." Maggie laughed. "I don't think so."

"Why not? We'll have a blast! Manis and pedis. Dinner at some fabulous restaurant. I read that time apart from your hubby is supposed to be good for a marriage."

No answer. Could she blame her? Maggie had a family and a big house in the suburbs. A break from her life would be a chore.

"I guess I can ask Marc to stay with Melanie for one night. It's not like I've had a single day to myself since she was born. He's always traveling for work, flying first class, staying in Ritz-Carltons around the world.... Can you believe she's already taken her first step?"

"Wow. It seems like only yesterday we were scoping out cute boys on campus, doesn't it?"

Maggie laughed. "All right. You and me, tomorrow night."

Chapter Fourteen

Ava looked up at the dome ceiling of Grand Central Station. The sun shone through sky-facing windows into the main concourse. The sheer size of the building, with its dusty light and wavy echo of overlapping voices, made her feel vulnerable, like a small fish in large aquarium.

Finally, Maggie appeared in a crowd from the Hudson Line track. Good, the same warm, familiar smile.

"It's so good to see you!" Ava hugged her as if no time had passed and they were still college roomies. "You look great!"

"If *fat* is what you consider great, then my secret is snacking all day, and my exercise regime is lifting an eighteen pound weight I call Melanie." She did a quick pantomime of holding up a baby.

Ava laughed. "That's so cute."

"Seriously! You're supposed to lose weight after childbirth, and I'm gaining it. If you were still getting married, they'd have to take out my dress an inch or two."

"For the amount of money it's costing me to cancel the wedding, you and I should have it. Just for fun."

Maggie's face lit up. "We should! A wedding to celebrate the moment, instead of the rest of your life. Get it? I'll throw you the bouquet and everything. It'll be great!"

"Oh, man. I'd be catching the bouquet at my own wedding."

A deserted smile lingered on Maggie's face.

"What's wrong?" Ava asked.

"The one regret from my wedding was not drying the flowers. That was the last time I received them. It's only been a few years, but Marc doesn't look at me the same way as he did then. He's not inspired."

"I don't believe you." Maggie still had those dark blue eyes, purple almost, and strawberry-blond hair that all the girls at school had envied.

"I'm not kidding. Moms with babies are invisible to the male race."

Maggie actually sounded depressed, and she had the perfect life. "Well, you're not invisible to me." Ava hugged her shoulders.

"Thanks." Maggie hugged her back. "But I'll be honest with you, Ava. The starved look isn't attractive, either. And your hair has gotten so long and...shiny."

"You mean stringy. I know. I've got to get my act together. Starting today! Come on, let's drop your stuff off at my place first."

On 22nd Street, their cab pulled up to Ava's welcoming committee: Chris, with that notebook, and the dog by his side.

"You have a homeless guy below your stoop," Maggie whispered.

"I'm aware of that." She made a point of not looking at him, hoping to avoid conversation.

Inside, they started up the five flights. "Hey, remember helping me move in?" Ava asked.

"Uh-huh, and I'm wondering how we managed it." Maggie was dragging her feet by the second floor. "How do you do this every day?" she asked, short of breath.

Eventually making it to the fifth floor, Ava unlocked her door, and they went inside. The sound of their footsteps emphasized the emptiness in her life.

"Oh, look!" Maggie exclaimed. "Your 'light' reading. Remember? We lugged those heavy crates full of books up all five flights! That must've been three or four years ago."

"More." Ava stared at her treasured love stories with their exotic settings, seeing only that her life had gone nowhere. "Well, everything will change. You know, now that Josh and I are through. Did I tell you? I met someone."

"Already? Aren't you supposed to suffer a little first? At

least a few weeks of self-inflicted solitude, wallowing in guilt and heartache?"

"No. I've suffered enough for Josh's love. Think of a rabbit chasing a carrot for five years. *Feed me! Feed me! I'm cute and fluffy!* I'm over it!"

Maggie laughed. "So is this new guy chasing you?"

"I think so. He's new to New York, so he might be a little lost. But he's good-looking, in a thin, washed-up kind of way. You know that look?"

"Definitely. Like Mick Jagger, when he was hot."

"Right, but Mick Jagger is eternally hot. Anyway, his name is Julian. I'm gonna show him around the city." She heard her voice bouncing off bare walls. He obviously wasn't calling.

Maggie just smiled.

"So, how's Marc doing? Is he warming up to being a daddy?"

"I guess, when he isn't working." She paused. "He had the family room renovated. That's something, I suppose."

"A family room! That's when you know you have it all." Ava realized that she was talking about an old dream, making a home with Josh. A flawed dream at the core; her family room would've become her prison.

What should you do after breaking your engagement? Find a new dream, one that sets you free.

Maggie seemed reluctant to let go of her overnight bag.

"Here," Ava said, "I'll put that in the 'bedroom' for you." Without moving, she set it down next to her futon. "If you drink enough wine tonight, you won't realize you're sleeping on plywood."

"I'll take back pain over a screaming child any night. Melanie still wakes me up, wanting her mommy."

"How adorable! Well, I promise I won't do that. Okay, so, here's the day's agenda: a rocking Marc Jacobs sample sale, sloppy burgers in Madison Square Park for lunch, manis and pedis, of course, and then dinner at Indochine. The place has been around for decades and is hip as ever."

"What are we waiting for? Let's go!" Maggie put her no-name handbag over her shoulder and started for the door.

Ava grabbed her Prada tote. "Thanks for coming into the city," she said and followed Maggie out of the apartment. "I'm really glad you're here."

"What are ex-bridesmaids for?"

7:00 p.m. Their cab stopped short at a traffic light. "Watch it!" Maggie snapped at the driver, as they braced themselves against the plastic divider. "I have a ten-month-old baby waiting for me at home!"

"Maybe we should buckle our seat belts," Ava said, helping her find the strap jammed between the seats.

"I'm so paranoid now," Maggie said, strapped in. "What if I break an arm and can't lift her? What if I die and she has to grow up without a mother? I hate living this way."

Ava buckled up, too, thinking of her geranium waiting for her at home on the fire escape. *A plant is a living thing.*

She skimmed the faces of people out on a Saturday night as their taxi moved down Park Avenue South toward Union Square Park and then Astor Place. "Maggie, do you think there's such a thing as Mr. Right?"

"Who knows, but I wonder if you'll find him. I think you're scared. Your parents divorced, and you're afraid of the same thing happening to you. I mean, when Josh proposed, you said yes, so you obviously thought he was Mr. Right. No?"

"He was the carrot; that's all I knew. I was too busy chasing after him to think much about it, too afraid of falling behind. Wait, that's it! If I meet someone and I'm *not* afraid, then I'll know he's right!" She pictured Courtney and Brad facing the pulpit with their arms interlaced.

"Except," Maggie pressed, "what if the fear is buried deep inside you?"

"Since when did you become a shrink? If it's *buried* deep inside me, then I'll put up a tombstone and consider it dead.

How's that?"

"You're so corny." Their cab pulled over on Lafayette Street. "Forget Mr. Right. Let's just have fun."

They stepped inside the restaurant, which looked like a moonlit Tiki bar, minus totems and the beach. "The perpetually hip restaurant *Indochine*!" Ava announced, remembering Phoebe, who actively believed trendy diversions from everyday life never failed to lift your spirits. Unfortunately, trendy diversions weren't cheap, and she couldn't afford to live according to Phoebe's rules anymore.

The air smelled like mango and soy sauce. Candlelight cast shadows on faces, creating masks, while palm fronds and birds of paradise bent low over the booths, as though bowing to the elite.

"I'm the only mother here," Maggie whispered as they waited to be seated.

"Then count yourself the lucky one." Ava scanned the crowd. So many ageless women in sexy little halter tops. Her own paisley silk camisole, designer jeans, and strappy stilettos seemed trying and unoriginal compared to Maggie's mommy style. Her flats, black knee-length skirt, and cherry-red sweater set had its own beauty, and Maggie wore it well.

Seated, Ava scanned the prices on the menu before looking at the food. A waiter came to their table. "Hello, ladies! I'm Sean, and I'll be your server tonight." He looked under-aged and perhaps happier to be there than she or Maggie.

"Order for me, Ava," Maggie said. "I'm so tired of choosing meals."

Ava looked up at their willing waiter. "We'll have your summer rolls, an order of crab cakes, and the ravioli to share."

"Perfect," Maggie said. "And a glass of chardonnay."

"Make that two," Ava said, handing back the menus. "Tonight's special."

"I guess you'll have to start cooking for yourself now," Maggie said once they were alone. "No more dinners out with Josh or his mother."

"That's exactly what I'll do. Get into cooking. Clip recipes and everything." Chris and his cutout recipe from *The Times* came to mind. His life clashed with the vibrant flowers, the meticulously prepared dishes, and the air of respect surrounding them now.

"Everyone loved your homemade mac-n-cheese at school," Maggie said.

"It was from a box."

"Still, you're good." Maggie was so sincere in her innocence. Their drinks arrived.

"Here's to life turned upside-down," Maggie said, raising her glass.

Ava did the same. A nod to her tanked wedding, she assumed, which definitely deserved it.

"It's true, everything changes when you have kids." Maggie lowered her glass and suddenly looked tired.

There was obviously more than one way to stand on your head.

As they were finishing the last ravioli, splitting it in half, their waiter appeared with two glasses of champagne, which they hadn't ordered. "Compliments from the gentleman at the bar," he said and breezed off, leaving them to draw their own conclusions.

Maggie sat up straight and blushed. "Oh?" Her attention shifted across the room. "I think I see our admirer. Don't look. I'll describe him. Mid-thirties, black hair, wearing a double-breasted suit with one of those power-red ties. *Very* handsome."

Josh? But of course Maggie knew Josh. Ava pinched the back of her hand. *Don't think of him!* She turned and looked toward the bar.

"No!" Maggie hissed. "We don't want to seem desperate. Glance toward the bar as you casually get up to go to the bathroom."

Too late. He waved. Ava smiled and continued on with the plan, going to the women's room. He was handsome. Maggie wasn't exaggerating.

Alone in the bathroom, her reflection stared back in the mirror as if it knew more than she did. What, though? Would she be ready when the right man presented himself? The idea of being *afraid* of love didn't make sense. Love was total acceptance...assurance...the pure happiness of children at play. She'd know it at first sight and live happily ever after... wouldn't she?

After trying to do something with her hair—fluff it out...tie it up?—she gave in to feeling dull and returned to their table.

The man from the bar was sitting in her chair, laughing with Maggie.

"Ava, I presume?" He stood and bowed. "I am Roberto. I hope you don't mind that I've joined your table." He turned out to be average-height and looked middle-aged, but the South American accent and blaze of confidence in his eyes had a persistent draw.

Maggie smiled, holding a glass of champagne. "Roberto is from Brazil."

"I *had* to top off your meal with Moët & Chandon," he said, as if it were the culture of his homeland to buy women champagne.

Their waiter was quick to fetch her another chair.

"He ordered us crème caramel, too!" Maggie exclaimed, giggly now.

So much for their girls' dinner. Maggie took a sudden interest in Brazil, its climate, language, status of women...

Ava remembered their college days: Maggie in the student union, making rounds from table to table, always socializing. "Are you thinking of giving up Scarborough for Rio, Maggie?"

"Don't be silly. I'm just interested, that's all. Brazil is so romantic!"

Ava leaned back in the spare chair they'd dragged to the table. Romance was beginning to feel overrated.

Dessert finished, Roberto insisted on paying their bill, which was a total break. Little did he know he was trying to impress a mom and an emotionally damaged woman in a lot of debt.

The thought raised a frightening question: Who would want to date her now?

"It's my pleasure," Roberto continued. "Now, shall we have a digestif at the bar?"

"Of course, we shall!" Maggie was beaming, young again and vivacious. Transformed, just like that.

Roberto stood. "A friend of mine from São Paulo is in town and I told him to meet me here. He will be thrilled to see me in such beautiful company."

"We'd love to meet your friend, wouldn't we, Ava?" Maggie nudged her arm.

Ava declined a sherry and sat with them at the bar, trying to ignore a bad feeling.

"So, Ricardo—I mean, Roberto—what do you do in Brazil?" Only Maggie could manage to be scatterbrained and attentive at the same time.

"I travel the world in search of precious stones. I suppose in pedestrian words," he said, letting out a dramatic sigh, "I'm nothing more than a jeweler. But tell me, lovely Maggie, what is your life's calling?"

"I'm a..." She looked at her glass.

You're a mother. Ava glared at her. Would she actually lie? Say something she'd regret?

Maggie, stalling, took a sip from her empty glass and giggled. "I'm a woman out of booze!"

The bad feeling kicked Ava in the gut. "Maybe we should go," she said, jumping up. "It's getting late and—"

"Shush. I haven't answered Ricardo's question. I mean, Roberto."

He leaned closer to her in breathless anticipation.

"There's no p-profound way to put it," she said, her cheeks blushing to match her sweater set. "I'm a...mom."

Roberto sat back in his chair.

Ava clapped. "I think there's nothing more admirable!" She took Maggie's hand. "Now are you ready to leave?"

"You go," she replied. "I'm having fun." The bartender refilled her glass.

"I'm not going without you, Maggie."

"To motherhood!" Roberto raised his drink.

"Hear! Hear!" Maggie all but slammed her glass into his.

"To motherhood." Ava sat back down, overruled.

A tall man approached them wearing dark glasses and a white shirt unbuttoned to his chest. "Getting into trouble, my friend?" He slapped Roberto on the back. He was younger and more muscular.

"Luis!" Roberto leapt out of his seat and they hugged. "Olá! About time, my man! Sit, sit. You must meet my new friends. This is Maggie, and this is..."

"Ava." It was clear where Roberto's focus lay.

"Ava, so happy to meet you," Luis replied. He had a slender face and a deep tan. "Forget this joint. I know where it's hot tonight." He looked straight at her. "I am telling you. It's *hot.*"

"Sounds good to me." Maggie stood—apparently ready to go after all. "Come on, Ava. It's only eleven, and there's nothing to do at your place."

An unfair comparison, though true.

It was crowded, with all four of them in the backseat of the cab. The smell of musky cologne was enough to make Ava woozy. Luis slid his arm around her back, which she allowed but wasn't sure she liked. Maggie didn't seem to notice Roberto's hand resting on her thigh. She talked nonstop, jumping from topic to topic: her "lost" career...motherhood...her husband who wasn't the dad she'd hoped he'd be. "I don't mean to brag, but I used to have a great body, before I had my little girl. Didn't I, Ava?" She looked down at her waist. "I have to lose a few pounds."

"You're beautiful," Roberto said, touching her chin. "Perfect."

The line outside the club, fifty deep, was not an issue. With Luis leading the way, they bypassed the velvet ropes and the thirty-dollar cover charge, entering a deafening beat. A barrage of strobe lights picked out moving bodies from the massive bi-level space.

"This could be fun!" Ava hollered, unable to resist the music.

"I'm sweating just standing here!" Maggie shouted, and they

danced on the periphery of the crowd.

"Come on." Luis pulled them farther into the club. "This way." They climbed a suspended staircase, and a shirtless man in a fur vest led them into a private lounge.

The place smelled of burnt wood and looked like a dungeon with rough walls and deep-set couches. Muted light trickled from amber votives burning on low-lying tables. The music was seducing. A waitress set out a bottle of champagne on ice without asking if they wanted it.

Ava looked around. No dance floor. Attractive people nonchalantly watched each other from their seats while talking with their friends.

"For you." Roberto handed Maggie a glass of bubbly.

"Who would've thought we'd end up here! Right, Ava?" She sipped her drink. "You never know with life, do you?"

"I'm starting to prefer knowing." Ava plopped down on the couch.

Luis planted himself next to her. "Why aren't you drinking?" he asked, slipping his arm around her shoulders. His eyes latched onto her mouth.

"I'm fine. Thanks." She sat forward to avoid his kiss. "I have a hypothetical question for you."

Luis took back the distance she had claimed. "I charge for questions," he said close to her ear. Wet lips tugged gently on her earlobe. Without warning, a sensual energy took over and she felt herself moving toward him.

"That's it," he whispered.

"Whoa!" She pulled back from his mouth, shocked by how intensely she longed to be touched.

"Why did you stop?" he asked, aghast, as if she had committed a crime.

"Because I don't know you, perhaps?" She took a deep breath. Reset. "So, I have a question."

"Ask me anything you like." He gave her his attention.

"All right. Would you date a woman, knowing she had debt of, well, seventy thousand dollars?"

"Is she good looking?"

"I don't know. Let's say yes, for argument's sake. And you could see yourself falling in love with her."

"No," he replied flatly. "But I'd sleep with her."

Ava cringed. "So what you're saying is that money matters more than love?"

"That much debt...it depends. On the sex." He went for her neck, trying to kiss a new trail to her lips.

She jumped to her feet. "I need a second opinion." It'd been a long time since she'd felt those initial tingles. She'd forgotten how they could senselessly take control.

The wall behind the bar was a giant fish tank. Instead of the usual tropical fish, however, two women in bikinis performed underwater ballet. Even stranger, no one paid much attention. What would impress this VIP crowd?

Ava found space at the bar beside a man and woman chatting, perhaps a couple, and ordered a Cherry 7UP. The question of whether anyone would date her with "that much debt" became a porthole to panic in her mind.

"Hi." She smiled at the couple. "Could I ask you both a question?"

"Sure," the woman replied. She had an open face and large, unblinking eyes.

Ava set her drink down on the bar. "Well, say you meet someone, and he or she has a lot of debt, like enough to be turned down for a mortgage. You feel a strong emotional attraction. Would you go with your feelings?"

The man laughed. "I wouldn't care, but I also wouldn't pay off her credit cards. At least not until we were married." He looked expectantly at the woman. "What about you? What if I had the bank chained to my wallet?"

"I might think twice."

"Come on. It should go both ways."

"I'm just being honest. I like your lifestyle."

He stared at her, perhaps rethinking their relationship. "Should I be flattered?"

Hearing a question with no right answer, Ava picked up her drink. "Uh, thanks for your input. I should find my friends."

Maggie and Roberto were entwined on the couch, making-out. "Oh, no." Ava recalled her own words to Maggie: *Time apart from your hubby is supposed to be good for your marriage.* This wasn't good.

"Come on, we're going." Ava poked her shoulder, which did nothing. She grabbed her arm and pulled. "Maggie!"

Roberto looked up, and Maggie opened her eyes, barely. "What? We're going?"

"Yes. Now."

Maggie struggled to get up from the low couch and fell back down. "I'm too dizzy."

"It's only twelve-thirty," Luis protested. "Who goes home at twelve-thirty?"

"Us." Ava glared at him.

"Okay, okay." Roberto helped Maggie to her feet. "We must take you home. No question. We will get a taxi and take you home."

"That's not necessary." Ava took hold of Maggie's hand, though she continued to lean against Roberto's chest.

"I won't hear of it," he said. "We have to know that you are safe."

"We can call you when we get there."

Ground-shaking percussion in the main club ended their debate. Outside, Roberto held Maggie upright, while Luis opened the door of a waiting cab. Ava glanced back at the bouncer managing the crowd at the door. She could get him involved, or just let the guys get their kicks as "gentlemen" and take her and Maggie home.

She started to get in, and then stopped. "Just so it's clear," she said, "there's no chance you're coming into my apartment."

The four of them, once again, squeezed into the backseat of a cab.

Luis went straight for her lips.

"Sorry, I don't kiss in cars," she said, pushing him away. "Motion sickness." She just might...all over him.

"Ah, so we save it for your stoop...and then your bed, if all goes well?"

"You're out of luck, Luis. I don't own a bed."

"No bed? Did the creditors take it?" He laughed and ran his fingers over her hand. "You're so soft, I don't need a bed."

Why didn't she get the bouncer on these horn dogs when she had the chance?

They arrived at her building, finally. Maggie was asleep against Roberto's arm. Luis handed the driver a ten and got out of the cab.

"Thanks for offering to pay, but you can keep the meter running," Ava said, scrambling out after him. She turned to help Maggie, but Roberto already had her in his arms, standing on the sidewalk. Luis shut the door and the cabbie drove off. "Wait!" She waved her arms, watching the yellow car disappear down the street.

As she turned to face her unwanted company, Luis scooped her up in his arms. "I've got you now!"

"Put me down! What are you doing?"

"Don't you want to be swept off your feet?" He held her like a bride about to be carried over a threshold. The irony hurt.

"Not by you!" She fought her way to the ground, but he kept his arms locked around her waist.

"You're a strong girl!" He laughed, tightening his hold.

Roberto, with Maggie passed out in his arms, hollered to them from the stoop. "Stop messing around and unlock this door! She's dead weight!"

"Leave her alone!" Ava felt sick as she struggled against Luis's muscular arms, his cologne rubbing into her clothes, under her skin. "Let go of me! Help!"

From the corner of her eye, she saw movement below the stoop. Chris stepped out from the shadows, holding a metal pipe. "Let her go. Now."

Ava stared in disbelief. He was going to fight these guys?

For *her*?

Luis tensed. "Who are *you*?"

"Just walk away and we won't have a problem." Chris looked at her and nodded. She felt ridiculous, helpless as a snared fish.

"Listen, dude," Luis said, "I'm her date tonight. Why don't you just drop the pipe and go back to your little hide-out?"

Chris moved fast and swung low. She heard a sharp *crack* and braced herself for pain when Luis dropped to the ground. He held his knee, moaning in agony.

"Are you hurt?" Chris moved toward her, still holding the pipe.

"I'm...I—" Words wouldn't come out.

"What's going on?" Roberto ran down the steps, while Maggie lay in a heap at the top of the stoop, her red sweater set hiked up to her middle, exposing doughy pale skin.

Ava ran to her. "Maggie! You have to get up!" She corrected the sweater and tried lifting her from under her arms. "Please— get—*up*!" It was no use.

She looked down at Roberto, bent over Luis, just below the stoop. They spoke in Portuguese, and then Roberto stood, his hands in tight fists. "Yo, freak," he growled at Chris. "You made a big mistake."

Chris held up his weapon, ready to strike again, while his dog barked, guarding the cardboard. Suddenly, it went for Roberto's ankles.

"Get the thing off me!" Roberto kicked it. The dog yelped, backing off.

"Don't touch my dog!" Chris charged Roberto, swinging the pipe. Lights went on in one of the apartments above. Roberto fell backward, just avoiding the metal bar striking his chest.

"Come on, Maggie," Ava pleaded. "Stand up! We have to get inside!"

"I just want to sleep," Maggie moaned, flailing an arm.

Chris stood over Roberto, ready to swing again. "It's time you stop picking on people and animals that are smaller than you!"

Roberto jumped to his feet and held up his fists. "It's time you put down the pipe and fight like a man!"

"I'm here to help Ava. You guys should leave before I cause serious harm."

Roberto didn't put his fists down, and now Luis had staggered to his feet,

"Go inside!" Chris shouted, his eyes on his targets. He looked dangerous with the pipe raised and strands of hair hanging over his face.

"Come on!" Ava pulled harder to get Maggie upright. "You can't sleep here!" Nothing worked. Her hands shook as she groped through her handbag for her cell phone. "I'm calling the police!" she shouted, fearing for Chris, that he would be the one arrested. But she had no choice. "I'm calling 9-1-1!"

Roberto held Luis back. "Forget this guy. He's just some bum."

An operator answered. "This is 9-1-1."

Ava gripped the phone to her ear. Luis held Roberto's shoulder, limping, as they moved down the dark street.

"Is someone there?" the operator asked. "You've reached 9-1-1—"

"False alarm. Sorry." Ava stopped the call.

Maggie half opened her eyes and saw the phone. "I need to call Marc." She tried to reach for it and missed. Ava helped her up against the door. "Where am I?" Maggie muttered.

"With me." Ava took out her keys. She wouldn't feel safe until they were inside.

"Are you all right?" Chris called out from the bottom of the stoop. His face glistened with sweat in the light from above.

"Thank you for helping. I'm really sorry." She jammed the key into the lock and the door opened, landing Maggie on the floor of the foyer.

"Oh, gosh! Sorry, Maggie!"

Chris ran up the stoop. "Can I help?"

"No! We're fine. Really." She dragged Maggie inside and made sure the door locked behind them.

Five flights turned into an endless climb with Maggie hanging off her shoulder. They finally made it into her apartment, and Maggie went straight for the toilet to boot. Minutes later, she lay asleep in her clothes, diagonal across the futon.

Ava changed into her rainbow pajamas and curled up on the floor with a blanket and pillow. Sleep felt far away. No one had ever fought for her before. For the first time in so long, she felt... important. She pictured Chris coming to her rescue...reading to her from *The Times*...asleep under the moonlight. He was as real to her as the mystery surrounding his life. And perhaps he was the kindest man in the world, but he lived on the streets.

Chapter Fifteen

Ava woke up on the hard, creaky floor of her apartment. *What the—*

"I'm definitely not telling Marc," Maggie said as if they'd been talking all night. "I mean, what would I say? That I didn't know what I was doing? I knew. In the beginning, anyway. A man actually hit on me, and it felt good!"

Ava remembered the Brazilian men. *Such creeps!* Her and Maggie's stupidity, she wished she could forget. And Chris, her knight with a lead pipe...that could've been a strange dream. She blinked at the clock. "It's six in the morning. Why are we up?"

"I'm going to Grand Central to wait for the next train." Maggie stuffed her sweater set into her bag and zipped it shut. "Thanks for giving me the futon last night. I feel bad that you had to sleep on the floor."

"It's all right." Ava sat up, achy all over. "Don't you even want breakfast?"

"And puke? No, thanks." Maggie started toward the door.

Ava scrambled to her feet. "Want me to go with you to Grand Central?"

Maggie stopped and turned, her eyes bloodshot and sad. "Ava, if you ever get married...well, you'll see. Forget looking for Mr. Right. You're just setting yourself up for disappointment. And kissing someone else doesn't change a thing, except you feel like dirt."

"Oh, Maggie." They hugged. *If she ever got married?*

Maggie pulled back. "You don't need to come with me to the train. I'd rather be alone."

"At least let me walk you outside." Ava went for her keys on the kitchen table.

"You're wearing rainbow pajamas," Maggie said, waiting by the door.

"No one will be out this early on a Sunday." She thought of Chris as she slipped on her sneakers, but he wouldn't judge her.

She and Maggie didn't talk going downstairs. Outside, the smell of coffee wafted from below the stoop. He was awake. Ava held up her pajama bottoms so they wouldn't drag on the ground. First she'd see Maggie off, then she'd thank Chris.

On the corner of 22nd and Tenth, they waited for a cab. "I'm so sorry for the way things turned out," Ava said, feeling to blame. "Does this mean you'll never visit me again?"

"It's not your fault, and of course I'll visit you—every five years."

"Hey, that's not funny! But if I'm still sleeping on a futon five years from now, shoot me. Seriously."

Maggie laughed. "Never! And if we have a girls' night without champagne and men, we'll have a great time. Or at least we'll wake up feeling good about ourselves." She hailed a distant cab. "Hey, about your canceled wedding, Ava, I admire that you're holding out for love. Even if it turns out to be a mistake."

"Thanks, but you could have a little more faith."

"When I'm hung over, I'm a realist." The cab pulled over and Maggie got in, her face drawn with worry and regret. "I still don't know what I'm going to say."

"He'll understand, after he cools off. You just have to trust in your love for each other." *Wasn't it Phoebe who told me that?* Phoebe didn't seem to have a marriage she could trust, and to make matters worse she knew what love should feel like.

Maggie waved as the cab pulled away.

Ava waved back and then hoisted up her pajama bottoms and returned to the stoop.

Chris, hidden in his Sunday *Times*, didn't see her approaching. His dog, however, watched her with its eyes full of suspicion, its tail flat to the ground.

She smiled uneasily. "Hello, there."

Chris looked up from his paper. "Nice pajamas! How are

you doing this morning?"

She glanced at her rainbows, suddenly embarrassed. "I'm all right, I guess. Thanks again for helping us out. It was kind of cool the way you took that guy down." She looked for a smile.

He chuckled. "I wasn't trying to be *cool*. But maybe I'll keep that pipe handy."

"You've come to my rescue twice now, if you count that rude businessman on the subway. I think I still have a bump." She touched her forehead.

"I seem to be at the right place at the right time, for you anyway." He took a sip of his coffee.

"Well...I just wanted to say thanks. So, thanks." She turned to leave, wanting to do or say something more.

"Did you call the cops?" he asked.

She stopped before going up the stoop. "No. I don't even know those guys' last names. It was just a dumb night. I should've ended it long before they insisted on taking us home."

He nodded. "The funny thing is, I found that metal pipe broken off of a bicycle rack last week and decided to keep it, just in case. I've been living on and off the streets for over three years and not once did I think about needing a weapon." He reached into a Whole Foods bag beside his suitcase and took out a can of Pedigree dog food.

"Are you from here?" she asked. "If you don't mind me asking."

"I was born and raised here, in the West Village, back when it was less trendy and more artsy. But then I moved to France for high school. Not my best years." He didn't say anything more on that.

"I thought I heard an accent. Sounds exciting to someone who's never been to Europe."

He went into his suitcase, retrieving a manual can opener. She caught a glimpse of a hefty book, *Larousse Gastronomique*, before he shut and latched the lid. Why the expensive dog food? And what about the cookbook and clipped recipes? Was cooking a hobby? Should she ask? The question seemed cruel, put to someone with absolutely no means of cooking. A former hobby? A dream?

"By the way," she ventured, "is there anything I can get you? For helping me out. I don't know what kind of food you like, but I'd be happy to pick up your favorite meal or something."

"No. Thanks." His dry tone made it clear that he didn't want her help.

Warmth spread over her face. "Sorry. I just feel indebted to you."

"You shouldn't." He opened the can of Pedigree, releasing the unsavory scent of liver and carrots. The dog lifted its head, gazing at its owner in utter gratitude.

"While I was growing up," Chris continued, "my father did all the cooking in our family. He had this crazy electric can opener from the fifties. It was sea green and made such a racket that I would run out of the house screaming, whenever he used it. I was maybe three or four at the time." He wiped the opener with a napkin and returned it to his suitcase. "My father would turn it on just to get me out of the kitchen."

"How mean! Does he still do that?"

Chris laughed. "He's found other ways to scare me away."

"Oh." Mom's cancer came to mind. Ava longed to be home with her, and to live without fear.

"So, what kind of can opener did you have growing up?" Did he know he was steering her memories toward better times?

"I grew up in an old farmhouse, upstate New York, and everything we owned was outdated." She pictured Mom and David trying to get the stubborn crank to turn on the pasta machine. Johnny Cash in the background.

"There are some decent wineries up around the Finger Lakes." He patted his dog as it wolfed down its slop.

"I guess. I've never been. I like upstate, but no place compares to the city."

He nodded. "Endless possibilities."

"Well, sure I can't even pick you up another cup of coffee?" She spoke without thinking.

He frowned, clearly not wanting handouts, or at least not from her. "I had my one cup today, thanks." He looked straight at her, flipping a lock of dark hair out of his brown eyes.

"I see." She didn't see at all but wasn't going to pry any further. "Thanks, again, for saving me," she said as she went up the stoop.

"You're making me out to be some kind of hero, Ava."

"Hey, if the pipe fits..." Sending him a smile over her shoulder, she slipped back inside.

Monday morning, the Job Market section of *The Times* was left on the ledge of the stoop. This time he wrote FOR AVA across the top. Smiling, she picked it up. A prominent star marked an article: "Some Work a Second Job, the Dream One."

The subway wasn't crowded, which meant she was running late. Fifteen minutes made the difference between fainting from a lack of oxygen and a quiet seat to read. She opened Chris's newspaper to the article he had starred and read as the train propelled through the tunnels:

If Only jobs are the ones people do after working to pay the bills. If Only jobs often don't pay, but money isn't the point. These jobs feed the soul. They make life worth living.

Ava read on. One man, a banker, helped out in the kitchen of his friend's cafe on the weekends. A publicist volunteered to teach yoga to children. A woman with a government job led a writers' group at her local Barnes & Noble. *If Only* jobs fulfilled deep yearnings.

She looked up from the article, remembering the story of Janusz Korczak and the orphanage he ran in Poland during World War II. He lived for those children. What did she live for? What could give her life meaning?

Dance.

The answer was easy. She had taken lessons since she could remember, but it didn't fit into her life now. Did Chris have an *If Only* job? What happened to his paying job? She tried to

145

guess his vice, and then went back to dreaming about dance, the challenge of wanting perfection, the euphoria mid-pirouette, the only time she felt complete...

The train stopped at 59th Street, and the doors opened. She ran off, back to reality.

Another day of extravagant handbags loomed ahead. Ava sat down at her desk and called the managing agent of her building—her third attempt. Finally, someone picked up.

"Hi, this is Ava Larson, and I've left two messages explaining that I no longer want to terminate my lease. I understand this is short notice, but my plans have changed and I need a place to live."

"Right. Larson. Someone will get back to you on that."

"Okay, but is the lease still available? Because I don't have anywhere else to go."

"I'll note that, and, like I said, someone will get back to you with more details."

"When?"

"Shortly, I'm sure. Thank you for calling."

"All right, but I'm not leaving, just so you know." Ava hung up. The woman didn't say she *couldn't* renew her lease, but her noncommittal reply was...unsettling.

The buzz of the intercom dispersed her rental worries. "I need you in my office ASAP." Steaming frustration seeped through the speaker with Bucksly's voice.

"Sure, I'll be right there." No overzealous hello, no laundry list, no morning jab about being twenty minutes late. More tough love? She went in for her sentencing, whatever it was.

Bucksly's office could've been campaign headquarters for the Bergdorf Goodman party. Framed advertisements and press clips dating back to the 1920s hung on his walls, while promotional tricks and trinkets littered his shelves and windowsills. It never failed to put her off.

She entered, feeling guilty. For what? Treason? So she dreamed about an *If Only* job dancing. She knew what she really needed was a second job waiting tables, or something, to pay off the wedding.

"What's up?" She stood in front of his desk.

"Can you explain to me what's going on with the Prada denim bag?" he asked, peering at the computer screen. "You know, the one with ostrich feathers."

"Right." She tried to think.

"We've sold through our entire stock in less than a week. It seems that someone with your login I.D. marked the style down sixty percent, final sale, storewide. Am I just over-worked and blurry-eyed, or are we giving away our number one bag of the summer as I speak?" He waited for her to respond, to set everything straight.

Had she, really? It might go down in Bergdorf's history as the worst mistake ever made. The president and CFO would hear about it, if they hadn't already. She faced the numbers and flashing flags on the computer with a racing pulse and wet palms. "I thought it was an old style."

"*Old*? It has ostrich feathers! Feathers are *in*. The bag is plastered above Times Square. You'd have to be blind to miss it! And we're out of stock!"

"Maybe the factory can turn around a reorder?"

"Have you also forgotten the lead-times on our product?"

"No, I just—"

"Eighty-four percent mark-up, gone! This is good-bye to year-end bonuses!"

"I don't know how it happened. I'm really sorry."

"A mistake like this...we can't afford it. Not in today's economy."

"There must be something I can do. If you just let me think, I'm sure—"

"You're fired, Ava. I'm sorry. I have to let you go."

She couldn't move or speak. This wasn't happening. It couldn't happen. "You've promoted me every year since I started. You said I could run this division if I wanted to."

"That's right, if you *wanted* to. Bottom line, this is a business, and I need someone whose heart is in it, fully committed. I'm sorry, Ava. This is hard for me, too, but I don't have a choice. If I kept you on now, I'd be jeopardizing my own job. I can give you two weeks to look for something else."

"Bucksly, wait. Hear me out. It's been tough these past couple of months, worrying about my mom, breaking my engagement..." She paused for air. "I'm dealing with a lot of changes, and I just need you to be a little understanding."

He shook his head. "I've been understanding. Now I have to put the company first."

"But I've worked around the clock for you! Isn't a person entitled to a mistake? I called in sick a half-day in the past three years. One half-day!"

"The decision has been made. Be thankful that you're not being asked to clear-out your desk immediately."

"I *need* this job! I have bills to pay! I'll have to move out of the city...or I don't know what!"

"I hate to sound cold, but that isn't my problem. My problem is keeping our division from going into the red. Ava, sometimes in life there are no second chances."

"I don't deserve this. I just don't..."

He had nothing more to say.

She turned and left his office, picked up her handbag off her desk, and walked out of Bergdorf. Perhaps no one suspected how out of control her life had just become. It wasn't apparent, yet.

The sun glistened in the pale blue sky. She started walking with no direction. Bucksly had been her mentor, her guide. And her cheerleader, in a way. How could he give up on her? How could he be so heartless?

She had screwed up, that's how. She deserved to be single, and she deserved to be sacked. No way would she call home about this. Mom needed good news. Hope. All she had to give was worry and more uncertainty. She was a disappointment as a daughter, too.

Maybe she'd have to move home...and admit she wasn't cut out for New York City. It was all she could do to fight back tears.

A church stood just up ahead, a church she had wandered into before, years ago, the day Mom was first diagnosed. A few minutes of serenity had helped her to have faith and keep going. She needed that same miracle now.

Street sounds—honking, hammering, a hundred conversations—ceased as she stepped inside the cool, dim sanctuary of marble and stained glass. Silence and the smell of burning candles embraced her.

She walked down the center aisle, high heels clicking on the marble floor. A seat in the back seemed like a good spot. She sat, looking up to the domed ceiling where paths of soft light, red, purple, and orange, flowed from stained-glass windows. Tears came to her eyes. Everything she'd worked for, lived for, had led nowhere.

It led her *here*, actually. Here was somewhere.

Now what, God? I've lost the Copelands, Bergdorf, and if I can't pay my bills, I'll lose Manhattan, too. Turn my life around, please! I promise to do things differently this time. Somehow. I'll be a better daughter. I'll get a job that makes a difference. I'll even vow chastity until marriage! If I make these changes, will You set me on the right path? God?

Wiping away tears, she lit candles. One for Mom to beat cancer. Another for love—he had to be out there somewhere. And a third for the strength to start a new life. She could pray night and day, but it was up to her to change.

Back to the commotion of midtown Manhattan. Her cell phone rang as she walked down the steps of the church, an unknown number. "Hello?"

"Is this Ava?" Julian's voice was unmistakable. "*The* Ava who likes cinnamon twists?"

"Just one, yes."

"Ha! You're sticking to your limit, I see. Listen, I can't talk right now. I'm at work and am about to meet up with someone."

"Work? So much for keeping your options open." Their previous conversation replayed in her mind.

"What's that?"

"You said you were new to the city and...never mind. Congratulations on finding a job."

"Oh, right. So, how about a late dinner tonight?"

"Tonight?" Her calendar was open, other than finding work. But was it right to accept on such short notice? Apparently, he wasn't in the mood for dating etiquettes any more than she was. "Sure, I can do dinner. How late, though?"

"Nine-thirty? I'll call you later. I have the perfect place in mind, real casual. It's a favorite, in Loisaida."

"Where?" Not a chance would she leave Manhattan on a first date, especially not after being attacked outside her own building.

"Loisaida. Lower East Side. How long have you lived in this city?" He laughed and hung up.

What happened to her showing *him* around? She walked back to the job she no longer had.

Chapter Sixteen

The restaurant was small, bright yellow, and practically empty. Not the ambiance typical of a first date. Ava squeezed by tables and chairs, following Julian to a back corner. Posters of Japan hung on the walls with yellowed tape. He'd said the place was known for its fresh fish, but nothing about it being raw.

The only other customers, a Japanese couple and a guy with a book, turned and stared. Maybe it was Julian's loose gray shirt and fitted jeans tucked into motorcycle boots. Or the sunglasses pulled back over stringy blond hair. He stood out, tall and thin, and his green eyes seemed to look at the world with amused skepticism.

"We almost have the place to ourselves," he said, pulling out her chair. "I prefer out-of-the-way places. Hidden gems, you know?"

"Absolutely." She sat as he pushed in her chair. It seemed a double bonus that he was a gentleman with a rebel image.

A scuffing sound from the kitchen grew louder as an old Japanese woman approached their table in flip-flops and socks. Julian handed back the menus, unopened. "I'll order for us both." His eyes narrowed in on hers. "I'm counting on you being adventurous, Ava."

"Go for it." Here was her test in spontaneity, her chance to take a flight anywhere.

He ordered in Japanese and then turned to her. "I'm gonna have a cold Sake. You?"

"Sure, let the adventure continue."

The old woman nodded, expressionless, and scuffled back to the kitchen.

"I should mention that I've never eaten raw fish," Ava said.

"I dated this guy for years who hates sushi, so I wasn't exactly encouraged to try it."

"First times are what keep life interesting!" He flashed her a photogenic smile and then sat back in his seat. "So, tell me about yourself, Ava. Are you an introvert or extrovert? Intuitive or logical? Dogs or cats? Who is Ava?"

She laughed, feeling overwhelmed in a good way. "All of the above, except for cats. I'd have a dog if I could afford one." She pictured Chris scooping top-shelf mush into his dog's bowl. "I'm not an introvert, but I'm getting used to living alone. And I'm inclined to make lists of pros and cons only to follow my heart."

"Hmm..." He nodded as if to music. "You're complicated, in a matter-of-fact way. Straightforward, walking backward. Not me. I trust the facts. I prefer crowds, and I'd take a cat over a dog any day. A cat is more self-reliant than a goldfish."

She laughed. "I think you and I have to count on the attraction of opposites."

"We'll see about that."

A sound of scuffling, and the woman appeared with their Sakes and two glasses of water.

"How did you hear of this place?" Ava asked.

"This joint? It's been my sushi go-to for years."

For years? "Wait, you told me at Krispy Kreme that you just moved here." She suddenly saw herself sitting across from a scam artist and noted the distance between their table and the door.

Leaning forward, he glanced around the restaurant and lowered his voice. "I had to lie. I was on assignment, trailing a suspect who went to Krispy Kreme every day, sometimes twice. I hate doughnuts, to be honest. Why do you think I asked for your help ordering? Well, other than I wanted your attention."

She pushed aside all disbelief and smiled. "So...you're a secret agent?" A scam artist was infinitely more likely, but she'd play along for now.

He put his hands on the table. "All right. The deal on me is I grew up in Brooklyn—"

"Hold on! Your entire story was made up? I feel like a fool

for believing you! From now on I want a sign, like a wink or a special word, whenever you're on assignment. Are you right now?"

He laughed. "No. And I'll tug my ear, like this, if I am."

"Perfect. It'll be like watching baseball, except exciting."

"I think baseball is boring, too. There's hope for us yet." He raised his Sake, and she clinked her miniature mug to his before taking a sip.

"Yuck! I'm sorry, but—" She downed her water. "Sake is *not* for me."

"Well, that 'first' was a flop, but I can help." He finished his Sake and took hers. "Anyway, I went out west to study pre-law, didn't love it, and then got a phone call that my little brother had been shot. He was an innocent victim of a hold-up. I came back to New York for the funeral and enrolled in the Police Academy. That was six years ago. I'm a cop. Mostly undercover."

Maybe he *was* being honest. The emotion in his voice when he spoke of his brother sounded genuine. "I'm sorry about your brother. How old was he?"

"Nicky was sixteen. I don't go a day without thinking about him. Sometimes I feel like I'm living for him."

"Fighting the same kind of crime that took his life. I'm sure he's proud of you."

Julian looked away.

"Do you do yoga?" she asked, moving on. "You were holding a yoga mat the last time I saw you. Your T-shirt read, *Namaste, Nincompoop.*"

"Not one of my better experiences. The lead didn't go anywhere, and I pulled my groin. Talk about a bad day at the office."

"I've never met an undercover cop before, that I know of." She imagined him busting prostitute rings and heroin dens— although for all she knew, he could be the dealer.

"Check this out." Julian lifted his sleeve to show her a bullet wound on his veined forearm, a scar across his calloused palm. "This one's a knife slash," he said, stroking it proudly. "A guy beating up his wife."

153

She cringed. "I see."

He watched her, saying nothing, amusement in his eyes.

"What are you thinking about?" she asked, feeling her whole body blush.

He sat forward. "You. Here's the thing, Ava. I love what I do, you know?"

"I wish I could say that." She wished she could say that she had a job, but no need to get into her personal life now. "So what's the best part about being undercover?"

"Two things, actually. Moving through the city incognito and the triumph after an arrest."

"You have unique job perks," she said. "Privacy and glory."

"I guess in the end it's the glory that gets me. The rush."

The old woman returned with their order, and Julian rubbed his hands together with excitement. "Are you ready for your next new experience?" He helped arrange the dishes so they'd fit on the table. "I'll tell you what's what."

Ava looked over his "adventurous" selection with an acute feeling of dread. "Are those fish heads?" A needless question. Wide-open eyes stared up at her, complete with gills and gaping mouths. It was the waking dead.

He picked one up and ate it. "They're delicious. Crunchy."

She couldn't watch. "The orchid petals are a nice touch. I love it when a chef takes the time to accessorize the food."

"The petals are dessert." He grinned, clearly enjoying her naiveté. "We'll start with the chuka salad. Real simple. It's seaweed in a sesame dressing."

Was she on a reality show? *The Bachelor* meets *Fear Factor*. If she could just swallow the food with a smile, she'd get asked out on a second date.

"Cheers!" He held up a mouthful of oceanic plant life.

"For me?" She felt the cold, slimy greens slide over her tongue.

"Good?"

She shook her head, swallowing it down with more water. "Maybe it's an acquired taste."

"Here, try the barbecue eel." Now he squeezed dolphin food

between chopsticks and dropped it on her plate, skin and all. The mashed liver Chris fed his dog looked more appetizing. "Eel is my favorite." Julian smiled, revealing distinguished laugh lines she hadn't noticed before.

"Please, don't make fun of my sushi skills." Foreign eating utensils made the challenge at hand even more difficult.

"You're doing fine; you've got great dexterity. Try picking up the eel now."

She poked at it. "So what do you look for in a woman?" A safer topic, surely, than what was on her plate.

"Hmm, good question. I look for a lot of things." He laughed again. "Not to sound picky. But I like women who aren't afraid to go for what they want and don't care what anyone thinks. Is that you?"

She thought about it. "Actually, no. Not if you look at my past, but it's definitely something I'm working on."

"I see." He nodded as if he approved. "And what are *you* looking for? In a man."

"My list is going to sound sappy compared to yours. But I'll just say it and not care what you think, right?"

"Ha! You've got me now. I'm all yours."

"Let's see if *you* qualify first." She paused, organizing her thoughts. "I'm looking for someone who's loving and kind and... has a deep passion for life." Finally, she could articulate what she wanted in a man!

"Only off the record will I admit that I'm kind. A deep passion for life, you've got your man. Now, as for physical traits, I'm into leggy brunettes with bright, oval eyes and long, dark hair." His smile was sly. "And you?"

She blushed uncontrollably. The eel glistened on her plate. "I like your look, too."

He smiled and finished the Sake. "I'm dating a couple of women at the moment."

"Oh?" Floored by his statement, she suddenly felt like a crumb beneath the table. Scraping together her morale and crawling back up onto her chair, she tried to continue the conversation. "Um, I'm kind of new to the dating scene. I guess that's what you do until someone sticks?"

"I hope I'm not being too outspoken." He craftily moved a mound of seaweed salad into his mouth.

"Uh...no, outspoken is fine. I like that you're honest."

"Good. How's it going with your eel?"

The glossy brown piece of fish kept slipping between her chopsticks. Never before had she tried so hard to get food into her mouth that she didn't want to eat. "So how many women are you dating?"

"Two or three. I'm sure you'll meet them at one party or another."

What?

"Are the women you're dating friends? I mean, don't most women get jealous?"

"Some. Are you the jealous type?"

"No, not normally." She wondered.

"Then there you go! Come out with me one night. It'll be fun, and you'll make some new friends."

"I will. I'd like that."

He leaned over his arms folded on the table. Faint lines around his eyes, light growth on his cheeks...to reach over and touch his face...

"If you really want to know what I'm looking for, Ava, it's to eventually settle down with one woman. And I'm not just saying that." Their eyes met, and she held his gaze to prove to herself, to him, and to the whole world that she wasn't afraid. *Bring love on!*

Following an impulse, she pinched the eel between her chopsticks and ate it.

Horror!

The flavor was barbeque, but the texture, wormy. Was it still alive? She gagged, covering her mouth, and then swallowed the thing whole, choking at the same time.

"Whoa!" He stood and slapped her back. "You okay?"

She drained what was left of her water and finished off his, as well. "I'm fine now." She willed herself not to throw up.

"Are you sure?"

"Yes, I think so. I got the little guy down, now I've just got to keep him down."

The old woman appeared as if by magic to replenish her water.

"So," Ava said after finishing another glass, "I'm also looking for the One. If that's what you mean by settling down."

Julian returned to his chair and threw his head back laughing. "Did you say the *One*? That's like trying to find your imaginary friend!"

"Okay, it has to be easier than impossible. Don't you believe in fate?"

"Definitely not. I make decisions." He sat back, folding his arms across his chest, making his opinion clear.

"What about when things happen beyond your control? Or when you have a gut feeling about something, as if the answer is being whispered in your ear?" She found herself leaning forward, pressing against the table.

"I suppose there's intuition, but it doesn't always pan out the way you expected. And you don't *have* to listen to it. My path is paved by facts. Evidence."

"Well, if there's no evidence, I go with my gut." Her canceled wedding came to mind, but she saw no reason to make an example of it. "Does dating take up a lot of your time?" A lineup of women flashed in her mind, all wanting exclusive rights to his natural high.

"Keep it fun. That's my motto." He popped a roll of orange, gluey-looking eggs into his mouth and swallowed. "Ikura. Want to try it?"

"Do you want to see that eel again?" There was a limit to impressing a guy. "You know what I think is the hardest part about dating? Getting past first impressions."

"Are you saying I'm too scary for you?"

She laughed. "I can handle you, so far."

"I'm glad to hear it. You looked like you were going to run for the door a while ago." He crunched down on another fish head. "I'll tell you something. I have no idea why, but this date feels a long time coming."

"We did happen to see each other twice at Krispy Kreme."

"Amazing! Except I was there every day on a job." He pushed his chair back from the table. "Back in a sec." He went to the men's room.

Ava reached into her handbag for her phone. Maggie had to know about this.

Text: *Out w/ UNDERCOVER cop...vry mysterious!*

A minute later, Julian returned from the bathroom and looked thrilled to see her. His energy was like drinking hot chocolate after coming in from the cold—invigorating, warming her inside out.

He glanced at his watch and then twisted in his seat to signal for the check. A tattoo, something serpent-like, crawled up the crevasse of his throat. His shirt-collar shifted and another one peered from around his neck.

"Julian, are the tattoos real or a part of your cover?" She touched her throat, imagining women's names etched into his skin: Lena, Sophia, Veronica...Ava in a bulbous heart stuck with an arrow.

"Ah, the tattoos!" He laughed, pulling back his collar, exposing dark ink on pale skin. "Now there's a life-commitment I didn't have trouble making. You'll get used to them."

"Will I?"

His eyes lit up. "You'll never guess what I did on my break today."

Went on a date was her first thought. "You busted someone."

"Almost as good. I received a long-anticipated delivery. The bed of my dreams! A California King topped four-feet high with two deluxe mattresses, forgiving springs, resistant coils, and layers of plush padding. My apartment is finally done, and it really feels like home."

Everything her futon lacked. But it wasn't clear if he was tempting her, or just happy to have a new bed. "That's great," she replied. "I bet you're looking forward to sleeping tonight."

Julian held out an orchid petal. "Here, you can't say I didn't give you a flower on our first date."

"You probably give them to all your dates."

He grinned. "And you probably get them! But how many guys tell you to eat it?"

"Another first." She bit off a petal. It tasted sweet, like a fruit. "What a nice surprise!"

He handed his card to the old woman without glancing at the total. "Thanks for coming out tonight, Ava. And for being adventurous."

"I'm glad I took a chance on a stranger." She was starving, but it was worth it. Was this the end, though? Thanks and good-bye?

Outside, the warm night air felt good on her shoulders. He lightly touched her back. "Can I see you home?" His voice was gentler now.

She tried to contain a smile. "Only if you show me your badge. I want proof."

"What?"

"I'm serious. I want to see it. You don't look like a cop."

"I'm not supposed to. Sure. Here you go." He pulled a New York City Police I.D. from his wallet. "Do you want to see the gun strapped to my ankle, too?"

He couldn't get any more attractive.

They traveled across town in a cab, Julian on his phone, rescheduling plans for later that night. He blamed work, but maybe she was the real reason.

A block from her apartment, she checked a text message from Maggie: *Shld be a law agnst mysterious cops. Be careful!*

Arriving at her building, Chris and his sidekick were sitting on the stoop, as though waiting for her to get home. Not now, not Chris. Feeling lower than a worm, she looked up to the stars, avoiding eye contact, as Julian walked her to the door.

"I hope I get to see you again," Julian said.

"Me, too." A naked light bulb above the front door shone on his face. She kept her voice low. "Thanks again for dinner."

Chris moved from the stoop to his cardboard. Over the ledge, she could see the dog's black-and-white tail.

Julian reached for her hand. "I have to be at work early tomorrow, so I can't stay for a nightcap." He simultaneously invited himself up and rejected the idea.

"I understand," she replied, while her mind turned circles. Would she have let him into her apartment? Should she let him *assume* she would've?

Stepping closer, he wrapped his arms around her waist. She was hardly aware of kissing him, as his lips moved over hers. It felt so good to be kissed, really kissed. "I actually don't need that much sleep," he whispered, with his hand lightly beneath her shirt collar, caressing her neck. "I have an idea."

"What's that?" She felt anxious to hear anything he had to say.

"Come to my place. Stay with me tonight."

Her mind scattered between yes and no. It was time to end the night, according to her promise to save sex until marriage. But the thought of staring at the ceiling in her bleak apartment, where there was all the room in the world to think about being alone and unemployed...would it hurt to check out his place and spend the night? She looked down to the dog's tail, wagging back and forth. "I should say no."

He kissed her once more. "Says who?"

"The little voice in my head." They could just cuddle. Talk. Get to know each other. "But it's a really small voice."

He raised his eyebrows. "I'd love to spend the first night in my new bed with you."

The word *first* almost sparked against her cheek. No other word could've made her feel more special. She was *first.*

"Wait a minute," she stepped back, catching herself from falling into an old pattern of jumping in too fast. "Can we take a walk? I need to tell you something." She needed privacy for this, away from Chris...and his journal.

They turned west down her street, taking it slow. Julian kept his hands in his pockets, already backing off.

"So, here's the thing. I made a vow to God and myself to save sex for marriage. And I want to keep it. I hope I'm not being presumptuous or anything, but I don't think it would be fair if I went home with you, got into your new bed, and then told you. I have to say, though, the decision has suddenly become a lot more difficult than I expected."

He stopped and looked at her, saying nothing. She felt lost and exposed. "Um, I'm not a virgin, if that's what you're thinking. Unfortunately. But I want love, and in my last relationship, sex only made it hard to see that we weren't right for each other. I mean, we weren't really in love."

"Okay, I can understand that."

"So..." She dreaded what would come next. "Do you want to cancel your invitation?"

Silence. He looked back in the direction of her building.

"Okay," she said, "at least now I know how you feel. I think."

"Hold on. This is a first for me, that's all."

"And 'firsts' are what make life exciting, right?" She couldn't resist giving him his own medicine.

He smiled. "They say in the Academy that sacrifice gets results. Maybe you have the right approach. I can respect that. And I'd really be a jerk if I reneged now."

"True." A flood of relief.

"I think you're smart not to go around having sex with every guy you date," he said, looking ahead, perhaps still thinking it through. "A lot of regret can come from that. And if you're ready to settle down, it probably makes sense." He turned to her. "Sure, I'm with you."

"You are? Really?" She studied his face and saw sincerity. "I have to admit, I'm shocked. Oh, no. Does this mean you're not attracted to me?"

He laughed. "Listen, I'm going on thirty-five. I've dated and slept with a lot of women. I don't *need* to have sex to get to know somebody. I think you're right. It interferes with the important stuff, like...personality."

"Integrity," she added. "And, above all, heart!" She stopped herself from jumping into his arms and kissing him all over. "If anything, this will be a date you'll remember."

He put his arm around her waist. "So should we christen my new bed? Figuratively speaking, that is."

"Let's go!"

Chapter Seventeen

"We're home!" Julian announced, as their cab pulled to the curb.

Ava looked out the window at a dark and deserted street. "I think I know why they call this neighborhood Hell's Kitchen."

"The story goes that two cops came up with the name, witnessing a riot. These streets used to be crawling with gangs and organized crime."

"But not anymore, right?" She hesitated and then got out of the cab. Desolate was the only word to describe it. Up ahead, cars sped down the West Side Highway. Beyond that, darkness, where the Hudson River flowed.

He pointed to a converted warehouse across the street. "I'm on the top floor."

"I see they kept the original façade." Black grime discolored the brickwork surrounding wide windows. By the moonlight, dark spots created the illusion of vacant eyes. She looked where she was walking, narrowly avoiding a spilled container of lo mein on the sidewalk. A couple of drunks stumbled down the street where a wire fence cordoned off a barren lot.

"Stay with me," Julian said, leading the way. She reluctantly followed, although making a run for it in this neighborhood didn't appear to be a better option. Next door to his building, an abandoned factory stood in ruin, boarded and defaced. A narrow alley running between the two structures ended in more darkness.

"That old slaughterhouse will be a high-rise condo one day," he said, admiring its potential.

"You think so?" Maybe she was overreacting. He was a cop,

after all.

At the entrance, he fumbled with a mass of keys on a silver chain and then unlocked two deadbolts. She followed him through the steel doorway, her heart beating faster. She'd felt a connection with Julian—based on what? She hardly knew him. He was a gentleman at the restaurant, and he promised to respect her vow. But did he mean it? Names like Bundy, Wayne Gacy, Manson, and Jack the Ripper crossed her mind.

"The best thing about my place is getting to it." He chuckled.

"I hope you're kidding." She was either being paranoid or insanely naïve. Was he a serial killer or the man of her dreams? One foot in front of the other, she was going to find out.

Down a cinderblock hallway, they came to a gated freight elevator. He pushed open clanging metal for her to step inside. As the lift crept higher, creaking through the cool airshaft, she felt like she was leaving the city far behind. It stopped with a bounce, and he pulled open the gate to a rough, poorly lit corridor. She held back, afraid to step out and let the lift go.

"Julian, maybe I should—"

"Just wait." He took her hand, urging her forward. With the gate fastened once more, her only escape eerily descended, leaving them in virtual darkness.

Julian unlocked large double doors and stepped aside for her to enter. "Mi casa es su casa!"

She walked into his warm home, her mouth gaping and eyes wide open, wishing it really were hers. A row of windows ran the length of the spacious loft, offering a view of the moon's reflection on the river, a silver path to heaven.

"Would you mind taking off your shoes?" he asked, switching on soft lighting.

"Oh. Of course." She looked down to dark hardwood floors and quickly slipped off her sandals. His motorcycle boots were already lined up on the doormat.

"Your place is amazing!" Unlike her life, his apartment was in perfect order. A sculpture in the center of the loft soared and twisted in metal and stone. "I love your art." His furniture looked unique, handcrafted, in earth tones with copper accents.

Every detail, balanced. She ran her fingers over the coffee table, a modern design of knotted wood and glass. It didn't make sense on a cop's salary, but maybe he had an inheritance.

"Do you have family here in the city?" she asked.

"My mom lives in Brooklyn with her latest boyfriend. You like that table? It's on commission. I know the artist, a total nutcase." He walked into the open kitchen.

"It's stunning. My stepfather would be down on his knees, inspecting every knot in the wood. He's a carpenter, although what he makes doesn't cost enough for your taste."

Julian laughed. "Expensive stuff looks good. You want beer, wine?" He opened the refrigerator. "OJ?"

Her body was still digesting the eel, or trying to catch it live in her stomach. "Water would be great, thanks."

She stood before high metal bookshelves that served a dual purpose of also partitioning the loft. A quick glance at the titles told her that he was into mystery classics: collections of Sir Arthur Conan Doyle, Dashiell Hammett, Dorothy L. Sayers, and—

She felt hands on her shoulders and quickly turned. "Oh! Hi."

"Hi." He bent over, kissing her earlobe, her neck, her mouth. She relaxed, leaning against his chest, loving the feel of his soft, moist lips on her skin.

"Are you tired?" he whispered.

"Yes. I mean, a little." She felt off-balance, on unsolid ground. "I'm sorry. May I use your bathroom?"

"Sure thing. It's just off the kitchen."

Here were the imperfections, the signs of a real bachelor. She put down the toilet seat and wiped it before sitting. There was toothpaste on the faucet, a splattering of water stains on the mirror. At least he wasn't *too* perfect.

Washing her hands, she looked at her reflection and saw an excitement she hadn't felt with Josh. Despite the heaps of stress she had on her shoulders, her insides felt light and bubbly. Her mind felt clear. He was into her. He respected her. She was doing things differently now, and it was working.

Back in the main room, Julian was nowhere in sight. A glass

of water had been left on the dining room table. She took a few sips and followed a rustling sound coming from the other side of the loft.

"Hello?"

Behind the wall of bookshelves she found the bed of *her* dreams with Julian lying on top of gray sheets in a pair of black briefs. His legs were long and muscular, his chest was smooth and lean. The serpent tattoos...well, they were there, too.

"I'm happy you came back with me," he said. His smile, his lips...they could just kiss...all night.

She let the tips of her fingers touch his sheets. "I'm happy to be here." Her eyes filled with tears at the sight of a man offering himself to her, his body, his warmth, his affection. She could barely stand beside him lying in his bed.

"Um, do you have a pair of shorts and a T-shirt I could sleep in?" Stripping down to her favorite pink underwear was out of the question.

He grinned, looking like he was about to say something, but thought better of it and leapt off the bed. "Coming right up."

He returned in seconds. "They might not look it, but they're clean."

Back in the bathroom, she slipped out of her jeans and top and into his too-big clothes. They smelled like laundry detergent and calmed her down, a little. Physical intimacy wasn't the priority now. It was deeper than that. It was finding love, like Courtney and Brad's solid connection. Good love. The right man.

Armed with a goal, she returned to the bookshelves of mysteries and, behind it, Julian.

He smiled when he saw her. "Would you believe me if I said you look incredibly sexy?"

"Do I?" She nervously touched the hem of her T-shirt. "Oversized PJs are usually for romance novels and ice cream in bed."

"You look hot. And I taste better than ice cream." He rested his hand on *her* side of the mattress. "Join me." He spoke in a low, seductive voice.

She slid in close beside him, taking shallow breaths. He wrapped his arms around her; they were chest to chest. His body felt warm. Hard. And eager.

He playfully bit her chin. "We can just hold each other...if that's what you want."

"Yes." Resting her head against his chest, face-to-face with the serpents, she felt his hands creep beneath her roomy T-shirt. A low, beastly moan came from his throat as his fingers slowly, gently moved over the curves of her waist, her stomach...and then as if he were cracking a safe, her body relaxed, opening to him from the inside out.

"Please," she heard herself say, clutching his naked back, feeling skin and bones. Their embrace became desperate, a struggle for more, and she gave herself to it, the last of her will surrendering silently to her body screaming out, *Yes!* Gone were those lonely years with Josh. Julian made up for them all. She couldn't deprive herself now. Not yet. Not ever again. Thoughts flickered like lights on the subway as his mouth pressed to hers, his hands sliding down...

"Stop." She attempted to push him away. "Julian...that's enough!"

"Right." He rolled over, and heavy breathing substituted words.

She resisted apologizing, but her fear of losing him grew as their heart rates normalized.

"Are you mad?" she asked softly.

"No...but I have a feeling I'm going to wake up tomorrow morning and wonder, did I really promise chastity?"

"It's got to be better than waking up *wishing* you had."

He turned onto his side, facing her. "That is true."

She let out a long exhale. "I don't know what it is with me, but when I meet someone I like, things move fast. Too fast. Like now."

"Don't worry about it. I'm exhausted, anyway...I haven't slept in days."

She decided against asking why. Her head already felt full of jumbled information, a collage of facts without a clear picture.

He curled around her, and they lay together like two pieces of a puzzle. In no time, she felt his chest slowly rise and fall. "Thanks for a great night, Julian," she whispered.

A foghorn droned over the Hudson River. She thought of the desolate street below and how scared she had felt riding up in the drafty freight elevator. His place wasn't at all what she had expected...but then, neither was he.

Chapter Eighteen

The misty air against her face felt like a cool cloth as Ava walked home from Julian's. It was 7:00 a.m., and she had the promenade along the Hudson River to herself. She dug her hands into the pockets of his hooded sweatshirt and smiled.

The USS *Intrepid* aircraft carrier hovered ghost-like in the low clouds on the water. Retired warplanes slept on the hangar deck. Just beyond it, a cruise liner sailed slowly and steadily out to sea. People waved farewell to Manhattan. Life felt surreal.

For now, anyway. She had to get through the day at work, and then muster the drive to update her resume. She had to embrace all hope and call home. But maybe with Julian in her life it wouldn't be so bad.

She headed east on 24th Street, turning into a gust of wind. Soon she'd see Chris. Of course, he would notice that she was wearing the same clothes from last night, under a man's sweatshirt. But she had nothing to be ashamed of. She'd kept her promise and had no regrets...except one. She had blatantly ignored him last night. It didn't feel right then, and it bothered her even more now. He had come to her rescue. Chris, of all people, didn't deserve to be disregarded.

On the corner of Tenth Avenue and 22nd Street, an old man was listening to Neil Diamond on his boom box. His music transformed Manhattan, slowed it down, gave it feeling. The man sat beside a small collection of used books spread out on the sidewalk. *The Alchemist* was one of them, the story of a boy on a journey to fulfill his destiny. She had read it years ago and still believed in its message of keeping faith. The book would make a good gift for Chris.

"Two for three dollars." The peddler said, tuning down the volume on his boom box.

She handed him the money and picked up *Don Quixote* for herself. Perhaps one day she'd want to read something more... enlightening than far-fetched love stories with steamy endings.

The man folded the bills into his breast pocket and increased the volume.

Miniature cyclones picked up dust from the street and whirled it about. Summer would fly by. Fall would come and then winter. What would happen to Chris? He couldn't go on living below her stoop forever. The thought of him gone gave her an empty feeling. It was selfish, but when she didn't have a girlfriend visiting or a hot date seeing her home, she liked him close by.

Arriving home, she gripped her "new" books and approached Chris. He glanced up from his morning paper and then calmly went back to the article he was reading. No hello, no smile. His dog pretty much did the same, not bothering to lift its head off the cardboard.

"Hey, Chris."

He looked up as though first noticing her there. "Oh, are we acknowledging each other today?"

"I'm sorry. I was caught up in this guy, Julian, and it was like my brain didn't want to let in any distractions."

"I promise I'll only take down the guys you want me to," he said, smiling now. "I'm glad I wasn't a 'distraction.'"

"I knew you weren't going to hurt him...never mind. Hey, you'd be proud. I made him show his police I.D. before I'd let him take me home."

"A cop?"

"A true blue. Is that what they call them?"

"Among other things."

"So...I have something for you." Her heart rate quickened as she handed him the book. "Don't tell me you won't accept it, or you already have it in that bottomless suitcase of yours."

"Ah, *The Alchemist*." He looked it over. "I read this my first semester in college, but I'd like to read it again."

College? "Where did you study?" She assumed he didn't finish.

"L'Université Paris-Sorbonne." He opened his suitcase and tucked the book inside. "What I remember most from the story is the alchemist telling the boy that the fear of suffering is worse than suffering itself. I didn't believe it at the time." He shut and latched the suitcase.

"Do you now?" she asked.

"Yes. Fear is unlimited and runs wild. Suffering has a beginning and an end."

Mom's suffering came to mind, as well as her own fear of how it might end. "Either one is hard to live with."

"Sometimes accepting your fear can feel good," he said, "and then suddenly it's gone." He jumped up. "Hey, I have something for you, too."

"You do?"

"A poem. Graffiti, really. Something I read on a school wall not far from here. The title is *Facing a Wall*, which I thought was clever, since that's just what I was doing, reading it. Anyway, it goes like this: *Facing a Wall. I take up my position: to make sense of that wall.*"

"Hmm...I like it. How about this one: *Facing a Wall. I step back to make sense of it all.*"

"Even better! You should become a street artist, Ava."

"That reminds me—I need to find a job."

"You're unemployed?" He sounded surprised.

"Just recently. A street artist sounds like fun, but I need something that pays."

"Right. That narrows your search. What field?"

"Good question. Listen, I am sorry about last night. It was a jerk move. I'm not normally that self-absorbed."

"That's good. I forgive you."

He seemed to mean it. She felt relieved, renewed even.

Orange-colored party leaflets from curbside garbage did a maypole dance at her feet. The words "Summer Bash" rallied around her.

"Our street is the last in Manhattan to see the collectors," he said, like he knew it for a fact, and maybe he did. She glanced up between the rooftops at clouds rushing in the wind, as if eager to be somewhere.

"It's going to storm," she said offhandedly.

"I'm hoping it'll blow over." He looked at his dog.

Where would they go? Not to a shelter full of hungry, worn-out men on narrow cots. Not Chris. There had to be someplace better.

His dog, faithfully keeping guard, had a silvery white muzzle, as if it had just buried a bone in a snow bank. She reached out her hand. "Hey, there. Are you a good dog or a bad dog?" An apprehensive shiver ran along its back before its fluffy tail began to fan. Trust won, it sniffed her fingers.

"I haven't even asked your name." She knelt down and saw in its eyes what she wanted most: to be loved.

It stood with a commanding *ruff*!

"Oh! Is that your name?"

Chris laughed. "Her name is Chickpea."

Chickpea's tail waved in affirmation.

"I like that name." Ava stroked her head. "Even though she's not the right color—sandy-brown or whatever."

Chickpea fondly nudged her hand.

"I got her when I turned twenty and she was only a puppy, about the size of a chickpea," Chris said as he took out a can of Pedigree from a Whole Foods bag. From his suitcase, the can opener, a butter knife, and a bottle of large yellow pills.

"Are you sick?" She didn't wish illness upon him, but it would explain a lot.

"Me? No, I never get sick." He mashed one of the yellow pills into powder with the knife. "It's a multi-vitamin, for Chickpea. She's missing her spunk." He gave Chickpea a firm pat, like a slap on the back. "Don't worry, old girl, I'll keep you going."

Chickpea glanced at him with adoration, and then gobbled down the ground meat and vitamin.

Chris sat back against the wall and sighed. "Some days I think something's got to give, you know? You stay focused, do everything right..."

171

Mom. Fighting bad cells with fresh juice and plenty of rest, trying every "miracle" drug, and keeping up hope. Ava pictured herself in Julian's stylish loft, in his spacious bed, a world away from Mom's war...and felt guilty for not doing her part. Which was what? How and when could she become the right kind of daughter?

"So now that your plate has been cleaned—and you're unemployed—what's your calling in life?" Chris's brown eyes glistened.

She remembered where she was and felt grateful for his company. "I was going to ask you the same question. I mean, what's your *If Only* job? You know, the article?"

"I asked first." He could be so stubborn.

"All right." She thought about sitting down beside him but leaned against the stoop instead. "When I was young, I dreamed of being a dancer. Took lessons and all that. I used to love to dance."

"Why do people grow up and stop doing what they love? That's what I want to know."

"Good question. I'd also like to do something that helps people, something that makes a difference in this world."

"Well, I say try for the top and see where you land." His eyes shone even brighter.

"You think so? You mean, just walk into Radio City and audition to become a Rockette?" She stood up a little straighter.

"Sounds like a good idea to me."

"More like totally nuts!" She smiled. He energized her—not in a sexual way, like Julian, but in a life way. "What about you?"

"I'm going to open restaurants around the world, starting here in Manhattan. French comfort food—a place where people can feel at home. And for every restaurant I open, I'll open a soup kitchen. Do you know the chef Alice Waters?"

Ava shook her head.

"She's older now, but when she was twenty-seven, she opened *Chez Panisse* in Berkeley with no restaurant experience, only a vision of offering good food and being a generous host. Forty-two years later, it's still in operation. She said we are

172

most complete when we are giving something away, 'when we sit at the table and pass the peas to the person next to us we see that person in a whole new way.' I get that."

Ava recalled Mom's advice on love...the greatest gift, if you give it back. "I get that, too." But restaurants around the world? Was he joking? She thought of the book in his suitcase, *Larousse Gastronomique*, the Bible of cookbooks. Still, restaurants around the world? Even one restaurant seemed highly unlikely. Of course, it was a dream; they were talking about dreams.

"Well, that's a fun *If Only*," she said, playing along. "What would be your specialty dish?"

"Gaudes!"

"*Toads*?"

"No." He laughed. "*Gaudes*. It's a type of porridge from the Swiss border of France. You pour it into a mold, let it cool, and then slice it and fry it with butter and sugar."

Her mouth watered. "Sounds even better than a doughnut!"

"Or cassoulet, made of beans, lamb, pork, duck, and sausage. I'd serve it with creamy potatoes au gratin. I like hearty food."

"Umm. I'm ready for dinner and it's only..." she glanced at her watch. "Oh, shoot! I have to get ready for my Been Fired From job." She ran up the stoop and stopped at the door. "Hey, I hope you conquer the restaurant business."

He smiled up at her. "And you show the Rockettes what you've got!"

"Right!" She went inside and sprinted up all five flights in a sudden burst of energy. Under her door was a bill stamped PAST DUE in red ink from the managing agent of her building. They definitely weren't going to renew her lease if she didn't pay her rent. It was time to find a new job, ASAP.

Chapter Nineteen

A bouquet of Narcissus greeted her like a symphony of little trumpet players from the security desk at Bergdorf. She half expected to hear "The Prince of Denmark's March," although going to work these days was hardly ceremonious. A solitary elevator ride meant it was after 9:15 a.m. She entered the 14th floor reception and met Rhonda's wide-open eyes. Word had gotten out.

"Ava, how *are* you?"

"Great! And you?" Just keep walking.

Nearly in her office, she heard someone cough, intentionally. She glanced back, meeting Bucksly's cold, impatient stare.

"Morning, Ava." His voice was loaded, safety off, ready to fire. "Interviewing already?"

"Not yet. Any news on ostrich feathers?"

"Nothing good. I'd still like your help in rectifying the mess."

First the mess of her canceled wedding and now this; she was getting too good at messes. "Of course. I'll do whatever it takes."

"Meet me in the conference room in twenty?"

"Sure." The next two weeks would feel endless.

Inside her office, she shut the door and faced the work on her desk. The Holiday Line needed to be finalized. Fall was getting ready to ship. Summer was in stores, some styles selling out, others slow. There were transfers to do, markdowns. Inventory had to move. But she wasn't a part of it anymore, and just being there felt like trying to get off a fast-moving ride.

Computer on, she Googled "Radio City Rockettes." Scenes from Christmas Spectacular popped up: "The Parade of the Wooden Soldiers," "New York at Christmas," "Magic is There."

Her heart opened to the possibility, and a surge of adrenaline awakened her senses. Everything appeared brighter. Her soul, in the image of her younger self, leapt inside her.

Catching her off-guard, her office phone rang, a double ring. "Hello?"

"Hello!" David talked on the phone as though it were a hollow can on a string. She tensed. He never called to chat.

"Hi. Is everything okay? Is Mom feeling better?"

"Can you come home, Ava?" His voice sounded gentle, painfully so.

She gripped the edge of her desk as though someone were trying to drag her away. "Right now? What's wrong? What's going on?" She could see herself on a Greyhound bus, could smell the bags of chips and feel the bristly stain-resistant seats. She'd be home in three-and-a-half hours.

"We're at Lourdes Hospital. You should get here as soon as possible."

The day she had feared for so long had come.

Walking down the white corridor to Bucksly's office, something told her that it'd be the last time. His door was ajar.

"I have to go home," she said as he looked up from his computer. "I'm not sure when I'll be back. It's my mom."

His hand drove through his hair, spoiling its artful disarray. He seemed to hate her life at this moment more than she did. "Do what you have to do. Today can be your last."

Thunder rumbled over the city. Chris could hope all he wanted, but this storm wasn't about to blow over. Heavy raindrops fell hard, and then ceased as the bus entered the Lincoln Tunnel. Ava watched lights go by in endless rhythmic procession, her eyes becoming heavy. She could forget why she was going home. Then rain again and New Jersey drenched and dejected. A wide view of Manhattan across the river in a wet haze of smog. A sad good-bye. *Don't think about it. Don't think about Mom.* "Food in your dish..." she whispered. Where was Chris now? Was he keeping dry? She let her thoughts turn static as the storm raged outside.

Hours later, her eyes opened to familiar streets. Ava stared out the window at the south side of town. Old Victorian homes, once prominent and proud, stood divided into apartments, occupied by many and cared for by none. Not much of downtown remained. Vacated storefronts lined the wide, empty streets. A bridal boutique, years out of business, still displayed a mannequin in an outdated wedding gown. Its vacant stare trailed hers. Memories of planning a wedding came back. She shook them off, and then remembered why she was home.

The bus pulled into the station. She had no energy to move from her seat, but then twenty minutes later she realized she had somehow gotten into a cab when it left her in front of the hospital. She could only assume she paid the driver.

People coming and going into the large yellow-brick building moved like apparitions in the afternoon sun. She clung to the details surrounding her: a bed of pink roses, newly cut grass, an ice cream wrapper stuck to a wooden bench.

Through a revolving glass door, she found the right elevator, found the right hallways. The room was just up ahead. She could see Aunt Janis and David waiting with Chuck, their pastor. Sorry, downcast faces corrected, brightened, when they saw her.

"I'm here." She didn't fully believe it herself.

"Ava!" Their hugs were long, eye-contact short. Of course, no one wanted to cry. It was time to stay strong, time to hearten.

"Go on in." David placed his hand on her back. She stepped inside the small foyer of Mom's hospital room, and the door closed quietly behind her. Two steps, and she stopped. The air was warm and smelled like over-ripe lilacs, Mom's favorite flower. A white bouquet decorated a rolling table beside her bed. Ava recognized the glass vase from home, where it had held purple lilacs on the kitchen table every spring.

A machine dripping something liquid into Mom's arm beeped, softly, slowly, continuously. Ava couldn't look at her face without crying, without making matters worse. She should've gone home more, been stronger for her. She should've cherished Mom's life while she still had it. *God, how can I make up for the things I should've done? Give me another chance!*

Minutes passed. She concentrated on a hangnail, as if pulling it would fix everything. Go to her. Say something. She made a fist and stepped forward. Mom turned to her: bald, gaunt face, yellow skin, eyes barely open. Just over a week ago they were trying on wigs in a cab, laughing, making the most of life. Any hairstyle would do. Go blond, go brunette...*just don't go.*

A tear made a run for it down Ava's cheek. Mom looked away. Standing there helpless, Ava fought her own heartache and fear, trying to speak, while the machine beside Mom's bed, in charge at this point, seemed to rush her, counting down the seconds: *ten, nine, eight...*

"I'm sorry—" Her throat clamped shut. She wanted to say something important: *I love you*, or *Don't be scared.* But her tears would start and might never stop. Shaking, she left the room.

David looked surprised. "Did you speak to her?"

"Why didn't you tell me sooner?" Ava walked away, the knot in her throat unraveling. Grief became anger.

"Ava, stop! Where are you going?" He followed her down the corridor as she continued walking with no destination. "This *is* sooner," he said, breathless, a few paces behind.

She reached a set of double doors and whipped around. "Her eyes are neon! And what are they dripping into her arm? I thought they had found a miracle cure. Why am I coming into this now?"

He didn't answer, but pressed his lips together as he looked back in the direction of Mom's room. Inhaling, he faced Ava again, his gray eyes tired.

She searched them for relief. Hope. Anything to lessen the strain building as every passing second as Mom's life slipped further and further away from them. "I just wish you had told me. I would've come home. I would've been stronger."

"Ava, you spent many good years with your mom."

"What am I supposed to do now? I can't even speak to her, David!"

"She knows you love her."

"But there's so much I haven't done..." She surrendered to her grief and sobbed.

He put his hand on her shoulder, guiding her back. "I don't know what to say, except...think of today as the most important day of her life. Do your best. She needs you now."

Back into the lilac-scented room. Mom turned toward the sound of her footsteps.

Ava noticed a chair beside the bed and sat while love pounded in her heart. She looked out the window. Evergreens trembled in the wind. Swaying branches beckoned as if death itself were calling. How would she say this final good-bye? How would she live with herself if she didn't?

Ava carefully laid her hand over Mom's hand. A poem she had wanted for her wedding came to mind. Reciting the words might be easier than speaking her thoughts, and might release the love trapped in her heart. She began in a whisper, "You, because you love me, hold fast to me, caress me, be quiet and kind, comfort me with stillness, say nothing at all. You, because I love you, I am strong for you, I uphold you."

Mom's lips parted, but no sound came out. They shared the silence. It was enough for now.

A gentle knock, and David entered, looking stunned. Traumatized. It hit her that he was losing his wife. Year after year, he and Mom had grown closer, needing each other more every day. Now they were suffering separate deaths, as though he couldn't go on without her. An all-consuming love.

Ava watched his tough carpenter hands shake touching Mom's head, watched him bend down and tenderly kiss her shrunken cheek. She felt in awe of him at that moment and wondered if she would ever let herself be so vulnerable. Was she strong enough?

Hours passed unnoticed. The sky outside the window went from rose to midnight blue. Night came fast. Aunt Janis walked cautiously up to Mom, her sister, and explained that the kids wouldn't eat if she didn't put food on the table. She'd be back in the early morning.

The room fell quiet again, except for the machine and David's footsteps as he paced. Every so often, he would stop and pray over Mom or relive a memory for her.

Ava sat in the chair beside Mom's bed, feeling imprisoned by her own fear of death and saying good-bye. Chris appeared in her mind, squatting below the stoop on 22nd Street. He believed that the fear of suffering was worse than suffering itself. It might be true, but could she get past the pain of letting go?

"Hey, Mom?" Fingers stirred against her palm. "Thanks for taking me to all those dance lessons." It sounded trivial...but it meant everything.

Sometime after midnight, David volunteered to bring up food from the cafeteria. Again, she and Mom were alone with life and death and the beeping machine—a little slower now?

Without warning, Mom sat up, her eyes wide open and incredibly bright. Hope leapt in Ava's chest; she had her back! Mom looked straight ahead, as if at something wonderful, and then raised her arms to the ceiling, or heaven beyond.

"Yes," Ava whispered in amazement, and for the first time in months, or maybe years, she felt calm. She didn't have Mom back, not in the flesh, anyway, but it would be all right. Mom was going to God, to a place of love and peace.

Then, as if being supported, Mom gently fell back down on the pillow.

Ava put her face to hers, feeling her stunted breaths. This was it. They had only these seconds left. "Go ahead, Mom. You can let go now. You're in our hearts. We love you so much, and we know you love us, too." Ava cupped her head in her hands, cherishing her baby-smooth skin. She kissed her face. "You taught me everything that matters. You taught me how to live."

She'd taught her how to love. Ava pulled away...and how to let go.

Chapter Twenty

Back in Manhattan, Ava unpacked her old jazz shoes from a box of memories: blue First Place ribbons, sparkling tiaras, Victorian-pink tutus, and dried roses. The shoes she had worn when she was eighteen still fit, melding to her feet.

It was hard to believe a week had passed. The familiarity of home and the whirlwind of the funeral still replayed in her head, and yet some things she could barely remember, like helping David make arrangements for the burial or packing up Mom's belongings for the Salvation Army. Perhaps those were only dreams. She took off her jazz shoes and slipped them into her gym bag. Thank God for the sun that morning. Rain would've been enough excuse for her to stay home and hide.

She pulled on stockings, a black leotard, and a pair of light blue running pants. Hair, back in a bun. A brighter shade of lipstick, rouge, eyeliner. She put on her sneakers and grabbed her gym bag. The address was 51st Street, between Fifth and Sixth avenues, the stage door entrance to Radio City Music Hall. She was actually going to audition for the Rockettes.

Outside, she looked for Chris under the stoop. He hadn't been around since she'd returned from home, but the cardboard and Chickpea's bowl told her he'd be back. What would he think of her now, in stage makeup, looking like a real performer—she hoped. He'd see that she was serious about finding her dream job. He'd tell her she'd top the competition and send her off with a big, earnest smile. She took a nervous breath and headed for the subway.

A long line of anxious-looking women waited outside the stage door at Radio City. She stood at the end, trying not to stare, while at the same time surveying her competition. They all looked like they could be Rockettes. Did *she*? Could she still do a high kick? She had stretched that morning, but wished she'd been able to take a few dance classes first, just to brush up.

The line started moving, and through a gray corridor, she entered a brightly lit dance studio, possibly as wide as a city block. A woman sitting behind a table at the back shuffled through printed forms from the online preregistration. "May I have your name?"

"Ava Larson. Um, I was wondering, do you happen to know how many they're hiring?"

"I don't. Sorry."

There had to be a hundred women vying for her dream. Some looked like teenagers and others appeared to be in their thirties. She hadn't felt this nervous since her last recital... seven years ago.

"Stand up straight, please." A heavy-set woman with flushed cheeks measured her height and wrote down 5'9" on the registration form. The requirement was between 5'6" and 5'10½". Did being tall give her an advantage? Maybe she had a shot at this. Just think, a Rockette, dancing on the same stage where Liza Minnelli and Frank Sinatra had performed. The Rolling Stones. U2.

"Your signature, please." The first woman pointed to the bottom of the form.

"Oh, right." She signed, agreeing not to hold them responsible if she were to twist an ankle or become heartbroken.

"You're number eighty-four."

"Thanks."

The choreographer, a real Rockette, introduced herself,

along with six other Rockettes: Emily, Annie, Angie...Ava's heart raced ahead of her thoughts. Not a chance she'd keep their names straight.

"We'll do a jazz sequence first," the Rockette in charge called out. "Those of you chosen will come back tomorrow for the tap routine. We're looking to hire thirty new Rockettes for spots on our Gold Team, Blue Team, and our Traveling Team. The jazz sequence is approximately eight minutes. After a twenty-minute lesson, you'll perform it four at a time."

Ava's fingers shook as she buckled the straps on her shoes. Would she pick up the routine in twenty minutes? Well enough to perform it flawlessly?

"Oh, God, please let me make it." Ava heard a prayer and glanced at the girl next to her. Long, skinny legs, flat chest, brown ponytail...she saw herself back in high school. The girl sought God's blessing with her eyes clenched shut.

"You'll do great," Ava whispered.

Hazel eyes popped open. "I've been waiting for this my whole life!"

Ava smiled and nodded.

A man with tanned skin and wavy hair sat down at the grand piano in the corner of the studio. A microphone was pointed at the strings.

"This studio is the exact size as the Grand Stage," the lead Rockette said. "Sixty-six-and-a-half feet deep. That's pretty big! Imagine you're on the real thing, performing for six thousand people!"

Ava stood in the middle, toward the back. The girl with the ponytail wove her way toward the front like a frantic mouse.

"I know it's a little crowded today," the Rockette continued, "but whether you're here now or one of thirty-six Rockettes on the Grand Stage, your movements must be controlled. Precision is key."

"Precision," Ava whispered.

"Let's begin!" Large sweeping chords rolled off the piano, and the lead Rockette began calling the routine. "Weight on your left foot, right knee crossed over left, hands on hips, elbows back. Hold. Face front, chin up, chest out, for one and two and three. Step wide with your right..."

The Rockettes led them through the moves and added on more; reviewed those and added on more, and more, and more. *Stop adding on more!* Ava's head spun. Covered in sweat, out of breath, she tried feverishly to get the details down, with precision. *Left cheek front, wrists bent, right arm always over left, fingers always splayed, and above all, smile!*

Twenty minutes later, exactly, auditions started. She sat at the back of the studio with the others and waited for her number. Eighty-four.

An hour passed and they were calling the twenties, thirties... her heartbeat had stabilized. Forties, fifties...a chill settled on her bare arms. Sixties, seventies...nearly four hours of nerve-racking anticipation. Watching the auditions didn't help her to remember the routine at all. So many of them fumbled, even got the moves wrong. Or did she have them wrong in her head? Finally, the woman from registration posted numbers 81, 82, 83, and 84.

Heart beating, hands sweaty and cold, Ava stood with three other women, all about her height, in the middle of the studio. The Rockettes sat behind a table at the front, holding their pens, ready to catch any little mistake. The piano man played the first cords of the accompaniment. She counted to four. Weight on the left, right knee crossed over left, hands on hips, elbows back for one and two and three. Step left, no right, follow with left, on toes...

She walked out of Radio City, head down. Not picked. Okay, it was her first audition. She was out of practice. Dance classes were a must—but no way could she afford them, now that she was unemployed.

The girl with the brown ponytail was on the sidewalk with

her mother, crying, refusing condolence.

Ava looked away and longed to call home. Except, without Mom, *home* didn't really exist anymore. Going for her dream of dancing, she felt lost on an overgrown path from childhood, and she had only herself to find the way.

Cars honking at a double-parked delivery truck brought her back to the city. She walked down Sixth Avenue and came to the supper club she had seen the night of Eve's Garden—and her sex tape fiasco. Remembering *that* mistake, it seemed she'd come a long way, even though she hadn't actually arrived anywhere.

According to the posters out in front of the supper club, *Girlz Senzational!* was still running. She imagined the "girlz" down in the dressing room between show times, chatting and laughing, having their hair and makeup done, and decided to go in. Behind the ticket window, a middle-aged man wearing jeans and a sports jacket leaned back in a swivel chair, texting on his phone. He had thick eyebrows and sideburns, almost a wolfish appearance. She suddenly felt vulnerable in her leotard and sweats.

"Excuse me?" she asked.

He looked up. "Yeah?"

"Do you have auditions?"

"Do you have an act?" Now he stood, looking her over.

"An act?"

"Have you seen any of our shows?"

"Well...no."

"You might want to see what you'd be auditioning for. This is a burlesque club. We do erotic acts, anything bizarre, vulgar. You know, S&M and that sort of stuff." His smile was vulgar. "Come up with something perverse, and we'll give you a shot."

"Sure. Thanks." She left as fast as she could without running.

Didn't the nightclub down the street have a *Talent Wanted* post on its door? That place might be starting closer to the bottom, but a start was a start.

The sign was still there, taped to tinted glass. The Encore. She'd never heard of it before, but that didn't mean anything.

As she reached for the door, it swung open and a striking

Italian-looking man nearly took her down. "Yo! Watch yourself!" he said, stepping sideways.

"Sorry." She moved out of his way as he rushed off. A Brooklyn accent. A silky white shirt and tuxedo pants. "Wait!" she called after him. "Can I ask you something?"

He stopped. "You talking to me?"

"Do you know when auditions are? And this place isn't burlesque, is it?"

He laughed. "No, it's not burlesque. Five-thirty, every Wednesday."

Before she could say thanks, he was walking away.

Every Wednesday? Sounded like high turnaround.

"Hey!" he said, moving backward as he talked. "They don't like it if you're late!"

"Thanks!" Given what she'd just been through auditioning for the Rockettes, it sounded easy.

Chapter Twenty-One

Ava checked under the stoop for Chris. A pep talk would've been nice. But his cardboard and Chickpea's bowl were the only signs of life.

She had pounded on fourteen theater doors, inquiring about auditions, and not one lead, other than The Encore. So many auditions were invite only. What she needed was an agent, someone with contacts. But agents wanted work history, credits, headshots. One even had the audacity to tell her she was too old! There had to be a starting point somewhere.

She pushed inside her building and checked her mail, dreading more bills. One envelope, resolutely business in nature, came from J. B. Copeland. Oh, no...Josh's revenge. She opened it to find a bill for $8,000 from Vera Wang, due July 3. He was true to his word. And he even threw in the $1,000 bill from The Moment bridal boutique. Her veil. Who would have thought it'd become a weight hanging over her head? Standing in the tiny foyer, she mentally calculated her debt.

In addition to the wedding, which was costing her nearly $75,000 all in, a number too large to feel real, she had $800 left on her school loans, $1,000 in previous credit card debt, and $1,700 owed for rent. *Why did I splurge on those Wicked tickets?* Cell phone. Electricity. And after being stuck with dinner at Raoul's, her bank account was overdrawn. She felt paralyzed, as though taking a step forward might cost her something.

No question, it was time to give up her *If Only* dream of dancing. Time to call headhunters and find something desk-bound in fashion. Anything to pay the bills, including a weekend gig, waitressing. In other words, no life—or at least not the life she wanted.

Going upstairs felt more laborious now than it did dragging inebriated Maggie. On the fifth floor, the bad news didn't end. A second rent notice with PAST DUE stamped in red ink lay at her door, only this time with a twenty-five-dollar late fee. July was a week away, and the managing agent of her building couldn't be bothered to call her back. Strangers could show up at her door, ready to move in. Where would she go? No one would give her a lease with the amount of debt she owed. How would she come up with a deposit?

Resisting the urge to tear up the notice, she went inside with a new mission. Laptop out, she sat down on a throw pillow, her back against the wall. Time to become the next sympathy case on eBay: *Vera Wang wedding gown and cathedral veil... never worn.*

The bathwater up to Ava's chin had cooled, and the dripping faucet was getting on her nerves. She hadn't seen Julian since their date eight days ago. He had called while she was home, the day of the funeral, and she'd told him she had family stuff to take care of. It didn't feel right to say more, but now she wondered where he was. Busy catching nefarious drug dealers? Or dealing with some family emergency of his own? Chances were, unfortunately, he was "keeping it fun" with his other dates. The thought discouraged her from calling.

Relaxation was *not* happening. She reached for her chamomile tea, and her cell phone vibrated against the bathroom floor. Dad, probably. She hadn't heard from him since Mom died, other than his e-mail explaining why he wouldn't be at the funeral.

An unknown number came up on her caller I.D. "Hello?"

"Ava! Are you back in the city?"

"Julian, is that you?" Pounding bass in the background was her answer. She scrambled out of the bath and snatched a towel, as if he could see her. "Where are you?"

"Come out tonight!" he shouted above music and voices.

"It's kind of late for a Tuesday."

"Nine is early. Am I interrupting something?"

"No, I was just taking a bath."

"Sounds good. Now get dressed. I'm out with friends and I'm missing you."

Problems vanished from her mind as she jotted down the address. Picturing a bar scene, she figured a pair of jeans and a fitted T-shirt would do. Sandals on, hair still damp, she ran out into the hot city night.

Still no Chris. And now his cardboard and Chickpea's bowl were missing. Stolen? Thrown out? Was he gone for good? She felt deserted for a second, utterly alone in the world, and then worried for him. Wherever he happened to be, she hoped he was okay.

Two stops on the R train and she found Julian's downtown hangout. The steel door seemed impenetrable, except for music spilling over onto the street. A bouncer opened the door for her. Inside, a band played on a dark stage at the back of a long candlelit lounge. She felt uncoordinated, maneuvering through the standoffish crowd, looking for the man who made her heart race and her palms sweat.

Large, garish paintings hung on rough walls. They looked like abstracts, until enlarged body parts revealed themselves: feet, hands, buttocks, thighs, some parts more recognizable than others. Searching the dance floor in front of the band and the booths along the sidewalls, she hoped for a small gathering of friends and a spot saved beside Julian just for her.

He stood in a crowd near the back. People talked and laughed,

Julian at the center of it all. He didn't see her approaching, and for a second, she felt like a groupie. A nobody. He had the same rebel look that he'd had on their first date and even appeared to be wearing the same clothes. She moved closer. Yes, the gray un-tucked shirt, those tight jeans, and his worn-in motorcycle boots. His face looked haggard. His hair, dirty. A hard day's work playing a drug addict? She was close enough to touch him now.

"Hi, Julian!" She had to shout.

"Ava!" He wrapped her in a zealous hug. "Finally! I'm a sucker for wanting the things I can't have." His breath felt hot against her skin. "You've been on my mind since you left my place."

She kept her face close to his. "It's good to see you, too."

"Come meet my friends." He took her hand and made random introductions, shouting above the music. "This is Mitch and Carrie, and over there, Keith, Jess, Helena..."

She smiled and shook hands with those within reach. None of them looked half as reckless as Julian. A petite woman with curly blond hair grabbed his arm like a significant other. Ava felt his hand drop hers.

"And this is Nina," he said.

Nina. She'd heard the name before...the first time she had called him. So this was the woman he had confused her with.

They shook hands. An old friend? Doubtful. Her low-cut top was an open invitation for more.

Julian disengaged from Nina and spoke into Ava's ear. "So I got you out of the bath?"

"The hot water felt good while it lasted. By the way, you're not undercover tonight, are you?"

"Am I what?"

Before she could repeat herself, Nina was nibbling on his ear, saying something and giggling. Julian nibbled back, sending Nina into orbit with laughter. Ava faked a sudden interest in the band. Maybe she was the jealous type, after all.

A woman sitting nearby with razor-short black hair and high cheekbones stared her down, somehow maintaining civility.

"I'm Helena," she said. "Helena Morganbesser." Her broad shoulders and raspy voice were anything but feminine. "I work with Julian."

"Really? Are you an officer, too?"

She half laughed, saying something that sounded like, "You're very cute."

"Ah, you've met Helena," Julian said, joining the conversation with Nina on his arm.

Helena ignored him. "I'm a prosecuting attorney."

"And she never loses." Julian gave her his star-studded smile.

"What would you do without me?" Helena replied. She turned to Ava. "What do you do?"

It was a good question. Ava took a deep breath and decided to go for it. "I'm a dancer." It sounded nice. She smiled at Julian.

He looked stunned, as if she were morphing into someone else before his eyes. The pause of heightened interest was like the ring of a chime...before it faded. His expression turned quizzical, probably wondering whatever happened to her "glamorous" career at Bergdorf.

"Well, I'm looking for a job as a dancer, on—or off—Broadway. Actually, if you know of anything, I could use some leads."

Helena shook her head with a patronizing smirk.

"You're full of it," Julian said and grabbed her hand. "I'll show you about dancing." Things were suddenly looking up again.

They lost Nina and fought through the crowd on the dance floor. Being pushed together from all directions wasn't a problem.

"I thought you were blowing me off last week," he shouted into her ear. A bass rhythm pumped incessantly through the speakers above their heads.

"I was home and..." She didn't want to talk about it. "Let's just dance."

In the middle of the mob, he pulled her close to his slender body. Wrapping his arms around her waist, he pressed his lips to hers. No tenderness. He wasn't gentle. But she wanted him, and she liked that he wanted her and no one else at that moment. In the dark, surrounded by strangers, it seemed as though she didn't have a life beyond his kiss, and that was fine.

Someone shoved Julian hard from behind. He stumbled, and she started to fall with him when he caught his balance and steadied her at the same time.

Nina faced them, not happy. "I didn't come out tonight to watch you be with *her*!"

"Hey, calm down," Julian said, reaching for her shoulder.

She brushed him away as if he were a wasp. "What's with you, Julian?"

"It's a party, Nina. Relax. I told you I'm seeing other people. Hang out. Have fun." The fast rhythm became a single note like a siren ripping through the speakers, while strobe lights moved everything in slow motion.

"If I was having *fun*, I wouldn't feel blown off!" Nina shouted. "I deserve better than hanging around waiting for you!" Light reflected in her tears. "I'm leaving!" The beat resumed, reaching new decibels at full speed.

Julian looked at Ava and shrugged. "Do you mind? I'll just walk her out."

"Uh, sure. I mean, no, I don't mind."

They left. Ava walked to the bar, feeling bad for Nina, in a way. No one wanted to be second choice. A smile crept over her face...but it felt fantastic being his *first* choice.

The mob was dense at the bar. Without Julian to hold her tight, a glass of water wasn't worth the pushing and shoving.

"Can I get you a drink?" a man asked, standing at her shoulder. He had a narrow face and steel-framed glasses. Wearing a pinstriped button-front shirt, he appeared too straight-laced for the venue.

"I'm totally dehydrated," she said. "I'd love a Cherry 7UP."

"Sure thing." He held out his hand to her. "I'm Marcus."

"Ava." They shook. "Are you from New York?" she asked, sensing he wasn't by his polished sun-kissed complexion and bright eyes.

"I'm from L.A. but just moved to SoHo. I'm starting a record label."

"Wow. That's pretty cool. What do you think of this band?"

"I think they rock. I signed them. Look, forget trying to get drinks here. I have a table in the VIP with plenty to quench your thirst, including Cherry 7UP. Whatever you want."

"I didn't know there was a VIP lounge."

"If you know the right people, there is. Come with me."

She could stand there counting the minutes until Julian returned, go back to Helena-the-prosecuting-attorney, or get something to drink and maybe meet some new people.

"All right. I'll go."

"Great. Follow me."

Chapter Twenty-Two

"So, Ava, are you here with someone?" Marcus shouted as he maneuvered through the crowd to the VIP.

"This guy I just started dating and a bunch of his friends," she shouted back.

Marcus turned abruptly, and she crashed into his chest.

"Sorry!" she said, stepping back.

"He isn't going to come after me, I hope." Marcus stepped back even farther.

"No, he wouldn't do that." She pictured Julian pulling the same jealous act as Nina, wanting her undivided attention. It was a flattering thought, but— "I'd be very surprised."

"Good."

They continued past the rest rooms and down a narrow corridor to a red door guarded by a woman in a cat suit. She had Rapunzel-esque hair and held a clipboard.

"Finally!" she said and kissed Marcus on both cheeks. "What took you so long?"

Marcus frowned deeply behind his steel-framed glasses. "The idiot never showed. I got sick of waiting. He'll call. He always does. Hey, meet Ava, a friend of mine." He turned to her. "Ava, allow me to introduce Princess Victoria."

"Hi." Ava reached out to shake her hand and received a kiss on both cheeks. The princess smiled but said nothing, as though she only spoke to people who were on her list.

"Come on." Marcus held open the red door. "I'm ready for some fun!"

Inside, red lighting gave everyone a devilish appearance. The room was small with red velvet couches against red walls. Even the carpet, red. In the center of everything was a black and red canopy bed where people sat puffing on hookahs, filling the air with a sweet cherry scent.

"My table is just over there." Marcus pointed to a group of guys and several tall, thin women, probably in their early twenties. Three of the women, variations of blond, danced on the ledge behind the booth, loving the spotlight.

"So, this guy you're dating, what does he do for a living?" Now Marcus was beginning to sound paranoid.

"He's a...club promoter." Even if Julian wasn't on duty tonight, she couldn't give him away.

"A promoter?" Marcus grinned like a boy talking about Lego or trains. "What clubs? Maybe I know him...or should know him."

"Oh, I'm not sure where. Like I said, we just started going out."

"Ah, I get it. You had a one-night stand and probably don't even know his last name. Right? Come on, fess up."

"Not exactly." Julian had mentioned his last name...what was it?

They stood before Marcus's table. "How about you, Ava? What do you do in this crazy city?"

"It's something I'm figuring out."

"Cool."

Forgotten drinks, mixers, and bottles of vodka covered every inch of the table. Marcus asked a server to bring a Cherry 7UP and a bottle of water.

"Thanks," Ava said. "And thanks for showing me the VIP."

"Meet my crew." He ran through names while she smiled and nodded, feeling the couple-year age difference as if it were ten.

Their drinks arrived right away.

"Finally!" Marcus drained his bottle of water. "So, what's on your agenda tonight, Ava? Do you party?"

"Actually, I just ended a long relationship, so I've been going out a lot more, meeting new people, rediscovering the city, in a way. Are you celebrating a birthday tonight or something?" She glanced at the door, half expecting Julian to stride in. He'd know about this room, wouldn't he?

A devious smile came over Marcus's face. "It's not a birthday party, but...I've got party favors! Check this out." He took a plastic bag the size of a quarter from his wallet and slipped it into her palm. "It's just a sample, but there's plenty more. Trust me."

"Oh." At first, she saw baby powder, confection sugar... drugs? "Thanks, but—uh—crack isn't my thing." She handed it back, suddenly very uncomfortable.

"*Crack?* No, no. You're funny. Let me tell you, this is the good stuff." His wide smile turned freakish. Demented.

She continued to hold the bag out to him, wishing he'd take it, and fast. "Really, I'm not interested."

"Keep it. You might change your mind. Seriously, I'm talking top quality. You'll love it."

She looked down at the little bag in her hand. Give it to Julian? Turn the creep in? "All right. You never know. Thanks."

"Don't mention it."

She set down her drink and took a step back. "Okay, well, listen, I should—"

"Relax. Hang out. I'm gonna pop into the men's room for a sec." He started to turn and then stopped, his attention on something behind her. She glanced over her shoulder.

"Of course I'd find this girl in the VIP!" Julian was all smiles.

"I didn't even see you come in." Her happiness stumbled over guilt. Here she was, caught with some random guy and holding drugs.

"Dude." Marcus looked at him as if he were a stray dog, obviously not making the connection. "This is a private party. Are you on the list?"

Julian laughed. "Ask Princess Victoria." He turned to her. "What's going on?"

"This is Marcus. He's just showing me around." She gripped the bag in her hand, hot enough to liquefy the powder. "Marcus, this is Julian."

Marcus looked from her to Julian. "Of course! You must be the promoter. Sorry about that, man. I'm new in town and forgot that looking five days hung over is cool! Where do you promote?"

She leapt into the conversation to save Julian's cover. "Jules, I totally forgot where you said you promoted parties." She tugged on her ear, hoping he'd catch on.

"That's funny," he replied. "I can't remember where I said I promoted, either."

Marcus put his hand on her shoulder. "Looks like you're seeing too many guys, Ava. Here's a tip—keep the facts straight."

"I'm an idiot," she said. "Hey, do you have any, uh, party favors for Julian?" She held out the bag of powder.

Marcus slipped on his elastic smile. "You bet. For a price, though. I can't hook up the whole club."

Julian looked at her, raised an eyebrow and grinned. "Are you telling me that you scored?"

"*I* didn't! But I thought you might." She winked at him.

He turned to Marcus. "What do you have?"

Now Julian was supposed to whip out his badge and throw Marcus down on the floor. Cuff him and read him his rights in front of her and everyone else. No? But what if Marcus had a gun? She suddenly wanted to leave the scene before it played out—but was too curious to go.

Marcus pulled yet another "party favor" from his wallet. "A hundred and twenty bucks, but I'll give it to you for eighty." He handed it to Julian. "The stuff's high-end. Trust me."

"Sorry, buddy, but I don't trust anybody." Julian reached into his back pocket, whipped out his keys, and with the tip of one, scooped up a small pile of the powder. She didn't think he would actually snort it, until he inhaled from one nostril like a pro.

Repulsion gripped her stomach as she looked away. Was *doing* drugs his job? Couldn't he just taste it from the tip of his pinky finger, like in the movies?

Julian nodded to Marcus, smiling, taking in the high. Marcus was slime, giving her free cocaine. *Escort him out of the club! Make a public spectacle of him! Be a hero!*

"We're in business." Julian counted out four twenty-dollar bills.

She watched the exchange of money for drugs, feeling too close to the action, and yet Julian acted as though she weren't even there. She'd had this nightmare before: surrounded by danger, unable to scream for help.

"Ava, how about I catch you later," Julian said, rubbing her back. "All right?"

She shivered as if caught in a cold draft. Twice in one night, she was being told to get lost. Nothing about *I'll call you later*. No sign to let her know that he was undercover, that she shouldn't worry.

"Have fun." She tossed the bag on the table, and it landed in someone's leftover cocktail. Marcus dove in after it.

"What did you say your name was?" Julian asked.

She walked away, confused and disappointed.

Outside, the night air was dense and clingy. A cab waited at a red light on the avenue, but she started to walk in the direction of home and just kept going. Her thoughts returned to the funeral, calling hours, and the flowers filling every corner of the parlor. David telling stories, his voice too loud. Everyone's sad laughter. Dad's absence. Memories came and went, the way a gentle ocean wave reached the shore and then quickly receded. Life had one constant now: Mom was gone.

Ava bit her lip to override the pain. Crying didn't help. Navigating life and all its vague pros and cons was only harder looking through tears.

Her mind quieted. The moon appeared above downtown buildings, blue-white and big as a balloon. It bobbed brightly above, while dark deserted streets fell behind. Tomorrow was a new day. She had headhunters to contact and her audition at The Encore, one last shot at dancing. Maybe Chris would be back with more street art, or another story from the news, like an article on how to live life without regrets. He had become her muse, as well as her bodyguard.

Turning onto 22nd Street, she had a feeling she wasn't alone. Glancing back, the shadow of a man came into her peripheral vision and she picked up her pace. Fear triggered her heart rate to spike. As she walked faster, the scuff of footsteps sounded nearer, gaining on her. *Run!* She took off in full-sprint.

"Wait! It's me!"

She heard his voice, the touch of a foreign accent, and slowed down to look back.

"Chris!" Excitement sparked in her chest, catching her by surprise. She stopped, and Chickpea appeared out of nowhere dancing at her feet. "Hey, girl!" Ava bent down and stroked her soft fur.

Chris came up to her, flipping his hair out of his eyes. "Hi, Ava!"

"Hi! I haven't seen you in forever!" She stood before him, and for a second, thought they might embrace.

"Over a week," he said. "I was beginning to think you had moved."

"I wouldn't leave without saying good-bye. I went home for a while, that's all." They walked together.

"Home to upstate?" he asked.

"Yes," she replied softly. He remembered. "My mom passed away. Breast cancer." Ava dug her hands into her jeans pockets, uncomfortable with the weight of her words.

"Oh. I'm really sorry."

"What a bummer thing to say. I'm sorry I put that on you. I haven't told anyone yet, and it just came out."

"I lost my mom when I was thirteen. A car accident. It's not something I usually tell people, either."

"Gosh, that must have been tough. So young."

"Yes, but not as difficult as living alone with my father. Anyway, that's another story. Are you okay?"

"I think so. Yes, I am. You know, my mom lived her *If Only* job. She was a music history professor and a fiddler in a folk band. I'll always have her life as inspiration."

"You couldn't ask for more than that. She sounds like an

amazing woman."

"She was." They paused at the stoop. "I had a strange night tonight," Ava said. "I was out with this guy I've started dating, who seems perfect in so many ways, but then he got his hands on cocaine and snorted the drug like it was no big deal, right in front of me. It was like watching him cut himself, or jump off a cliff. And I just stood there."

"That's awkward. The guy obviously wasn't thinking of you."

"The strangest part is that he's a cop."

"The cop who showed you his I.D.?"

"Yes, him, and right now he could be arresting the dealer, or he could be getting high with him. I've no idea."

"Maybe he needed to know it was real, and he's trying to get to the source. Or he's got a serious problem. Or both. You could try and talk to him about it."

"I might give him the benefit of the doubt. Innocent until proven guilty, I suppose."

"Can't hurt to hear him out. But at the same time, I'd trust your instincts." Chris looked at her and then to the sky. "Did you happen to catch the moon tonight? It's huge."

She looked up between the buildings, but the moon wasn't visible from where they stood. "I did. It was so bright and full." With Chris, it was easy to feel good about life, to have hope. "By the way, were you following me home?"

"Was I following you? Well, let's see," he said, leaning against the stoop, as if they might sit down together and figure it out. "We were both headed for this building, and you were walking in front of me, so yes, technically, I was following you home. Is that a bad thing?"

"No. Maybe you're *supposed* to be following me, like a guardian angel."

He smiled. "Sure. Just don't call me a hero."

"All right." She started up the stoop. "Oh, by the way, the Rockettes didn't happen."

"Too bad for them. That's great that you went on the audition, though. What's next?"

"An Off-Off-Broadway cabaret club. Five-thirty, tomorrow.

Could be something."

"Definitely. Let me know how it goes."

"I will." Was he any closer to becoming a renowned restaurateur? Afraid of putting him on the spot, she didn't ask.

Inside her apartment, the night with Julian replayed in her mind. Maybe she should call. Let him know that she understood. That she cared.

His line rang, but he didn't pick up.

Chapter Twenty-Three

The Encore. Nonexistent on the Internet, no website, not even a review. Ava pictured the name in lights and with a little man in a tuxedo and top hat, leaning on a cane. A tourist trap? A members-only club? She shut down her laptop. She'd just have to go and find out.

Putting off corporate America another day was a bold move. Irresponsible, really, like a student skipping school on the brink of expulsion. But she wasn't ready to give up on Broadway and had gone out looking for open calls. No such luck. Not for a moment did her feet feel the smooth leather inside of her dance shoes. Not one dance move! With every agent she contacted, it was the same conversation: *We'd like to see a demo reel. No headshots? You need a resume.* If someone would just give her a chance!

The light on her cell phone was blinking...a missed call from Phoebe? Ava stared at the familiar name as a rush of emotions, from longing to apprehension, passed through her heart. There was no message, unfortunately. She had probably dialed Ava's number by accident, so no point in calling her back. She shouldn't hope for Phoebe's forgiveness.

Only a half hour to make it to The Encore on time. It could be her big break. She dressed in her stockings, leotard, and light-blue running pants. Gym bag with jazz shoes, all set. She ran downstairs.

Eighteen hours had passed since she had left Julian at the club, and not one phone call. No text. No voice mail. Not even a hang up. Was he hurt? Dead? Or *really* inconsiderate. She wanted to write him off, for peace of mind. But how could she, not knowing if he was even alive?

She stepped outside her building.

"Ava!" Chris stood at the bottom of the stoop, holding three yellow roses.

"Flowers?" She went quickly down the steps to meet him.

"Not exactly a dozen, but...they're for you." He held the roses out to her and she took them.

"But...why?"

"I was thinking of your mom."

"Oh, thank you...so much." Tears came to her eyes, no stopping them. She instinctively stepped toward him, and he opened his arms. They embraced.

"I'm sorry," he whispered. His warmth calmed her.

She pulled away, flushed, and looked at the roses. "Thank you...for caring."

"They're a little wilted. I've had them for a few hours."

"They're perfect." She remembered where she was. "Oh, I have to go. I'll be late for my audition. Thank you, Chris. It means a lot." She walked for the subway, yellow roses in hand. Before turning the corner, she glanced back.

"You'll do great!" he shouted with a big smile and gave her a thumbs up.

Ava yanked on the tinted glass door. Locked. "What?" She reached for her cell phone, fearing she had her days mixed up. *Wednesday, June 30th, 5:23 p.m.* The guy did say every Wednesday, didn't he?

Down the street, a steel door looked like it could be a stage entrance. One hard tug and it opened. With her gym bag and Chris's roses, she squeezed inside and stood in darkness until her eyes adjusted.

A deserted lounge and dark stage came into focus. On the stage, a grand piano lurked in the shadows. Tacky wall-to-wall carpeting in blue and gold swirls matched the tattered upholstered chairs surrounding round tables of varying sizes. The sunless air was stale, like an old man's breath drenched in Scotch. Decades of progress had bypassed the club. Just standing in the entrance, wondering about its purpose, she lost track of time.

A door opened, and she turned abruptly as a man appeared from a room marked OFFICE. He had a pronounced upper lip and thick neck. His faded brown three-piece suit fused with the once-classy atmosphere of the lounge.

"Uh, hi," she stammered.

"Yeah?"

"I'm here to audition?" Oops, bad protocol, questioning her intention.

"There." He pointed to a red-carpeted flight of stairs to the left of the stage, leading downward.

"Is the club open?" she asked.

"What's that?" He had started to turn away.

"It doesn't look like you're open to the public."

"We open at six. You'd better get downstairs if you want to audition." He waited in the doorjamb for her to make a move.

Here goes. She went down. Finally, the red carpet...in a low hallway with cement walls. She followed the sound of overlapping voices to a large, brightly lit room. Her heart rate quickened. A swarm of half-naked women crowded a wall-length mirror, putting on makeup and doing their hair.

"Let's go, ladies!" A voice like Lucille Ball's rang above the chatter. "Ten minutes and you're all upstairs. Brianna, why aren't you dressed? Customers aren't going to come looking for you down here. I want everyone giving her best tonight. No excuses!" She waved a schedule, gold bangles clanking around her wrist.

It was the woman she had seen outside the club, talking on her cell phone. *This joint's not about pretending you're someone special.* A satiny pink blouse was tucked into yellow pants, showing off her slim figure. Years prior, she must have been pretty.

"I'm here to audition." Ava extended her hand, proper interview fashion, and received a cool, limp hand in return.

"Yeah, fine. I'm Rose, the house mom. Everyone calls me Mama Rose."

"Like Mama Rose, who lives to see her girls make it on Broadway? I saw *Gypsy*, twice." In another life, it seemed. The Shubert Theatre...Phoebe.

"Hold your pants. We're not exactly on Broadway. I run *this* show, down here in the dressing room. Are those roses for me?"

Ava felt her cheeks flush. "Oh, actually, they're a gift...from a friend."

"Right. We get flowers down here all the time. Hopeful admirers and all. Sometimes I feel bad for the poor guys. Wait by my desk. I'll get you a vase."

Ava walked to the bulky metal desk covered with pins and spools of thread, bandages, Tampax, and a large bowl of assorted candy. Two women stood nearby in tight jeans and high heels, carrying designer bags. Counterfeit Hermès, actually. They returned her smile, kind of. Auditioning, too? Both looked exotic, perhaps Russian or Czech. But this was nothing like the hundred-plus competition auditioning for the Rockettes.

She held tight to her roses as she watched the women in the dressing area pull lavish gowns from dented metal lockers. Some of the lockers were decorated with photographs and postcards, costume jewelry hanging from plastic hooks. There didn't appear to be a height or weight requirement for the dancers, although all the women were attractive, short or tall. Conversations flowed in Spanish, Russian, French...possibly an international show.

"Not a bad deal." One of the other women waiting touched a satiny black evening gown that hung on the wall. It had rhinestone straps and a price tag of $140. Next to it, a stretchy floor-length leopard-print number that tied around the neck went for $120. It seemed she'd have to invest in some fancy dresses, if she got the job.

"Five minutes!" Rose shouted, returning with a vase filled

with water. "We open in five minutes, ladies! I want everyone upstairs on time!" She turned to Ava, holding out the vase. "Plop those poor things in here."

A woman burst into the room and began frantically tearing off her clothes at her locker.

Rose frowned. "You're late, Chloe. That's a twenty-dollar fee."

"Come on, you know I have to run here from class on Tuesdays. Give me a break!"

"A break? You get a break, and I'm giving *everyone* a break. I want twenty dollars, and you have four minutes to get upstairs!"

Chloe looked on the verge of tears.

A woman with black hair and red-rimmed glasses working at the makeup counter approached Chloe. "I'll do your makeup for free," she said, "just as soon as I'm done with Georgia." Georgia, in a glittery red gown with a side-split to her thigh, sat in front of the mirror, short a false eyelash.

Rose set the flowers on her desk and looked at Ava. "Just don't forget them at the end of the night." She sat down with a sigh.

End of the night? How long would the audition take?

"All right, let's get started here." Rose pulled some forms from a drawer. "I need each of you to sign a release and write down your contact information. A picture I.D. is mandatory to audition, and so you know, our acts involve singing."

The karaoke part sounded fun. Ava signed the form and showed Rose her driver's license. "What is the audition, exactly?"

"I'm getting to that." Rose addressed the three of them. "We often let our girls come in with their own acts, but this one is a house favorite, and we recently lost our 'Michelle Pfeiffer.' Supposedly, she followed her fiancé to Bali. Good for her, bad for us. But that's how it goes." Rose glanced toward the lockers, as if she expected any one of the women getting ready to suddenly run off to Bali.

"Anyway, it's a piano act we call 'The Best of The Fabulous Baker Boys.' What you do is dance on top of our Steinway while singing Michelle Pfeiffer's version of 'Makin' Whoopee.'"

Ava squinted, wondering if she heard Rose correctly. She knew the song from the old '20s musical *Whoopee!*, about the demise of a marriage. It was a classic, though not what she considered a particularly uplifting song. And she had to sing it while dancing on *top* of a piano? Impossible.

"The words will be on a prompter," Rose continued, "but you'll get the lyrics down real fast. The challenge is performing the number with your body, heart, and soul, like Michelle Pfeiffer in the movie. Did any of you see it?"

None of them had.

"Google the video. It's a jaw-dropping act. Think enticing. Tantalizing! Any questions?"

Ava raised her hand. "Did you say on *top* of the piano?"

"I did." Rose looked at her with raised eyebrows, as if waiting for the next question.

Ava took the opportunity. "I think I would perform the number much better if I danced *next* to the piano. Is that an option?" Just the thought of being on top of a grand piano created a virtual tilt-a-wheel ride in her mind. And, besides, there wasn't the space on a piano to do the moves she'd spent her youth perfecting.

"No, it's not," Rose replied flatly and went on. "The club pays ten dollars an hour, and then, of course, a fifteen percent service charge is added to each food and drink order. Customers are encouraged to tip on top of that, as well, and most do. You'll perform on stage three times a night. Some girls alternate between different acts, if that's something you want to work toward. When you're not on stage, you're waiting tables."

Ava nodded. That she could do. Go figure, waitressing at TGI Fridays throughout college had become more valuable an education than her liberal arts degree.

"My spiel is almost done," Rose said. "At the end of the night, you tip out to your busboy ten percent of your tips, and to the bartender, me, and Giovanni, our Entertainment Director, ten dollars each, or more if you're so inclined." She smiled.

"Don't forget about me!" the woman in red spectacles called

from the makeup counter.

"It's twenty if you want Maryanne to do your face." Rose glanced at the clock. "They'll be ready for you soon. Have I left anything out? Oh, take-home can range from not much to upward of a thousand, depending on the night and what kind of regular clientele you have."

"A thousand dollars for waiting tables?" Ava blurted out. "What kind of 'entrées' do you serve?"

"Oh, no whoopee here. No hanky-panky whatsoever. In fact, we have a No Touching rule. If a customer gives you trouble, one of the hosts will escort him out at once. But if you get someone who wants to talk, go for it, let yourself care, or at least act like you do. The idea of love can be just as powerful as the real thing."

"I see," Ava said, seeing a serious dilemma. Did paying for a lie make lying okay?

"Now, go on and change, and then show Giovanni your best Michelle Pfeiffer." Rose collected the release forms.

The two Russian-looking women opened their gym bags and pulled out slinky gowns. Ava looked down at her jazz shoes, stockings, and leotard.

"What are you waiting for?" Rose asked.

"I don't think I brought the appropriate clothes." She glanced at the gowns for sale hanging on the wall. "I really don't have the money to buy a dress. Could I borrow one?"

"I think we can work something out, this one time. Listen," Rose lowered her voice, as if she were about to tell a secret, "I have a good feeling about you for this act. You look a little like Michelle. Those high cheekbones."

Ava imagined herself clinging to the piano for her life. "Actually, I'm not sure this is the job for me."

"Give it a shot. There's a first for everything."

Ava nodded. And firsts were what made life exciting, according to Julian, a man who may have overdosed on excitement.

She thought it over. Healthy tips could help her financial problems, and working nights would allow her to take dance lessons and go on auditions. Get headshots, build a resume. "All right," she said. "I'll audition. But I'll need to borrow a dress."

"Here." Rose took the leopard-print off its hanger and handed it to her. "You can pay for it at the end of the night. There's a box of high heels behind Maryanne's makeup station, shoes left here over the years. I'm sure you'll find something."

Opposite the mirrors, Ava found an empty locker and got undressed. Standing in her flashy new gown, she looked pale and felt exposed...and then there was the problem of the piano.

Chapter Twenty-Four

Glitzy high heels were the shoes of choice at The Encore. Ava searched through the box. There had to be something a little less...showy. Gold stilettos with tassels? Mile-high Lucite platforms? Black high-heel shoe-boots with studs? No, no, and no. Buried at the bottom, she found a pair of beige open-toe sandals, only a half-size too big.

"You're up!" Rose shouted from her desk.

"Can I run to the ladies' room first?"

"Make it fast."

The bathroom attendant, a middle-aged woman with thinning black hair, arranged an assortment of deodorants, breath mints, and used lipsticks. She kept her eyes on her task, humming to herself. Handwritten memos were taped to the mirror: *Tell Giovanni before you go on break! No drinking, and that includes champagne! Dinner available in the kitchen. ALL performers must work two Sundays a month, no excuses!*

Ava looked at herself in the mirror. Plain Jane. The Girl Next Door. *Un*exotic. She shook out her hair, trying for a wild look. After all, she was wearing leopard-print.

A tall blond woman stepped out from one of the stalls. Like an angel in a pageant, she had platinum ringlets draping her back.

"Hey, love your dress," she said as she washed her hands. "I've been thinking about buying it, myself." She wore a beaded white gown, and a string of pearls hung to her chest.

"Thanks. Yours is really nice, too. What's your act?"

"Tonight I'm doing Billie Holiday's 'I'm Gonna Lock My Heart.' You know, *and throw away the key...*" she sang in a full, melodic voice. "Of course, I look nothing like Lady Day, but they let me perform her because I can. Mostly I do off-Broadway stuff." She stared into the mirror, fixing a curl. "I'm in between contracts at the moment and need the money. You know, sometimes you just need a job." She bent over to tighten the straps on her white patent leather heels and spirals tumbled around her slender shoulders. "What brings you here?" she asked, upside-down.

"I kind of fell into this place. I used to work in fashion, and now here I am, auditioning."

"So you're looking for a new job, something completely different." The angel-looking Holiday sprang upright. "That's great."

"To be honest, I'm looking for new everything," Ava said. "A new me, new love..."

"Whoa, you're asking a lot of this place. I'd keep love on your prayer list, if I were you. I'm Billie. Angie in real life." She glanced at the clock hanging crooked on the pink tiled wall. "Oh, I've got to get upstairs before Mama Rose starts throwing late fees at me as if they were knives. See you up there!"

Ava took a deep breath and went back to find Rose. The Italian-looking man, who had nearly taken her down the day before, stood outside the dressing room in white tie and tails.

"Here she comes," he said, talking into a two-way radio. He turned his narrow eyes on her. "You ready? Everything all right?"

"I'm okay. A little nervous—"

"Let me tell you something. When you get upstairs, you're gonna have to be a lot better than 'okay.' There's nothing interesting about being 'okay,' not to our customers, anyway. Know what I'm saying? Here's the deal: you are exactly where you want to be, you're happy, and whoever you're serving is the only man alive."

"Right. I get it."

"The name's Giovanni, Director of Entertainment. I'll show you where to go."

"Thanks, because I'm totally lost here." She followed him

down the red carpet in her skin-tight dress and four-inch heels, struggling to keep pace.

"Don't forget to sparkle!" Rose shouted after her. "Think *enticing!*"

"Thanks...Mama Rose." This would take getting used to.

"So, what's your name?" Giovanni asked.

"Ava."

"Nice to meet you, Ava. From now on you'll be Michelle. That's your stage name, providing you get the job."

"Oh. Okay." Her legs shook going up a narrow spiral staircase that ended in darkness.

"The MC is Chris tonight," Giovanni said, climbing the stairs ahead of her. "He'll introduce you when you go on stage."

Hearing Chris's name took her back to the stoop, the two of them talking about life and living their dreams. What were the odds that he was an MC here, too embarrassed to tell her that he wasn't working in his *If Only* field? Odds were, she and Chris were just a couple of dreamers.

"Auditions are live." Giovanni stopped at the top of the stairs. "We have a handful of regulars who come in early on Wednesdays just to see them."

"In case I wasn't nervous enough," she said, looking around. The stage curtain was closed. By the floor lights, she could make out the looming grand piano. Lounge music and women laughing made the unseen club come alive. A restless energy seemed to permeate the heavy red curtain and settle on her chest.

"The Best of The Fabulous Baker Boys is ready," Giovanni said, back to his two-way radio. "You can introduce Michelle." The lounge music quieted. He motioned for her to follow and approached the piano.

Giovanni sat down on the bench with a flip of his tails. "Ready?" he whispered.

She took a deep breath, and before she could exhale, a pulley creaked from above and the curtain reeled open. She stepped into the spotlight directed at the piano, stunned by the sudden brightness.

"Welcome Michelle!" the MC announced, sounding nothing

like *her* Chris, which surprisingly was a letdown. He stood stage right, addressing a scattered audience. "Our last audition to perform Michelle Pfeiffer's 'Makin' Whoopee' is willing and able, we hope." The crowd chuckled. "So, let's give her a big round of applause!" He backed off the stage.

Golden lights made faces glow as if cast in bronze. She broke a sweat from anxiety alone, though the spotlight was sweltering hot. Her legs begged to give out.

Giovanni played the opening chords, while Ava, hands shaking, took the mike from its stand and moved for the piano bench. *God, help me.*

One foot up and then another, visibly lacking balance, she made the climb of her life. Finally, she stepped up on top of the piano and immediately went down on all fours, sitting with a thud. A quick scan of the audience and she noticed an older man seated just below the stage. He watched her with wide eyes, as though fearing for her life.

Eyes locked on the prompter, voice quivering, she sang the words, trying her best to captivate, sparkle...oh, and to be enticing.

Another bride, another June, another sunny honeymoon, another season, another reason...for makin' whoopee...

She swayed to the music, as stiff as a metronome. Her audition wasn't happening. She was a joke of a performer. Why did she think she could go back to dancing? This wasn't even dancing!

Caught between her fear of holding back and her fear of letting go, she felt paralyzed. All eyes were on her, and definitely Giovanni's. *Engage!* She wanted to scream at herself. *Move or get off the piano! Make this happen or go back to fashion!*

Her legs dangled awkwardly off the edge of the piano, pining for solid ground, when a decisive "Booo!" came from the audience. Sheer panic felt like she'd been slapped across her face. She wasn't going to get the job, another rejection.

A lot of shoes, a lot of rice. The groom is nervous. He answers twice. It's really killin' that he's so willin' to make whoopee...

Focusing on the music, she started to feel the rhythm and slowly began to move. A sense of control came over her and with it, awareness. Clarity. She took full breaths and swayed to the sound of her voice, letting emotion unfurl from deep inside and letting go of fear. The decision turned out to be easy: commit to her dream and make it happen. There was no giving up.

She swiveled her legs around and shimmied her shoulders, as if shaking off the past five years with Josh. Awakening unused energy made her skin tingle. Her muscles felt strong and determined, dedicated to the moment and all its potential. With arms outstretched and head held high, she sang out, proclaiming her own revolution:

Another year, or maybe less. What's this I hear? Well, can't you guess? She feels neglected. And he's suspected...of makin' whoopee!

The older man seated below the stage nodded in approval. If all she ever achieved were these three minutes on top of a piano, gaining her own sense of power and passion, it'd give her life significance. As if her dream of dancing depended on this one triumph.

Hearing applause and even some cheers, she smiled at her audience and looked for someone she might know, hoping for the impossible...that Mom could see her now.

The music stopped. Shakily, she crawled back down, all the way down to solid ground, feeling electric. Alive.

Giovanni turned to her once they were backstage. "You're hired. You can start now if you want, or go down and talk to Mama Rose about getting on the schedule."

"I'll start now."

"Great. You're Section 7. I'll make sure the MC has you on the circuit, and the girls on the floor will show you where everything is. It's a straightforward menu, and the pace is pretty relaxed. Have fun with it. Oh, and be backstage at seven-thirty, ten-thirty, and one a.m. That's when you're on."

"Okay. Thanks. Thanks a lot." Her heart pounded in her chest as she walked down the short flight of stairs that led to the club.

Now for the waitressing part.

Male hosts in tails escorted customers across the blue and gold carpet to their seats. She saw Billie laughing with two men dressed in crisp jeans and ten-gallon hats. Big tippers? Was there any way to tell? Billie talked to them with her whole body, including her ringlets. She showed stage presence, not once dropping a starlit smile. As soon as she sashayed away from the table, Ava pulled her aside.

"Hi! Can you tell me which is Section 7? I made the audition!"

"I saw! Didn't you hear me whoop and holler? You pulled it off in the end, girl!"

"Thanks. I'm still in shock."

"See those five tables closest to the stage?" Billie asked, pointing. "That's your section: the single, those two doubles, the four-top, and the six-seater front and center. Good tips, but the farthest from the kitchen, which is all the way at the back and to the left. We've been splitting Section 7 since the last Michelle left. It happens a lot. Girls come and go."

"Right. Do I need a pad and pencil for taking orders, or something?"

"Oh, boy. This place is no Four Seasons, but it isn't the Moonstruck Diner, either! You'll remember the orders. Most importantly, chat with the customers, work it, you know?" Billie touched her arm. "Come with me and I'll show you how to enter orders into the system. The computer is totally antiquated."

They seemed to glide in their gowns and heels to the back of the lounge. The first act hadn't started yet, and Natalie Cole's "It's Only a Paper Moon" spiraled down from the sound system overhead.

"Is there a cover charge to get in here?" Ava asked.

"You bet. Forty bucks a head. Some customers have annual memberships, which sell for seven hundred a pop."

Ava counted eight waitresses on the floor. Busboys balanced trays of food and drinks for the early crowd, which mostly consisted of older men.

"I wish I were doing more dancing," Ava said, "but as far as waitressing goes, it seems ideal."

"Oh, that reminds me," Billie said. "We don't wear garters here. You know, around the thigh? It's a rule. Tips go in the office. Phil or Keith, the owners, will give you an envelope with your name on it. Someone's always there, so nothing gets stolen."

Entering orders into the system was a cinch. Ava practiced saying her name, "I'm Michelle!" as she approached her first customer, the older man who had watched her from below the stage. He had a head of silvery hair and a long face. His ribbed sweater and wide cords gave the illusion of girth to his slender frame. Perhaps he was a retired professor or journalist. Or a small business owner. She was about to say hello when the MC stepped out on stage and announced, "The Boswell Sisters!"

The curtain opened to an enthusiastic applause dominated by a stout man with a shrill whistle. Ava ducked out of view, while on stage three identical-looking black women in frilly white dresses and coiffed hair sang their number.

Ava noticed her customer's thin lips curve into a smile. When the song ended, she tried again.

"Hi, I'm, um, Michelle!"

"Yes, I know. I always sit in Michelle's section, only you have brown hair, and my old Michelle was a blond. Pull over a chair."

She did and sat beside him. "Well, I'm not going to dye my hair blond, so don't get any ideas."

"I wouldn't ask you to do that. Just don't leave town without saying good-bye. When I found out the old Michelle took off, I almost stopped coming here. How could she be so heartless? We saw each other here every night for a month! I have to assume it was an emergency."

Ava recalled that she was replacing the act of a woman who ran off to Bali to get married. If love constituted an emergency, then he assumed right. "I can tell you one thing," she said, "I'm doing everything I can to stay in town. But if Manhattan gives me the boot, I'll let you know before I go."

"Why would this city want to part with such a beautiful woman like yourself?"

She blushed in the shadow beneath the stage. "Because New

York City loves money more than beauty."

"Nah." He shook his head. "You have a lot to learn."

She looked at the little man dining out alone on a Wednesday night and fell in love with New York City a little more.

"Can I trust you with a secret?" she asked.

His eyes gleamed. "Certainly."

"You saw my audition, right? Well, at first I thought I was going to fall off of that piano. I had no faith in myself. But I pushed through."

His smile broadened. "Look at that, she's brave, as well." He held out his hand, painting her with his eyes. "I'm Ron. It's a pleasure to meet you." They shook. His long face held bloodhound eyes, pathetic and loving.

"I'm glad I can be your new Michelle," she said.

"Now, here's *my* secret," he whispered, leaning toward her. "My wife died, and throughout my year of mourning, I went to temple every day, sometimes two or three times, to thank her for being a good wife and for loving me. I had almost no social interaction at all. It was my duty to her. As of a month ago, I'm free to live again, free of grief and free of guilt. Free to be happy, Michelle. That's what I am."

"A whole year, giving thanks..." Ava replied. She had thought she had mourned Mom's death throughout her cancer, before she even died. But maybe she hadn't begun to grieve, or to thank her.

"The bonds we form take root deep within our souls," Ron said. "They are what nurtures us and keeps us from blowing over. We have to care for them. So, like I said, don't you go leaving me without saying good-bye!" He laughed, while his eyes begged *don't leave me.*

"I'm not going anywhere," she assured him and suddenly felt a huge responsibility. "So, what would you like to eat?"

"The lamb, please, and coffee, black."

"You've got it." She left to enter his order into the system.

Strangely enough, it seemed she'd made a friend...but would he tip?

2:00 a.m. Downstairs, the party continued in the dressing room. Women laughed and sang like girls as they squirmed out of their dresses for the night. Complaints about customers became jokes.

"Your performances went really well," Billie said, her locker only a few down. "They loved you." She twisted her hair back into a loose bun. Wearing a black velour jogging suit with matching black Nike's, her angelic quality diminished. "It looks like you've found your new job."

"For now, yes." Ava shut her locker. She was taking home $270 and a new dress, after paying back Rose the $120 and tipping out. One hundred of what she made came from Ron, a new bill folded into an origami crane. She had been surprised to find the little piece of art on his table after he had left. It struck her as both peculiar and sweet.

"I think this place just might save me," she said, walking with Billie out of the dressing room.

"There you go again!" Billie raised her hands in protest. "You still think working here will give you a life!"

"In a way, it might." Chris had managed to find a life under her stoop. Why couldn't she find one here?

Back upstairs, a bouncer hailed a cab for each woman and wrote her name in a log, along with the number of the cabbie. As Ava was getting into her cab, Mama Rose stepped outside, waving yellow roses. "I think you'll want these!"

"Yes!" Ava ran back. "Thank you! I forgot."

"You know what they say. It's the man *behind* your rose that makes your rose so special." Mama Rose's eyes twinkled under the streetlight.

Little did she know.

Chapter Twenty-Five

Another call from Phoebe and no message. Ava worried as she rode home in a cab from The Encore. What if Phoebe wanted to reconnect but was afraid to go through with the call? Or the Piranha could have skipped town from embarrassment over the canceled wedding. Phoebe could be alone and depressed. With prescription drugs...

Ava returned her call, not caring that it was three in the morning. The line went straight to voice mail. "Phoebe, it's me. I hope everything's all right. Call me when you can, okay? I'd like to talk."

She paid the cabbie and got out in front of her building. Chris was sound asleep, wisps of brown hair dancing on his cheek with a gentle wind. Seeing him curled up under his russet blanket, with his inflatable pillow and his loyal companion, life looked so simple.

Going up the stoop, her legs burned and her throat felt dry and scratchy from talking. But The Encore sure beat a desk job, and if she made $270 in tips five nights a week, she'd have her rent paid in less than two weeks. The rest could go toward living, and debt.

Inside her apartment, she dropped her gym bag on the floor. Makeup plastered to her face, dried sweat, layers of perfume on her skin...she'd wash up later. She flopped down on her futon, and the conversations repeating in her head faded until she couldn't hear them anymore.

219

A loud pounding sound pulled her out of sleep. Ava sprang off her futon, blurry-eyed, and scrambled for the light switch. The noise stopped. Was she dreaming? Outside her window, darkness, and a few cars soaring down the avenue, trailing red lights. The time on her phone read 4:00 a.m. She had only been asleep an hour.

The pounding came, again. *Bang! Bang! Bang!* Someone was outside her door, trying to get in. Chris? She pictured him asking for a glass of water. Or Julian, back from the dead? She envisioned Roberto and Luis looking for revenge and began to shake. That loose lock could break any moment...the door could bust open.

Think. She found her gym bag on the floor and took out her cell phone, although she should look through the peephole before calling for help. It wasn't a crime to knock on someone's door. "Patron Saint of Security, please be with me." She tiptoed down her hallway.

Every creak of the old wood floor made her cringe. Nearing the door, she held her breath, expecting another knock like the blast of a gun. But all was quiet. Maybe whoever was out there had given up and gone away? She wrinkled her brows, made her hands into fists, and peered through the peephole.

A tall man wearing a navy business suit and pale-yellow tie stared at his phone. She froze, afraid to move or breathe. From what she could see, he looked like Julian, except clean-shaven and with short hair—or was it slicked back? Either he was undercover as a businessman or she was losing her mind, seeing him in every stranger that knocked on her door.

The man suddenly stepped forward and looked through the peephole, as if trying to see into her thoughts.

"Agh!" She jumped back and covered her mouth.

"Ava! Open the door. It's me!"

"Julian?"

"Who else? I thought I'd stop by to show you my other side. How about opening the door?"

His *other* side? She watched her trembling hand release the lock and turn the handle. The door swung open, and he snatched her limp body up into his arms. Like a drug taking effect, she felt good all over, far beyond sore muscles and shot nerves.

Then her mind switched on. "Where have you been?" she asked, pulling away. "And why didn't you call?"

"Surprises are more fun."

"For you maybe. I just had a heart attack. And I've been worried about you, Julian. What happened the other night? You didn't give me the sign. Remember?" She tugged on her ear. "Were you undercover or what?"

He burst out laughing. "I'll tell you what, the next time I buy cocaine off of someone, assume I'm undercover." He grabbed her around the waist and raided her neck with kisses.

Now she was laughing, enjoying his absurd attention.

"Seriously, this is the first chance I've gotten to see you. You expect me to wait until morning?"

"No." She smiled.

"And tell me you didn't have a good time last night on the dance floor." He held her, swaying, as if there was music.

"Dancing with you was the highlight, for sure." If only it had lasted more than a few minutes. Still in his arms, she remembered Nina running out of the club in tears, and Julian following after her.

He suddenly pulled back. "Hey, thank you for the fantastic lead! I never know what to expect with you, a vow of chastity, a drug link..."

"So what happened? Did you arrest that guy—Marcus? Become his best friend? I still think you could've sent me a text or something. The last I saw you were snorting cocaine, which isn't good. And now look at you! A suit? Who are you really, Julian?"

"Just a different dress code. I was in court all day."

"Locking up Marcus?"

"Man, you're really obsessed with Marcus. No, today was routine, a probation violation and other boring stuff. Marcus I'm still working on. He's my 'in' to a bigger ring. Very nice work, by the way. I owe you one."

"You sure do."

"So, are we going to stand in your hallway until the sun rises? Or do I get to see the rest of your apartment?"

"This way." She gestured toward her living/bedroom.

"You don't have a roommate, do you?" He moseyed down her hall.

"No, I have this palatial studio apartment all to myself." Was he hoping to stay the night? He still had that cheetah-like quality, the way he moved, slinked, so attractive in a dangerous way. Only now he looked more the type to settle down.

He stood in front of her futon, a pensive expression on his face. It would've been better if he just made fun it.

"All right," she said, breaking the silence, "let's get this out in the open. My place is a dump compared to yours."

He flipped over a throw pillow on the floor with his foot. "Not everyone is into furniture."

"Well, I think a futon qualifies for furniture. Feel free to sit."

He took off his shoes and jacket and lay back, feet crossed, looking totally at ease. "I can chill here, no problem."

She sat on the edge of her futon, feeling tense and uncomfortably warm. And somehow wide-awake. Just the thought of kissing him and a burning frustration deep in her abdomen made her want to squirm out of her skin.

Julian shifted over onto his side, giving her room to lie down next to him.

Smiling uncontrollably, she slid in, facing him, this other Julian. "So, are you hiding your tattoos?"

"Do you think you can find them?" His lips turned up at the corners, sneaky-like.

"Maybe, if I looked." She loosened his tie, not one hundred percent sure she should. There they were—nostrils flared, bared fangs, soulless pupils, and silvery scales. Tempted further, she began unbuttoning his shirt, when he rolled over onto his back.

"So, anyway," he said, talking to the ceiling, "after you left the club, Marcus and I hung out until closing, and then continued the night at an after-hours party with a couple of his buddies."

"Oh? Was that necessary—to get evidence or something?"

"The guy thinks I'm his best customer! I went home at six in the morning, jumped into the shower, and worked a full day. Don't ask me how I do it."

"I think I know, and it scares me."

"Seriously, the guy has fallen for me. He thinks I'm a party promoter."

"Right, because I told him that's what you do."

"Did you?" He looked at her, surprised. "I missed that. Well, tonight I got him into a Sony BMG party at the Soho House. *Real* exclusive. It took me a few phone calls to get him and his crew on the list. But was he impressed! Pushed a gram on me, free."

"Did you take it?"

"I told him drugs are bad for you, laughed out loud, and then took it. Of course, I took it. But I wasn't about to pull another all-nighter, although I might as well have. I'm so tired, I can't sleep. Sometimes I'll have insomnia for days before I finally crash."

"Sounds awful. How often do you do cocaine?"

"You talk like I *want* to do it." He sat up. "Ava, you can't freak out over my work. If you start worrying about me, you'll spend all your time worrying. I take a lot of risks. Drugs is just one of them, and I can't be calling every hour to let you know I'm okay. I shouldn't even be talking to you about it."

"I'm not freaking out," she said, sitting up as well. "All right, maybe a little. It's just—health first, right? What if you become an addict?"

"Won't happen, trust me. I'd never throw my life away to drugs. I see that kind of stuff all the time."

"Isn't that what all addicts say?"

In one movement, he pinned her down and kissed her lips hard until it hurt. "You wouldn't hold my career against me, would you?" he whispered against her cheek. His breath smelled like strong mouthwash and felt hot on her skin.

"No," she replied, letting him win and winning his affection. "I like that you're a cop. It's admirable and courageous and... attractive."

He brushed his lips over hers, over her ear...her collarbone...

moving toward her heart. She sighed from sheer pleasure and closed her eyes.

He pulled back, like ripping a Band-Aid off in one swift motion, thinking you can avoid the pain. "Did I tell you I was in court today with Helena Morganbesser?" he asked. "I think you met her. My friend, the D.A."

Ava took a long breath, fatigue rushing in. She couldn't keep up with his insomnia. "Sure, I remember her." Razor-short hair and hard eyes. A first impression she wouldn't call positive.

"That woman is a warrior. I'm not kidding. No mercy." He spoke as if talking about his favorite superhero.

"You mean she's a feminist?" Ava asked, her impression of Helena swelling to Wonder Woman dimensions.

"Whatever a feminist is. All I know is she's a fighter in the courtroom, and she's winning on a predominantly male playing field."

His admiration for Helena hit like the blow of a wrecking ball. Ava pictured herself in the leopard-print dress, fighting her own fears on top of a piano. Why had she considered The Encore an accomplishment? She had felt proud...of what?

Julian looked at her and suspicion flashed in his eyes. She felt guilty before knowing the charge.

"So, what's with all the makeup?" he asked. "A date? A new job?"

"Oh, shoot!" The wrecking ball on its back swing. She ran for the bathroom.

"Hey, you can't hide the evidence now." He stood in the doorway, prohibiting her from shutting herself in. "Look, it's your business what you did tonight, but for the record, you've got nothing to hide. Not with me. Okay? If you were out on a date or whatever, fine. Just tell me. Were you?"

She looked up from the sink, her face dripping-wet. "I wasn't trying to hide anything. I just forgot about the makeup." She dried off with a towel.

"And..."

"And I got a new job."

"That's a good thing, I assume."

"Yes, absolutely. I'm dancing, more or less. At this place on Sixth Avenue called The Encore." She pointed to her garment bag on the floor. "Tonight was my first night."

"The Encore? That old cabaret? Is it still there?" He went to her bag. The leopard-print dress was a wrinkled mess. "Right," he said, examining it. "The waitresses perform in chintzy evening gowns and hang all over the customers."

Chintzy? "I'm not hanging all over anyone. I perform Michelle Pfeiffer in *The Fabulous Baker Boys*—on top of a piano. I got a loud applause, actually."

"Way to go! A fan club of dirty old men."

"All right, I know it's not Radio City Music Hall, but the job is perfect for now. I can pay my bills and still have my days free to audition."

He let the dress drop to the floor. "Come on, The Encore is as close to stripping as you can get without taking off your clothes!"

"I don't see it that way at all!" His interrogation squeezed her into a corner. She wanted space—away from his judgment.

"Seriously, Ava, you're a hypocrite—keeping a vow of chastity while basically selling sex for tips."

"Wait a second, you're calling *me* a hypocrite? Hypocrisy is you doing the drugs of the dealers you're busting!" She'd said too much, gone too far.

"I should go." He walked to the door. "I thought...forget it."

"Julian, I have to start somewhere. I'm going for my dream, a career in dance. You're not being fair."

"You're not being honest. You said that you admire my work, but you don't trust it. You don't trust me. I'll see you later." He left, shutting the door behind him.

She could hear his footsteps fade in the stairwell. Sinking down onto her futon, she let him go.

Chapter Twenty-Six

The next morning Ava opened her windows to the smell of warm garbage. Not the fresh air she was hoping for on a sticky-hot day. Out on the fire escape, her neglected geranium was a goner. She gave it water anyway. Was Julian's criticism fair? Hanging all over men...a stripper...a *hypocrite*?

She sat down at the kitchen table and iced her instant coffee. A nearby church chimed its daily noon service, twelve dongs, until the final note hung in the air. Everything was still. Chris's yellow roses, standing tall now in a vase on the windowsill, glowed in a ray of sunlight.

Forward to the end, and then forward again, Mom used to say.

Ava sighed. *Thank you for your little sayings, Mom, powerful enough to restore hope.*

She turned on her computer and Googled *The Fabulous Baker Boys*, which took her straight to a video clip of Michelle Pfeiffer in the "Makin' Whoopee" scene. The clip was three minutes, and from beginning to end Ms. Pfeiffer was in the moment, every word, every move, born from her soul. The audience didn't breathe, or so it seemed. Perhaps she was breathing for them. For those three minutes, she could've been the life force for everyone watching.

Ava sat back in her chair and thought of Ron, her first customer...free to live, free to be happy. Was there such a thing as being free to love? According to Maggie, yes, and fear was her solitary confinement.

But how could she *not* fear for Julian? If she expected him to accept her, then she had better accept him without question—or keep looking. Ava shuddered at the thought of a life spent searching for perfect love. Why did it seem that God was singling her out when it came to finding a life-partner? She had faced her fear of death, supporting Mom when it was time to let go. She was actively in pursuit of meaningful work. She even risked rejection to uphold a vow of chastity. What else was there? What else was she supposed to achieve or overcome?

Ava took out her mobile. Maggie answered right away.

"Hey, I was just about to call you." Her voice missed its usual effervescence. "Any luck with auditions?"

"Open your laptop," Ava said, desperate for another opinion. "Ready? Now Google Michelle Pfeiffer in *The Fabulous Baker Boys.*" A minute later, she could hear the music through the phone. *Another bride, another June, another sunny honeymoon...*

"I saw the movie," Maggie said. "What about it?"

"That's my new job, at a cabaret in midtown. I think things are finally falling into place."

"On top of a piano? *You?* I can't picture it."

"Exactly, that's the whole point. I'm embracing life, no boundaries, no judgments...no fear!"

"You sound like a Nike ad, but that's great. I'm super happy for you. Confused, but happy."

"I'm going to stick with it, Maggie. I can do this and stay true to myself."

"There's more to the job than a piano, isn't there?" Maggie said.

"Yes. I also waitress, and the club has an all-male clientele."

"Ava, I understand that you're set on dancing, but this job seems like a giant step into the unknown and potentially dangerous. Is it worth it?"

"There are tons of bouncers, rules, and precautions. I'll be fine."

"I don't know. The type of men who go to those places... they become obsessed. What if one of them follows you home?"

"It won't happen. Trust me!" This was *not* the pep talk she was hoping for. "So, what about you? Have you told Marc yet?

It's going on two weeks since our girls' night of regret."

"No. He's in Chicago this week for work. I couldn't tell him before he left—he might not come back!"

"Maggie, I know it's hard, but—"

"I'll tell him. I promise, as soon as he gets home. The confession is eating my brain alive. I can't live with it any longer."

"Then stop putting it off! You can stay with me if he kicks you out of the house."

"No offense, but that's *not* an incentive." Melanie cried in the background. "She's up. I've gotta go."

"Call me once you've told him, or anytime."

Back to the video. Ava filled her lungs with air, as if readying to plunge into deep waters. Michelle Pfeiffer wore a red dress, earrings like chandeliers, and a sparkling bracelet. Ava took in the whole ensemble. If she was going to do this, she'd do it right...and for under $200 dollars. It'd be an investment in her career. Phoebe, of course, would say it was impossible to buy an evening gown for under $1000. What she didn't know was that when it came to art, good food, and shopping, Manhattan had many secrets.

Ava looked at her phone lying quietly on the kitchen counter. Nothing from Phoebe, not even another hang up. There was no telling what was going through her mind at this point, and it was really frustrating, like listening to music turned down so low you couldn't make out the song. Perhaps she was still angry and seeking revenge. Or was she reconciled and wanting to make peace? Ava forewent tact and tried again. This time, Phoebe answered.

"It's you!"

"Phoebe, hi. Am I calling at a—"

"No! I'm so happy to hear from you. In fact, I was just thinking we should get together. Today."

"Today?"

What should you do after breaking your engagement? Remain friends with his mother?

"Just a little lunch," Phoebe said.

That could mean a side salad and a three-hour chat, but it didn't matter. "Sure. That would be nice." Ava thought of Josh's reaction. A clandestine friendship with Phoebe would be ridiculous.

"Shall we meet at Fred's, say one o'clock?" Phoebe suggested one of their old favorites, as if nothing had changed and they still had Josh in common.

Ava dropped her leopard-print dress off at the dry cleaners and then walked to the subway. It felt strange going to Barney's department store now that she was out of the industry, even if she was there for lunch and not to spy on the competition.

On the top floor, the scene at Fred's was simultaneously chatty and composed. Men and women, ranging in age from early twenties to golden age, wore their designer labels like badges, suggesting degrees of power. Phoebe, likely dressed in Chanel, would rank high.

"Table for one?" the host asked.

"No, I'm meeting someone, a woman in her late 50s, dark-brown hair with red highlights. At least that's how it was a few weeks ago." Inspired by chocolate covered cherries.

He smiled. "Phoebe Copeland. Right this way."

She followed him to a corner table. Jackie O sunglasses matched Phoebe's black and white Chanel-logo dress. Ava went to her with open arms.

"Sweetheart!" Phoebe stood and wrapped her in the floral scent of No. 19. Forgiveness felt like a homecoming, and they hugged as if it had been years. "Oh, Ava. I thought I'd never see you again!" She slipped off the sunglasses, revealing bloodshot eyes.

"I was afraid of that, too." Ava sat down at their table. "Phoebe, are you okay?"

"I'm not sure how to answer that. I have my health, but... sweetie, how do you look so composed?" She dabbed her eyes with a tissue.

"I don't know. Maybe because I've come to accept certain things in my life."

"Well, if there's one thing I wish I could take back, it's

barging into your office that day, screaming like a woman off her antidepressants. I might be heartbroken and feel like I'm losing my mind, but it was wrong. Can we put that behind us?"

"Phoebe, trust me, it was behind us the moment it happened. I understand how upset you are. I do."

"Well, you don't know everything." Phoebe looked up as a waiter appeared. "Oh, right. Food. Ava, do we need menus, or should we order the chicken breast like always?"

"The chicken, like always." Returning to a healthy diet wouldn't be a bad thing.

The waiter noted it and poured two glasses of water.

"And two Diet Cherry 7UPs," Phoebe added and winked at Ava.

"Did you tell Josh we're having lunch?" Ava asked.

Phoebe shook her head. "I didn't. He's in Las Vegas...his bachelor party." She looked down.

"His what?" Ava's mouth hung open, and for a second she thought she was being forced into marriage. "But the wedding is...off, of course. Right?"

"Yes. Yes, it is. He's celebrating anyway. I know. It's callous and wrong. Please, he's not turning to me for advice. He hardly talks to me at all. It's as if he blames me."

"He can't blame you for our breakup. If anything, you were a reason *not* to call it off. I didn't want to lose you."

Phoebe reached across the table for Ava's hand. "Well, that's not going to happen. We're friends, and Josh will just have to accept that."

Ava imagined him shrugging it off.

Their drinks arrived. "Here's to us!" Phoebe said, balancing an unsteady smile. "By the way, I tried calling you at work. Rhonda said you were no longer with Bergdorf. Is this true?"

"I got canned."

"Goodness! That can't possibly be true!"

"Don't worry, I've found something else, something temporary. I'll be fine."

"Temp work doesn't pay. Are you still in the fashion industry at least?"

"I'm a waitress-slash-performer at a cabaret." She didn't expect Phoebe to approve, but was intent on telling her the truth, for better or for worse.

"Is it safe?" Phoebe asked, wrinkling her nose, as if she could smell the club from where they were.

"Very safe. The place is legendary. Old school, like Cipriani's on Fifth Avenue, kind of."

"I don't know. I hate to think of you working late nights." Phoebe looked down at her hands. "And I understand that you're paying for the wedding." She met Ava's eyes. "How are you surviving?"

"There's always a way, isn't there?" Chris appeared in her mind, sound asleep under the moonlight. "Listen, let's not talk about money. Can that be a rule?"

"I'm worried about you, that's all." Phoebe sipped her drink, her perfect eyebrows creased. "What does your mother say about all these changes?"

Ava gathered her breath, knowing there would never be a good time to tell Phoebe, and it would be worse to wait.

"I need to tell you something. My mom...Phoebe, she passed away." Ava winced as dismay seized Phoebe's hopeful expression. For the first time, she understood how exhausted Mom must have felt consoling her all those difficult years.

"No." Phoebe covered her mouth with her hand. "I—I'm so sorry." Tears came, again. "She was such a lovely woman. I can't believe it...all of a sudden, and now she's gone."

"I lived in fear of getting that phone call," Ava said after a while. "It took years, but then it happened so quickly. It's strange, but I haven't really cried since the last time we were together, in the hospital room. Even at the funeral, I felt dry inside, kind of hollow and airy. There was a day of calling hours, a few days of sorting and rearranging, and now it's over."

"Sweetheart, I honestly don't know how you're handling everything."

"I just am. In a way, I feel grateful. Phoebe, I saw her reach for God, just before she died. I know she's safe."

"Oh, that's wonderful. You were with her. You saw her off."

Lunch was set down before them, and they ate in silence. Tears rolled down Phoebe's cheeks, one and then another. "I can't stop crying. I'm sorry, I just..." She patted her eyes, smearing mascara.

Ava dipped her napkin in her water and reached across the table. "Here, let me help." She gently wiped away the makeup under Phoebe's eyes. "Is there something else bothering you? I have a feeling there's more."

Phoebe sniffled. "I can't hide anything."

"Okay, rule number two in our new friendship." Ava looked straight at her. "No hiding feelings."

Phoebe took a deep breath and sat up straight in her chair. "Ava, I need to ask a favor. You don't have to say yes—"

"Anything. Of course. What is it?"

"Can I stay with you for a while?"

"You mean in my apartment?"

"Not long. Just a few days or so. I need a place where I can sort things out, away from Barry and our circle of friends."

"Well, yes, of course. You're welcome for as long as you want. But you've never seen my apartment. It's small. And unfurnished."

"If it's good enough for you, it's good enough for me. I hate to impose. I'd go to a spa, but I don't want to be alone and surrounded by strangers right now. I feel so lost."

"Is everything all right with Mr. Copeland?"

"No. We had an argument and he blocked me access to our savings account. Can you believe it? How dare he!" Phoebe's hand shook as she sipped her soda. "It's not just that. You can call me batty, or just plain immature, but I want him to miss me. I want him to come after me, for once. To appreciate how much I love him!"

"You're not batty at all. You're doing what you feel is right. You're listening to yourself for once! Phoebe, I fully support you and am thrilled to have you as a roommate."

"Thank you, Ava. Thank you so much."

"So, we'll have to share my futon, or else buy an air mattress." Her mind raced, imagining the impossible. "I only have one closet. Will that be a problem? And there's this homeless guy living below my stoop. Just so you know. He's really nice, though. I can introduce you."

"Oh, that's probably not necessary."

"He'll make you feel at home, trust me."

Phoebe put down cash for the bill. "And I'll pay your rent. I'm not totally broke."

"Of course you won't! You're my guest."

"I insist on giving you something."

"You're treating me to lunch. That's enough. Thank you."

The host retrieved Phoebe's Louis Vuitton luggage from the coat check.

"You're already packed?" Ava asked.

"Just some essentials. I didn't think you'd send me out on the streets." Phoebe put her arm around Ava's shoulders and squeezed. "Thank you."

They took the elevator to street level, and reality hit. Phoebe would be going home with her. Josh's mother. She should be panicking! But she wasn't. As long as she didn't let Phoebe take over her life, it could work and they could have a *real* friendship. That was what she wanted all along.

"I have a little shopping to do before I go to work tonight," Ava said. "Do you want to come with me?"

"Of course! A shopping spree is exactly what we need."

"A spree? No, I don't have the money—oops, I'm not supposed to mention money. Forget I said that. All I need is a dress and a pair of four-inch heels."

"*Four* inches? Okay. Well, we're here at Barney's. Why don't we look around? Or would you rather go downtown to Jeffrey's?"

"Neither. We're going to a store you've never been to before." It was like putting Phoebe on a leash. "It's just two stops on the subway."

"On the *subway*?"

Outside, Phoebe hailed the first available cab. "You made two rules, now it's my turn. When you're with me, we take taxis. Now let's go." They squeezed in with her suitcase.

I ALWAYS *Cry* at *Weddings*

On 31st Street and Fifth Avenue, Phoebe stood on the sidewalk, shading her eyes from the sun while peering into Cheap Jack's. "Ava, sweetheart, are you sure you want to go in there?"

"Don't be ridiculous. It's a famous vintage clothing store. They have name brand stuff going back to the '20s. You'll love it. Come on." Ava held open the door as Phoebe stepped inside.

"Good grief!" She held her nose. "I feel like I'm in someone's basement."

Cheap Jack's did have the distinct odor of "old." And the volume of clothes, sorted by decade, would require work if they were going to find anything. Poor Phoebe, accustomed to sipping champagne in dressing rooms.

"Once you get over the initial shock, it's a find, trust me. Look, there are couches if you need to rest. They even do custom tailoring."

"Ava, you've changed since breaking your engagement. Now you're taking *me* places." She smiled. "So, what is it you're looking for?"

"An evening dress. Think *enticing*. Salacious!"

"Really! Oh, fun." She went straight to the '80s and pulled out a long red dress. "Look at this! Vivienne Westwood, Gold Label. And only seventy-five dollars. Dear, you could wear this number to the Grammys!"

It could've been the dress in the video. Rhinestone straps and an open back..."It's perfect."

Phoebe handed it to her and continued browsing. "Look! Diane von Fürstenberg from the '70s. Fifties Chanel. I'm a vintage shopper and didn't even know it!" She pulled out dresses from every era.

"I don't have time to try on all that," Ava said.

"Who said *you*?" Phoebe replied. "These are for me!"

"Go crazy." Ava found a pair of dangling earrings and matching bracelet that shimmered in the light. Twenty dollars for the set. She went into the dressing room to change, feeling like Clark Kent in a phone booth, about to step out not as Superman, but Michelle, the Piano Dancer!

"What do you think, Phoebe?" She turned in front of the mirrors and couldn't stop smiling.

"Beyond red!" Phoebe dropped her pile of dresses on the couch and stared. "Now, did you say you need it for work?" She cocked her head to one side, no doubt trying to visualize her waiting tables.

"It will do the job, trust me."

Ava changed back into herself and found Phoebe sitting on the couch in her pile of dresses. "Are you taking a break?"

"I'm fooling myself, buying all these dresses. I'm old! My breasts sag. I have wrinkles, and my husband doesn't want me anymore." She broke down crying.

"That's not true, Phoebe. You're a beautiful woman, inside *and* out." Ava moved the clothes out of the way and sat down next to her. "I'm sorry. I feel to blame for all this."

Phoebe sat up and looked her in the eyes as if she had reached a decision, or somehow found new courage. "No. I understand why you called it off. I do. You felt insignificant with Josh, as though your needs, your feelings, and your opinions didn't count as much as his. And it just wasn't worth it."

"Oh, Phoebe." Ava hugged her, filled with relief. And empathy.

Chapter Twenty-Seven

They climbed inside a southbound cab, Ava with her Cheap Jack's package and Phoebe holding her Louis Vuitton luggage.

"I don't know what to do with myself," Phoebe said, looking like a girl traveling alone for the first time.

"You're entering a new phase in life!" Ava said, feeling resolute about Phoebe's independence. "All you need to do is keep moving forward."

"Right. Forward. I knew that I could somehow figure it out with you."

"Just think, you're free to make your own choices. You can do all the things you've always wanted to do."

"I thought I *was* doing the things I've always wanted to do," Phoebe said, despondent. "But I suppose I can find new things." She fanned herself with a rock band flyer she had absently picked up at Cheap Jack's. The AC in the cab was no stronger than if they were blowing air on each other.

"You know what?" Phoebe said after a while. "When he comes running after me, he's going to be surprised. I'm going to take up hobbies, meet new friends, maybe even volunteer. I'll be a changed woman, and I'm not just talking about a new hair color!"

"Good." Ava tapped on the plastic divider. "You can stop here." The cab swerved to the curb on First Avenue and 13th Street.

Phoebe paid the fare with her bankcard. "Thank goodness I still have money in my checking account," she said. "Barry only locked me out of our savings."

"He can't be too worried about you if he sees you're spending money." Ava questioned the longevity of Phoebe's "big" change.

"Oh, I must be leaving a paper trail wherever I go!" Her expression turned pleasantly sneaky. "But he'll never guess where I'm staying."

They stood on the sidewalk, Phoebe a glitch in the East Village flow of grungy students and weathered longtime inhabitants. "It must be a hundred degrees out and you're not even shiny," Ava said, wiping her forehead.

"The right makeup, sweetie. Hey, aren't we shopping for shoes now?" Phoebe looked around as if Bergdorf or Neiman's might pop up.

Ava pointed to Gabay's Outlet. "That's right, and this is the place."

An hour later, Phoebe sat on the floor amidst the wreckage of opened shoeboxes. She held up a pair of Jimmy Choo four-inch red stilettos as if finding a survivor. "Look what we have here!"

Ava crawled over boxes and tissue paper to examine the shoes. Three delicate gold chains draped the top and one hung from the ankle strap. She slipped them on, and they fit perfectly. "Watch out, Michelle Pfeiffer!"

"Yahoo!" Phoebe cheered.

"And they're a steal for one twenty-nine." Ava took them to the cashier and put the forty dollars she was over-budget on the only credit card she had that wasn't yet maxed-out.

After a cab ride to the west side, she led Phoebe into a drug store around the corner from her apartment. "This will only take a minute."

She found the hair aisle and glanced over boxes of dye before deciding on the one that pictured a woman with radiant cherry-red hair. "See, Phoebe, I'm with you on this journey of self-improvement."

"You're going red!" Phoebe shrieked. "I love it!"

Ava paid, and they went back out into the piercing sun. As they walked down 22nd Street toward her building, Ava noticed a woman trailing three beautiful children, two girls and a boy, holding hands. She watched them pass by. "You know, sometimes I have this fear that I'm not meant to get married and have a family."

"Funny. I was just thinking the same thing about grandchildren. At least you can have children on your own. Sperm donors are very popular nowadays."

"I'm too traditional for that. But if I do have children, you can be their grandma, okay?"

"Can I, really? Oh, Ava, I'll be the best grandma!"

"I have no doubt you will be."

"They can call me Fefe. Goodness, we need to get you married! Who do I know?"

"No one! Sorry. I appreciated your introduction to Josh, but this time I want to find my own future husband."

"Fine. Just get on it, already!"

Ava laughed. "Oh, sure, coming right up." Only Phoebe could get away with such an exasperating comment.

Her building was just up ahead. The sidewalk looked like a graveyard for gum. Grimy vans and delivery trucks paraded the streets with WASH ME! and other more graphic messages written on them in spray paint or finger art.

"Welcome to authentic city grit," Ava said, unable to ignore it with Phoebe at her side. "I bet you can't find litter around Central Park West like you can here."

"It's charming," Phoebe said. She looked exhausted.

Ava stopped walking when they reached the stoop. "That's too bad. Chris, my homeless friend, isn't here just now. I wanted to introduce you to him."

"Where do you suppose he is?"

"I don't know, but he sure keeps busy." They went inside. "Are you ready for your workout, Phoebe? I forgot to mention the five flights up. Here, let me take your suitcase. I'm used to this."

Rounding the third floor, Phoebe stopped, gripping the banister. "This is so good for me," she gasped. "I keep thinking, what if Barry chases after some fit woman half my age, instead of chasing after me? How am I supposed to compete with *that*?"

"I didn't think wives had to compete for their husbands. You're beautiful, Phoebe, at any age. And you're more fun than anyone I know."

They started climbing again, and Ava took her arm for the last flight.

Unlocking 5C, she stopped before opening the door and turned to Phoebe. "I'll understand if you change your mind and want to go somewhere else."

"Don't be silly and open your door."

Ava led her inside, watching for a reaction. Phoebe moved slowly, looking up at the paint-chipped ceiling and down to the warped wood floor.

"I keep the windows open for a cross-breeze," Ava said. "It can get pretty stuffy in here."

"It's a quaint little apartment," Phoebe said, turning on her unbeatable spirit. "I'll think of it like camping. My first venture into the wilderness."

"You could look at it that way. I'm sure we'll have fun. We always do."

Phoebe took her hand. "Thank you for letting me stay with you. I can't face my friends right now...all the gossip. I love them, of course—just not when they're talking about my problems. And I *am* the hot topic these days, what with... everything."

"I know." Ava hugged her—bubbly, vulnerable Phoebe. "You're safe from all that with me." She went to her hope box. "Now, let's get you settled. I have an extra set of keys in here for you." She handed them to her, Josh's set. Who would've thought?

Next, she went to the closet and pushed her work clothes to the back. "And here's some hanging space. If you need more, we can get rid of these suits."

"Don't be ridiculous. You'll be back to corporate America in no time, making decisions that will change the course of fashion."

Ava looked at her straight-faced. "Let's hope not."

Phoebe waved her off and went to explore the refrigerator. "What do we have here? A turkey wrap, half-eaten. Cheese, looks like Munster. And all-natural peanut butter. Good for you, buying the real stuff. Oh, and a container of milk, out-dated. I might go grocery shopping while you're at work."

"Feel free." Ava glanced at the clock. Only two hours before Rose's time-check in the dressing room. "I've got to get this dye on my hair. Make yourself at home, all right? Take whatever you need."

Forty-five minutes later, Ava dashed out of the bathroom in her robe. "Well? Am I a redhead, or what?"

Phoebe, sitting on the futon, looked up from her *Cosmo*. "You did it! That's a very bold color, Ava. *Very* bold."

"Do you like it?"

"You know how I love color. And you've got color! Where's your makeup?"

"Oh, they have makeup at the club. There's even a woman who will do it for you for twenty dollars."

"You mean that *used* stuff the bathroom attendants put out for tips? No, no, no." Phoebe climbed off the futon, rather awkwardly. "We've got work to do." She went into a black Chanel cosmetic case and pulled out brand-name makeup from Yves Saint Laurent to NARS: gothic eyeliners, lipstick called Burnt Roses, base, bronzing cream, and even a luminizer to fake "fresh." She lined them up along the vanity like a brigade. "You can't be willy-nilly about this. Not with hair like that."

Ava peeked at herself in the mirror from time to time, watching as her oval eyes became wider...her cheekbones more pronounced...her lashes, longer, thicker.

Phoebe pursed her lips, dabbing and smearing with the intensity of an artist. "I used to be really good at this. You know I worked at Elizabeth Arden, eons ago, before I met Barry. I did his sister's makeup for her wedding and ended up going as his date!"

"I love that story," Ava mumbled, trying not to move her lips.

"Six months later we were married and the feature of The Vows column in the Sunday Style section of *The Times*! Of course, I've told you all that." Phoebe stepped back to admire her work. "I hope Barry is somewhere remembering the good times. You're all set, sweetie."

"I'm sure he is." Ava pictured him keeping obsessive watch over Phoebe's checking account. She peeked at herself in the mirror. "Wow! I actually look rested! Thank you!"

"I'm not as good as I used to be. You're just an easy subject."

Ava checked the time on her phone. "I have to grab my stuff and go. Will you be okay?"

"Worry about yourself. I'll keep camp."

Ava rushed outside in jeans and a T-shirt. The red dress awaited its debut in a garment bag. Her new shoes and jewelry were tucked away in her gym bag. She wasn't "Michelle" yet.

Glancing over the edge of the stoop, she smiled. Chris was reading *The Alchemist*. She went quickly down the steps. "Do you recognize me?"

"Hey, Ava." He brushed his hair out of his eyes. "Wow!"

She casually swept a red lock off her shoulders. "What do you think?"

"You're a redhead!"

"I know! I got the job at The Encore! I've been dying to tell you."

"You made the audition! Congratulations!"

"Thanks." She clutched her bags, remembering Julian's reaction. Would Chris think less of her, too?

"I have a question for you," he said, jumping up. "Real quick."

"What is it?"

He paused, staring at her, and then actually blushed. "Sorry. It's a little shocking, to be honest. You look good, of course, just not at all like yourself...or at least how I knew you."

"I decided it was time I stood out."

"Absolutely. You made it to the stage, Ava. You're on your way!"

"I suppose. I mean, it's not my *ideal* job. But a start is a start."

"No truer words spoken. So, where can I get tickets?"

241

"Oh. No, it's not like that. I'll explain later, okay? I can't be late." She started down the street.

"Wait, my question!" He followed after her. "I've seen you buying food from the deli on the corner. Is that where you do all your shopping? Fruits and vegetables, too?"

"Yes. Pretty much."

"Okay, well, they apparently receive their vegetable delivery once a week. They're probably buying them from suppliers who are loading on the pesticides. It isn't just a matter of taste. We're talking about long-term health. I'd consider going organic if I were you."

"Good tip. Thanks."

"Whole Foods Market is only a few blocks away." He pointed up the street.

She looked in the other direction and flagged down a taxi for the sake of time. "Whole Foods, right."

"Pick up a garlic crusher, while you're at it. I have a recipe that will send your socks, or dance shoes, flying!"

She laughed and got into the cab. His passion for life always surprised her.

"You'd be amazed what you can make on your own," he said through the cab's open window. "And I was thinking maybe we—"

"Another time. I promise." As the cab sped off, she turned in her seat. Chris was strolling back to his cardboard, hands in pockets, head down, saying something to Chickpea.

Chapter Twenty-Eight

Ava ran down the red carpet and made it into the dressing room with five minutes to spare. *Phew.* No late fee.

"Hi!" Billie wiggled into a lacy gold gown, momentarily stuck getting it over her hips. "There's. No. Room to. Breathe in this thing!"

"It's beautiful, though. Where did you buy it?" Ava smiled as she hung up her dress, remembering Cheap Jack's with Phoebe.

"Ladies!" Rose trampled their conversation. "I suggest you stop chitchatting and get dressed." She looked at her watch. "You have zero minutes to get upstairs to your tables."

"I just need to change," Ava said, doing the same wiggle dance into her dress.

"See you up there." Billie shut her locker and started out of the dressing room. "Hey, I love your wig, by the way. You go, girl!"

"I'd loan it to you, except it doesn't come off!" Ava called after her and did a double take in the mirrors. She looked hard-edged. Cold and brazen. Chris was right; she didn't look like herself. Of course, that was her goal...only, something about it felt wrong, as though she were now hiding from her true self.

Out on the floor, only three tables were seated in the club, and not one in Section 7. Her jewelry sparkled. Her red dress and shoes gripped her body, raring to go, but she had to sit and wait...and hope for tips to walk through the door.

A Caribbean woman sang Nat King Cole, while Ava shivered from the AC. Crossing her arms and legs conserved some body heat but wasn't doing anything for her debt.

A lanky brunette named Ella sat next to her, cuddling one

of the votive candles for warmth. "This place drives me crazy. You're either so cold your nose runs, or you're sweating your buns off."

Ava smiled, appreciating the camaraderie. "I hope it picks up. I feel like I'm in a club for bored women in evening gowns."

"That's a good one!" Ella laughed. "My guess is that it will pick up soon. Thursday nights are normally hopping."

The woman on stage closed her eyes as she sang, perhaps imagining herself at Carnegie Hall, or singing to her love. Ava followed Ella's example and cupped a candle close to her chest. As 6:00 became 6:45, telling each other that the night was still young didn't help.

"Is this place still your saving grace?" Billie asked, stopping by to say hello.

"It feels more like my golden prison," Ava replied, regretting her investment in her new career. Even a good deal on a dress was a bad one if you weren't making money. "Have you ever had a night when you didn't make enough to tip out?"

"Anything's possible here," Billie said. "But you tip out regardless."

Around 7:30, customers started coming in, and the penguins got busy seating people. The Best of The Fabulous Baker Boys was up. Ava shook off her chill and went backstage.

"Ready?" Giovanni asked in the shadows. "Bet we have a full house before the curtain closes, so give it your all."

"I'm not performing for the audience," she whispered back. "I'm doing this for me—so you can be sure I'll give it my all."

"Let's see it then," he replied, and they walked to the piano. With that flip of his tails, like a concert pianist, Giovanni sat down at the bench. She picked up the mike as the curtain reeled open and the MC announced, "We all love 'Makin' Whoopee,' so let's give a big welcome for Michelle!"

A few people clapped. The music started, and with her heart pounding in double-time, she softly, slowly sang:

Another bride, another June, another sunny honeymoon...

She stepped up onto the bench, and then again beside the keys. Another step and she was standing on top of the piano, the mountain peak of her life. Fear crept up her chest as if wanting to get in on the glory, but she wouldn't let it take over. This was her time to shine, and to be a brazen redhead, if that's what she wanted.

The groom is nervous. He answers twice...

She swiveled her hips, moving down, until gracefully, she rested on her stomach. She could just see Michelle Pfeiffer in the video, while she herself crept low like a stalking cheetah, stealing across the watery black surface of the piano. Blood red strands of her hair fell over one eye. She rested on her elbows and sang to Giovanni:

Picture a little love nest, down where the roses cling...

He looked up from the keys and smiled, mouthing the word, *Wow!*

She rolled over onto her back and sat forward without missing a beat. Then, while swaying her hips, she moved to standing for the final verse. Singing out, taking full ownership of the moment, she stood tall, and yes, she felt proud. Julian didn't know what he was missing.

But don't forget folks, that's what you get folks, for makin' whoopee!

With her chest rising and falling, Ava anticipated that breath-catching silence before a burst of standing applause, just like in the video.

Someone clapped, and then others joined in. No one shouted *Hooray!*—except for Billie, who even whistled. Ava took her bow. The curtain closed.

"Well?" she asked Giovanni, wiping her forehead with the back of her hand.

"Very nice," he said and proceeded to put on his two-way radio. "The wig works, surprisingly." He headed for backstage. "Good luck on the floor!"

After a glass of water, her heart rate returned to normal and she was ready to start making money. Two middle-aged men sat in her section. One had a trimmed beard and was occupied with his iPhone. The other, a handsome man in a *Twilight* sort of way, with light-brown hair and sideburns, watched as she walked toward them.

"Hi! I'm Michelle." She offered him her hand.

"Steve. Nice to meet you." His handshake was gentle. "You're a natural on that piano, Michelle."

She laughed. "If you only knew."

"I know one thing. You have beautiful feet." He stared at them, as if fixated.

Looking down, she had to assume he meant her shoes. "I just got them today. They're pretty extreme, aren't they?"

His eyes twinkled, laughing. "Yes, I find your feet to be *very* extreme. But did you say you just got them today?"

"Oh, you mean my *feet*, as in ankles and toes. Got it." She felt a little repulsed but kept talking. "What you should admire is my dress. It's brand new by vintage standards."

"It's all right. You know what I think, though? Fabric is flat." His gaze slid down her legs. "But the curved underside of a woman's foot..."

"All men have their thing, I suppose," she said, wanting to use her feet to walk away. Rose's speech came to mind: let yourself care, or at least act like you do...he'll tip.

"So, how did my feet do on top of that piano?" she asked in an attempt to play along.

"Mesmerizing. In fact, after that hard workout, you should give them a break."

His friend stood up and pointed to his phone. "Got to go. She's not having it. See you tomorrow."

"Later," Steve said, and then turned to Ava. "Take a seat."

"I'm sorry," she said, trying to avoid his invitation without being rude. "I haven't even asked for your orders. I hope your friend wasn't annoyed."

Steve snorted. "Only at his wife. Food can wait. Relax a minute, unless you have other customers to get to." He seemed to know her section, as they both glanced at her empty tables.

"I'm all yours." She forced a smile and sat down in his friend's chair. The rest felt good. "There's nothing like breaking in a new pair of shoes over an eight-hour period."

"Has anyone ever told you that you have dancer's feet?" he

asked, staring at them. "Those high arches."

Not her feet, again. "Are you a dancer?" she asked. "Most people don't think about the underside of feet."

"No, just an admirer." His focus remained downward.

"I always thought my feet were too big," she said, self-conscious of his steady gaze. "It makes shoe shopping no fun at all."

"I'm not interested in shoes."

"So what are you interested in, besides feet?" she asked, desperate to steer his thoughts in another direction, preferably upward.

"Giving you a foot massage." He looked at her, unabashed. She shivered. "Why would you want to do that?"

"To make you feel good. Why else?" Dimples winked at her when he smiled. "It would be my pleasure."

"Sounds wonderful, but I can't take my shoes off. It's against house rules." *Thank goodness!*

"Your strappy shoes won't get in the way." He reached down and pulled her right leg up onto his lap.

"There's also the No Touching rule," she said, trying to reclaim her foot.

"That's only if you don't *want* to be touched, and why wouldn't you want a massage? Relax. I give them to all the girls." With the tips of his fingers, he tickled her sole. She squirmed and laughed, though it wasn't funny.

"Really, Steve, you don't have to." Did the other girls like it?

His eyes shone with excitement. "Close those worried brown eyes of yours. I can see the tension in your shoulders, neck... your whole body."

No kidding! Even if she wanted to close her eyes, they were on guard. He made circles around her ankle. She cringed. He swirled his finger in between her toes. She giggled, miserable. How dare he sigh with pleasure?

Ron, the free-to-live widower was seated in her section. Finally, an excuse to leave.

Using force, she took back her foot and stood. "Thanks, Steve! That was wonderful. Now, can I take your order? I hear the lamb is good."

"You should enjoy the gifts you have, Michelle. Beautiful feet won't last."

"I suppose they won't, but neither will my job if I don't get back to work."

He gave her a sour grin. "The coconut shrimp appetizer, the filet, well-done, and whatever you have on tap."

After entering the order, she went to Ron's table. "How nice to see you—and so soon!" she said, putting her hand on his hunched back.

He turned in his seat. "Ah, Michelle! Did you say *soon*? If one is counting the minutes, then 'soon' is never soon enough."

She laughed; it was like being courted by a Renaissance man. "Good point. And, unfortunately, you missed my performance."

"You go on at ten-thirty," he said, "don't you?"

"Yes, that's right."

"I'll be here."

She smiled and took a seat as the lights above dimmed and the MC stepped into the spotlight on stage. "Next we have Dixie singing a new song in her repertoire: Julie London's 'Cry Me a River.' Let's hear it for Dixie!"

The curtain opened to a petite woman with strawberry-blond hair framing her pretty, round face. She wore a white wedding gown, and her curvaceous figure, much like a dollop of whipped cream, gave her the appearance of a sweet dessert.

Ron leaned over to Ava during the performance. "It's good to see your smile, Michelle," he whispered. "You have what I call a...*real* smile. It was the first thing I noticed about you. I said to myself, now there's a sincere woman."

"Thank you," she mouthed in reply, conscious of their proximity to the stage and disturbing Dixie's performance. Ron was like a child, only able to focus on what interested him.

"Genuine," he added. "That's the word I'm looking for."

Ava nodded and put a finger to her lips, while Dixie sang her last line:

"Well?" Ava said, facing him once the curtain had closed, "do you notice anything different about me from last night?"

He stared at her face. "Well, I'll be. You were a brunette before, weren't you? My memory is a bit drafty."

"That's right, I went from a brunette to voilà!" She shook out her hair.

"Didn't you say you wouldn't dye your hair for me?"

"I wouldn't dye my hair *blond*. I wanted to stand apart from your last Michelle." She realized her lie; she wanted to stand apart from her past self.

"I'll tell you how you can be different from the last Michelle," Ron said.

"I know. Don't go without saying good-bye." One table over from them, Steve with the foot fetish devoured his coconut shrimp. She quickly looked away, repulsed.

Ron reached out and carefully touched her arm. "Just don't go."

Ava smiled and felt bad for him. She *had* to say what he wanted to hear; that's what he was paying for, no?

Two more of her tables were seated. "Ron, what are you in the mood for tonight?" she asked, standing up. "The lamb again?"

"Other than your smile, let's see…" he glanced over the menu. "I'll have the chicken cordon bleu and coffee, black."

She took his order to the kitchen. Was she bringing happiness to his lonely existence, or only false hope?

2:30 a.m. A bouncer wrote down her name and the number of her cab. She got in with $160 in her handbag. Steve had left her $5, apparently figuring in the spa treatment. Even with Ron's hundred-dollar origami swan, she couldn't break $200. It was only one night, but then maybe Billie was right: The Encore wasn't the place for high expectations.

Chris was sleeping peacefully when she arrived home. Chickpea opened her eyes and gave a wag with her tail. Ava smiled back. She wanted to tell Chris all the details of her night, from mastering Michelle Pfeiffer to sacrificing her comfort zone for a man with a foot fetish, and then disappointing him anyway. She wanted to tell him about Ron, his dead wife, and his yearlong dedication to temple and giving thanks...about his strange loyalty and even stranger tips. She hoped Chris would see some value in her work, and take her happiness into account, unlike Julian.

Standing there, a voyeur of sorts, she caught herself caring about a homeless man's opinion. He was the only one who believed in her, without question or speculation. Then why was she afraid to tell him where she worked? Leaving Chris to sleep, she went up the stoop.

Inside the dirty-yellow foyer, she noticed a small package taped to her mailbox. *What in the world...?* She tore it open and found a garlic crusher with a note that read: *Try it.* She stared at the shiny appliance, which glistened under the dingy hall light like a lifeline.

Clearly, Chris had a thing for cooking, only how would that help her?

Chapter Twenty-Nine

Ava blinked away sleep. Nearby, Phoebe sat cross-legged on the floor in a stream of dusty sunlight, eyes closed.

"Phoebe?"

Her eyes popped open. "Sweetie, good morning!"

"Is it still morning?" Ava strained to read her bedside clock.

"Barely. I think it's after eleven. I was just meditating. Something I've always thought of trying." She had on a green kimono.

Every muscle in Ava's body complained as she sat up on the futon. "Meditation? How does it feel?"

"Oh, intense. Today I focused on all the things that annoy me about Barry."

"Phoebe, I don't think that's how it goes."

"At least my mind didn't wander. And it helps me to stay strong."

"Well, it's a start, and that's what counts. By the way, have you heard from him?"

"Nothing." Phoebe got up off the floor, leaving the patch of sunlight, and sat down beside Ave on the futon. "I left after saying some mean things, which I'm sorry for now. It hurts that he hasn't called."

"Oh, Phoebe." Ava put her arm around her. "I know how difficult it is when you can't even agree there's a problem."

"He disregards whatever I have to say. I feel so much anger toward him, sometimes I want to scream!"

"You know what? I think you should. Scream. The woman living below me is practically deaf. The man across the hall is never home. Go ahead and scream. Scream all you want!"

"Really? Now?"

"Yes! Let the whole city hear you!"

Phoebe pounded her fists on the futon and gave a squeaky starter shout, before screaming loudly enough to put more cracks in the ceiling. "He refuses to see my side of anything! I can ask. I can beg. I can demand. I get nowhere! What else can I do but walk away? If I don't stay strong now, he'll never take me seriously!"

"You will," Ava said, this time believing it. "And I think if Josh is ever going to have an honest relationship with his father, he'll have to see you do it first."

"You're so right. He's only ever seen me trying to appease Barry." Phoebe exhaled a long breath. "Enough about me. Sweetie, you look exhausted. Just because you're not getting married this weekend doesn't mean you don't need your beauty sleep. I put some cucumber-infused eye-patches in the refrigerator last night. They'll do wonders. I'll grab them for you." She popped up and headed for the kitchen.

"That's okay. Right now I need a shower and breakfast more than anything else." Ava stood and stretched sore muscles throughout her body.

"Oh, dear. I should be serving you breakfast in bed." Phoebe glanced anxiously at the electric stove with two missing knobs. "It's just that we're lacking the basic ingredients."

"I really don't expect you to make me breakfast, Phoebe."

"I was going to go shopping this morning and stock your refrigerator, but then I looked out the window. I'm just not that comfortable with your neighborhood yet. So I meditated instead."

"I'm glad. I would rather do my own grocery shopping. I need more than bottled water, raw almonds, and sprouts."

"Very funny. So tell me how work went last night. Did everyone love your dress?"

"Not everyone." Ava thought of her foot massage and shuddered. "But I liked it." She went into the kitchen. "Do you want some coffee? It's instant. Sorry."

"No, thank you. I'm giving up coffee as part of my meditation regimen. Something else I've always wanted to do."

"I've always wanted to be a professional dancer." Ava poured a cup for herself and opened her laptop on the kitchen table. "So I'm going to find an audition today even if it's for the dancing penguins in *Mary Poppins*."

"I'm sure that's a coveted part," Phoebe said. "*Mary Poppins* is a classic."

Ava clicked on *Dance.net*.

"I still can't believe you lost that fabulous job at Bergdorf." Phoebe joined her at the table. "You were so good, and at the very helm of fashion! Maybe I could talk to someone in corporate, someone at the top. You know, I am a Preferred Shopper."

"I don't want to go back. I'm finished with handbags."

"But, why?"

"Because I believe there's something more out there for me," Ava replied, scanning a list of auditions for open calls. "Hey, here's something." She pointed at the screen and read: "NYC Arts Center, 800 Washington Street, Friday, July 2, 10:00 a.m. to 6:00 p.m. Must be between the ages 24-32 and have training in jazz and modern dance. Television advertisement. Some pay."

"Oh, by all means, *go!*" Phoebe exclaimed.

Ava smiled. Mom would've said the same thing.

"So are you going?" Phoebe urged.

"It'd be great exposure, and just the resume builder agents are looking for. Hey, you should come with me. We'll make it an outing, unless you want to continue with your meditations."

"And give up a behind-the-scenes glimpse of the arts? Think of me as your loyal fan. I'll just be a few minutes getting ready." She took out her toiletry bag, a miniature suitcase. "You know what, Ava? This is just what I need. Positive distraction." She disappeared into the bathroom.

Ava clicked on eBay. It'd been three days, and not one bid on her dress and veil. Besides seriously needing the money, she couldn't hold them at Vera Wang and The Moment bridal boutique forever. Relist. She took her minimum bid of $800 down to $400, a wedding steal.

Phoebe was still in the bathroom. Ava opened her gym bag and found the garlic crusher beside her red shoes. Chris. She smiled, remembering the package taped to her mailbox in the foyer. Maybe she'd make him garlic stuffed mushrooms or garlic mashed potatoes. Stir-fry chicken and vegetables in a garlic sauce. It was something to look forward to. She hung her dress outside on the fire escape to air. She'd have to wear it again that night.

Ava pulled her hair back and changed into her stockings, leotard, and jogging pants. As she slipped her dance shoes into her handbag, Phoebe stepped out of the bathroom in a white Chanel pantsuit with violet trim and large gold buttons.

"Wow, smashing outfit!" Ava said. "They're going to give *you* the job!"

They started downstairs, excitement going with them.

"I know what we should do." Phoebe gripped the banister as she managed the stairs, just barely, in her white open-backed pumps. "Breakfast at Le Pain Quotidien. Wouldn't the parfait with granola and fresh berries taste delicious right now? You'll need high-energy food before your audition, and I'm working up an appetite just getting out the front door!"

"Sounds perfect."

Outside, Ava looked over the ledge of the stoop for Chris. "First I want to say hello to a friend." He was writing in his notebook, focused, unaware of being watched. "Hello, down there!" She waved. "Am I disturbing you?"

He looked up and smiled. "Please, do!"

She went down the steps with Phoebe following closely behind.

"Good morning!" Chris said, meeting them at the bottom of the stoop.

"Good morning. I want you to meet my friend, Phoebe. She's staying with me for a while."

"Hello." He held out his hand, while at the same time, Chickpea offered her wet nose.

"Oh, my!" Phoebe, clearly overwhelmed, took a step back.

Chris scolded Chickpea. "Where are your manners?" He turned to Phoebe. "I'm sorry. You don't have to worry, though. She's friendly."

"It's nice that you have each other," Phoebe said. "Are you able to feed her regularly?"

The implication was painful. Phoebe was just being "Overprotective Phoebe," but Chris would hear the insult.

"On the contrary," Ava said before Chris could reply, "you wouldn't believe Chickpea's diet. It's better than my own!"

No one spoke, perhaps preoccupied with smiling. If only Phoebe could see the real Chris—how smart and honest and considerate he was. "Chris has come to my rescue so many times, it's embarrassing."

He looked down at his scuffed sneakers. "I wouldn't say that."

"Really?" Phoebe glanced uneasily at his suitcase.

"Hey," Ava said, "what was that great advice you gave me, inspired by Kafka? As long as your dog has food—"

He laughed. "It's Chickpea's motto: as long as there's food in your dish, life is good."

She nudged Phoebe. "At least we're not starving!"

"Of course not!" Phoebe exclaimed. "Oh, I'm sorry, I wasn't even thinking..." She plunged into her Chanel handbag and came out with her wallet, both violet on white to match her suit.

"No!" Ava put her hand on Phoebe's. "That's okay. Really, it's not like that."

"It isn't?" Phoebe blinked several times. "I guess I don't understand. Don't you need money?"

Chris smiled. "Don't worry. I'm guilty of confusing people. But I think the rule with charity is that usually someone asks for it first. Or else it's given anonymously."

"That's a good rule. Right, Ava?" Phoebe put her wallet back inside her handbag. But she wasn't finished with Chris. "We're having fun making up new rules: no talking about money; no hiding feelings; and no subways. That's what we've got so far."

Now he looked confused. Ava tried to collect her thoughts. What was it she had wanted to say to him? There was something...

Phoebe donned her reporter face, pensive while curious. "So, Chris, what do you do about using the—"

"Oh, the audition!" Ava exclaimed. "We should go, now."

"You're really going for it, Ava," Chris said. "That's great. I'm sure you'll find what you want."

"Thanks." His words felt like nourishment. "We'll see you later."

"Nice meeting you, Phoebe." Chris seemed sincere, which spoke for his ability to read people.

"Oh, likewise! Wonderful."

They walked to the corner to hail a taxi. That could've gone better. Phoebe still saw Chris as nothing more than a homeless man.

Le Pain smelled like hazelnut coffee and glazed tarts. They took two seats at the communal table.

"Two parfaits and two skim lattes," Phoebe ordered before the waiter could set down menus.

"I thought you gave up coffee!" Ava exclaimed.

"I did, and I will again later. I'm just not giving it up right now."

"Oh, I see. You're just cutting back on *my* coffee."

"Sweetie, all humor aside...I really don't like to think of you coming home at three in the morning with that man there, as nice as you think he is."

"I feel safe coming home so late *because* he's there, Phoebe. Chris is someone I can trust. He's a friend."

"I told myself when I came to stay with you that under no circumstances would I interfere with your life. But your safety is most important, and I'm worried about you."

"Believe me, Chris is the last person to hurt anyone." The image of him swinging the metal pipe came to mind...Luis buckling in pain. "Well, not without reason, anyway."

"My point, exactly. He might find a reason!"

Parfaits and lattes arrived. "Well, I can't move into a new apartment right now, and I can't make *him* move, so I guess I'll just have to...I don't know, carry Mace."

"Good idea! Let's buy some today. My treat."

"I was kidding."

"Sweetie, if I've learned anything in life, it's to expect the unexpected. For example, who would've thought we'd be roommates?"

"Or that I would have a job dancing on top of a piano."

"Or that I'd be exploring the Buddhist's way!"

All too soon their breakfast was over. They scraped the bottom of their fountain glasses for every last seed and berry, and then Phoebe reapplied her lipstick. "So, are we ready for your audition?"

Ava laughed. "Okay, if you're ready, then I am. Let's go!"

Chapter Thirty

"Oh, look!" Phoebe gasped. A woman in purple tights did a front split, midair, in the center of the dance studio. Ava nodded and watched. The performance was impressive, but not intimidating. This audition would be easier than the Rockettes and not nearly as terrifying as The Encore.

She waited her turn, comfortable in tights and a leotard, feet safe in her old jazz shoes. The dance studio, full of sunlight, energized her. She felt at home for the first time in many years.

Phoebe leaned over and whispered, "You can tell the judges that I'm your agent." She looked the part, drawing plenty of attention in her white pantsuit with large gold buttons.

"You're hired," Ava whispered back.

Twelve dancers, men and women, waited ahead of her. It wouldn't be a long wait; each audition was only two minutes. "It's videotaped," Ava said, keeping a low voice. "That's what the woman at registration said. And it's freestyle."

"Videotaped? Can I buy a copy?"

Ava chuckled. "It's for the judges."

"Oooh! A spectacular leap!" Phoebe applauded and then caught herself. "Oops. Sorry."

"Promise me you won't cheer when it's my turn," Ava said, not taking her eyes off the competition. Only three to go.

"I'll try not to," Phoebe replied.

Two...one...

"Here goes." Ava walked to the middle of the studio and faced the man with the video recorder.

"I'm Ava Larson!"

The music began and her body started moving before she

even recognized the groovy 1970s rhythm of "Boogie Nights." Amazing. Only two shifts at The Encore and she was practically on autopilot, ready for any spotlight. Just to dance with her feet on solid ground seemed to give her an advantage, and it felt like being reborn.

The music faded out. The judges *had* to love her.

"Thanks," one of them mumbled.

She waited, breathing hard. A standing ovation wasn't protocol, but not even a smile? A nod?

"We have your contact information. You'll get a call in the next few days if we're interested."

Euphoria evaporated.

A tall man in mauve tights walked onto the floor, ready for his two minutes. A song from *Sgt. Pepper's Lonely Hearts Club Band* filled the room. Maybe only she thought her audition went well. Phoebe, of course, would gush praise.

"I don't want to talk about it," Ava said before Phoebe could open her mouth. They walked outside.

"But you were wonderful! Judges are *supposed* to be aloof."

"I appreciate your optimism, Phoebe, but let's forget it."

The Meatpacking District held its own auditions for the most posh hotels, exclusive clubs, and upmarket boutiques. She didn't qualify for in-style wearing jogging pants, and Phoebe walked on the cobbled streets in her pumps like someone on stilts.

"I could never be hip downtown," she said, clutching Ava's arm. "Unless a twisted ankle is the new craze!"

"I have an idea," Ava said. "Yoga. For you! We can pick out a colorful mat and some Zen-looking clothes." She pictured Julian in his *Namaste, Nincompoop* T-shirt and regretted their argument. It was more a misunderstanding than a fight. He judged her without seeing her act, and she worried about him more than she trusted him. They had a vow to wait for marriage and an undeniable attraction. It was too good not to hope for a second chance.

"Me, do *yoga*?" Phoebe replied, as if the suggestion were to climb Mount Everest. "You need to be flexible. I couldn't do that."

"Phoebe, that's what it's for! You *become* flexible. Anyway, you need to get out, meet new people."

"I don't know...I've had the same friends for so long, making new ones feels almost unnatural. Maybe I should stick with solitary hobbies for now."

"Hey, I just made a fool out of myself on videotape. If you want to move forward in life, you have to try new things. You've started meditating, advance to yoga, and before you know it, you'll be making pilgrimages."

"Fine, yoga." She sent Ava a look as pointed as the toes of her open-backed pumps. "And you did *not* make a fool out of yourself in your audition."

A little city air and her red dress hung ready for The Encore. Phoebe had changed into her kimono, all set for another night of somber reflection.

"Thank you for doing my makeup again," Ava said, standing with her bags, ready to go. "While work is slow being my agent, you can double as my stylist."

"I'll put on as many hats as you need," Phoebe said. "Ava, I know you don't want to talk about it, but you were something else in that audition. I saw a whole other side of you. Expressive. Explosive!"

"I wish the judges saw it that way."

"It's a TV commercial. They have a certain look in mind. You're probably too pretty! And don't rule it out so fast. They said they'd call over the next couple of days, and it's only been a few hours."

"I just have a feeling I won't hear from them."

"You'll get work dancing. I bet everything I have on it. If I'm wrong, you'll find me below your stoop, living with that man and his dog."

"Chris and Chickpea." Ava started toward the door and stopped. "Will you be all right here alone?"

"Oh, sure. If I get bored with meditating, I'll just browse your library." They looked at the crates of feel-good romance novels and laughed. "This is nice, Ava. I'm really getting to know you now."

"Not only that," Ava replied, "we're getting to know ourselves."

Phoebe nodded. "Have a good night at work, and be careful!"

Outside, Chris was sitting on the stoop with *Gourmet* magazine, the July Fourth issue. Reminders of her former wedding were everywhere, as the countdown officially ended this weekend.

"Hi, Ava," he said, setting down the magazine. "Rushing off to work?"

"I have some time today." She sat down next to him, holding her bags on her lap. Their meetings between the events of the day felt like islands in rough waters. Chickpea nudged her hand. "What a sweet dog you are." Ava patted her head and then looked at Chris. "Listen, I'm sorry about this morning. Phoebe is kind of sheltered, but she's possibly the kindest woman you'll meet in New York City."

"I like her. No apology needed."

"But I wanted her to see what a great person you are, and she was so...nearsighted."

"Ava, it's not even worth talking about. I'm sure if she's staying with you, we'll get to know each other over time."

Ava smoothed down Chickpea's fur. "She's so fluffy, and she smells like lavender. Did you wash her today, or put tea in her water?"

"Actually, I took her to Downtown Doghouse for a bath and proper grooming. It's about time we cleaned up our act."

Ava stroked Chickpea's feather-soft fur, estimating the price for a proper grooming. Seventy dollars, at least. How did he afford it? *She'd* wash Chickpea for that much money.

"So, speaking of acts," Chris said, "tell me about your new job."

"My new job? Well...sometimes it's so cold my nose runs, and other times I'm sweating buckets." She fingered the dry ends of her processed hair. "Do you think we could talk about it later?"

"Sure. Whenever you want."

"Thanks. You're always understanding."

He glanced at his notebook. "I probably have my father to thank for that."

"Is he understanding?"

Chris laughed. "Actually, no. He *requires* a lot of understanding."

"Oh. I guess my father does too, come to think of it. I should probably try harder to understand him." She thought of Mom's last advice, given when she was still well enough to talk: *Don't give up on your father. You'll regret it. Keep trying, and don't stop loving him. Promise me?*

"Your smile, Ava. It's getting away!" Chis grabbed the air as if catching dandelion fluff.

She laughed at his pantomime, and he reached over and touched her lips with his fingers, gently. "There. It's back," he said.

She blushed, looking down. "Thanks for bringing it back."

"Your smile is important to me. I look forward to it every day."

She could say the same...but didn't. "Hey, I went on an audition this morning, a TV commercial for the New York Arts Center."

"TV! Did you tell them you don't watch TV?"

"No." She laughed.

"Sounds great, Ava. I hope you get it."

"Thanks. At least I'm trying. So, how's the restaurant business?" She ventured the question, worried that it might be difficult or even painful for him to answer. If going for a dream job was a challenge for her, it had to be impossible for him.

"Well, I'm still working at the *Rainbow Room*, but I've got something in the works."

"Wait. You work at the *Rainbow Room*? At the top of Rockefeller Center?" She imagined a busboy lugging tubs of dirty dishes.

"I'm the sous chef," he replied matter-of-factly.

"No kidding! What is that?"

He chuckled. "The assistant to the executive chef."

"Really?" He had to be making this up. "How can you handle a job like that living *here*?"

"I have my ways." He smiled and picked up his magazine.

"Okay, I have to ask or it will drive me nuts: if you have a steady job, then *why* are you living here?"

"One reason is to save money, but it's a personal choice, too. A matter of needing space. You might think I'm a born bohemian, but it's not a lifestyle I want to keep forever."

"I can't imagine waking up outside," she said, being honest, "although I suppose you could look at it like camping." She pictured herself down-and-out on the streets, ignoring society's disdain, no privacy and utterly alone...forced self-reflection. It was a lot like leaving Josh, actually.

What should you do after breaking your engagement? Survive.

"Being a *sous chef* sounds pretty impressive," she said, turning her thoughts back to Chris and his life. "At least you're not starting at the bottom."

"Oh, I've been at the bottom. I've had every job there is in a restaurant, starting with busboy when I was fourteen. I've been a waiter, an expediter, a pastry chef...I've prepped vegetables, chopped salads, and butchered meats. I could run my own restaurant with my eyes closed—there's not a doubt in my mind. But it takes a lot of capital, and, of course, the right partner."

"It will happen one day." She put her hand on his arm, following an impulse to touch him. Solid, warm...she pulled away. Did he really work at the *Rainbow Room*? Could he actually open a restaurant? French comfort food? Josh used to say she was gullible.

"So, Ava, anything *new* in your life, something you came upon last night?"

"Oh! I've been meaning to tell you! The garlic crusher! I love it!"

"I was hoping you got it. Garlic. Now there's a vegetable that's good for everything, from healthy skin to immunities, not to mention a strong heart."

"Really? Well, one of these days I'm going to make a meal with it. Will you join me?"

"A home-cooked meal? Are you serious? I'll be there!" He took a bundle of celery stalks from a Whole Foods bag and broke off a piece for Chickpea, who ate it skeptically. "The vitamins don't seem to be doing anything for her. It's a vegetable and dry food diet now."

"Poor girl." Ava rubbed her tummy. Chickpea sighed deeply, looking up with dreamy eyes.

"Here's an idea." Chris's eyes glimmered with excitement. "I'm taking Chickpea to the My Dog Loves Central Park County Fair tomorrow. Want to come along?"

Chickpea's tail wagged wildly at the mention of "park."

"Tomorrow?" The invitation came as a surprise. "What is it?"

"Once a year city dogs get together on the basketball courts by the Great Lawn in Central Park for advice from the best vets in Manhattan. Okay, maybe they just want the free rawhides."

Now Chickpea sat and stood three times in succession.

"It sounds like fun. Sure, I'll go. I haven't been to the park all summer."

"Tomorrow at one o'clock then."

"It's a date." Not a real date, of course. She stood, wishing she hadn't said that. "Right. So, garlic...you know, I happen to be pretty good in the kitchen. You might be surprised."

"I'm ready whenever you are." Light shone in his midnight eyes beneath unruly hair.

"Okay. Soon." She moved for the street. Not sure how to feel about garlic dinners, dog fairs, or anything, she quickly set off for The Encore.

Chapter Thirty-One

Ava zigzagged through women curling weaves and fastening wigs...applying fake-eyelashes and bottled tans. She went to her locker. No Billie tonight, unfortunately, which raised the question: who would whistle and cheer for her?

The women getting ready were younger and louder than the previous nights. Most of them she didn't recognize, as if it were a different club on the weekends. She stripped down to her underwear and pulled up her dress, faster at it now than when she had started.

A busty woman with light-brown skin and long black hair twirled a gold sequin choker around her finger. "*Va a ser una fiesta esta noche!*"

"Savanna, stop goofing off!" Rose sounded particularly on edge as she called orders from her desk. "What do you think this is? Carnival?"

"Yo, my people celebrate Ponce. Do you hear me speaking Portuguese?" The other women giggled. "Mama Rose, you are *loco en la cabeza!*"

"My *head* is just fine," Rose replied. "Michelle, you need to sign in. Everybody, two minutes and you're upstairs! Giovanni called down, and they're already seating customers. You won't be sitting around complaining about the AC tonight."

Ava fastened her jewelry and slipped on the red shoes. Hustling upstairs, she set a new goal: $300, to make up for last night. A hurried breath and she entered the club, stepping into the unknown.

Six large men, more wide than tall, were seated in her section. They looked like defensive linemen, despite pastel golf shirts. She reviewed her mental checklist: you're happy, you're exactly where you want to be, and these guys are the only men alive. None of it was true, but she could follow Giovanni's instructions.

"Hi! I'm Michelle, the lucky gal who will be looking after you guys tonight!"

"Howdy, ma'am," they replied with big smiles and thick southern accents. One of them started singing, "Where'd You Get that Red Dress?"

"I get the feeling you're not from around here," she said.

"Ah, gee-wiz, is it that obvious?" asked the one sitting closest to her, putting on an even heavier drawl. He had white-blond hair and a flushed face. "We're all from Alabama, and our buddy Craig here is about to get hitched." He stood and swatted Craig in the head with a riding whip. "Tonight we're showing him the time of his life in New York City!"

The guys burst into a chorus of *Yahoos!*

"Where dreams are made!" she exclaimed, jumping into the New York spirit with them. "So, what's with the riding whip?"

"The groom gets a swat every time someone says 'marriage,' or any word with the same meaning." The white-blond guy stood and got Craig on the other side of the head.

"Poor you!" she said, although he didn't even wince. His tanned skin looked like worn leather, and the goatee fit perfectly with his tough demeanor. "I hope it doesn't hurt too much."

"Which one, marriage or the whip?" one of the guys burst out, and Craig felt the sting.

"Thank ya, kindly," he said to her, "but I can take it." His friends whooped and hollered on his behalf. "We're all staying at the Marriott up the road," he continued, "and when we asked about some good, clean entertainment and decent food, the concierge told us to come on down here."

"He's so 'whipped,'" one of the guys exclaimed, "his fiancée gave him a list of things he couldn't do. Not only did he read it, he's following it!"

"I don't see any reason for a strip bar," Craig said. "Y'all want to pay big money for nothing but frustration, go on ahead."

"You guys will have a great time here. Our first act should

be starting any minute, and I go on at seven-thirty."

The white-blond guy sitting closest to her with the whip put his hand on her lower back. "Sugar, we'll be looking for you on that stage, for sure. What kind of act do you do?"

She excused the pet name as a cultural difference, but removed his hand from her back. "You'll have to wait and see. Now, do you fellas want to start with drinks or are you ready to order?"

Orders taken and repeated, she turned to go enter them into the system. One step and her bum got the whip. "Ouch!" She spun around, ready to knock someone off his seat.

The same guy chuckled, holding his little black *toy*. "How could I resist?" he asked.

"I'm afraid you'll have to *resist*. Hands—and whips—must be kept to yourself." She shook from her core, completely unnerved, but smiled politely.

"Yes, ma'am." He went for her backside again, but pulled away when she tried to stop him. "Just checking!"

"Please," she said and glanced around for a bouncer, an oversized penguin, anyone. No one suspected a problem. There wasn't a disagreement. Her table laughed, and she kept up a smile. "You guys are too much." She walked away, still feeling the sting.

Orders entered, she found Ron in her section, waiting at his usual table. Grateful for his kindness, she took a seat beside him. "You're early!" He wore black corduroys tonight and a maroon sweater.

"I couldn't wait to see you. Could there be any other reason?"

She smiled and shrugged her shoulders. "You look very nice. How was your day?"

"Well, I read the *Daily News*, played a little solitaire, heated up my usual split pea and ham soup, and then...this is boring."

"Were you going to say you did origami?" she asked.

He looked down at his hands and blushed. "That's my secret."

"I loved the crane, and the swan, too! It was such a shame to have to unfold them."

267

"It's just a hobby." He waved it off, grinning like a proud boy. "Tell me about your day."

"Okay, well, today I went on an audition, which is exciting. I thought it went great, until I saw the judges' deadpan faces. Totally unimpressed." She made herself laugh. "But you never know. I should keep up hope, right?"

The light in Ron's eyes went out. "So you're trying for something better already. Why am I surprised? Of course you are." He sighed. "Michelle, I wish you all the luck this city has to give."

She touched his arm. "Thank you, Ron. That means a lot to me."

He took her hand in his. "I have an idea."

"An idea?" She wanted her hand back.

"Give me your telephone number. That way we can keep in touch. I'll give you mine, as well. You can call me when you hear about the audition, or whenever you just want to talk."

She envisioned him sitting beside a landline telephone, waiting, hoping, afraid that if he went to the bathroom, he'd miss her call. "I'm sorry, Ron." She carefully pulled her hand away. "But I don't give out my number. It's nothing personal against you. I don't give my number to anyone."

"What do you mean you don't give your number to anyone? Am I just *anyone*?" He touched his chest.

"I mean I don't give out my number here. I don't even think it's allowed."

"Who would know?" he said, leaning toward her, and then lowering his voice. "I thought we had a connection."

"We do, and I enjoy your company, Ron."

"Then there's no harm in a phone conversation." He raised wiry gray eyebrows.

"I still think it's best if we only talk here, where—"

"Where you're paid to talk." His gaze moved to the stage. "Please don't tell me I'm just a part of your act."

"Of course not! I think you're a very special person."

"I'm old and I'm foolish, that's what I am. I should stick to my solitary life, going to temple. There's no freedom for an old man. Forget happiness."

"You have every right to be happy!" She reached for his arm. "You're a good man, Ron. I just can't give out my phone number. It wouldn't be fair."

"Who's playing fair here? I finally get it. Every man who tips well is 'special.' It was the same with the last Michelle. This is nothing more than work for you women, nothing more than money and lies." He stood and took a hundred dollar bill in the shape of a heart out of his coat pocket. "Here, money." He tossed it at her.

A bouncer came over. "Is there a problem?"

"No." She held out the heart to Ron. "Please take it. I thought coming here and seeing me made you happy, and that was enough."

He shook his head and walked out, hunched over, alone.

She watched him leave, holding back tears. She had contributed to his sorrow, his loneliness. Her work did nothing to help others. It did nothing.

She walked to the office, undoing the tight folds of the heart, and put the hundred-dollar bill in her envelope. Going back to her section, she felt outside the music, the laughter and chatter. Everywhere she looked women were teasing and flirting and batting fake eyelashes. This scene wasn't hers, and she would never fully become it.

Wanting to run out of the club and forget that she ever tried to revive her love of dance, she approached the bachelor party, gathering all the strength she had from a deep breath.

The guys shouted above each other, laughing. The black riding whip *snapped* and *snapped*.

She turned on her smile, ready to react should they even point it at her, when someone tapped her on the shoulder.

Spinning around, she met the wide-open eyes of the Piranha. "Mr. Copeland?"

"Ava?"

Her mind went into reverse, trying to connect her past with the present. It seemed impossible that Josh's father could exist here.

Tell him I'm someone else. Walk away. Leave the club and never return! She didn't move or speak, like a hunted animal hiding in its environment.

"I suppose you're not 'Ava' here," he said, standing tall, broad, intimidating.

"Mr. Copeland! I'm sorry. I wasn't expecting to see you here." She concocted a facial expression that said *how nice!* As if they had run into each other at a coffee shop and everything was as it should be: no red gown and four-inch heels, no canceled wedding or hurt feelings.

"Occasionally I take clients out for dinner and entertainment." His bulging eyes seemed to pin her down. "What are *you* doing here?"

The absolute futility of trying to explain herself to him had an immediate effect; she stopped caring what he thought. Relief rushed through her as if she had fixed a leaky faucet after years of hearing it drip.

"Frankly," she replied, "I don't need to tell you why I'm here. Why do you even want to know?"

His eyes scrutinized her, while his forehead creased with judgment. "You're obviously in serious trouble. You've ruined your hair, you have makeup plastered all over your face, and you're squeezed into some cheap dress. Clearly, you're out of control and need professional help."

"Excuse me? Red hair is something I've always wanted; your wife did my makeup; and this 'cheap' dress is brand name!"

His mouth hung open before he spoke. "Phoebe did your makeup?"

"Mr. Copeland, do you even know where she is?"

"Don't insult me. Of course I do. She's with you. You were the last person she spoke to before she set the house alarm and left."

"Well, just so you know, she's doing great. She's taken up yoga and meditation, and she's meeting new people." Phoebe's painful introduction to Chris came to mind. "She's doing the best she can, and I'm really proud of her, starting an exciting new life on her own. So don't feel you have to worry about us for a second."

His face went white. "Well." He cleared his throat. The Piranha, stumped? "I'm going to leave. It's a shame to see you like this, Ava."

"The name is *Michelle.*"

He excused himself at his table and left the club.

A new energy flowed through her body, making her feel shaky and charged at the same time. She had actually stood up to Mr. Copeland. And shook him up, too! He had to be calling Phoebe right now, begging her back. There would likely be a note when she arrived home: *He loves me!* Ava felt a surge of excitement...even though she'd miss her roommate.

After pulling off a flawless second act, she went on a much-needed break, helping herself to the free salad and pasta in the kitchen.

"You look tired, my lady," her busboy said, taking a soda break himself. Bart was Jamaican and had a family back in Portmore.

"I'm wiped-out," she said. "I've been here three nights in a row."

"That is nothing. In four months, you'll be working night after night, no problem. I know for a fact. You get immune to all this noise and hustle and bustle." He waved his arm in the air, as if making it disappear.

And the lies, too? She doubted it.

They could hear Sinatra singing "New York, New York" upstairs. "I work," Bart said, "but really I sleepwalk." He laughed out loud.

1:00 a.m. Ava went backstage for her final performance. Bart might have had a point; she felt hazy, even as the curtain opened. But the words came easy to her now, and she climbed up on top of the piano with almost no fear of losing her balance. *She sits alone most every night. He doesn't phone her. He*

271

doesn't write...

She sang for her audience, while they watched, completely still, forgetting their drinks, their meals and conversations. She was their escape, for the moment. They hung, suspended above everyday life, onto her every word, every move, every breath.

Savoring their undivided attention, her focus fell to a back corner of the lounge where a familiar face stole her next inhale. It couldn't be. But his boyish grin was unmistakable. Julian stood watching her, arms crossed over his chest.

A chill spread through her body, leaving her weak and shaky. *Just one more verse.*

Gripping the mike, she carefully moved to a seated position, palms sweating. It suddenly felt like the first night all over again.

He says he's "busy." But she says, "Is he?" He's makin' whoopee!

With her legs folded to one side, she leaned back on her free hand and grasped air. Balance gone, she tumbled over backward and hit the stage with a *THUD!*

The audience gasped; the spell was broken. The curtain closed.

"I'm okay." She reached for Giovanni's hand.

"Are you sure you can stand?" A smile shone beneath his concern. "No injuries?"

"Go ahead and laugh. I'll be fine. Just help me up."

He pulled her to standing. The seam of her dress was torn, but nothing that couldn't be mended. The impact of the fall she'd feel in the morning, without a doubt.

"I'm going back out on the floor," she said, thinking of Julian. "I can finish the night."

"I wouldn't push it," Giovanni said.

She walked off, holding in the pain.

Julian laughed when he saw her. "Talk about going out with a bang!" He gave her a tentative hug. "Are you all right?"

"What are you talking about? That was a part of my act."

He smirked. "Oh, really? I hope they pay workers' compensation."

She took in his black jeans and turtleneck, the evening-shadow on his cheeks enough to call a beard. It made him look artsy, sophisticated even.

"So...are you actually here to see me?" she asked.

"Aside from the howler, you weren't bad. Only you *really* are a hypocrite, singing about making whoopee."

"They get married in the first verse, if you were listening."

"Sorry, I missed that. Too distracted by the wig." He moved a damp strand off her cheek.

She didn't have the energy to correct him about the wig. "You didn't answer my question. Or maybe you're here undercover."

He drove his hand through his hair, looking at her as if trying to see past the tight dress, the heavy makeup, the dyed hair. Could she blame him for disliking her in this place?

"I'm here on my night off," he finally replied. "It's good to see you."

"It's nice to see you, too."

"Sorry for the other night." He flicked a piece of lint off his sleeve. "I was tired and...not myself."

"I know you're only doing your job, Julian. And you're doing your best."

"Like I've said from the beginning, I put my work first. I have to." He reached for her hand. "Listen, can we get back on track, forward ahead?"

"I'd like that."

His lips brushed hers, and a longing to collapse in his arms moved her toward him—when she remembered where she was and pulled back. "Not here. I could lose my job."

His eyes flashed frustration. "Maybe I'd be doing you a favor."

"Not if I lose my apartment because I can't pay my rent."

"Whatever," he said as if it couldn't happen. "Come back to my place when you get off, or better yet, leave with me right now."

Wouldn't she like to. Just forget her customers, forget her bills, forget her vow to wait, and lose herself in his arms, on his luxurious, king-size..."I can't. And to be honest with you, Julian, I'm exhausted. I need to finish my shift and crawl home to bed. I'm taking a few nights off from this place after tonight. I promise."

"Sleep is a lame excuse in my book. But do what you have to do." He leaned over and ever so lightly kissed her cheek. "I'll catch you later, 'Michelle.'"

She watched him go, her hand on her tailbone throbbing in pain. It was worth his apology. So worth it.

2:45 a.m. Ava trudged upstairs to her apartment, carrying her bags and the $480 she'd made in tips. The guys from Alabama treated her right in the end. Goal accomplished? Legs numb, a bruised bum, her body couldn't take any more.

She quietly shut her apartment door and tiptoed down the hallway, wondering if she still had a roommate. Phoebe lay asleep on the futon. No note.

Chapter Thirty-Two

The city disappeared, and green treetops became the sky. Ava walked beside Chris into Central Park, while Chickpea, on her leash, led the way to the dog fair.

"I'm a little off-balanced," Ava said, still feeling her injury. "I have a bruised tailbone—a minor casualty on the job."

"I'm sorry to hear that." Chris held out his arm. "Consider me your walker."

She glanced at his tanned forearm...hesitated...and then linked her arm in his. "Thanks." It helped.

"Speaking of your new job," he said. "Are you up for talking about it? You've definitely got my curiosity."

She smiled. "I think I can put it into words."

"Is it ambiguous? Wait. You're a mime!"

She laughed. "No, actually I'm—I'm a waitress, and I perform on top of a piano."

"As in cabaret?" He raised his eyebrows with genuine surprise.

"You're probably thinking I've sold out and will never be a real dancer. Or that I'm out of control, what with losing my mom and my job. I mean, who knows? Maybe I am. How can I know if I'm making the right decisions?"

Chris suddenly released her arm and stopped walking. "Can we back up this conversation? I'd like to be a part of it."

She stopped as well and noticed the trees shading their path... the benches where New Yorkers paused...the giant boulders on which children announced, "I'm on top of the world!"

She looked at Chris. "Sorry. You're right."

Chickpea, impatient, pulled them onward.

"Okay, so let me get this straight," Chris said. "You're performing. You're paying your bills, and you're going on auditions. Where does 'sold out' fit in?"

She glanced down and smiled; he got her. It felt as if the entire city hugged her at that moment.

"I assume you like the job, right?" He hooked his arm in hers again, and they walked.

She met his questioning gaze and thought of Ron hunched over, leaving the club. "The problem is that I don't like what the customers expect from me. I refuse to be their play toy. I won't give out my number, and I *don't* want a foot massage, thank you very much."

"I see."

"But it's been good for me, too. I never thought of myself as enticing, especially on top of a piano. But I am, inhibitions aside."

"So you like the artistic element. I'm sure I would, too—from the audience, that is." He winked at her.

"Stop, you're making me blush!" She shoved him.

"Hey!" He pretended to stumble, and then tripped over Chickpea and fell to the ground. Chickpea, barking, jumped on top of him, either in rescue mode or just having fun. "You're a lot of help!" he said, laughing, and struggled to get up with her sitting on his chest.

Ava laughed until in tears. "I'd give you a hand, if it didn't hurt to bend over. It even hurts to laugh!"

Chris finally shoved Chickpea off and got back up on his feet. They caught their breath as he brushed the gravel from his jeans.

"What I really want is to do something that makes a difference," she said as they continued walking. "I want to inspire people, to help them realize their potential. I know how it feels—to be afraid to try for what really matters to you. It's like you have a treasure to share but can't get the lid open. Once you experience your best, though, you become captain of your ship. The world is yours!"

Chris nodded. "I'm captain of my ship, and I know exactly

where I want to go—only my ship has been known to sink."
He laughed.

"I'm captain of my ship," she said, laughing, again, "but singing 'Makin' Whoopee' isn't going to get me anywhere!"

"'Makin' Whoopee'? This gets more intriguing all the time!"

"I'll tell you what's intriguing...the tips. But that means playing a role that can be seen as a lie."

He looked at her, the curled ends of his hair brushing his shoulders. "You have good intentions, Ava. I believe doors will open for you, when the time is right."

"I hope so. At least I didn't go back to fashion. Doing what you know isn't always the answer in life, either. I'd be getting married to the wrong guy this weekend if I stuck to that rule."

"Married? This *weekend*? You really are about change these days!"

Chickpea's leash was taut as she pulled them forward. "We're getting close," Chris said, holding her back with visible effort.

"Come on, then. Let's go!" Ava charged forward, wanting to put distance between today and past hurts. Chickpea burst into a sprint, taking Chris with him.

"Ouch!" Three strides into her idea and pain put an end to it. "Okay, that wasn't smart." She hobbled along, holding her lower back. "I really wasn't thinking."

Chris backtracked with a reluctant and confused Chickpea. "Are you all right?" he asked, taking her arm. "Do you need to sit?"

"No. Sitting isn't good. I think we'll have to *walk* to the fair, slowly." She leaned on his arm with half her weight, and they fell into a one-and-a-half step rhythm.

"So, you broke your engagement?" he asked.

"Yes, and I have nearly seventy thousand dollars of debt to prove it."

"Wow. Then congratulations on your new job!"

A gust of wind blew their hair into their eyes. Chickpea stuck her nose in the air like an airplane in takeoff.

"I had the most loyal dog when I was young," Ava said. "Pearl was part collie, part Russian wolfhound. We had her for fourteen years."

"Fourteen. That's nice. I've had Chickpea for eight years and would give anything to have her for eight more."

"What do you do with her when you're at work?" Ava asked.

"A friend of mine takes her. This really cool woman named Gretchen."

"Oh." Of course he had friends...or maybe a girlfriend. "That's good." Was Gretchen homeless, too?

She held tighter to his arm as they crossed the road where bikers and skaters whizzed by, making the six-mile loop around the park. Safe on the other side, Chickpea resumed the lead.

"So is Gretchen a friend from work?" Ava ventured the question, dying to know.

"I know her from the Church of the Guardian Angel," Chris replied matter-of-factly.

"You go to church?" she blurted out, as if she expected him to blame God for his leaky ship.

"I wandered into their soup kitchen one day and was appalled by the food. Talk about tasteless and mushy. So I joined the church and asked if I could volunteer mornings to help out. I'm their 'unofficial' chef. You'll have to stop in sometime. If you're not homeless, they ask you to donate. But you can be my guest. You're probably in more debt than most of the people getting free meals."

"That's a scary thought, but please don't make an exception for me." She thought a moment and then added, "I used to go to church."

"I suppose my motivation was hunger. I went to the soup kitchen and had a meal, but I ended up finding something like a family."

She nodded, craving family more than ever.

"Anyway," he continued, "that's where I met Gretchen, the woman who takes care of Chickpea. She runs a home for teenage girls that offers workshops with women professionals—lawyers, doctors, actors...any role model who's willing to donate her time. It's called All for One."

"That's a great idea. So many people are out there making

a difference...I'll be one of them, one day." Wind rustled the leaves. She could hear a merry-go-round and children cheering. "Chris, can I ask you a personal question?"

"Oh, no. Wait. Let me guess. Where do I go to the bathroom?"

"No! But maybe just as stupid. Never mind."

"Go ahead. Ask away. Do you want to know where I shower?" A couple walking ahead of them glanced back. Chris smiled. "At church. Since I help out with the soup kitchen, they let me use the bathroom in the rectory."

"I've wondered how you keep so clean, but that wasn't my question. I was wondering where you'll go when the weather changes? You know, like Mary Poppins. The open-ending of that movie always bothers me."

He smiled. "Fall is my favorite season in New York, so I prefer to spend as much time as possible outdoors. December through March, however, is another matter. Last year, I housesat for a friend, and the year before last, I spent it on the streets of Marseilles, in southern France. I worked in a B&B that winter, which was a blast. Anyway, I'll be sticking around here this year."

"That's good. I hope. For you, I mean. I hope it works out for you." Flustered, she let go of his arm. "The pain's gone down," she mumbled. "Thanks."

"No worries."

They stopped at the Great Lawn and looked over the sea of sunbathers and Frisbee throwers. "Ah, where New Yorkers make believe they're vacationing," he said.

"Thanks for inviting me, Chris. I'm glad I came along."

He pointed to the left of the lawn. "There it is."

Through a patch of trees, she could see their destination. It looked like a street fair, only under trees and full of dogs. As Chickpea pulled them forward, the yapping and howling grew louder. At the entrance, a basset hound added to the natural scents of the park. "Sorry about that," Chris said. "I never stay too long."

"I'm not in any rush."

A golden retriever's tennis ball rolled up to them, and Chris gave it a toss. Ava laughed as a small heard of Chihuahuas surrounded a Saint Bernard. "I feel like I'm in a Walt Disney movie: *101 Dogs of Different Breeds!*"

Chickpea circled her ankles, overexcited. "Hey!" Caught up in the leash, Ava grabbed Chris again for stability. Something about being close to him felt good. Easy. Her hand lingered on his broad shoulder. He looked at her, smiled, and then helped her to untangle.

"We better keep moving before Chickpea goes nuts and one of us sprains an ankle. That's the last thing you need." He kept a tighter rein.

They walked along the booths. He didn't seem interested in buying anything, although a doggie bed would've been nice for Chickpea.

"There must be a vendor for everything a dog could want here!" she said. "Toys, leashes, grooming services, organic food—"

"There she is." Chris plowed through the crowd, dragging along Chickpea, who wanted to investigate every smell.

"Who?" Ava hobbled after them, weaving between dogs and owners. "Where are we going?"

He stopped in front of a booth with a sign that read: *Ask Dr. Nguyen.* There was a line. "Do you mind waiting?" he asked. "She's supposed to be one of the best vets in the city, and I need a second opinion on vitamins."

"Absolutely," Ava replied. He certainly obsessed over Chickpea. But not like the women with their pooches peeking out of Louis Vuitton carriers. Somehow it seemed more selfless with Chris.

When it was their turn, Dr. Nguyen kept a stoic expression as she looked over Chickpea. "Sorry, but a daily vitamin won't make your dog young again. No such miracles."

"Well, yes, but will it *help*?" he pressed. "Maybe I should double up on the dose?"

Dr. Nguyen raised her eyebrows. "You might just have to let her be an older dog. It looks like you could increase her diet, though. Give the poor thing a bone."

Chris looked down at Chickpea as they walked away. "Sorry, girl. You deserve better than celery stalks." He walked straight to the booth where they were giving out all-natural biscuits. Chickpea got two.

"Now it's my turn to choose a booth," Ava said and led them to the French crêpes. "Nutella with bananas, please."

"Make that a double." Chris pulled a worn leather wallet out of his back pocket.

"No, I'll pay." She took a crinkled ten out of her handbag. "After everything you've done for me—"

He put his hand over hers. "Please, let me pay. You're my guest."

"Well...all right. Thank you."

They left the fair with their treats, meandering through the park in the direction of home. She bit into her crêpe, savoring the nutty chocolate cream and bananas.

Down a narrow and winding path, where a small cove nestled a pond, they stopped to watch a family of ducks nudge the lily pads. No one else was around. "I see you with a pen and notebook all the time, Chris. Are you writing a book or something?"

He didn't answer right away. Perhaps she was getting too personal. For someone living without any privacy, he was certainly a private person.

"It's just a journal," he finally replied. "A collection of details, really. Every day is full of them, if you stop to notice. I write the good ones down."

"That's interesting." Think of the details she could collect from The Encore: a lonely man's origami money; the sigh of pleasure from a man with a foot fetish; the sting of a bachelor party's riding whip. She'd have to live with these details. They were a part of her story now.

She skipped a stone in the water three times, making ripples.

Chris skipped one five times. "Maybe I'll use my journal in writing the biography of your life on 22nd Street." He smiled.

"That would turn into a book of blunders." She threw a stone as hard as she could, just making it across the pond. "You know,

I used to think you were writing the story of a homeless man. This is going to sound ridiculous, but I used to call you 'Joe,' as in Joe Gould. Have you heard of him?"

"Didn't someone write a book about him? *The Secret of Joe Gould*, or something like that?"

"Do you have a secret?" she asked. It had to be captivating, though maybe sad or disturbing.

"Who doesn't have a secret?" he replied. "But I think wondering what it could be is more interesting than knowing."

"True." Apparently his secret would remain one. The sun sparkled like glitter on the water. Ducks moved through the shade of a weeping willow. "It's like we've wandered into a secret right now."

"One of those moments you try to go back to again and can't," he said, looking into the distance.

They woke Chickpea from a powernap and walked on in silence, leaving the cove behind them.

The city on Central Park South was pandemonium. Bellboys at The Plaza Hotel whistled down cabs, and limos waited, double-parked out front. A wedding. Thank goodness it wasn't hers. At this point, she'd prefer a chat on her stoop to a dance in the Grand Ballroom.

They walked south on Fifth Avenue with Chickpea trotting alongside of them. A group of French tourists filled the sidewalk, taking photos, while tired-looking horses hitched to buggies ignored it all. Chris reached for her hand, and she held fast, not caring what people would think if they knew. He was a "street person"—so be it. His touch somehow calmed her and made her feel alive at the same time. She'd hold on and not think about anything else.

Back at her building, something felt different. Their casual acquaintance had deepened. Now what? Chris stood next to his cardboard looking lost, as if he'd forgotten how to live on the street.

She stopped before going up the stoop. "Thank you for the best day of my summer so far."

"If you're not working tonight, Chickpea and I are walking over to the Hudson River to catch the fireworks. You're welcome to come with us."

She had planned on staying home to keep Phoebe company—and to wait for the holiday to pass. Or maybe Julian would call, although she couldn't count on that. He probably had to work. "Sure, I'll go. I wasn't going to celebrate the Fourth this year, but why not?"

"I would've thought that this year in particular you'd want to celebrate your independence."

"That's true. Count me in!"

"Hey, Chickpea, are you up for the fireworks this year?" He ruffled her fur. "They make her a little jumpy."

"Oh, you'll be safe with us, Chickpea." Ava squatted down and hugged her, receiving a wet kiss on the cheek in return.

"Want to meet down here at seven-thirty?" Chris asked.

"Perfect." She walked up the stoop, noticing the crumbling steps as she went.

"Hey, let me know if you hear about that audition for the Arts Center," he said.

"I will. Maybe I'll get lucky."

"I think it's more about having faith." He pulled his suitcase out of a black plastic garbage bag tucked beneath the stairs, his own demonstration of faith.

"By the way," she called down from the top of the stoop, "I haven't forgotten about that garlic dinner I owe you."

"When you feel like it. I'll be right here."

"I know where to find you." She went inside, smiling.

Chapter Thirty-Three

The smell of bleached mold in the stairwell stung her eyes and nose. A few hours with Chris in Central Park and she'd forgotten the stark reality of her life. He had the power to make her believe everything was as it should be, and she could accomplish anything. Maybe he knew the truth.

She rubbed her lower back. The task at hand was getting upstairs. As she climbed, the feel of his hand—warm, strong, worldly—stayed with her, and the way their fingers linked so easily. She wasn't sure who had initiated contact. It was more of an impulse, like a sneeze she didn't know was coming. And then everything felt right. But it wasn't.

She reached the fifth floor and found her door ajar. Phoebe had called from the hair salon—refusing to divulge July's new tint. That was a half-hour ago; she wouldn't be back already. And if she were home, she would *not* leave the door open.

Ava went inside. "Phoebe? Are you home?" At the end of her hallway, sunlight pushed through grimy windows, casting a dusty spotlight on...Julian? Now clean-shaven, he lounged on her futon in a navy suit and red tie, reading *Cosmo*. For a second, Ava thought she was looking at a life-size advertisement.

"Who's Phoebe?" He set the magazine aside but didn't get up. "I don't remember you having a roommate."

"Julian, how'd you get in?"

He stood up, a proud smile spreading over his face. "You weren't home, so I let myself in."

"I see that. You picked my lock? I should call the police."

He laughed. "That would be redundant."

"Oh, so you have the right to break and enter—"

He moved swiftly toward her and snuck his arms around her

waist, kissing her lips. She felt his power and control and didn't resist, expecting the thrill she always felt when they kissed. But his mouth was dry and tasted like metal.

"You've surprised me, again," she said, pulling back. "Couldn't you call first, for once?"

"The surprise is on me." He touched her hair. "So, you're really a redhead?"

"Hey, if I can get used to your tattoos, then you can get used to my hair."

"Fair enough. Red has its appeal." He loosened his tie. "Come with me to a party tonight. It's at my friend Helena's place—you know, the D.A. She has *the* rooftop for catching the fireworks."

"I wish you had asked me sooner. I have plans." Of course she wanted to go with him, but did he think she'd be sitting at home, waiting for his invitation? Even if that was the original plan, he shouldn't just assume it, and now she actually had plans, with Chris.

Julian glared at her. "You said last night that you were taking the weekend off. I took that to mean you'd be spending it with me." The laugh lines around his eyes—or anger lines, such as they were—quickly softened. "I really want you to get to know my friends, Ava. No crowds, no loud music. Do I have to beg? It's a holiday. Who else would you spend it with?"

She hesitated, not able to explain her friendship with Chris.

"Do I have a yes?" Julian pressed.

"Of course I want to meet your friends, but...it's just that... okay, plans can be broken. I'd love to go with you."

"All right!" He playfully nudged her arm. "I knew you'd say yes."

Disappointing Chris would be hard, and she had looked forward to their evening, but with Julian she could have a future—and apparently his friends would play a big role in it. Helena's party could be the deciding factor.

He checked his watch. "I'll pick you up at seven. I'm off. Gotta get my car from the shop."

"I didn't know you had a car."

"Dodge Challenger, '79. Olive green, chrome rims, you'll love it." He took her hands in his. "So, a fresh start?"

"Yes. Take Two." Three? Four? What did it matter if everything came together in the end?

Ava crawled off the futon before her eyes were fully open. "What time is it?"

Phoebe was in the kitchen, sipping tea. "You're up! It's five to seven, dear. Do you like my hair? It's called Buttercup Blond!"

"Julian will be here any minute!" Ava bolted for the bathroom, but then stopped halfway and turned to Phoebe. "It's a fabulous look! We should go out one night and celebrate our new colors, maybe see *Hairspray* or something. But right now, I've got to get ready, fast." She went into the bathroom, keeping the door open.

"What's the big rush?" Phoebe called from the kitchen. "You're not working tonight, are you?"

"No, but I have plans to go out, like now. Actually, it's a date." She wasn't going to lie, even though she knew it had to hurt Phoebe.

"Oh." *Silence.* "Is he nice?"

"If I say yes, it doesn't mean that Josh *isn't* nice." She ran a brush through her hair, exciting flyaway strands. "To be honest, I'm still getting to know this guy. I've been out with him a few times...we'll see."

"It's funny, but I can't help feeling a little jealous. How could anyone be better than my Josh? But I know, I know. It's not about being *better*. It's about being in love." She sighed. "So who is this new guy? What does he do?"

"He's a cop, and he's full of surprises. It's exciting, some-times."

"Oh, sweetie, you don't want that. Dating a cop means a lot of drama and not a lot of paycheck."

"Phoebe, I'm looking for the right connection, not the right career." She tore through her closet. Nothing felt right. Too dull. Too revealing. Dated. Not flattering. She had to pick out something, now. Go bold. Diane von Furstenberg. An Easter gift from Phoebe. She ran her fingers over the long silky fabric, pistachio-green with faint lavender lilies, cut deep down her spine. It demanded attention.

Her cell phone rang as she pulled the dress on over her head. "Hi!" she answered Julian's call while deciding on a pair of open-toe pumps. "I'll be right there."

"I'm double-parked. Where are you?"

"Coming down now." She hung up the phone and grabbed her handbag, not caring that it didn't match her outfit. "Do you remember this dress, Phoebe?" She did a quick spin.

"Of course! I gave it to you for Passover. You look beautiful, absolutely gorgeous."

"Thank you. Are you staying in tonight?"

"Oh, there's a party I could go to, but I might just stay here. Don't worry about me."

"All right." Ava started to leave, and then stopped. "I'm sorry things didn't turn out the way we had hoped with Josh, but I do believe they've turned out for the best, for all of us."

"I know. Have fun, sweetie. And be careful, okay?"

Ava hobbled downstairs. In the foyer, she tried to place a feeling of regret...

Chris. Breaking their plans felt like the wrong move, but she had to give Julian preference, or they'd never get things off the ground.

Outside, the perfect summer evening made her feel even worse.

Chris saw her coming down the stoop and jumped up. "Ava! Wow! You look amazing. The fireworks won't compare."

"Oh, thanks." She noticed Julian waiting in his muscle car.

"You're a little early," Chris said, "but we can take our time walking over to the Hudson. Probably best with your injury."

"Chris...I have to cancel for tonight. I'm sorry." A dismal feeling cut a new path through her heart, but it was too late to turn back. "It's just that Julian, this cop I've been seeing,

invited me to a party and I said I'd go. I mean, I'd like to go."
"Sure. That's fine. No problem." He seemed sincere, although, yes, disappointed.

"Thanks for understanding." She heard a car door open, and they both watched Julian approach. He was minus jacket and tie now, and the top buttons of his shirt were unbuttoned, allowing an occasional peek at the serpents. Straight-laced melting into rebel-look.

"What's going on?" he asked and looked at Chris...the cardboard...Chickpea and her dish. "Hey, buddy. There's a good soup kitchen not far from here. Church of the Guardian Angel, on Tenth Avenue."

She tensed. Canceling their plans just got worse. "Sorry. Chris, this is Julian."

Chris offered his hand to him and they shook. "Thanks for the advice, Julian. I volunteer there regularly. Excellent food."

"Chris works at the *Rainbow Room*," she chimed in. "He's the sous chef."

Julian stared, momentarily baffled. "Interesting." He slipped his arm around her waist. "Well, we're out of here. Take care, man."

Chris's eyes met hers. "You really do look amazing, Ava. Have a good night."

It was hard to leave, but Julian led her away. "Drugs," he whispered. "Same old story."

"No. Not Chris."

"You know him?"

"Yes. Well, not entirely, but—"

"Trust me, these guys will make up anything."

She crawled into the white leather interior of Julian's Dodge, and they sped off down the street.

At Eighth Avenue, uptown traffic came to a standstill. "This could take hours," Julian grumbled. "So much for seeing the fireworks."

"They don't start until after nine. I'm sure we'll make it." She felt pressured to turn his lousy mood around. "So, how's your lead going with Marcus? Are you close to a major bust, or can't you talk about it?"

"Everything's going according to plan. I'll let you know when I have something to tell." He touched her dress. "You're making quite a statement, by the way."

"A *statement*? What am I saying?"

"You're saying...I don't know. Fresh. You could be in a soap commercial."

Was he serious? Was it good to be in a soap commercial? "Those people are usually in the shower, lathered in...soap."

"Good point." He nodded, watching the road. "I meant you look 'all natural.' Forget it. So, anyway, what's your stage name again?"

"Michelle. As in Michelle Pfeiffer in *The Fabulous Baker Boys*."

He laughed. "That's right. Talk about a bad movie."

"For a bad movie, it won a lot of awards."

He didn't reply. Traffic was stop-and-go, like their conversation, and tension escalated. "Move it!" he shouted out the window, slamming his fists against the steering wheel. He glanced her way. "I can't stand it when drivers block the intersection." He stuck his head back out the window. "Yo, idiot! I could take you in!" Another blow to the steering wheel and he looked at her, frowning. "Not to say this traffic is your fault, but I really hope you're not the type of woman who's always late."

"Sorry. I took a nap and overslept. I've had almost no sleep this week."

"I go days without sleep."

"Well, you're borderline insane," she said, assuming he'd get that she was kidding, or at least exaggerating.

"What makes you say that?" he asked, no hint of a smile.

"I don't know. You're nocturnal. And you have a wild side." Time for a new topic. "So, how long have you known Helena?"

"About a year. Okay, here's the deal with Helena. You might as well know. I met her on a case, and we went out afterward. One thing led to another, and let's just say it became a habit. She's not waiting for marriage. You can trust me on that."

"I see." She envisioned Julian on a jet airplane taking off

for the horizon, getting smaller and smaller. "Well, that might explain the bad vibe I got from Helena at the nightclub," Ava said after the image had faded.

"I doubt that. Helena doesn't want anything from me." They waited at a red light. Julian stared out his window.

"Do you want anything from her?"

"She's too independent for my taste." The light changed, and they were moving again. Barely—in more ways than one.

It was after eight o'clock when they finally pulled into a private entrance. Julian jumped out of the car, leaving the engine running. A small-statured man in maroon with brass buttons opened her door. "Welcome!" Behind him, a modern condominium pierced the hemisphere like a polished spear. She got out of the car, careful not to step on the hem of her dress.

"Hello, my friend," Julian said to the concierge. "How's your old lady's foot healing?" He obviously spent time here.

"Good evening, Detective Knox," the concierge replied. "Painfully slow, I'm afraid. She calls to tell me about it every hour." He slid into the driver's seat. "Pick up tonight?"

"That's right," Julian said. "Could be late."

"Have a happy Fourth!" The concierge drove Julian's car toward the underground parking garage.

As they rode the steel-plated lift, a silent fan blew cold air on the back of her neck. Julian put his hands on her shoulders and started massaging. "Your back feels like a plank of wood."

"Your 'friendship' with Helena isn't the best kick-off to her party."

"Everyone has a past." He gave up on her shoulders.

Floor PH. The elevator stopped and the doors opened. A capacious but characterless hallway stretched before them. They walked to a wide metal door, and Julian rang the bell twice.

"Hold on!" Helena's scratchy voice came from beyond.

Ava shivered and wished she'd brought a sweater, some sort of protection. "Did you tell her you were bringing me?"

The door flew open. "Since when do you knock?" Helena asked, smiling at Julian. Her focus landed on Ava, and the smile faded. "Why didn't you tell me you were bringing a friend? You know I hate surprises." Her red and orange poncho-inspired silk dress, undoubtedly haute couture—Pucci or Alexander McQueen—draped her body. Her "look" was a moveable screen, or barricade, as she stood in the doorway.

"This is Ava," Julian replied.

Helena raised her painted-on eyebrows at him, blatantly ignoring the introduction.

"Helena, I *told* you I was bringing someone. I did. I left you a voicemail."

"Of course. Ava. How nice." Helena produced a smile and then put it away.

"I hope I'm not intruding," Ava said. "We met a few weeks ago at—"

"I remember. You're the dancer, right? I see you've changed your hair." Saying nothing more, Helena escorted them through her high-ceilinged living room hung with wall-sized works of contemporary art. A bold red dot. A sweeping black smear. "I call them my Pride and Joy." She paused to admire her collection. "The red dot is Pride."

"And the black one is Joy?" Ava tried to take her seriously.

"Black humor! Don't you get it?"

The raucous laughter of friends floated in from the patio. "Can we just get to the party?" Julian asked, showing his impatience.

"Look who's on edge," Helena said. "Work getting to you, Jules?" She led the way out back, her red and orange dress waving before them like the flag of an adversary.

On the veranda, candlelight danced on a table of cast iron and cracked glass. A dozen or so friends clinked their goblets above half-empty bottles of wine and a picked-over spread of figs, wafers, chorizo, and brie. They had a direct view of the Empire State Building beaming the colors of the American flag.

And yet, she wished she were with Chris, watching the fireworks on the banks of the Hudson. She didn't need the perfect view.

Julian took off to the bathroom, leaving her with his friends and no introduction.

"What are you in the mood for?" Helena looked her over. "I have a Geyser Peak Cabernet and a fantastic Trimbach Alsace."

"Water or seltzer to start would be great, if you have it."

"Everyone, this is Ava!" Helena announced to the company in general, handing her a glass of white wine. "Take a seat. Make yourself known."

After an awkward wave to "everyone," Ava sat at the table where there was an open spot next to her for Julian.

"Hey, babe!" he returned, sleeves rolled, edge off.

Babe?

"Having a good time?" he asked.

"A blast. I just met everyone, I guess."

"Great. You'll love them." He walked past her and squeezed in at the head of the table, next to Helena. At once, they were into a conversation, voices dropping to a whisper.

Ava took a sip of the wine she didn't want, and a warm hand brushed her thigh.

"Whoa!" She jumped in her seat, splashing wine down her front. A new reflex from The Encore. At least she stopped herself before she exclaimed, *No touching!*

Everyone stared.

"We don't bite!" Helena laughed.

"Real sorry," said the woman to Ava's left. "I was just wiping some crumbs off my lap. Want a fig?" She offered a bowl.

"Thanks."

"I'm Jess." She was fair and petite. "I didn't mean to frighten you."

"It was my fault," Ava replied sheepishly. "Stress, I guess. Men..." She glanced over at Julian. He tossed her a grin, while saying something to Helena.

"Oh, don't expect anything from *men*," Jess replied. She had big, bright eyes and a cheery voice that carried. "It's the only way you'll be pleasantly surprised!"

"Or you could expect to be surprised and then get blown away," Julian said, slipping into their discussion. "You never know."

"Exactly." Helena poured herself another glass. "This guy throws on a suit and tie, and he's the spitting image of a family man. Blows me away every time."

"The suit comes and goes," Julian said. "Tomorrow you won't be able to tell me apart from the dealers."

"Speaking of which," Helena said, and their whispery conversation resumed.

"All right, you two," Jess cut in, pointing the cheese cutter at them. "If you're going to whisper sweet nothings about the judicial system all night, then taxi it back to the office, or wherever you conduct business."

Both the cutter and Jess's pointed comment were ignored. Julian didn't make *anything* easy. Then again, he'd say she was acting jealous. *Was she?*

"So, what do you do?" Ava asked Jess, paying no attention to the obvious. She could be a cool girlfriend. She'd show them.

"Advertising, the creative end, and I just got this new boss who is totally—"

An explosion went off, and the sky rained red, white, and blue streaks of fire. Everyone cheered. Helena popped the cork on a bottle of champagne and announced, "To life, liberty, and the pursuit of happiness!"

Julian got up from the table and disappeared inside. The bathroom again? What about his rush to catch the fireworks? Maybe he had calls to make for work...or a bad stomach. Asking might make her sound suspicious; she wouldn't risk that.

"How did you and Julian meet?" Jess asked.

"At Krispy Kreme, of all places. He picked me up along with a couple of doughnuts. It had to be fate." Ava smiled.

"He hates doughnuts," Helena hissed, like a coiled snake ready to strike.

"I know," Ava bit back. "He told me."

"Well, that makes the story even better!" Jess exclaimed.

Julian rejoined the party to another explosion of color in

the sky. "America the beautiful!" he said, his eyes as bright as the sparklers. Was he doing drugs? Was she losing her mind?

"So, Ava, what kind of dancing are you doing?" Helena asked. She heard a loaded question. "Mostly I'm going on auditions, learning that success doesn't happen overnight." Screamers spiraled to the earth.

"It must be nice, not working." Helena spoke, waving a flute of champagne. "I wish I could wake up whenever I felt like it. Schedule a court case, or not, depending on my mood. You have no idea, the hours I work as a litigator."

"It must be stressful. I do have a job, though. I work at The Encore, which can be grueling, too. In a different way." Crackles went off above her head, hundreds of little pops, as if the stars had burst out laughing.

"The Encore?" Helena cocked her head to one side, the way a dog gathers information from a scent.

"You've never been," Julian quickly replied. "It's a dive."

"What do you do there?" Helena asked, and all eyes turned to Ava.

"Well, do you know Michelle Pfeiffer in—"

"She waitresses," Julian cut in. "Let's be real, Ava." He turned to Helena. "Hey, tell everyone about that last case we worked on. It's a good story. The guy was up for..."

He hardly looked at her. Everyone got into the "good" story, while fireworks boomed in the background. She stood up from the table, legs shaking. "Excuse me, but I promised I'd stop by another party tonight, so I should get going. Thanks, Helena, for having me over."

"If you're sure." Helena rose with a send-off smile: big, warm, and entirely insincere. "Jules, can you make sure she finds the door all right?"

"I'll be fine, and don't worry, I'm not going to make off with your Pride and Joy."

"Ava, wait." Julian followed her through the living room and out the door. "What's going on? Why are you leaving so early?"

"Well, to be honest, I realize you're not the One." She pressed the down button at the elevator.

"Come on, Ava..."

"I'm pretty sure you're attracted to me, and you said yourself you want the things you can't have, but I really don't think you're interested in who I am."

He laughed. "Whoa! I'm totally lost."

"No, you've lost me, *Jules*." She stepped into the elevator.

"You're being ridiculous." He followed her inside. "Honestly, you're the most sensitive woman I've ever met. You really are! What are you so insecure about?" He blamed her, while she felt the pull of gravity on the long ride down.

Ground floor. She stepped out and faced him. "Listen, I spent a lot of time with a guy who wasn't supportive of what I do or believe, and it's really not fun."

Julian shrugged. "I just don't get why this job is so important to you."

"Maybe that's something I'm figuring out, but do you think your judgment and disregard is *helping*?"

He shook his head, refusing to see her for herself.

They stood at the curb, while the concierge hailed her a cab. It was a balmy summer night, perfect for taking a stroll with the one you love.

"I'm gonna stay at the party," Julian said.

"I didn't ask you to leave with me."

A taxi pulled up. The little man in maroon opened the door. Before getting in, she turned to Julian, "You know what? I realize where I went wrong."

"I could've told you that. Leaving the fashion industry, for starters."

"No. I thought since you agreed to wait to have sex, you were the One for me. You know? That rare gem." She got into the cab, holding open the door. "It's a start, and I'm *so* glad we waited, but a true gem is someone who knows how to be a friend."

She shut the door and lowered the window. He remained standing on the sidewalk.

"Speaking of which," she said through the window, "I have a very good friend waiting for me at home."

Her street was dark and quiet. Chris was apparently still out celebrating. She slumped down onto his cardboard and buried her face in her hands. The day had started so right at the dog fair; her life always came into focus when she was with him. Now nothing made sense. What did she see in Julian to give him so many chances? And what if she was leading Chris on by wanting his friendship, and leading Phoebe astray by taking her in?

She looked up. A man walking his dog passed by on the sidewalk. The lit tip of his cigarette looked like a firefly. He didn't notice her watching as she crouched low, tucked into a shadow. Homelessness was Chris's privacy. She finally understood his desire for autonomy and discretion, going for his dream.

She looked at her street from his viewpoint. Everything appeared larger and closer, as if within grasp. Even the scrawny trees wanting rain looked taller and stronger. She discovered the moon between two buildings that seemed only inches apart. Were these the details that inspired him? That he kept in his journal? She'd give anything to be privy to all the little miracles in his life. Insightful, mysterious, funny...or even mundane. How did God show himself to Chris? What kind of detail was *she* in his book? A small one, easily forgotten? Or was she an everyday detail, the kind he couldn't live without?

She closed her eyes and rested her head against the cool façade of her building. Would it be so horrible to fall asleep right here? Several distant explosions sounded in the direction of New Jersey. She opened her eyes as a cascade of colored stars lit up a corner of the sky. Here was life turned upside-down. Oddly enough...it was a clearer perspective than her usual one.

Chapter Thirty-Four

Ava sat outside on her fire escape with a cup of coffee, squinting into the morning sunlight. It had only taken her a few weeks to figure out that Julian wasn't the One, a huge improvement over her five-year learning lesson with Josh. She watched two pigeons flirt on a neighbor's window ledge. Their tiny heads couldn't possibly allow for much brain development, and yet when they chose their mate, it lasted for a lifetime. The decision had to be instinctual, or from the heart.

From inside her apartment, she could hear someone knocking on her door. She didn't move to answer it. Julian? Back to apologize? That would be Take Too Many. Not a chance. Anyway, he wouldn't knock; he'd just break in.

She climbed inside through the window and tightened the drawstring on her pajamas. Phoebe's Post-it lay on the kitchen table: *Yoga. P.* Maybe Mr. Copeland was outside her door...on a white horse and bearing roses. She'd serve him instant coffee while they waited anxiously for Phoebe to return.

She looked through the peephole and caught her breath. *Chris?* It was the first time she'd seen him *in*side. And not only that, he had gotten a haircut. She peered harder through the tiny hole.

His fierce, dark eyes observed her door below long, equally dark brows. His prominent cheekbones and the set path of his jawline were like a mark of lineage...even Chickpea, sitting at attention by his side, seemed proud. Ava pulled back, suddenly dizzy, as if ascending new heights.

He knocked again and she opened the door, much too fast. "Hi!" Her cheeks burned at once. "Sorry, I was outside...on my fire escape."

Luckily, Chickpea in her wiggle dance insisted on Ava's full attention. "Ruff!"

"Hey, girl!" Ava gave her a rubdown, taking the opportunity to collect her thoughts. Chris always had the potential to be attractive, but she never thought he would rise to it. His homelessness suddenly became more confusing.

"Ah, the rainbow PJs." He grinned. "Good morning, A. Larson of 5C. It was my first guess. 'Ava Larson' has a nice ring."

"Your hair is short!" she blurted out, unable to control her volume. "You look good! I mean, the cut. It's nice. Well, if anything, I can see you now." She patted Chickpea, again avoiding eye contact.

"Thanks." He leaned against the doorjamb. His white T-shirt, self-possessed air, and easy posture hadn't changed. "Enough about my twelve-dollar trim. I stopped by to see if you wanted to come to the soup kitchen with me at the Church of the Guardian Angel. They have an excellent Sunday brunch, which I prepared this morning."

"A soup kitchen?"

"It's like going to church, except there's food." His eyes made their own appeal, lively, full of hope.

Yes, she wanted to go with him. "Well, all right, since you went to the trouble of climbing five flights to invite me."

He laughed. "I don't know who was panting more, me or Chickpea."

"Then you both needed the workout. I just have to get dressed. When do we leave?"

"Fifteen minutes. I'll wait for you outside." He headed for the stairs.

"Hey, Chris?"

He turned. "Yes?"

"Thanks for asking me."

"Anytime."

Outside, Chris waited with Chickpea on her leash. "You cleaned up fast!"

"I'm excited to try your food," she said, rubbing Chickpea's nose.

"One day you will." His smile reflected the sunlight. "At the soup kitchen I'm limited by the budget and the menu. It's not *my* food."

"I understand, but I'm still hungry."

They started off, Chickpea leading the way. "It's just two blocks from here," Chris said. "An easy walk."

"Oh, then it must be the church bells I hear from my apartment," she said, "year after year, chiming the hours."

"We've been listening to the same music." He glanced her way and smiled. "I never tire of them."

He didn't reach for her hand, the way he did yesterday after the park. What did she expect, after blowing him off to be with Julian last night?

Chickpea took the lead, glancing back periodically as if to say, *come on!*

"What's the rush, Chickpea?" Ava asked. "Did Chris tell you how long it's been since I've been to church?"

He laughed. "Dogs do have good intuition. But that's not what her rush is about."

The Church of the Guardian Angel came into view, a yellow-stone structure with four columns on either side of the portal. Ornate sculptures surrounded open double doors, both a warm and intimidating welcome.

Chickpea's urgency suddenly became clear. A Golden Retriever tied to a tree out front jumped about, exuberant over their arrival.

"Hey, boy!" Chris gave the dog a pat. "Meet Willard, Chickpea's boyfriend." Willard pulled at his leash to get closer. "Hold on, guy. She's not going anywhere." Chris tied Chickpea to the tree, and the two dogs were instantly nose-to-nose, tails at high mast. "Now don't get all tangled up like you did last week!" He turned to Ava. "You should have seen them. They could barely move."

She laughed, feeling more at ease. "I like your Sunday routine."

"At least now you know where the church bells are coming from." He double-checked Chickpea's leash and glanced warily up and down the sidewalk. "All right. Let's go in." They climbed the front steps and entered the open doors.

Clear-paned windows gleaming sunlight gave the church a sense of lustrous magnificence. The vaulted ceiling with redwood beams drew her attention upward, and she gazed into the high arches. Ahead, two life-sized marble angels guarded either side of the altar.

"Where are the pews?" she asked, staring at rows of foldout tables and chairs, and hundreds of men and women focused on eating.

"They removed them in order to get more use out of the church." Chris led her down a short corridor to an industrial-looking kitchen, where the slop line was in progress.

"We've passed the eight hundred mark!" a man shouted from a back entrance. He held up a small counter in his palm, and then continued checking people in for a meal. Volunteers in paper hats and aprons cheered as they worked the assembly line, serving up scrambled eggs, cuts of a fresh ham, and pancakes with a blueberry sauce option.

"That's nothing," Chris said, standing beside her. "We've served over fifteen hundred meals on a Sunday. They have to turn the church over four times throughout the two hours in order to feed everyone."

"Hey, Chris! Jump in line for a meal!" one of the volunteers called out. The hefty man beamed happiness as he scooped scrambled eggs onto plate after plate.

"That's Bob, and over there is Sandy and Alice and Susan... Everyone, this is my good friend, Ava!" Chris announced. "I'm recruiting her for the kitchen!"

Warm smiles and welcomes came from every direction of the bustling kitchen.

"I'm told I can make a decent mac-n-cheese," Ava replied, feeling instantly at home, "but maybe I should start out serving."

"Start out with a good meal!" said the woman on pancake duty.

A surprisingly young-looking guy, maybe a teenager, let them cut the line. "Hey, big C," he said to Chris. "The grub looks mad good, as always."

"Let's see how it tastes!" Chris laughed, and in no time they had full plates and were being offered tea, coffee, or orange juice at the beverage table.

A lot of the patrons knew Chris and stopped them to say hello. Eventually, they found seats at a table near the front of the church.

A short-statured man with ginger hair and freckles stepped lightly onto the altar and approached the podium. "That's Father Gallagher," Chris explained. "He sneaks in a short sermon every half hour or so throughout brunch."

"Hello, friends!" Father Gallagher, wearing jeans and a T-shirt, opened his arms wide. Conversations quieted until there was only the sound of cutlery *clinking* on plates.

Ava stared ahead, and her focus rested on the rough wooden cross hanging above the altar. Father Gallagher's voice faded from her mind as flashbacks of The Encore, talking and laughing with men, some of them utterly lost in their search for love, filled her with a dark and groundless sorrow. She didn't help them to see a better life; she was just as lost.

I'm so sorry. I put money before humanity...and I haven't been honest with myself.

A cool tingling sensation spread over her arms. Mom appeared in her thoughts, vivid, as if with purpose. *I love you, Ava.* It was as if Mom knew everything, and maybe now she did. Clearly, love didn't hide, not even behind death. Love surrounded her, even here, and if she opened her heart it would grow in her life in ways she couldn't imagine. Ava stared at her food. Somehow she knew that...but not how to open her heart.

Chris glanced at her and smiled as Father Gallagher sang out: *May the Lord, mighty Lord, grant and keep you forever. Grant you peace, perfect peace, faith in every endeavor!*

As they filed out of the church, two men, unshaven, with mismatched clothes and tattered knapsacks, came up to Chris. The smaller of the two, with brown skin and gray hair, spoke up. "Well, hello, Chris! It's about time you got yourself a girlfriend. Who's the lucky lady?" His wide smile showed missing teeth.

"Ava is a *friend*, Mike, if that's okay with you. What's with the pressure to find a girlfriend?"

"All the time you spend cooking for us, you should be feeding someone who's special to you, that's all. In other words, get yourself a life, man!" Mike turned to her. "Pleasure to meet you, Ava. You got yourself a good friend, anyway."

She smiled. "I feel real lucky."

Father Gallagher stood outside on the steps. "Welcome," he said and clasped her hand with both of his. "We hope to be of service to you here at the Guardian Angel." His eyes showed empathy, concern. Did he think she was in trouble, or even homeless, like Chris?

"Thank you. I'm happy just to be here."

Chris waved over an older woman with long yellow hair, like filaments of gold. "Here comes my friend Gretchen," he said, "Willard's owner, and the one who watches Chickpea. She volunteers every Sunday with some of the girls from her shelter."

"Hello!" Gretchen walked toward them, smiling and waving. "Another exemplary show of bravery, leaving Chickpea tied out front!"

Chris turned to Ava. "The hardest part about living on the streets is leaving Chickpea alone, even if it's only for an hour.

Just the fear that someone might take her..."

Gretchen laughed, shaking her head from side to side. "*Every* time he sees me tying up Willard, he asks if I worry about dognappers. I hate to break it to you, buddy, but our mutts ain't pedigree!"

"I still don't like to leave her." Chris untied both leashes and handed Willard's to Gretchen.

"Admit it, you treat Chickpea like she's your first-born!" Ava laughed out loud.

"I said the same thing!" Gretchen giggled like a young girl. "Chris, one day, you'll be an overprotective father." She was a lot like Dr. Lindquist, the hip grandma type, wearing jeans and carrying a hot pink duffle bag. She was small in stature with a round middle and flushed cheeks. Not the tough-looking woman one would expect to see running a home for wayward girls.

"Anyway, this is my friend Ava." Chris touched her arm as he said her name, and she felt lucky.

Gretchen put her hands on her hips. "I could've guessed that! I feel like we've met already. Chris has mentioned you, once or twice." She extended her hand, and they shook.

"He's told me about you and your work, too," Ava said. "All for One sounds amazing!"

"I consider it my Tough Love project. It's the hardest thing I've ever done, and I love it!" Willard, sitting beside Chickpea, yawned. Gretchen got down on one knee to scratch his back. "Silly boy, you get so excited over Chickpea, you have to nap afterward." She stood, a little out of breath. "So, I hear you're a dancer, Ava. And you've trained your whole life."

"Oh, well, yes. But only now am I actually doing anything with dance."

"Let me tell you something. It's never too late. I started All for One five years ago, at the age of fifty-eight! If I had thought it was too late, over a hundred teenage girls would be doing nothing with their lives right now, many in abusive relationships. Or on the streets. Now they know someone cares about them, and some have gone on to careers and stable families of their own!"

"That's amazing." Again, Ava felt pulled into a dark place, thinking of the men she led further astray. The fake names. The illusions of glamor. But it paid her bills...

Gretchen looked down at her watch. "Oh, I have to go. A wonderful pediatrician named Dr. Emmy Roads is giving a workshop on infant care today at one o'clock. We have eleven pregnant women in our care and four who have recently given birth. Life must go on! So, Chris, will I be seeing Chickpea this week, as usual?"

"You sure will. Thanks, Gretchen."

"I always say two dogs are easier than one. Hope to see you again, Ava." She wobbled off with Willard following along.

Ava walked with Chris in the direction of home, Chickpea at their heels. The city was quiet, giving the sparrows center stage for a change. Ava breathed in the sunny day. "You know what I feel like doing?"

"The way you're prone to change lately, I don't have a clue what you feel like doing."

"I want to make that meal I promised you. With garlic. Do you have plans tonight?"

"Now I do! That sounds great. You can bring it downstairs to my place, if you want, and we can have a picnic below the stoop."

"Okay!" It seemed like a fun idea, and a perfectly natural place for them to have a meal. "Around seven-thirty?"

"Super. Is there anything I can do to help?" he asked. "I want to contribute to the groceries, too."

"No way. This time it's all me. In fact, I'll even go to Whole Foods."

"At least let me get drinks. I can make a ginseng raspberry iced tea that will renew every tired muscle in your body."

"That would be perfect." She didn't ask how he would manage to make it, trusting he knew a way. "But you don't have to do anything fancy," she added. "We're having a picnic, not a meal at the *Rainbow Room.*"

They stopped in front of her building, and Chris reached for her arm. "Hey, I hope going to the soup kitchen helped a little," he said, "with losing your mom and all. It's a good place."

"Yes, it did. I was reminded that, despite appearances, I have everything in life I need."

He smiled at her. "I hear you. We just have to realize it."

She turned and started up the stoop. "See you at seven-thirty."

Inside, it occurred to her that she and Chris had more than just a stoop in common; they had a prayer.

Chapter Thirty-Five

Mist glistened on the row of greens at Whole Foods Market. Ava picked up a basket and set out to shop. Three cloves of garlic should be sufficient. Why not? Peppers, onions, and tomatoes for the stir-fry...butter, anchovies, and cream for a hearty Bunyaculta. Oh, she'd impress this chef! Next, free-range chicken cutlets and angel hair pasta...whole wheat? No, gluten free. Italian bread from the bakery, still warm. Fresh basil and Parmesan cheese. Nothing but the best for Chris today.

Back home, she opened the windows, welcoming a late afternoon breeze. Bing Crosby crooned on the radio across the way. She went out onto the fire escape and coaxed her geranium back to life with water, refusing to give up on it.

As she climbed back inside through the window, buttercup-blond Phoebe came into the kitchen. "I like your neighbor's choice in music!" She sat down at the table with her new favorite lunch, Tofu Tikka Masala from the local Indian restaurant. "If Bing knows anything about love, I guess pain is par for the course." She tucked a napkin into her olive-green yoga wear.

Ava put water on the stove to boil for the pasta. "Except he says you must have *showers*, and I've been getting steady rain!"

"That's nothing," Phoebe said, cutting her tofu with a knife and fork. "Try flash flood warnings!" They laughed.

"Phoebe, when you smile the sun comes out."

"You're too sweet. But why, may I ask, are you doing all this cooking?"

"My friend bought me a garlic crusher, and I'm making him a meal. Chris, the homeless man."

"Oh, good heavens. I swear, Ava, if you were my daughter, I'd put you in counseling."

"That's funny, Mr. Copeland said something similar when he saw me at the club." Immediately, she realized she had forgotten to mention it.

"When was this?" Phoebe asked.

"I'm so sorry. I forgot to tell you. I saw him at The Encore Friday night. He was there with clients. We only talked a minute. He knows you're with me. I would've told you right away, but you were asleep when I got home, and then with the Fourth it totally slipped my mind. I'm sorry, Phoebe."

"Sometimes Barry and I think alike," she said softly, and then sure enough the clouds rolled in and her sunny face darkened.

"He didn't like my new hair color," Ava said, trying to lighten the mood.

Phoebe fell quiet, while it undoubtedly sank in that he hadn't called. She might have to start over for real. Heartbroken, it wouldn't be easy.

"Hey, Chris and I are having a picnic. Do you want to join us? Everything's organic. Very healthy."

"A picnic? With that hairy man out front and his scruffy dog? I'd rather not, thank you."

"They cleaned up—a haircut, professional grooming...you should see them!"

Phoebe shook her head.

"If you're sure, then I'll save you the leftovers." Ava's voice dropped. "I heard garlic is good for the heart."

"Save *him* the leftovers." Phoebe stood up from the table. "I think I'll take a hot bath. My muscles are sore, and I'm not up for talking just now."

"You hardly touched your food," Ava said, worried for her.

"My appetite is gone." She disappeared into the bathroom. Ava watched the door close, wondering if separation was actually the right choice after so many years of marriage.

Crushing clove after clove of garlic, she stirred it into the sauce, into the veggies, and over the chicken. Soon the bare-wall smell of 5C was replaced by the warm aromas of an Italian eatery...a kitchen in Venice...a home.

Chopped basil and grated cheese over everything, and her

meal was done. Garlic enough to taste for the rest of the week, and definitely a meal they'd never forget!

Now how to get it all downstairs? She emptied a crate of dreamy love stories, and with the food in plastic take-out containers, everything fit. Paper plates, napkins, knives and forks. Anything forgotten?

She walked to the bathroom and called through the closed door, "Phoebe? I'm leaving. Are you okay? We can all eat here if you'd rather not be alone."

"Alone, please," Phoebe called back.

Ava paused, listening to the trickle of bathwater. "Are you going to call him?"

"I can't make him love me, Ava. Go and have fun with your street friend...and stay in public places, please."

"Okay. I'll see you later."

Ava made it downstairs without spilling a thing. A push through the front door and she called out, "Dinner is served!"

Chris rushed to help. "And I thought *I* was resourceful!"

Again, she avoided eye contact, struck by his looks. Feeling awkward and self-conscious, she reminded herself that they were just friends. It was easiest to think of him as her homeless friend. Establishing that boundary felt safe—if only he looked the part.

He set the crate down below the stoop, and something else felt wrong. The passersby and Sunday evening traffic demanded their attention. An ambulance raced down the avenue, its siren prohibiting conversation. Filth, everywhere.

Chickpea stood and sniffed the food, while Chris spread his russet blanket over the cardboard. His suitcase became the table.

"Have a seat." He patted the blanket, which looked raggedy up-close. Chickpea found a spot, salivating.

Ava hesitated, and then sat down in the spot saved between them. "It doesn't cushion the concrete much." She laughed, a desperate attempt at humor. "I should be used to hard surfaces, sleeping on a sack of potatoes called a futon every night."

"And this is doubled up!" He slapped the cardboard twice.

"It's amazing what you can get used to, isn't it?"

Wedged between Chris and Chickpea, her back to the wall, she suddenly felt stuck.

He pulled out a large plastic water bottle filled with a pink liquid and set it down on the suitcase. "For some reason, I figured you would bring glasses."

She jumped to her feet. "Oh, I didn't even think of glasses! I'll run back upstairs. Or, how about we just eat in my apartment?" Phoebe would have to accept his company.

"It's too nice to be inside." He took a paper plate for himself and set one down for her. "Who needs glasses? I don't mind drinking from the bottle if you don't."

"Here?"

"Sure. We don't want all this delicious food to get cold. Plus, I'm famished!"

A man shouted from his car in Spanish to a woman across the street. A couple jogged by, their breathing loud and labored. She couldn't do this. "I have an idea. How about we walk to the piers on the Westside and eat by the water? We can be there in ten minutes."

"You don't like the ambiance here?" He looked genuinely surprised.

Seriously? "All I'm saying is there are other places. You know? The piers are quiet. And they have benches."

"All right. I get it." He cleared off the suitcase, opened it, and took out Chickpea's leash. She wagged her tail enthusiastically.

"I think Chickpea's on my side." Ava hoped he wasn't mad.

"That's no surprise. The pier it is!"

She walked Chickpea, and he carried the crate. They headed west, toward a swirl of color, as the sun took its long bow, introducing a beautiful night. People turned to the aroma of their meal. Even a winded bulldog wrinkled his nose in curiosity. If anything, garlic was in the air.

Nearing the water, a blazing horizon suffused the city in rose, lavender, and gold. The facing buildings sparkled and glowed. "Life feels magical right now," she whispered. The tension was gone.

"I think we've stumbled upon another secret," he said, "like the pond tucked away in Central Park."

"Only with you, Chris."

"How about right here?" he asked once they made it to the water. A weathered bench on a deserted pier jutting out over the Hudson felt like the perfect spot for their picnic, despite Phoebe's warning to stay in a public place. Ava nodded.

Chris started unpacking the crate while she opened containers of food. Below them, gentle waves slapped against wooden beams. Ahead, the sun bled colors like molten lava over lazy swells.

"So how was your Fourth?" he asked.

"Let's just say I won't be seeing the cop anymore. How about you? Did you catch the fireworks?"

"Not literally, but I did see them."

"Very funny." She couldn't help but laugh. Josh never cracked silly jokes. "You know what I mean."

"A co-worker of mine lives in a high-rise about five blocks south of here, right across from the water. He and his wife throw a party every year. We had a great view, but guess who turned into a big howling baby?" He ruffled Chickpea's fur. "She 'caught' them from my lap on the couch."

"Oh, no! Chris, I forgot all about Chickpea. Her dinner. Not even a bone!"

"Don't worry, she already ate." He reached for the plastic bottle. "And she had her daily bone." He took a sip. "Homemade raspberry iced tea. I could have added a bit more lime, but it's still good. I toast to you." He passed her the bottle.

"This is crazy." She tasted the tea—sweet with a touch of citrus—and passed it back, laughing at herself. "To friendship."

Chris raised it high. "To *If Only* jobs!"

"Look at us, like new-wave pirates with herbal tea for a bottle of whiskey!"

He laughed. "I'm glad you like it."

They dished out the food. Chris took a mouthful of pasta, chewed and swallowed, eyes watering. "Crusher works!" He reached for the tea.

"Is it on par with the *Rainbow Room*?"

"Oh, much more potent. I'll be going for seconds, though. Don't worry."

They ate, watching the sun go down. Chickpea rested her head on Ava's knee, a show of affection, gentle and trusting. Chris smiled. "She likes you."

Ava stroked her silky fur to the soothing hum of life surrounding them.

"So, why did you choose my building?" she asked after a while. "I remember it was April first when I first saw you."

"You remember the day?" He looked surprised at first, and then smiled, nodding his head. "I get it. April Fool's Day."

"No! I'm not joking. Odd things stick in my head, like dates and poems."

"Poetry and the day I arrived...I like that." His eyes became playful.

She looked out at the water, blushing, and then faced him. "Actually, I wasn't thrilled about it. Seeing you there made me feel conflicted and uneasy. I didn't like to think about the hardships that must've landed you on the streets, and yet at the same time I was plagued with curiosity."

"I don't think hardships—like my mother's death or my father's difficult personality—'landed' me on the streets; they just made me who I am. I guess I don't talk much about my troubles because I don't find them all that interesting. You're better off being curious. But to answer your question, the reason I chose 'your' building is kind of random. I was already living on the streets, and one day, while sitting on your stoop to eat a sandwich, I came up with the name for my first restaurant. I figured it had to have good energy, so I made it my home."

"Really? What's the name?" Even if his restaurants were just a dream, she wanted to know.

"I won't tell you or anyone else, not until I announce the grand opening. It's not for superstitious reasons. I don't want the name talked about until there's a reason for talking about it. Like the food, it needs to be fresh."

"Of course. That makes sense."

He went for a second helping of Bunyaculta. "So, I'm sorry to hear that your date was a flop," he said and then took a bite, chewed, and swallowed. "Although I can't say that I liked the guy. Too much ego for my taste."

"We didn't see eye-to-eye on things. Our jobs, in particular."

Chris took a swig of tea. "A job shouldn't get in the way of dating. Relationships aren't about the *facts*." He passed her the bottle.

"I know that, now. The connection wasn't there, beyond an attraction, and even that soured." She drank and passed back the bottle. "Maybe if I keep an open heart, rather than an open mind, one day I'll be planning another wedding...or eloping at City Hall."

"No wedding?" he exclaimed. "You've got to celebrate— friends and family, good food, the cake!"

"That would be nice," she said. "Hey, like Father Gallagher sang this morning, *faith in every endeavor*. Right?"

He nodded. "Faith in every endeavor."

She looked up to a vestige of moon visible in the sky as the sun gave way to the stars. "'Hand in hand, on the edge of the sand, they danced by the light of the moon,'" she recited softly to herself.

"Ava..." He leaned over and kissed her, just once, gently on her mouth. His warm lips touched hers so carefully it seemed at first that he had only asked to kiss her and not actually done it. She hesitated kissing him back, and a sudden wind sent her paper plate into the water, floating away.

"I wasn't expecting that." She looked down at her empty hands.

"The wind can catch you off guard." He pulled strands of hair back off her cheek. "I can do it again."

Should she cross that line? Allow his homelessness into her life? It was a *fact*, and relationships weren't built on facts...but it was a big one. Independence and savings aside, how could anyone choose such a life? She felt fear and doubt take over.

"Your friendship means so much to me," she said tentatively. "I can tell you anything, and I *want* to tell you everything. In fact, you've influenced my life more than any friend I've ever had."

"But—" He waited for the real answer.

"I'm not sure I'm ready for anything more." Happiness seemed to slip through the planks of the pier and sink to the bottom of the Hudson. "Maybe it's just bad timing."

"I see. But I can't be your friend and wish we had something more. That would be too difficult for me, and dishonest to you."

Who was being dishonest? She wanted to be with him more every day. He understood her. He inspired her! But he was homeless, and likely a dreamer. Did she know him, really?

They cleaned up what was left of dinner. She moved slowly, mostly getting in the way. Chris nudged Chickpea, and the three of them retraced their steps back to 22nd Street in silence.

"Thanks for dinner, Ava. You're a good cook." He handed her back the crate.

"I'm glad you liked it." She went up the stoop. "Bye, Chris."

As the front door closed behind her, an empty feeling took root in her chest and began to grow.

Chapter Thirty-Six

Ava lay on her futon, still in her PJs, listening to the church bells chime the hour...ten chimes...eleven...twelve. If she didn't pick up more nights at The Encore or find a new job, she'd have to ask Phoebe for food and rent money. *No way*, she thought, *I'll turn to the streets first.*

Another Post-it lay on the kitchen table when she finally gave up on sleep and got up at noon: *Yoga! P.*

Ava made a cup of instant coffee and took it with her cell phone out onto the fire escape. A heavy gray sky seemed to meld with the sidewalk below. Hopeless weather. She dialed and waited for Maggie to answer.

"Hi, it's me."

"Ava, you got me at a good time—Melanie's napping. What's going on?"

"Remember the homeless man in front of my building? The one who saved us from those two creeps after the nightclub?"

"Sure, I remember some guy shacked up below your stoop. He was kind of cute, I think."

"Right!" Ava felt energy start to flow through her body again. "He got a haircut and is actually good-looking. I'm not kidding. Like storybook." She giggled. "But that's beside the point. He's a great guy. Intelligent, understanding, considerate...and really fun to be around. Okay, granted he's 'out there,' as in a total dreamer. But he does have a job—at the *Rainbow Room*."

"First of all, he's 'out there' as in homeless. And, secondly, I read that the *Rainbow Room* closed."

"That can't be; the place is an all-time classic. He said he's the sous chef, which is the assistant to the executive chef." A siren screamed from a nearby street.

"Let me guess," Maggie shouted through the phone, "you're out on your fire escape. Listen, why am I getting the lowdown on your homeless man?"

The siren passed. "Well, because I think...I think I love him. I'm in love with him, Maggie."

"What?"

"I don't care where he lives."

"You love the guy under your stoop? That's hilarious! Ava, you're not thinking clearly."

"I know! I got scared and let him get away!"

"From the stoop? What are you talking about? And what happened to the 'mysterious' cop? I've heard of the rebound relationship, but this is like that kissing game, Spin the Bottle. Here's my advice. Keep spinning! You can do better."

"Okay, now try to open your ears and listen. Chris and I became friends over the past month, like *real* friends, and then yesterday he made a move, I spun the bottle, and it landed on 'let's just be friends!'"

"The right answer."

"No! I made him feel like he wasn't good enough, but he *is*. Now our friendship is over and I feel completely lost. I can't imagine my life without him."

"All right, fine. Then go downstairs and tell him that."

"You think so?" Hope sparked. "It's not too late?" A thick drop of water landed on her forehead. She looked skyward for rain or a leaky air conditioner, and an ear-splitting crack of thunder vibrated through the fire escape.

"Are you still there?" Maggie asked.

Ava shakily climbed back inside still holding the phone. "That was scary. Anyway...are you sure it's not too late to apologize?" She tugged hard on the wooden window frame, closing it.

"You won't know until you try. I think you're crazy, chasing after some bum, though. Or maybe not? Who am I to tell you what's right? My marriage is far from perfect. Marc and I are in counseling."

315

"Jeez, Maggie, I'm really sorry." Rain fell like a screen over the windows, and the city disappeared from view.

"It hasn't been easy," Maggie said. "I finally told him about our weekend...that I wasn't faithful."

"Oh, I'm so proud of you, Maggie! It must be a relief."

"I suppose. We both agree we need help, which is a start. As for your 'homeless' love, I don't know. You listened to your gut when you left Josh. Why stop now?"

"Exactly! I needed to hear you say that. Thanks. I'm going outside to make things right again. And I'll bring him in out of this rain!"

"Just think, you can get married on your stoop."

"Right, if you officiate, play the flute, and bake the cake, I might be able to afford a stoop wedding! Talk to you later."

Ava threw her rain slicker and boots on over her PJs and grabbed her handbag. She flew downstairs, taking the steps two at a time. There was no time for a sore tailbone now. Bursting outside, the downpour wet her hair before she could pull up her hood.

Chris wasn't there. His cardboard and Chickpea's bowl, gone. *Gone?* She looked under the stoop, hoping to see his suitcase wrapped in a black plastic garbage bag. Nothing. There was no trace of Chris or his dog.

Panic swelled in her chest, squeezing her heart. He was the only stability in her life. He believed in her when no one else did. After everything she'd been through with Josh and bad dates, why didn't she trust herself when it felt right? Life showed her love and she followed her fears!

Without thinking, she pushed through the veil of rain toward Eighth Avenue, looking in every direction for Chris. She couldn't search the whole city. For all she knew, he had left for the south of France. Then she remembered—the *Rainbow Room*, of course.

At the curb, people hovered under their umbrellas, anxious for cabs that weren't coming. She ran north for the subway and saw a VACANT light moving down the avenue in a wet haze.

"Taxi!" Let anyone try and take it from her. She slid into

the backseat at a red light, rainwater dripping off her face.
"Rockefeller Plaza, please!"

They didn't get far. At Time's Square, traffic inched forward.
"Can we try a different way? Maybe go east?"

The cabbie looked at her through the rearview mirror.
"Whatever you say." In other words, it wouldn't make a
difference.

The urgency to find Chris and apologize was unbearable.
He'd understand. He'd give her a second chance. "I'll get out
here." She handed the driver a ten, and he pulled to the curb
at 44th Street. Back into the rain.

Soaked through and winded, she entered the GE Building at
49th Street, between Fifth and Sixth Avenues. The dark marble
corridor had a shadowy feel and voices sounded muffled,
despite the brightly lit shops siding up to it. She signed-in with
security and showed her driver's license before being directed
further.

In the elevator bank, she hesitated. Sixty-five floors to the
top...but it was the only way to find Chris. The doors of the next
available lift opened. Filling her lungs with air, she stepped
inside.

Her stomach dropped as the lift sped higher, beaming her to
the top of Rockefeller Plaza. She recalled photos of the *Rainbow
Room* and articles she'd read. Then there was that scene in
Sleepless in Seattle where Annie breaks her engagement to
Walter in full view of the Empire State Building. Though she'd
never been, Ava could picture the grand dining room, a whirl
of music and whimsical cocktails. Couples dancing under an
illuminated dome ceiling, while lights like confetti sprinkled
the revolving dance floor.

Light-headed, stepping off the elevator, she was struck
by the quiet. Perhaps their lunch crowd was more subdued?
She looked down at her yellow boots and slicker, her sodden
rainbow PJs peeking out at her knees. Hardly formal attire, but
she never had to think about what she wore with Chris.

Through ornate double doors, she cautiously entered the
main dining room. Deserted. Chairs stacked on tables. The only

light came from windows overlooking a soaked Manhattan. Obviously they didn't serve lunch, but shouldn't staff be preparing for dinner? Or the tables set, at least?

"Hey, we're closed." A man wearing a black suit and gray tie stepped out from the dark stage.

"Oh. When do you open? I was hoping to speak to someone who works in the kitchen. His name is Chris. He's the sous chef." Her voice sounded small in the large, dead-still restaurant.

The man moved toward her. "You misunderstand. We're no longer in business. Security should have told you." He smiled politely at her, the way hosts were trained to smile at guests, even the annoying ones.

"Oh." Maggie was right, though it must have just happened, if employees were still around. "Do you happen to know where I could find him?"

"Who are you looking for?"

"Chris? Your sous chef?"

"Christophe, perhaps? Christophe Bayonne-Larousse?"

"I don't know his last name, actually." She had never asked. "He has brown shoulder-length—I mean, short—hair, and he's in his late twenties, I believe."

"Christophe Bayonne-Larousse was our sous chef. Pardon me, but I have some business to wrap up . . . and you're not supposed to be here."

She took a step back. The name didn't fit the Chris she knew, but then she knew so little about him, so few facts. It sounded very French. He had said he was born in New York but moved to Paris for high school—not his best years, she recalled.

"I'm sorry, but could I ask just one more question? Do you know where I might be able to find...Christophe?"

The man shrugged. "Try the restaurant Autumn Leaves in SoHo. Greene Street. I haven't been, but that's what I hear."

A quaint French bistro came to mind...worn wood floors with miss-matched tables and chairs. Flowerboxes and a chalkboard out in front with the day's special: GAUDES. She hurried out of the Rainbow Room, excited by the possibility that Chris's *If Only* job had become a reality. But was he really Christophe

Bayonne-whatever?

The subway was running despite rainwater seeping into the tunnels. Shooting downtown on the number 4 train, express, it seemed she was chasing a figment of her imagination. But it was Julian who believed looking for the "One" was like looking for your imaginary friend. She had more hope—more faith—than that.

On Greene Street, parked limousines lined up in front of a pristine brick townhouse with Autumn Leaves engraved on a gold-plated plaque beside the door. Not exactly the French bistro with a chalkboard out in front that she had envisioned. Pulling back the hood of her rain slicker, she went in.

Live music greeted her—a woman singing in French with a guitarist accompanying. The warm, vibrant restaurant had a full house and an atmosphere that said, *Never mind what's going on out there. You're here. You've made it.* Had *Chris*? And what if he didn't want to see her? He'd left without saying good-bye, no forwarding address. Now here she was, showing up *after* his dream of owning a restaurant had come true. Why would she be welcome?

The airy interior drew her farther inside with skylights and chamomile-yellow walls. Modern lamps and antique gardening tools clinched the French countryside décor while upholding a classy ambiance. Two long wooden tables hosted large parties, friends and family among sunflowers in glass cylinders. If this did belong to Chris, he had achieved his dream of hospitality, heart, and the aromas of home...a chalkboard above the open kitchen read: Raclette, Bouillabaisse, and Tarte Tatin.

"Your reservation?" the host asked with a concerned smile, looking her up and down.

Strands of wet hair hung over Ava's shoulders like marinated red peppers. But what did appearances matter at this point?

"Are you waiting for someone?" the host tried again, just as cordial.

"I'm sorry. Yes, well, no...I was wondering, could you tell me if the owner is here, Christophe...Bayonne-Lamoose?"

"Christophe Bayonne-*Larousse* is expecting you?" the host asked, sounding doubtful.

"Yes. You can tell him that Ava Larson is here." Lying felt warranted.

"Well," he hesitated, "he's right over there, talking to a customer." The host escorted her to a robust older man with a shapely black beard. He looked extremely dignified, but he wasn't Chris. Before she could react, he excused himself from the customer and quickly took her aside. "*Gourmet*? We have been eagerly waiting your arrival. You obviously suffered getting here in the rain. Where is the photographer?"

"Actually, I—"

"Fine, fine. We will start without him. Come meet the staff. Everything is going wonderfully, despite Mother Nature's tears." He steered her toward the open kitchen.

"No. I'm sorry. I've made a mistake." She turned abruptly and ran for the door, but customers coming in blocked her way.

Glancing back, she heard the large man reprimand the host, "Who was that woman? You cannot just let anyone wander in here off the street. It is opening night!"

Dusk closed in on the misty rain as she walked the long blocks home. No glittery sidewalks, no golden brushstrokes, no liquid sunset. No Chris. Bucksly's proverb rang in her ears: *Sometimes in life there are no second chances.* She shook it off, not ready to give up.

Back home, she checked her mail before going upstairs. Behind the little metal door was a white envelope from the managing agent of her building. Finally, they were getting back to her. As she read the letter, her stomach filled with dread as heavy as cement.

STATE OF NEW YORK
COUNTY OF NEW YORK
To: AVA LARSON

YOU ARE HEREBY NOTIFIED that your tenancy of the following premises, to wit: The property at 324 WEST 22ND STREET, APT. 5C, together with all buildings, sheds, closets, out-buildings, garages and other structures used in connection with said premise, will terminate on AUGUST 1ST OF THIS YEAR. Under new management, the building will be demolished for a new construction. You are hereby required to surrender possession of said premises to the undersigned on AUGUST 1ST.

Elias Schneider, Landlord

Ava stared at the official paper in her hand in disbelief. Was this how people became homeless? Had she unknowingly fulfilled the equation? The accumulation of bills after a breakup, a lost job in a tough economy, and a real estate boom too big to include her. So simple, and so final.

Chris had said her life was all about change...Ava's hand trembled, holding the letter. Whether she wanted it or not, there were more changes to come.

Chapter Thirty-Seven

Sublets were cheap and small and overcrowded, and they went like free biscuits at the dog fair. Ava drew a red line through another rental in *The Voice*. She got up and went to the refrigerator, feeling frustrated and hungry. Reaching for the milk, her hand brushed the leftovers from her garlic dinner with Chris, a week old. How could she go through life missing him? Every hour, she wondered where he was, and what might have been if she had followed her heart.

"Good morning!" Phoebe walked into the kitchen dressed in a gray pantsuit. A simple gray pantsuit. No logos.

"You look like you're going on a job interview," Ava said.

"Good! Because I am. I'm interviewing to give free makeovers at Saks Fifth Avenue. You know, on the ground floor, where all the action is. It's a paying position, if I sell the makeup."

"You are?" Ava stared at her in disbelief. Phoebe was joining the drudgery of the workforce, at retirement age?

"I know, Saks is a direct competitor," Phoebe went on. "Can you forgive me? They have an opening."

"Competitor? You mean of Bergdorf? Don't be silly. I don't care about that. I'm surprised you want to work, that's all."

"I worked before I met Barry. Elizabeth Arden, remember?"

"Oh, I have no doubt you would be good at it. I'm sure you'll get the job."

"I have to admit I'm a bit nervous. Makeup is so subjective. Some women are never happy with their appearance, no matter how much foundation you put on...anyway, try to guess where I bought this suit." Phoebe modeled it with her eyebrows raised in childlike anticipation.

Ava smiled, relieved to see that she was pushing on despite

Barry's silence. "Is it Calvin Klein? Or does Chanel have a new CK-esque line?"

"Sweetie, Chanel doesn't copy. I bought it at Zara! I'm shopping on a budget now." She took her Greek yogurt from the refrigerator and mixed in flax seeds. "The quality is surprisingly good for what you pay."

"You're actually *looking* at the price tags?" Ava pulled a box of oatmeal and brown sugar from the cupboard. "Phoebe, are you just trying to be supportive of me...with all this 'budget' talk?"

"It's not 'talk.' I need to work. The one bank account I have access to is quickly going down. If Barry is writing me off, I have to be careful. I don't want to become a burden to Josh. I would *never* do that."

"You could sue Mr. Copeland for leaving you." Ava fired up the stove and rigorously stirred milk into the oats. The way he ignored Phoebe was infuriating.

"*I* left him," Phoebe replied. "And how could I sue? I still love him. Becoming enemies would ruin me, not being broke."

"I understand." Ava crumbled brown sugar over her steaming porridge. "Well, if you're really watching your spending now, there's one thing you need to know—it *is* possible to be happy on a budget. There are always reasons to smile, and most of them are free, like heart-to-heart talks, beautiful sunsets, long walks..." Ava realized she was thinking of times with Chris and fell quiet.

"I agree. The things in life you *can't* buy. The stuff of real happiness." Phoebe took her empty bowl to the sink, pushed back her sleeves, and washed it. "Barry will not only see a change in me, he'll see one in my checking account balance, as well. It will grow!"

So she was still hanging on. "Even if Mr. Copeland doesn't have the eyes to see it, you're an amazing woman, Phoebe. Don't ever forget that."

"Sweetie, you're too good to me."

Ava blew on a spoonful of oatmeal and tasted it...almost as good as when she was a child. "Oatmeal was my mom's specialty. I love the sweet, woody smell...it reminds me of home."

Phoebe went over to Ava and hugged her shoulders. "The best thing you can do is keep her traditions alive. Keep *her* alive in your heart."

"Thanks. I am."

"I'd have some, except it's not on my Perfect Yogi Diet." Phoebe sat down at the table with her. "Darling, how is your apartment search going?"

"I'll find something. I *have* to. I know you don't want to hear this, but I'm more worried about finding Chris. Without him and Chickpea, one apartment is the same as the next, and not at all appealing to me."

"Please don't talk like that, Ava. It scares me. You *need* a home. A safe, clean, preferably furnished home."

"All week I've looked at sublets, gone on auditions, sent out my resume to headhunters, and worked late nights at The Encore. No matter how I fill my time, my life feels empty. I miss him."

"Sweetie, you're talking to a woman who left her husband to get his attention, and he let her go. I know what pointless feels like. What you need to do is make a new plan. Sign up for a dating service or join a singles club. Have fun and see what happens! I started out meditating, and now I can't imagine my life without yoga and wheatgrass."

"You're right, Phoebe. I know you're right." Again, she thought of Mom. It would've been her advice exactly. In a way, it seemed Mom was there having breakfast with them.

"Now, as for a home," Phoebe continued, "I'm meeting a real estate broker today. I've asked to see a two-bedroom apartment on the west side. No doorman. Nothing fancy. Why don't you take one of the bedrooms and we'll split the rent?"

"Phoebe, I love you, and you're surprisingly easy to live with, but I refuse to move in with you. There are acceptable and unacceptable ex-mother-in-law relationships, and that definitely would be crossing the line. I found a sublet in Brooklyn, $500 a month, sharing a one-bedroom with two other women. Not ideal, sleeping on a pullout couch in the living room, but I'll have my own closet, off the kitchen." Her cell phone rang.

Phoebe checked her watch. "Oh, I have to go!" She jumped up. "We'll talk more about that kitchen pantry for a closet later."

Ava stared at the caller I.D. on her phone. Two rings...three. "Hi, Dad."

"Hello, Ava. We haven't touched base in quite some time."

"Since the funeral. And that was an e-mail."

"Yes, well, I'm sure it was a hectic time for everyone. The funeral is behind you now, I suppose. I still can't believe she's passed on. At times I even forget."

Ava stood up from the table. "The memorial service made it real. I wish you had been there, Dad. You were a big part of her life." She heard the front door open and gently close; Phoebe off on her job interview.

"At one point I was a part of her life, yes," Dad replied. "But your mother and I parted ways a long time ago. It wouldn't have been right for me to be there. I explained that in my e-mail."

"I'm just saying you were missed." Had she reverted back to childhood, wishing her parents were together, one last time?

He sighed into the phone. "You're first on my prayer list these days, Ava."

"Thanks." She stared out the kitchen window at her lone geranium.

"So, are you and Josh still in touch?" he asked, sounding hopeful.

Anger triggered in her chest. She imagined throwing her cell phone like a skipping stone in Central Park. Dad would *never* understand her decision to cancel the wedding, or her feelings for Chris.

"No, I haven't seen Josh, only his parents." She tried to keep frustration out of her voice, to have patience...to be understanding. They didn't speak that often; she couldn't expect him to know what to ask and not to ask. "Mostly, I've been focused on my new job," she said.

"Oh? Are you working two jobs now?"

"I'm no longer with Bergdorf. I switched careers, actually. Remember how I used to love dance?" Please remember...and have a little faith.

"Good grief, Ava, you were a girl then. How are you managing with your bills and that rent you pay?"

"I've found temporary work, and as for my rent, I'm looking for something more affordable, maybe a sublet in Brooklyn."

"That's sensible, I suppose. Just don't become content in a go-nowhere job to get by. Send out your resume. Make to-do lists. Television off."

"Right." He'd forgotten she didn't own one. "So, how are you doing?" she asked. "How's Kelly?"

"We're fine. The girls keep us on our toes." His tone lightened up. "You wouldn't believe their soccer schedule. We have to squeeze college tours in between away-games."

"That's great they love it so much. Maybe they'll play in college, too."

"It's a possibility. Well...keep me posted on your new career. E-mail is best while you're looking for work."

"All right. I love you, Dad."

"Okay, then. Bye, Ava." The line went dead.

Mom used to say, "If you hand that man an armful of love, he'll file it under miscellaneous." And then she'd add, "But at least he'll file it."

Ava threw her phone down on the table. She tugged the kitchen window open, stuck her head outside and screamed, "No more *at least!*" She shouted at her neighbors, over the rooftops, to the pigeons taking flight. "I'm sick of settling!"

The radio across the way was silent. Cars stopped honking. No sirens to cause alarm. The city listened...and would hold her to that moment.

Her hand shook as she reached for her phone on the table and pressed CALL BACK. She made a promise not to give up on him, and she'd keep it.

"Is there something else, Ava?" Dad answered, as if their five-minute conversation had covered her life and Mom's death and everything in between.

"Yes." Her voice wavered. "I've come to realize a lot about myself over the past few weeks. I think that happens when life-plans fall through and you lose the people you love, the people you depend on."

"I know you've been through a lot, Ava, but there's not much I can do."

"I'm not asking for your help. I just want...I want a real relationship, where we talk honestly about our lives and how we feel, where we see each other from time to time."

"Ava—"

"I swear, ever since the divorce, you've written me off emotionally. I've spent most of my life aiming for your approval, hoping one day I'll be good enough. I even fell in love with a man who kept his feelings from me. Just like you. It's become a bad habit in my life!"

"You can't blame me for Josh. That's not fair."

"I'm not. I'm blaming you for putting duty before love."

"Now wait a second," his voice rose. "Of course I'm going to feel a sense of duty. I worry about you! And now your life, such as it is; I feel I should fly to New York and get it back on track. But I can't. You're a grown woman, and I have a responsibility to my work and family here."

"You're seeing it all wrong. I'm finally doing what I want with my life. Maybe it looks like I'm not making progress, but I am. I know what I want, and I'm going for it! I wish you could see that."

"It's hard for me to see what is positive about living on the verge of bankruptcy and homelessness. But it's not right for me to place judgment; I know that much as a parent. All I can do is pray, Ava."

"Good! Then pray for God to open your heart!" She hung up.

The sun was out, fighting the clouds for space. Ava walked

to the Church of the Guardian Angel, longing for the love and assurance she had felt last Sunday. And then there was the chance of seeing...

She imagined standing in the food line, asking for the pancakes, and Chris appearing out of nowhere to fill her plate. He'd lean over and whisper, *I was hoping you'd show up.*

The daydream made her feel light and giddy, as if she were going to a ball instead of a soup kitchen.

On Tenth Avenue, the little tree came into view...with Willard and Chickpea tied to its trunk. She walked faster, heart pounding, church bells chiming. Finally, a chance to redeem herself!

Chickpea danced at her feet. "Hey, girl! I'm happy to see you, too. We'll catch up after breakfast, okay?" She could see the side entrance and a line of people anxious for a meal, but she went inside the main doors to see if Chris was eating at one of the foldout tables.

A man, perhaps in his eighties, wearing a rumpled grey suit and wool scarf, greeted her. "Welcome!" he shouted with a broad equally rumpled smile. "The line starts outside, but come with me, if you'd like, and I'll sneak you in through the kitchen."

"Thank you." She scanned the church for Chris. He should've been easy to spot, if he was there. Mike with the toothless grin waved from his seat. She smiled and waved back. Maybe Gretchen had brought Chickpea...maybe Chris was avoiding her.

"Are you here for a meal?" the older man asked, waiting for her to follow.

Ava looked again at Mike, hunched over his tray, scooping scrambled eggs into his mouth with a spoon. "If you could use a volunteer, I wouldn't mind helping out," she replied.

Inside the large kitchen, the smell of sweet pancakes and buttery eggs was familiar to her now. The vibrant smiles and the high energy uniting the volunteers' group effort was the norm here, as well. Stopping to face her, the older man asked, "Young lady, what is your name? I'll introduce you to Father Gallagher."

"Thank you. I'm Ava." Long yellow hair pulled back in a net

caught her eye. "I see a friend," she said. "If you'll excuse me for one minute."

Gretchen was working the assembly line, slicing and dishing out ham. Ava walked up behind her, so not to interrupt the flow of brunch. "I see you're busy," she said. "I just wanted to say hi. I've come back."

Gretchen turned and smiled. "I'm glad. Grab yourself an apron, hat, and hair net and start handing out ham!"

Ava moved quickly, anxious to join in with the others. There wasn't time to ask about Chris.

Two hours later, Ava and Gretchen dished up their own plates and went into the full church to eat. "I feel like I've just finished a long run," Ava said. "Repetition is hard work!"

"Can't say I know how it feels to do a long run," Gretchen said, laughing, "but I'm pooped out!"

As they found seats, Father Gallagher jumped up to the pulpit. He had a hopeful air about him so that his eyes, even his freckles, seemed to glow. Looking out over everyone, he took a deep breath and proclaimed, "God doesn't give a hoot!"

Rustling quieted.

"He doesn't care what you've done, or the things you've said. He doesn't care *how* you got here, why, or if you're just here for a meal. You're here! And whether you know it or not, your heart is changing. It's opening, learning to trust. God isn't going to ask questions. He's not going to look at you with doubt or put you to a test. He wants you to find your way with His loving guidance. Accept it, you're loved! You always have been and always will be. No matter what."

Ava thought of Chris. He had taught her not to be afraid when love didn't look the way she expected it to, when it required nothing more or less than faith. He had shown her unconditional love through example: through acceptance. Could she finally take his lessons to heart? A miniscule voice inside her head whispered, *You can. You can live in faith, not fear.*

When they had finished eating, Gretchen took her hand. "Come outside with me. I'd like to talk, if you have a minute."

"I have all the minutes you'd like," Ava said, hoping the topic would be Chris.

Out in the sunshine, she and Gretchen walked to the little tree, while Chickpea and Willard greeted them with countless tail-wags.

"Chickpea is sure happy to see you!" Gretchen said, untying both dogs.

"Is she going to the soup kitchen for Chris now?"

"He was here early to help in the kitchen, but then had other engagements, I assume. Come here, Willard. Stop getting all tangled up in Chickpea's leash!"

"I hope he's all right. Chris, I mean. I haven't seen him since last week."

"Oh, he's fine. Working a lot. A new restaurant, he tells me. I don't ask too many questions; Chris talks when he's ready. Anyway, all I know about eating out is my local diner, seven o'clock every Friday night. They have a plate of spaghetti and meatballs ready when I walk in the door. There's nothing better."

Gretchen paused, as though thinking of her next words. "Ava, I was wondering, do you have any interest in getting involved in All for One? From what Chris tells me, my girls could use a mentor like you. In fact, a few weeks ago I was praying about getting a dance project off the ground when Chris mentioned he had met a friend, a dancer."

"Did he? I would love to get involved! Yes!"

"Just yesterday I found a studio, near Macy's." Gretchen did a little victory wiggle. "So my next step is to find help running it. I was going to ask Chris how to track you down, and here, today, you show up beside me in the soup kitchen!"

"I'll give as much time as I can," Ava said with genuine excitement. "What kind of dance do you have in mind?"

"Well, this would be more than volunteer work. I need someone to run the program. You'd teach classes, plus find volunteer instructors to give their time, ideally some high-profile names, and then coordinate an end-of-the-year recital. A lot of my girls have children, and I'd like classes for them, as well. Perhaps you could include different styles. Maybe even yoga. I'm full of ideas but can't dance to save my life!"

"I can do all of that!" Her heart danced for joy. "And I believe anyone can learn to dance."

"Perhaps, with the right teacher." Gretchen winked at her. "The recital will be great for publicity, and branching into dance will make All for One eligible for a whole new category of grants and donations. I can't pay much, especially in the beginning, but you won't only be teaching dance, you'll be teaching these young women how to dream. What do you say?"

"Yes! Gretchen, trust me, I believe in dreams, and dance recitals are what I know best."

Gretchen pulled a pamphlet out of her backpack. "E-mail me your contact information. Can you come by the studio Tuesday morning for a mini interview, say nine o'clock?"

"Tuesday at nine. I can't wait. Thank you so much for the opportunity."

"See you Tuesday." Gretchen left with Chickpea and Willard trotting along on either side of her.

"Wait!" Ava almost forgot about Chris.

Gretchen and the dogs stopped and turned.

"When you see Chris, would you please thank him for introducing us? And tell him...I miss him."

Gretchen smiled and gave thumbs up.

The moment she turned away, Ava did a triple pirouette. "Yes!" Her heart was opening, and it felt like everything she wanted in life was within her reach. She twirled again. Let people stare. This was the Big Apple!

Back home, Ava got out her laptop and checked eBay. Finally! Someone bid on her dress and gown, $400 for both, the minimum. Well, $400 cash in the bank was better than hoping for $8,000.

She took a deep breath and started posting. *Prada handbags: Zip-Top Bowler—gray calf leather, top handles, chain detail; Cervo Antik Hobo-Tote—brown leather, shoulder straps; Nappa Hobo—black lamb leather, brass-tone hardware, chain braided shoulder strap; Nylon Heritage Messenger—black nylon with tonal heritage jacquard, adjustable and removable strap. Minimum bid: $300 ea. All authentic, made in Italy. Just like new.*

After an hour posting on eBay, she had a pounding headache. About to shut down her computer, an e-mail came through from Dad. She imagined his anxiety-provoking advice and felt even worse: gaps on your resume can't be erased! Falling behind with your bills can hold you back for the rest of your life!

But his message was brief: *Ava, I'm praying you'll find the job you want. I love you. Your Father.*

She pressed SAVE.

Chapter Thirty-Eight

Ava stopped at her local newsstand. *Time Out New York* featured "Hot Summer Spots for Cool Eats." She picked up a copy and flipped to a spread of select restaurant reviews.

"You want magazine?" The Pakistani man who owned the stand glared at her. She went into her non-Prada handbag for two dollars, rummaged through loose change, and came up with $1.50. She didn't work last night, Sunday night, and had been too ambitious putting what she had earned last week toward bills.

"Can I just glance through it for a second?" she asked. "I'm short on cash."

"Why should I give away my magazines? That is not good business. You pay, you read."

"I'll give you what I have if I can just look through it." She showed him her quarters.

"No." He waved her off as if she were a gnat.

"Take it." A woman waiting to buy Oprah's magazine held out fifty cents.

Ava hesitated. Accepting the handout seemed to make her desperate financial situation official. She looked again at the magazine, and her hand reached for the money. "Thanks. That's really nice of you."

The city felt kind and generous today.

Walking down the sidewalk, she scanned the reviews. *Christophe Bayonne-Larousse and Son Get Together to Create Autumn Leaves*. Her eyes stopped on the photo. Chris! He was smiling, proud, beside the large, bearded man she had met under false pretenses. That man was his *dad*? Side-by-side, Chris did resemble him, minus the beard and probably fifty pounds. Chris had on his usual checked pants and white T-shirt, as if the photo had been taken beneath her stoop. Autumn Leaves received a rave review, but there was some doubt as to whether the father-son team would last.

She raced through the article, wanting to know everything at once: Bayonne-Larousse Senior was a long-celebrated chef in France. He produced the hit television program, *Cuisine avec Papa*—or *Cooking with Dad*—and wrote the children's book series starring Christophe, "the mischievous boy who blunders his father's baking." Mr. Bayonne-Larousse's nickname throughout France? "Papi."

Grandpa? As in warm and jolly? She started to doubt she had met the same man, but continued with the article: after Chris graduated from L'Université Paris-Sorbonne, he went to work at his father's Paris restaurant, *Tulips*, as the dessert chef. Two years later, Chris walked out on the job. They tried again with *Lillies*, where Chris stepped in as manager. The restaurant closed its doors after eighteen months. Chris left Paris for New York to see the end of an era at the *Rainbow Room*, working his way up to sous chef. Now father and son were at it again, this time as partners of Autumn Leaves, the hot new French restaurant in SoHo.

Autumn Leaves is a gorgeous space for people to enjoy the things in life that really matter—family, friends, and good food. Father and son have invested heavily in their dream of owning a restaurant together. Let's just hope they've sorted out their differences.

So the night she was there aggravating "Papi," opening night, no less, Chris was but a few steps away in the kitchen! Excitement ignited inside of her, and then just as fast, fizzled out. Instead of being invited as his guest to the opening, she had intruded in her rain slicker and pajamas...only to be chased out by his father, embarrassed and confused.

She stuffed the magazine into her handbag and walked quickly for the subway. If Chris was confident enough to kiss her *before* announcing Autumn Leaves, she could be brave

334

enough to show her true feelings after the fact.

The dining room was set and ready for the first customers. A man, apparently the florist, pushed through the front doors with an armful of sunflowers. She scooted in after him and made it three steps into the dining room when Mr. Bayonne-Larousse advanced from the kitchen. "*You*, again?"

Was he talking to the florist? *Please?* The young man in a company polo shirt mumbled, "Good afternoon, sir," and busied himself with the flowers.

She stood in the direct path of Mr. Bayonne-Larousse's furious glare. Where was "Papi," the author of children's books? He made the Piranha look like a guppy! At least Mr. Copeland tried to hide his scorn.

"Um, I'm—"

"No solicitors! How did you get in here?"

"Oh, I'm not selling anything. I'm here to see Chris. We're friends. If I could just—"

"The answer is no! We are running a restaurant." He moved toward her with outstretched arms. "Can you see?"

"I understand," she stammered, taking a step back. "I just wanted to say hello. I promise I'll only be a minute."

"This isn't some coffee shop! You don't 'pop' in to say hello. Please leave. Now!" He pointed at the door, unrelenting.

She couldn't give up. "Is there a better time for me to come by, perhaps? When you're not so busy? Or maybe I could just take his phone number?"

"If you are his friend, then why don't you *have* his number? Who are you, anyway? Why do you keep coming in here?"

Chris stepped out of the kitchen, wearing a chef's hat and apron.

"Hi!" She couldn't believe he was standing in front of her. The past week without him had felt like years.

"Hello, Ava." He walked toward them, barely acknowledging her. "It's fine, Dad. She's not going to steal our recipes. I'll meet you in the kitchen, two seconds."

Mr. Bayonne-Larousse held his breath, turning red with anger, and then exploded, "I cannot believe we're having this conversation! We open in two hours. Two hours! If the kitchen isn't ready, it won't catch up!"

"Yes, I know that, and I'm not worried."

"Did you forget we're booked solid? That *Food & Wine* is reviewing us! I thought we were in agreement, business first! Instead, you stand here and chat?" His voice rose higher in pitch, as if building to some terrible consequence. Would they go their separate ways again? Over *her*?

"I'll just leave. It's okay." She couldn't convince her legs to walk away.

"I'd like to talk to her, Dad. You're overreacting."

Mr. Bayonne-Larousse became an orchestra conductor with his fast sweeping arm movements. "I'm going back to France! *La tension me tue*! Killing me!"

Chris shook his head and sighed.

"Fine!" Mr. Bayonne-Larousse turned a deeper shade of purple. "What about the cassoulet?"

"You'll have to trust that I'll get it done. I'm your partner, remember?" Chris looked at his dad with compassion, patience. "Can you give us one minute?"

"Unbelievable!" Mr. Bayonne-Larousse walked back to the kitchen and pushed through the double doors. "*I'll* finish the cassoulet!"

"Please don't!" Chris called after him. Still composed, he had his eyes on her now. "Sorry about that. How are you, Ava?" He seemed colder. Stress, maybe...or the spark had died.

Courage left her. "I'm good. I mean, great. I suppose." She felt lost in his world and couldn't think past having found him. What did she come here to say? Say something!

"Fantastic hat!" she exclaimed. "Hey, now I *know* you can cook!" It sounded so shallow. She needed *proof*? A hat?

"I guess." He looked back toward the kitchen.

Thank him! Apologize! Beg him back! But she had already rejected him. Why would he listen to her now? She stepped aside, allowing fear and doubt to take over, again. "I'm sorry, barging in like this. Maybe I should go."

He nodded. "I should get back. Life is hectic these days, to say the least."

"I understand." *Give me another chance!* "It's a beautiful restaurant. Oh, I'm such a schmuck! I haven't even said congratulations! You did it, Chris! We're standing in the middle of your dream this very moment!" Acting on an impulse, she flung her arms open wide and spun in a swirl of skylights and sunrays slicing yellow tones.

He smiled, the smile she knew and loved. "Thanks, Ava."

"I feel silly for spinning like that." Her heart beat fast. Her eyes didn't want to leave his bright face.

"Ideally, when spinning, don't stop until the world becomes your carousel. That's how I do it."

She laughed, aching to touch his broad shoulders, to inhale the fragrance of herbs and spices on his skin...just to feel close to him again.

"Thanks for stopping by," he continued. "My dad isn't easy to deal with, as you can see, but I couldn't think of partnering with anyone else."

"Of course—he's your father."

"The cassoulet!" Clanging pots and pans echoed from inside the kitchen.

"I'm sorry, Ava," Chris said, backing away. "It's good to see you again."

"You, too." She felt a tightening in her chest...regret leaving its permanent mark. "Wait! I was just thinking, since I don't see you around anymore, maybe we could plan something. Any dog fairs coming up?"

"No, no dog fairs on the horizon." He walked backward as he spoke. "It'd be great to get together again, but to be honest, it's bad timing..."

The taste of her words to him was rancid.

"Time is up!" Mr. Bayonne-Larousse hollered from the

kitchen.

"I've got to go. Take care, Ava." Chris disappeared through the swinging doors.

No rain check. No effort to keep in touch. She'd had her chance, and now he didn't want anything to do with her. Losing him felt like an unexpected death, too late for saying *I'm sorry* or *I love you.*

Out on the sidewalk, a tear rolled down her cheek, making way for more. She walked along bustling West Broadway, conscious of the eyes of strangers, feeling utterly alone.

Her cell phone rang, and hope leapt inside her chest. Chris! He could've called Gretchen and gotten her number. She reached for her phone in her handbag. An unknown caller.

"Hello?"

"A, do I have news for you!" Nick, the orchestrator of her blind date—the meal she was reminded of on her credit card bill—shouted through the phone. "And don't ask me why, but you're one of the first people I'm telling. Well, almost the first."

"Telling what?"

"Me and Puppy are getting married! Seriously! It was a ring or the door. So, guess who went shopping at Tiffany's last week?"

"Good for you!" She forced excitement through her vocal cords. Even Nick could find love. Murder by self-pity, a pathetic and all-the-more-painful way to go.

"You *have* to come to the wedding. I've got tons of single guys lined up."

"Absolutely." Was he purposely rubbing it in? "Sorry, Nick, but I can't talk at the moment." Her finger moved for the power button on her phone. No more.

Walking the streets, she let the tears fall. Let the city stare. With every step, Chris felt farther away, more firmly secured in her past. Maybe he had fulfilled his role in her life, and she was supposed to let him go. But her heart desperately held on.

Chapter Thirty-Nine

Holding a bundle of daisies, Ava looked up at the red brick building with large arched windows. Pink ballet slippers hung in the second-story windows, along with a purple and white sign: All for One. She smiled. Finally, she felt close to her *If Only* job.

Up a wide, sweeping staircase, she found studio 202 and knocked on the door. It opened at once.

"Welcome!" Gretchen hustled her inside. "Flowers! For me?"

"Yes, for your dance project." Ava handed her the bouquet and looked around the rough, bare studio.

"Well, can you see it?" Gretchen beamed with pride.

Ava set her handbag down on the floor. "I'll have to give it a try to know." She slipped off her sandals, walked to the center of the studio, and did a triple pirouette. "Yup, it works!"

"Wow! On bare feet, no less!" Gretchen, round and stout, attempted a twirl—a rather lopsided twirl. "I've never taken a dance class in my life, but I like the way it feels!"

"You can be my first student." Ava showed her again, and then, surprising herself, did the entire Rockette audition, as if she'd been rehearsing the moves every day.

"Fantastic!" Gretchen clapped. After a moment, her expression turned serious. "Be honest with me, though. Can you make this place work?"

The studio needed mirrors and a ballet barre, for starters, and the worn wood floor begged for a good sanding. But Ava could see a self-conscious woman in a fabulous red dress, much like herself at The Encore, dancing as if it were the pinnacle moment in her life. And maybe it would be.

"The studio itself is spacious," she replied, "and you've got southern exposure. Is there a bathroom? A dressing room?"

"The bathroom is down the hall, shared with three other businesses. But it's quite big and has a shower room and lockers. We'll have to find a dance hall for the annual recital. That is, one loaned to us as a charitable donation."

"Is there a budget for renovating the floor?" Ava asked. "Adding a ballet barre and mirrors? Music?"

"We can't spend extravagantly, but yes. I have grant money to get started."

"Then, yes! I believe we can make All for One: *Dance* a reality! I know a good carpenter from upstate who could do the job for a fraction of what you'd pay someone here in the city. He's my stepfather, and I think he'd like a little out-of-town work."

"Great! Now, here's the deal. I can pay you $25 an hour, as a part-time employee. You'll set up a schedule and teach as many classes as you can, not going over thirty hours a week. You'll have to factor in time finding volunteer dance professionals to teach yoga, mamba, whatever the girls are interested in trying. I wish I could pay you for more hours. I understand that you have to live."

"And I have steep bills, unfortunately." Ava put her sandals back on. "I have an idea. What if a few nights a week I used the studio for public classes? I'd charge a competitive rate and pay you a percentage, for rent. I think people would like the idea of giving a portion of their lesson fees to All for One."

"Hmm...interesting. I'll run the idea by my lawyer. It just might work."

"I'll do whatever it takes to make it work. I think it's a miracle we found each other."

"The miracle is Chris," Gretchen said. "He introduced us."

Ava remembered being at the restaurant...and failing to thank him for Gretchen. Failing, yet again, to overcome fear and show her true feelings.

"Well, I must be off," Gretchen walked to the door. "I have an appointment with a lovely school principal who might do an education seminar, and then an art dealer, very chi-chi."

They left the studio, and Gretchen locked up. "So the next step is for you to meet the girls. How about stopping by our headquarters tomorrow morning? Eight o'clock would be perfect. You can join us for assembly and breakfast. After that, we'll get down to the nitty-gritty—I'll need a criminal background check, references, the 'fun' stuff."

"I'll be there tomorrow at eight o'clock. I'm looking forward to it."

Out on the sidewalk, they parted for their separate ways. "Wait, Gretchen? I was wondering if you had Chris's address. I'd like to thank him in person."

"I do, actually." Gretchen went through her backpack and took out a thick black address book. "He has a new place, a big improvement from the street, I hear—with a roof and everything!" She laughed. "Let me see...he gave me the address about a month or so ago."

"A month ago? He was still living under my stoop then."

"Like I said, I don't ask. He must've had a reason for hanging around your stoop." Her eyes twinkled. "Here we go, under 'Chris,' of course." She gave a Ninth Street address in Greenwich Village.

Back home, Ava pulled her old Burberry bag out of the closet and started packing: bottled water, toothbrush, toothpaste...

"Are you going back out already?" Phoebe sat at the kitchen table, peering at the computer screen in her search for an apartment. "The question is where am *I* going? Nothing I've seen feels right."

"Tell me about it," Ava said, upsetting a pile of sweaters on a shelf inside her closet. She might need something warm; the temperature could drop at night. "Oh, you'll be glad to know that I let the Brooklyn sublet go. It would've taken me over an hour on the subway to get into Manhattan every day." She dropped a pullover into her overnight bag.

"An hour travel-time? Goodness, no. That's not acceptable.

I want you close by." Phoebe looked up from the computer and opened her eyes wide. "Why on Earth are you packing?"

"Would you mind if I told you my plans later? I'll probably be back tonight. Tomorrow morning at the latest." Chills raced up her neck as she imagined spending the night out on the street. A blanket, snack food...

"That means you're doing something I wouldn't approve of. You're not getting back together with that rude cop, are you?"

"No. I'll give you all the details tomorrow. We'll probably have a good laugh over it." She emptied her cardboard hope chest and tore the sides so that it opened flat. Perfect.

"*Now* what are you doing?" Phoebe asked, exasperation creeping into her voice.

"Details tomorrow, I promise." Was there anything else she might need?

"You can be so annoying, Ava. At least tell me how your meeting went today. Did you see the dance studio?"

"Oh, it's a dream! But it's going to take work." A change of clothes, in case she had to go straight to All for One in the morning. Oh, and a good book, not a romance. She was ready for *Don Quixote.*

"I'm done on your computer." Phoebe went to the kitchen window and looked out at the fire escape.

"Thanks." Ava sat down at the table. "I just want to check something."

"Take it. I'm only pretending to be independent...hoping I won't have to follow through."

Ava twisted in her seat and reached for Phoebe's hand. "Hey, you're doing a great job. It might feel like pretending some days, but you're focused on your *own* life now. Not how your life fits into Mr. Copeland's busy schedule."

"I suppose that's true." The corners of Phoebe's lips turned up, touching on a sad smile. It was as if she no longer trusted her own happiness. Turning away, she put water on for tea. "I'm a Yogi now, and that won't change," she said softly.

"Exactly." Ava couldn't convince herself, either. She pictured Phoebe doing backbends at 80, and growing old alone. She deserved security, and to be with the man she loved.

Ava logged onto eBay. Her dress and veil were up to $403, a whopping $3.00 increase. She moved on to her other posts. "Look here!" she said, hoping to distract Phoebe from thinking of Mr. Copeland. "A bid on one of my Prada handbags, $300 for the Zip-Top Bowler!"

"I don't want to know," Phoebe replied. "It pains me that you have to sell your only valuables."

"It did sell at retail for $2100. But I only paid half of that with my Bergdorf discount. To think I spent so much money on something I didn't need!"

"That's not true. Women need handbags like they need their own identity." Phoebe fell quiet, steeping her teabag at the counter. "But I do miss him."

"I'm so sorry you're hurting." Ava shut down her laptop and went to Phoebe's side. Right or wrong, the heartache they suffered was her doing, and there was nothing she could do to mend it or to speed up the healing process. "You could try meditating out on the fire escape. You might feel like you're levitating." She looked for a smile.

Phoebe glowered at her. "You will not catch me crawling in and out of that window like some cat."

"Just think how independent cats are!" Ava went into the living room and picked up her Burberry bag and cardboard. It was time.

Phoebe watched from the kitchen doorway. "Today I'll meditate on your safety, although so far my meditations don't appear to be working."

"I know it's not easy, what you're going through." Ava gave her a kiss on the cheek. "But you're doing everything right, and things will change. They always do."

"I'm holding out for that laugh tomorrow...whatever you're up to. And don't do anything foolish!"

Ava struggled down the stairs, catching the cardboard on the railing and getting stuck around the turns. In the foyer, she quickly checked her mailbox: two business envelopes. She stuffed them into her bag and kept moving.

Survival gear in tow, she headed for the subway. A few steps and a strong wind raging down her street from the Hudson grabbed hold of her cardboard. It slipped out from under her arm and took flight. "Oh, shoot!" Dodging pedestrians, she ran to a parked car where it finally lodged under a wheel. *What a novice!* She pulled it out, grease marks and all, and considered carrying it on top of her head. Another strong gust and she might fly to Greenwich Village.

Chris's new address was home to renovated brownstones, the kind of places people owned and held on to. "Finds." His building had long-paned windows, perhaps the originals. Flower boxes grew impatiens: purple, blue, and white. Six floors up, a rooftop greenhouse reflected the sun, and a large yellow umbrella suggested outdoor space.

She assessed the patch of lawn in front, which was enclosed by a knee-high iron rail. It had homeless potential, though rather exposed. Glancing about for protesters, an alarm system, mines—who knew what—she stepped sheepishly over the rail and laid out her cardboard. At least he didn't live in a doorman building. She could just hear the one-sided conversation: *Hey, you! Move along! Take your problems somewhere else.*

No one would ever guess that she was out on the streets for love. Technically, she *was* homeless. The days were numbered on her apartment, and aside from shoddy illegal sublets, she couldn't find a landlord in the city who would approve her for a lease. She'd have to crash Maggie's family room, or give up All for One and move back home with David. It seemed the fall after breaking up with Josh would never end.

A man and woman holding hands walked by and then turned for another look. Obviously, homelessness wasn't the norm in this neighborhood. If she had worn a bikini and sunglasses, she could've passed as a local sunbather. Her little patch of green was only partially shaded by the big elm at the curb, and when the wind moved the clouds along, the sun beamed down.

She took out *Don Quixote* from her bag and opened to the first page. *In a certain village in La Mancha, which I do not wish to name, there lived not long ago a gentleman...*She set the book down, distracted by a loud thought: HAD SHE LOST HER MIND?

Opening the mail she had brought might provide a feeling of normalcy, although it was likely more bills. Or, worse, what if *creditors* were after her now? She'd been late with her rent and had missed a few credit card payments. All for One required a thorough background check. Would Gretchen overlook bad credit?

Ava couldn't bear more bad news, especially feeling vulnerable on this Greenwich Village stage. The envelopes went into hiding, deep inside her handbag.

Ava sat down on the cardboard and stared absently at the knee-high iron rail surrounding her. The question remained: how long would she be a prisoner of Love?

Fifty pages into *Don Quixote*, her stomach started to rumble. A granola bar and an apple made for a sufficient snack. Crackers and peanut butter would be dinner. Only an hour or so had passed, and her butt ached as if she were sitting on an abscessed tooth. She stood to stretch her legs. How did homeless people do this?

She looked up the street for Chris. He didn't appear to be coming home for lunch. Chickpea was probably with Gretchen, so he wouldn't be stopping by to walk her.

Ava glanced east and then west, although only minutes had passed since she had last surveyed the situation. He would likely arrive from the east. But there were plenty of stops he could make on the west side: groceries, dry cleaning, the pet store, anything really. Perhaps he had plans to meet up with friends after work. If the last reservation finished at midnight, then an hour to close up, maybe longer...even if he came straight home, she'd have to wait twelve hours! Giving up would feel worse, though. This was homelessness...waiting, hoping for change.

Six hours down. Her fingers were sticky with peanut butter. The sky was growing overcast. Two hundred pages of *Don Quixote* read, and she felt as disillusioned on her quest to win over Chris as Don Quixote on his quest to salvage chivalry. She stood, jogged in place for a minute, stretched a bit, and sat back down. A cagey-looking neighbor across the street stared at her from a first-floor window. Every dog pulled at its leash, wanting to stop and sniff. She was an anomaly, an outcast, a threat.

Dusk settled in around eight. People were still coming home from work or happy hour. Some had already been out for a jog and returned, perhaps surprised to see her still sitting there. Not having a home was exhausting. It seemed the world was in her face, staring her down, demanding answers. She closed her eyes. Just for a minute...

Darkness confronted her upon waking, and she jolted upright, finding a man standing over her in a policeman's uniform.

"Excuse me, miss. Are you okay?"

"Oh, I must have fallen asleep." She was holding her handbag as if it were a parachute chest pack. Groggy to the point of feeling drunk, she fished her cell phone out of her bag and checked the time. "I can't believe it's midnight."

"Are you locked out of your apartment?"

"No, I just...thought I'd see what it's like to be homeless."

"Right," he replied, skeptically. "Well, you can't experiment here. Do you want a ride to a shelter?"

"No, that's okay. I think I'll just go home." She stood on stiff legs and gathered up her things, trying to appear normal.

Once she was no longer on the property, the cop got back inside his police car and drove off. A terrible thought followed her down the street. Chris could've come home while she was asleep. He could've seen her and just left her there. That was how homelessness really went.

Her legs felt weak, her hips sore, her tush...did she even have one anymore? Carrying her flattened hope chest under her arm, she hobbled down into the subway.

Chapter Forty

Dazed and achy, Ava carried her cardboard and overnight bag up the stoop of her soon-to-be-former building. Laughing with Phoebe over her homeless idea would *not* be fun. *How daft of you!* Phoebe would say. How true. She had struck out with Chris, one, two, three.

The ivy, waving in the wind, seemed to want her attention. Did it somehow know its days were numbered? Strangely enough, her building felt like home now, a place with memories. Three-twenty-four West 22nd Street...where she had learned to let go of the things she didn't need—Josh and Prada handbags—and had rediscovered her life, following a dream.

She felt around in her handbag for the front door key and heard a scraping sound come from below the stoop. She looked behind her. The moon's light through low clouds shone like a dying candle on her street. No one was out, windows dark. Holding tighter to her bag and cardboard, she dug deeper for her keys, worried that they had fallen out in front of Chris's building.

Scratch. Scratch. That sound again.

She glanced over her shoulder as a flash of brown and white barreled into her legs. "Chickpea!"

In the midst of deliriously loving and sloppy kisses, she saw Chris in his old chef pants and a glowing white T-shirt, standing at the bottom of the stoop. "Hi." She stared at him, awestruck.

He smiled. "I thought I'd say hello to the old place."

Was she imagining him? After twelve hours on the streets, had she truly lost her mind?

He joined her on the top step. "Actually, I was hoping I might see you, Ava."

"You're kidding! You'll never guess where I was tonight."

"Don't tell me I missed your Broadway debut..."

"When that happens, you'll be in the front row. No, I was sitting outside your building, waiting for *you*! For twelve hours!"

"Why would you do that?"

"For so many reasons! To show you that I care about our friendship. To thank you for opening a new door in my life and..." She hesitated as her old fear of rejection crept back. "... and to ask for another kiss?"

He looked away, and her heart followed his gaze back down the stoop. "Chris, I'm sorry..."

He closed his eyes, shaking his head from side to side. "It's not that."

"I went looking for you the morning after our garlic dinner! I knew then—"

"Ava." He quickly turned and reached for her hand. "I trust your feelings. I just can't contain mine."

He wrapped her in his arms, and they kissed—slow, tender kisses—as her joy became desire, like sampling a delicacy.

"I don't believe in coincidence," he whispered.

She rested her head on his broad shoulder, inhaling the scent of rosemary and garlic on his skin. "I'm sorry I doubted you."

He pulled back. "You had every right to be skeptical of me. I knew you didn't fully understand my life, but living a secret had become a habit for me. My co-workers, my friends, no one knew where or how I survived. With you, though, it was out in the open, and it didn't matter. We had a connection. So I forgot that I was asking you to take a leap of faith when I kissed you."

"Who's the one taking a leap of faith? My life isn't exactly stable. But, like you said, it isn't about the facts. The right connection is a feeling that won't go away, that you can't live without. I was so lost when you left!"

They sat down on the top step. Chickpea too. Trees lined the dark street like a parade of shadows. "I can't believe how long I waited for you," she said, thinking back over the day. "Did I have the right address? Ninth Street in the Village?"

"That old brownstone is where I grew up, before we moved

to Paris. I'm staying there with my dad now, although we more or less live at the restaurant."

"I don't know how you managed on the streets. The ground is seriously uncomfortable!"

"I've toughened up over the past three years, that's for sure. You can imagine how badly I wanted this restaurant, for myself and for my dad. Autumn Leaves is a new beginning for us both—in Manhattan, where dreams are made."

"Yes! Except, what did your dad think of your homelessness?"

"I didn't tell him. If he had known, he would've searched every stoop in the city until he found me. I told him after the fact; I gave him my journal."

"Of course." She smiled.

"Ever since my mom died," Chris explained, "seventeen years ago, he's been Super Dad, my best friend, my irate employer... he even made me the main character of his books. Well, now he's getting to know me apart from himself, and I'm not the mischievous boy who blunders his father's baking!"

She laughed. "I'm going to learn French just to read them."

"You won't have to. He's having them translated into English."

They were both quiet for a moment. "So, you've been without your mom for seventeen years," she said softly. "It's hard to imagine." She could still hear Mom's voice, as if she had only just spoken to her: *Go out and find someone more like yourself, Ava. You're free!* Mom had to be looking down now, happy...and proud.

"You'll never forget her," Chris said and gently laid his hand on hers.

Ava looked into his eyes and smiled. "I know."

"Wait here." Chris jumped to his feet and ran down the steps.

"Where are you going?" she asked, laughing at his impromptu burst of energy.

"I have something for you." He disappeared below the stoop.

"Don't tell me, a potato masher. Or, no, a lemon zester!"

He returned with a cold pack and thermos. "Gaudes and

coffee! Are you hungry?"

"I'm famished!"

"Our stoop picnic, at last." He poured two cups of coffee, and then unwrapped two slices of a sweet-smelling, sticky cake.

"Oh, I just know this is going to taste amazing!" Her mouth watered.

He held up a piece for her to take a bite.

She leaned forward...bubbly with happiness and anticipation. It could've been her wedding day.

It was the middle of the night, and despite the fantastic dose of sugar and caffeine, Ava felt exhausted. "I should get to bed," she said, resting her head against Chris's shoulder. "I'm meeting Gretchen at All for One tomorrow morning."

"Hey, I'm glad it's working out!" he said, enthusiastic.

"Thanks to you I'll be running their dance program." She remembered the two unopened envelopes in her bag. "If my interviews and everything goes well, that is."

Chris gathered his cold pack and thermos, and they both stood up. "I hope to see you soon, Ava." He kissed her and pulled back and then kissed her again.

The mystery was gone; she knew him now, and with her arms wrapped around his waist, feeling his soft lips on hers, she loved everything about him.

"Good night, Ava." He watched her walk up the stoop and then waited with Chickpea until she found her key and opened the door.

"Good night, Chris."

Going up the stairs, Ava reached into her bag for the envelopes. She was in love, and nothing, absolutely nothing else mattered.

The first letter was another eviction notice. Nice of them to send a reminder. She crumpled it up before sticking it back inside her bag.

Continuing her climb, she looked at the second envelope. It was from a Gregory R. Greenberg, Esq. Her guard shot up and she froze in the stairwell. Why would a lawyer contact her?

She forced herself to open the letter. With her heart in a panic, she skimmed the contents for a lawsuit titled Joshua Copeland vs. Ava Larson. "Please, no," she whispered. "Don't bury me..." Her eyes tripped over the words: *enclosed within... cashier's check...$75,000...benefactor...anonymous.*

What? She read it again, and then again, and still couldn't believe that she was holding a check for $75,000 in her name. A thick rope dangled before her—a way out of her wedding pit! Except, who sent it?

Not Phoebe, unless...oh, no. That would explain why her bank account had suddenly gone down...the job interview and shopping on a budget.

"I won't take it!" Ava said out loud, tearing the check into pieces. "I don't care if Phoebe planned every minute of the wedding, I won't let her pay for it. The mistake was mine!"

Ava ran up the stairs, jammed her key into the lock and burst into her apartment. Phoebe lay asleep on the futon in her green kimono.

"Phoebe," Ava whispered, shaking her shoulder. "We have to talk."

Phoebe shot up. "Sweetie? What's wrong?"

"You don't have to get a job. I won't accept the money. The canceled wedding is my responsibility. I'll pay it off, even if it takes me the rest of my life."

"What money, sweetie?"

Ava suddenly felt dizzy. "Do you know Gregory R. Greenberg?"

"Our family lawyer, but I haven't spoken to Gregory since...I guess it was Kitty's wedding."

The Plaza. Ava remembered Josh complaining that Greenberg was seated at Table Four, or some acceptably low number. "Phoebe, your lawyer issued a check made out in my name for $75,000...from an anonymous benefactor. I'm positive it didn't come from Josh; he recently sent me two bills, and if it didn't come from you, then that leaves...Mr. Copeland?"

"He wants me back!" she gasped. "It's what I asked for—that we help you with the wedding!" Phoebe jumped off the futon and started packing her bags.

"Wait a minute. Did you leave him because of *me*?"

"I left him to take a stance. But you gave me the platform. And the courage."

"Then why send the check anonymously?"

"He's not going to fully concede, of course. Sweetheart, I've got to go. Thanks for taking me in, and for turning my life upside-down. You're a darling!" She hugged Ava with all her new strength before running out the door. "Bye!"

Ava looked at the destroyed check. *Oops.* He'd issue it again, hopefully. She was still flat broke and homeless, but it felt good, so good, being forgiven for the canceled wedding and knowing that Phoebe and Mr. Copeland were a couple again.

Chapter Forty-One

The Glass Houses. As in, people who live in glass houses shouldn't throw stones? Ava entered the granite and steel lobby in her red dress from The Encore. It was a beautiful Indian summer evening in November, with deep eggplant and rich pumpkin popping the City's palette. Just the night for celebrating love renewed. The invite said *Formal Best ~ Bright Colors*, and Phoebe would accept nothing less for her second wedding.

What should you do after breaking your engagement? Accept a wedding invitation from his family to prove:

1) No hard feelings.
2) You've moved on and have never been so happy and fulfilled in your life.
3) Your love for them was and always will be real.
[Clause: Just be sure to go with a date.]

Ava breathed deeply until her dress tightened around her chest. She hadn't seen much of Chris over the past few months, what with All for One and Autumn Leaves demanding their time. The most they'd done together was grab coffee in the morning or stroll the city late at night. This would be their first wedding and something like a real date. Plus, she'd introduce him to Phoebe, again, only this time without his cardboard.

Unfortunately, he'd be late—a private party at the restaurant.

The woman at reception, as polished looking as the steel panels lining the lobby walls, directed her to the elevators. The Copeland wedding was on the 21st floor. Ava rode up alone. The Glass Houses, a part of the Chelsea Arts Tower, was just three blocks from her old apartment on 22nd Street—now a demo site. The city was always changing, morphing into something taller and grander, and she was changing with it, downgrading from her apartment, working harder, and spending less—saving money, for once.

The elevator door opened to a sprawling loft enclosed by glass walls that gazed out over the electric artwork of the city at night. Ava stepped into the room and stopped. The tables and chairs, the yin-yang centerpieces, the glasses and plates and cascading chandeliers were all white or made of glass. The guests brought the color, as specified in the invite. How clever of Phoebe to reverse the decorations. Mingling with her friends, dressed all in white, she provided the backdrop for them to shine. And they did, like splashes of paint in motion.

"There you are!" Phoebe breezed cloud-like over to Ava. "Come in!" Her silvery-white hair reflected her age but didn't detract from her beauty.

"You look ravishing!" Ava opened her arms.

"Oh, sweetie!" They hugged.

"Congratulations, Phoebe, you've got your wedding after all!" Ava glanced behind her. "Where's Mr. Copeland? I assume you've dressed him in a white tuxedo."

"He refused." Phoebe took her hand. "Come on. Shall we get past the first hello after a breakup? Josh is at the bar."

Ava had convinced herself that seeing Josh would be easy, up until now. She was in a better place. She loved another man. She had no regrets. So why the knot in her stomach? She felt overeager and rigid at the same time, the precise ingredients for an awkward moment.

"Ava, hello." He wore a grey tuxedo with a rose-colored tie and cummerbund and looked surprisingly happy.

"Hi, how are you!" She moved to kiss him on the cheek, stopped, and then started again. "Oh, sorry!" They looked like they were trying to pass each other on a sidewalk.

Josh smoothed over her rocky start with his confident double-cheek kiss, minus emotion. "This is Charlotte," he said, stepping back.

His date was a redhead, which felt like a low blow, especially as Ava's dye-job was starting to grow out. Charlotte was a natural red and pretty in a rosy-pink dress. "Nice to meet you." They shook, and Ava worried she would crush her soft, pale hand.

Mr. Copeland joined them. "Good to see you, Ava." He actually seemed to mean it.

"We have news!" Phoebe beamed with an excitement that surpassed her renewed vows. "I'm just finding out about it myself. Joshua, do you want to tell them?"

"I've asked Charlotte to marry me," he said point blank and took Charlotte's hand in his, but instead of holding her hand, he held it out for Ava to see.

The ring. Her eyes followed his lead, while she dreaded the sight of her engagement ring on someone else.

Thank goodness. A stunning arrangement of diamonds glimmered in an antique setting. "It was my great-grandmother's," Charlotte said, admiring it lovingly.

"The wedding will be at Charlotte's family's home in North Carolina."

"I'm not allowed to plan this one." Phoebe had that dog-on-a-tight-lead look, but it didn't last. "At least I had my moment planning your wedding, Ava. And, of course, my own weddings!" She rubbed Mr. Copeland's back. "I just might have to throw us a wedding every year!"

"Don't expect me to be there," Mr. Copeland grumbled.

Charlotte blushed, perhaps embarrassed by Phoebe's unconventional enthusiasm.

"Did you come alone, Ava?" Josh looked at her over the rim of his whiskey glass.

The question seemed to be on everyone's mind as they waited for her response with wide eyes.

"Chris should be here any minute. He had to finish up at the restaurant."

"Are you still seeing him?" Phoebe asked with lingering skepticism from their days on 22nd Street. "Chris is the co-owner of Autumn Leaves."

"Really." Josh nodded and frowned at the same time, his maximum show of approval. "How did you meet?"

A small *squeak* escaped Phoebe's lips.

"You've probably seen him before," Ava replied. "He lived below the stoop of my old apartment building. He was homeless by choice."

Charlotte covered her mouth.

"There's a story on it in *Time Out* magazine," Ava continued. "He says homelessness gave him a certain privacy and helped him to stay focused on his dream of opening a New York restaurant."

"No, that's just wrong." Josh put his hand on top of Charlotte's, as if their conversation was too graphic for her. "I wouldn't trust anyone who lived on the streets."

"Neither would I," Charlotte said. "I mean, how could you?"

"He wasn't hurting anyone or doing anything wrong. Chris is the most grounded, reliable person I've ever met."

"Ha!" Mr. Copeland burst out laughing. "I'm sure he's 'grounded.'"

"You can all meet him tonight and *then* form an opinion. Fair enough?"

"Yes, that would be fair," Phoebe said, although she had already met Chris several times.

"So, you're no longer living in the same apartment?" Josh flagged a waiter for another drink.

"I have a room at All for One, where I teach dance. It's a women's shelter on 34th Street near Macy's." The Encore was behind her now, although it would never be forgotten. God forgave her for playing to the weakness of men for money, and at the expense of her own comfort level; she was sure of it in her heart, but she'd pray for those men seeking love and fulfillment between the flashing lights in dark clubs.

"You told me you had found a nice, furnished studio apartment!" Phoebe exclaimed, bringing Ava back to the moment.

"That's exactly what it is, except I share a bathroom. There are a lot of women in the shelter just like me...can't afford the rents in this city or are in-between jobs. For others, of course, it's more complicated, but it's only temporary. I'm building up a client base in my dance classes. Most important, I love what

I do."

"I'm so proud of you, sweetie. Oh, there's Aliza, the real DKNY PR Girl! She's featuring our renewal on her blog!" Phoebe dashed off for her interview, while Josh got into a work conversation with his father. Ava noticed the terrace and excused herself to get some air.

A six-piece band played ABBA's "Take a Chance on Me," while ladies in bright dresses and high heels scurried onto the dance floor. Ava stepped outside and filled her lungs with cool air. The sun's warmth from the day had escaped into the cloudless sky. Stars seemed to go on forever. She looked out as far as she could see and quietly declared, "I'm on top of the world!"

Couples on the terrace held each other, entranced and content, as if they were conduits between the city lights below and the stars above. Maybe the real purpose of love was to channel kindness, generosity, and acceptance from Heaven to the human race. Some people felt it. Others didn't know how to let it flow.

Ava felt a tall presence standing behind her and then a hand on her shoulder. Turning around, she met Chris's dark eyes reflecting the moon's power.

"Hi!" Seeing him, tears came. She brushed them away.

"Ava, you're crying?"

"Oh, you know, it's a wedding...and I'm happy."

"Then I'll cry with you," he said. And they embraced, becoming a conduit of love.

Acknowledgements

I'd like to start by thanking Johanna Masters, English and drama teacher, organist, fiddler, karate black-belt, and my mother. Thank you for giving me your passion for life. You are the reason I'm a writer. You're my first editor, and you've seen me through every draft with unwavering faith.

Thank you also to Jonas Nilsson, my husband, travel partner, and best friend. You believed in me from the day I said I was quitting my job to write a book. You've made my dreams possible, and you continue to show me the world, expand my thinking, and encourage me to go for more. I Always Cry at Weddings is about a fun, selfless, and open-minded love. Thank you for being my inspiration. I love you.

I wouldn't be writing this acknowledgement if it weren't for my dedicated and talented publisher and editor at WhiteFire Publishing, Roseanna White and Dina Sleiman. Roseanna, I love the cover! I'm also grateful to be working with Claire McKinney and Larissa Ackerman of Claire McKinney PR. Thank you for seeing the book's potential.

David Allen Sullivan, thank you for the poetry you give to the world. I'm grateful for your permission to reprint "Warnings" from Strong-Armed Angel (Hummingbird Press) in the front of my book.

I also want to thank the following individuals for their guidance and inspiration along the way: Adam Sexton, Willard Cook, Bill Contardi, Carolyn Fireside, Mikhail Iossel, Jeff Parker, Josip Novakovich, Cheri Peters, Ian Frazier, Susan Shapiro, Alice Phillips, Cherry Provost, Jill McCorkle, Diane Johnson, Wendy Lawton, Joyce Magnin, Nicole O'Dell, Ane Mulligan, Narelle Atkins, Marion Ueckermann, Elaine Stock, Connie Mann, Paula Mowery, Janet Sketchley, Paula Vince, Valerie Comer, and Bonnie Calhoun.

Thank you to my New York friends: Laura and John Moore,

I ALWAYS *Cry* at *Weddings*

Alison Strong, Caroline Coleman, Lyndsay Hanchett, Nicole Baumgardner, Justin Stiver, Russell Terlecki, Sachin and Gayatri Shah, Jilian Gersten, Greta Bouterse, Kristine Bell, Robert Goff, Mathew McAlpin, Benny Williams, Emlio Collins, the Kleeblatts, and Carl, Anna, and Anton Linderum.

Sincere thanks, as well, to my London supporters: Sarah and Thomas Tarnowski, Daphne and Claudio Siniscalco, Michiel and Florentine Kotting, Shirley and Dave Palmer, Millicent Villiers, Victoria Sylvester, Suzy Lui, Heather Garni, Louise Hall, Noemi Maupertuis, Katrin Roskelly, Rosie Bichard, Man-Ching Fung, Nancy Spencer, Kay Petersen, Carlo Centurione-Scotto and all the wonderful Mums and Dads at Hawkesdown House.

To my little heartthrobs, Lucas and Axel. You guys make me stronger and wiser every day. Thank you, also, Solveig and Göran and Tim and Nancy for your love and support. Michael and Mary, my summer in L.A., way back when, gave me a sense of independence I'll never lose. Sue, Teri, Tami, Karen and Katherine, you are models of strength and the best sisters and support network I could ever want. I feel so blessed with you in my life. And, finally, I am eternally grateful for the woman who first showed our family how to love and sacrifice, how to have patience and grace, how to persevere, and how to pray. Grandma Murphy, you always encouraged our strengths and always stepped back so that we could shine. Now your spirit is a shining light in our lives.

I Always Cry at Weddings is dedicated to my father, John Goff, who passed away in 2000. He dedicated his life to his family and giving to those who are less fortunate. He was a father, husband, and boss, but most of all a good friend to us all. Thank you, Dad. This one's for you.

To help support schools for orphaned children and those living in poverty, Sara Goff started the charity Lift the Lid. Their mission is to help improve education and build confidence through writing and self-expression. Part of the proceeds from *I Always Cry at Weddings* will go toward this cause. Meet the students at www.lift-the-lid.org.

Discussion Questions

1. How does New York City play a role in the story? And how does the setting shape Ava's life?

2. How many different sides to the city do you see in the story? Which side stands out the most?

3. How is trust a theme in the story? Has Ava been lied to?

4. Is Ava and Chris's relationship plausible? Are they a good couple?

5. What is Maggie's role in the novel besides Ava's best friend and maid of honor?

6. Was The Encore an important first step or a total miss-step? Did you lose respect for Ava while she was dancing on the piano?

7. Does Ava's faith in God play a significant role in her journey to finding love and meaning in life?

8. What warning signs did Ava miss with Julian?

9. Compare and contrast Ava's mom and Phoebe?

10. Is the theme of "weddings" significant in modern day America? Have you been to a wedding that didn't feel sincere? What was the most sincere wedding you attended, and why did if feel meaningful?

11. If Ava and Chris get married, do you think they will have a big wedding? Personal vows? How might they make their wedding different?

12. After reading *I Always Cry at Weddings*, how would you describe unconditional love?

13. Do YOU always cry at weddings? Why?

If You Enjoyed *I Always Cry at Weddings*,
You May Also Enjoy:

The Good Girl
by Christy Barritt

What's a good girl to do when life goes bad?

Sailing out of Darkness
by Normandie Fischer

Love conquers all? Maybe for some people.